MICHAEL CHABON
THE YIDDISH POLICEMEN'S UNION

By Michael Chabon

THE YIDDISH POLICEMEN'S UNION

MICHAEL CHABON

HARPER

An Imprint of HarperCollins*Publishers*

HARPER

An *Imprint of* HarperCollins *Publishers*
10 East 53rd Street
New York, New York 10022-5299

Copyright © 2007 by Michael Chabon
Glossary copyright © 2008 by Michael Chabon and Sherryl Mleynek
ISBN: 978-0-06-149360-7

First Harper international paperback printing: March 2008
First Harper special printing: May 2007
First Harper hardcover printing: May 2007

HarperCollins® and Harper® are registered trademarks of HarperCollins Publishers.

P.S.™ is a trademark of HarperCollins Publishers.

Printed in the United States of America.

Visit Harper paperbacks on the World Wide Web
at www.harpercollins.com

10 9 8 7 6 5 4 3 2 1

To Ayelet,
bashert

And they went to sea in a Sieve.
—EDWARD LEAR

Nine months Landsman's been flopping at the Hotel Zamenhof without any of his fellow residents managing to get themselves murdered. Now somebody has put a bullet in the brain of the occupant of 208, a yid who was calling himself Emanuel Lasker.

"He didn't answer the phone, he wouldn't open his door," says Tenenboym the night manager when he comes to roust Landsman. Landsman lives in 505, with a view of the neon sign on the hotel across Max Nordau Street. That one is called the Blackpool, a word that figures in Landsman's nightmares. "I had to let myself into his room."

The night manager is a former U.S. Marine who kicked a heroin habit of his own back in the sixties, after coming home from the shambles of the Cuban war. He takes a motherly interest in the user population of the Zamenhof. He extends credit to them and sees that they are left alone when that is what they need.

"Did you touch anything in the room?" Landsman says.

Tenenboym says, "Only the cash and jewelry."

Landsman puts on his trousers and shoes and hitches up his suspenders. Then he and Tenenboym turn to look at the doorknob, where a necktie hangs, red with a fat maroon stripe, already knotted to save time. Landsman has eight hours to go until his next shift.

Eight rat hours, sucking at his bottle, in his glass tank lined with wood shavings. Landsman sighs and goes for the tie. He slides it over his head and pushes up the knot to his collar. He puts on his jacket, feels for the wallet and shield in the breast pocket, pats the sholem he wears in a holster under his arm, a chopped Smith & Wesson Model 39.

"I hate to wake you, Detective," Tenenboym says. "Only I noticed that you don't really sleep."

"I sleep," Landsman says. He picks up the shot glass that he is currently dating, a souvenir of the World's Fair of 1977. "It's just I do it in my underpants and shirt." He lifts the glass and toasts the thirty years gone since the Sitka World's Fair. A pinnacle of Jewish civilization in the north, people say, and who is he to argue? Meyer Landsman was fourteen that summer, and just discovering the glories of Jewish women, for whom 1977 must have been some kind of a pinnacle. "Sitting up in a chair." He drains the glass. "Wearing a sholem."

According to doctors, therapists, and his ex-wife, Landsman drinks to medicate himself, tuning the tubes and crystals of his moods with a crude hammer of hundred-proof plum brandy. But the truth is that Landsman has only two moods: working and dead. Meyer Landsman is the most decorated shammes in the District of Sitka, the man who solved the murder of the beautiful Froma Lefkowitz by her furrier husband, and caught Podolsky the Hospital Killer. His testimony sent Hyman Tsharny to federal prison for life, the first and last time that criminal charges against a Verbover wiseguy have ever been made to stick. He has the memory of a convict, the balls of a fireman, and the eyesight of a housebreaker. When there is crime to fight, Landsman tears around Sitka like a man with his pant leg caught on a rocket. It's like there's a film score playing behind him, heavy on the castanets. The problem comes in the hours when he isn't working, when his thoughts start blowing out the open window of his brain like pages from a blotter. Sometimes it takes a heavy paperweight to pin them down.

"I hate to make more work for you," Tenenboym says.

During his days working Narcotics, Landsman arrested Tenenboym five times. That is all the basis for what passes for friendship between them. It is almost enough.

"It's not work, Tenenboym," Landsman says. "I do it for love."

"It's the same for me," the night manager says. "With being a night manager of a crap-ass hotel."

Landsman puts his hand on Tenenboym's shoulder, and they go down to take stock of the deceased, squeezing into the Zamenhof's lone elevator, or ELEVATORO, as a small brass plate over the door would have it. When the hotel was built fifty years ago, all of its directional signs, labels, notices, and warnings were printed on brass plates in Esperanto. Most of them are long gone, victims of neglect, vandalism, or the fire code.

The door and door frame of 208 do not exhibit signs of forced entry. Landsman covers the knob with his handkerchief and nudges the door open with the toe of his loafer.

"I got this funny feeling," Tenenboym says as he follows Landsman into the room. "First time I ever saw the guy. You know the expression 'a broken man'?"

Landsman allows that the phrase rings a bell.

"Most of the people it gets applied to don't really deserve it," Tenenboym says. "Most men, in my opinion, they have nothing there to break in the first place. But this Lasker. He was like one of those sticks you snap, it lights up. You know? For a few hours. And you can hear broken glass rattling inside of it. I don't know, forget it. It was just a funny feeling."

"Everybody has a funny feeling these days," Landsman says, making a few notes in his little black pad about the situation of the room, even though such notes are superfluous, because he rarely forgets a detail of physical description. Landsman has been told, by the same loose confederacy of physicians, psychologists, and his former spouse, that alcohol will kill his gift for recollection, but so far, to his regret, this claim has proved false. His vision of the past remains unimpaired. "We had to open a separate phone line just to handle the calls."

"These are strange times to be a Jew," Tenenboym agrees. "No doubt about it."

A small pile of paperback books sits atop the laminate dresser. On the bedside table Lasker kept a chessboard. It looks like he had a game going, a messy-looking middle game with Black's king under attack at the center of the board and White having the advantage of a couple of pieces. It's a cheap set, the board a square of card that folds down the middle, the pieces hollow, with plastic nubs where they were extruded.

One light burns in a three-shade floor lamp by the television. Every other bulb in the room apart from the bathroom tube has been removed or allowed to burn out. On the windowsill sits a package of a popular brand of over-the-counter laxative. The window is cranked open its possible inch, and every few seconds the metal blinds bang in the stiff wind blowing in off the Gulf of Alaska. The wind carries a sour tang of pulped lumber, the smell of boat diesel and the slaughter and canning of salmon. According to "Nokh Amol," a song that Landsman and every other Alaskan Jew of his generation learned in grade school, the smell of the wind from the Gulf fills a Jewish nose with a sense of promise, opportunity, the chance to start again. "Nokh Amol" dates from the Polar Bear days, the early forties, and it's supposed to be an expression of gratitude for another miraculous deliverance: Once Again. Nowadays the Jews of the Sitka District tend to hear the ironic edge that was there all along.

"Seems like I've known a lot of chess-playing yids who used smack," Tenenboym says.

"Same here," Landsman says, looking down at the deceased, realizing he has seen the yid around the Zamenhof. Little bird of a man. Bright eye, snub beak. Bit of a flush in the cheeks and throat that might have been rosacea. Not a hard case, not a scumbag, not quite a lost soul. A yid not too different from Landsman, maybe, apart from his choice of drug. Clean fingernails. Always a tie and hat. Read a book with footnotes once. Now Lasker lies on his belly, on the pull-down bed, face to the wall, wearing only a pair of regulation white underpants. Ginger hair and ginger freckles and three days of golden stubble on his cheek. A trace of a double chin that Landsman puts down to a vanished life as a fat boy. Eyes swollen in their blood-dark orbits. At the back of his head is a small, burnt hole, a bead of blood. No sign of a struggle. Nothing to indicate that Lasker saw it coming or even knew the instant when it came. The pillow, Landsman notices, is missing from the bed. "If I'd known, maybe I would have proposed a game or two."

"I didn't know you play."

"I'm weak," Landsman says. By the closet, on plush carpet the medicated yellow-green of a throat lozenge, he spots a tiny white feather. Landsman jerks open the closet door, and there on the floor is the pillow, shot through the heart to silence the concussion of bursting gases in a shell. "I have no feel for the middle game."

"In my experience, Detective," Tenenboym says, "it's all middle game."

"Don't I know it," Landsman says.

He calls to wake his partner, Berko Shemets.

"Detective Shemets," Landsman says into his mobile phone, a department-issue Shoyfer AT. "This is your partner."

"I begged you not to do this anymore, Meyer," Berko says. Needless to say, he also has eight hours to go until his next shift.

"You have a right to be angry," Landsman says. "Only I thought maybe you might still be awake."

"I *was* awake."

Unlike Landsman, Berko Shemets has not made a mess of his marriage or his personal life. Every night he sleeps in the arms of his excellent wife, whose love for him is merited, requited, and appreciated by her husband, a steadfast man who never gives her any cause for sorrow or alarm.

"A curse on your head, Meyer," Berko says, and then, in American, "God damn it."

"I have an apparent homicide here at my hotel," Landsman says. "A resident. A single shot to the back of the head. Silenced with a pillow. Very tidy."

"A hit."

"That's the only reason I'm bothering you. The unusual nature of the killing."

Sitka, with a population in the long jagged strip of the metro area of three point two million, averages about seventy-five homicides a year. Some of these are gang-related: Russian shtarkers whacking one another freestyle. The rest of Sitka's homicides are so-called crimes of passion, which is a shorthand way of expressing the mathematical product of alcohol and firearms. Cold-blooded executions are as rare as they are tough to clear from the big whiteboard in the squad room, where the tally of open cases is kept.

"You're off duty, Meyer. Call it in. Give it to Tabatchnik and Karpas."

Tabatchnik and Karpas, the other two detectives who make up B Squad in the Homicide Section of the District Police, Sitka Headquarters, are holding down the night shift this month. Landsman has to acknowledge a certain appeal in the idea of letting this pigeon shit on their fedoras.

"Well, I would," Landsman says. "Except for this is my place of residence."

"You knew him?" Berko says, his tone softening.

"No," Landsman says. "I did not know the yid."

He looks away from the pale freckled expanse of the dead man stretched out on the pull-down bed. Sometimes he can't help feeling sorry for them, but it's better not to get into the habit.

"Look," Landsman says, "you go back to bed. We can talk about it tomorrow. I'm sorry I bothered you. Good night. Tell Ester-Malke I'm sorry."

"You sound a little off, Meyer," Berko says. "You okay?"

In recent months Landsman has placed a number of calls to his partner at questionable hours of the night, ranting and rambling in an alcoholic dialect of grief. Landsman bailed out on his marriage two years ago, and last April his younger sister crashed her Piper Super Cub into the side of Mount Dunkelblum, up in the bush. But Landsman is not thinking of Naomi's death now, nor of the shame of his divorce. He has been sandbagged by a vision of sitting in the grimy lounge of the Hotel Zamenhof, on a couch that was once white, playing chess with Emanuel Lasker, or whatever his real name was. Shedding the last of their fading glow on each other and listening to the sweet chiming of broken glass inside. That Landsman loathes the game of chess does not make the picture any less touching.

"The guy played chess, Berko. I never knew. That's all."

"Please," Berko says, "please, Meyer, I beg you, don't start with the crying."

"I'm fine," Landsman says. "Good night."

Landsman calls the dispatcher to make himself the primary detective on the Lasker case. Another piece-of-shit homicide is not going to put any special hurt on his clearance rate as primary. Not that it really matters. On the first of January, sovereignty over the whole Federal District of Sitka, a crooked parenthesis of rocky shoreline running along the western edges of Baranof and Chichagof islands, will revert to the state of Alaska. The District Police, to which Landsman has devoted his hide, head, and soul for twenty years, will be dissolved. It is far from clear that Landsman or Berko Shemets or anybody else will be keeping his job. Nothing is clear about the upcoming Reversion, and that is why these are strange times to be a Jew.

2

While he waits for the beat latke to show, Landsman knocks on doors. Most of the occupants of the Zamenhof are out for the night, in body or mind, and for all that he gets out of the rest of them, he might as well be knocking on doors at the Hirshkovits School for the Deaf. They are a twitchy, half-addled, rank, and cranky bunch of yids, the residents of the Hotel Zamenhof, but none of them seems any more disturbed than usual tonight. And none of them strikes Landsman as the type to jam a large-caliber handgun against the base of a man's skull and kill him in stone-cold blood.

"I'm wasting my time with these buffaloes," Landsman tells Tenenboym. "And you, you're sure you didn't see anybody or anything out of the ordinary?"

"I'm sorry, Detective."

"You're a buffalo, too, Tenenboym."

"I don't dispute the charge."

"The service door?"

"Dealers were using it," Tenenboym says. "We had to put in an alarm. I would have heard."

Landsman gets Tenenboym to telephone the day manager and the weekend man, snug at home in their beds. These gentlemen agree with Tenenboym that, as far as they know, no one has called for the dead man or asked after him. Ever. Not during the entire course of his stay at the Zamenhof. No visitors, no friends, not even the delivery boy from Pearl of Manila. So, Landsman thinks, there's a difference between him and Lasker: Landsman has occasional visits from Romel, bearing a brown paper bag of *lumpia*.

"I'm going to go check out the roof," Landsman says. "Don't let anybody leave, and call me when the latke decides to show up."

Landsman rides the elevatoro to the eighth floor and then bangs his way up a flight of steel-edged concrete steps to the roof of the Zamenhof. He walks the perimeter, looking across Max Nordau Street to the roof of the Blackpool. He peers over the north, east, and south cornices to the surrounding low structures six or seven stories down. Night is an orange smear over Sitka, a compound of fog and the light of sodium-vapor streetlamps. It has the translucence of onions cooked in chicken fat. The lamps of the Jews stretch from the slope of Mount Edgecumbe in the west, over the seventy-two infilled islands of the Sound, across the Shvartser-Yam, Halibut Point, South Sitka, and the Nachtasyl, across Harkavy and the Untershtot, before they are snuffed in the east by the Baranof range. On Oysshtelung Island, the beacon at the tip of the Safety Pin—sole remnant of the World's Fair—blinks out its warning to airplanes or yids. Landsman can smell fish offal from the canneries, grease from the fry pits at Pearl of Manila, the spew of taxis, an intoxicating bouquet of fresh hat from Grinspoon's Felting two blocks away.

"It's nice up there," Landsman says when he gets back down to the lobby, with its ashtray charm, the yellowing sofas, the scarred chairs and tables at which you sometimes see a couple of hotel residents killing an hour with a game of pinochle. "I should go up more often."

"What about the basement?" Tenenboym says. "You going to look down there?"

"The basement," Landsman says, and his heart describes a sudden knight move in his chest. "I guess I'd better."

Landsman is a tough guy, in his way, given to the taking of wild chances. He has been called hard-boiled and foolhardy, a momzer, a crazy son of a bitch. He has faced down shtarkers and psychopaths, has been shot at, beaten, frozen, burned. He has pursued suspects between the flashing walls of urban firefights and deep into bear country. Heights, crowds, snakes, burning houses, dogs schooled to hate the smell of a policeman, he has shrugged them all off or functioned in spite of them. But when he finds himself in lightless or confined spaces, something in the animal core of Meyer Landsman convulses. No one but his ex-wife knows it, but Detective Meyer Landsman is afraid of the dark.

"Want me to go with you?" Tenenboym says, sounding offhand, but you never know with a sensitive old fishwife like Tenenboym.

Landsman affects to scorn the offer. "Just give me a damn flashlight," he says.

The basement exhales its breath of camphor, heating oil, and cold dust. Landsman jerks a string that lights a naked bulb, holds his breath, and goes under.

At the bottom of the steps, he passes through the lost-articles room, lined with pegboard, furnished with shelves and cubbyholes that hold the thousand objects abandoned or forgotten in the hotel. Unmated shoes, fur hats, a trumpet, a windup zeppelin. A collection of wax gramophone cylinders featuring the entire recorded output of the Orchestra Orfeon of Istanbul. A logger's ax, two bicycles, a partial bridge in a hotel glass. Wigs, canes, a glass eye, display hands left behind by a mannequin salesman. Prayer books, prayer shawls in their velvet zipper pouches, an outlandish idol with the body of a fat baby and the head of an elephant. There is a wooden soft-drink crate filled with keys, another with the entire range and breadth of hairstyling tools, from irons to eyelash crimpers. Framed photographs of families in better days. A cryptic twist of rubber that might be a sex toy, or a contraceptive device, or the patented secret of a foundation garment. Some yid even left behind a taxidermy marten, sleek and leering, its glass eye a hard bead of ink.

Landsman probes the box of keys with a pencil. He looks inside each hat, gropes along the shelves behind the abandoned paperback books. He can hear his own heart and smell his own aldehyde breath, and after a few minutes in the silence, the sound of blood in his ears begins to remind him of somebody talking. He checks behind the hot-water tanks, lashed to one another with straps of steel like comrades in a doomed adventure.

The laundry is next. When he pulls the string for the light, nothing happens. It's ten degrees darker in here, and there's nothing to see but blank walls, severed hookups, drain holes in the floor. The Zamenhof has not done its own wash in years. Landsman looks into the drain holes, and the darkness in them is oily and thick. Landsman feels a flutter, a worm, in his belly. He flexes his fingers and cracks the bones of his neck. At the far end of the laundry room, a door that is three planks nailed together by a diagonal fourth seals a low doorway. The wooden door has a loop of rope for a latch and a peg to hook it on.

A crawl space. Landsman half dreads the phrase alone.

He calculates the chance that a certain style of killer, not a professional, not a true amateur, not even a normal maniac, might be hiding in that crawl space. Possible; but it would be pretty tough for the freak to have hooked the loop over the peg from inside. That logic alone is almost enough to persuade him not to bother with the crawl space. In the end Landsman switches on the flash and notches it between his teeth. He hikes up his pants legs and gets down on his knees. Just to spite himself, because spiting himself, spiting others, spiting the world is the pastime and only patrimony of Landsman and his people. With one hand he unholsters his big little S&W, and with the other he fingers the loop of rope. He yanks open the door of the crawl space.

"Come out," he says, lips dry, rasping like a scared old fart.

The elation he experienced on the roof has cooled like blown filament. His nights are wasted, his life and career a series of mistakes, his city itself a bulb that is about to go black.

He thrusts his upper body into the crawl space. The air is cold, with a bitter smell of mouse shit. The beam of the pocket flash dribbles over everything, shadowing as much as it reveals. Walls of cinder block, an earthen floor, the ceiling a loathsome tangle of wires and foam insulation. In the middle of the dirt floor, at the back, a disk of raw plywood lies set in a circular metal frame, flush with the floor. Landsman holds his breath and swims through his panic to the hole in the floor, determined to stay under for as long as he can. The dirt around the frame is undisturbed. An even layer of dust lies over wood and metal alike, no marks, no streaks. There is no reason to think anyone has been fooling with it. Landsman fits his fingernails between the plywood and the frame and pries off the crude hatch. The flashlight reveals a threaded tube of aluminum screwed into the earth, laddered with steel cleats. The frame turns out to be the edge of the tube itself. Just wide enough to admit a full-grown psychopath. Or a Jewish policeman with fewer phobias than Landsman. He clings to the sholem as to a handle, wrestling with a crazy need to fire it into the throat of the darkness. He drops the plywood disk back into its frame with a clatter. No way is he going down there.

The darkness follows him all the way back up the stairs to the lobby, reaching for his collar, tugging at his sleeve.

"Nothing," he tells Tenenboym, pulling himself together. He gives the word a cheery ring. It might be a prediction of what his investigation into the murder of Emanuel Lasker is bound to reveal, a statement of what he believes Lasker lived for and died for, a realization of what will remain, after the Reversion, of Landsman's hometown. "Nothing."

"You know what Kohn says," says Tenenboym. "Kohn says we got a ghost in the house." Kohn is the day manager. "Taking shit, moving shit around. Kohn figures it for the ghost of Professor Zamenhof."

"If they named a dump like this after me," Landsman says, "I'd haunt it, too."

"You never know," Tenenboym observes. "Especially nowadays."

Nowadays one never knows. Out at Povorotny, a cat mated with a rabbit and produced adorable freaks whose photos graced the front page of the *Sitka Tog*. Last February five hundred witnesses all up and down the District swore that in the shimmer of the aurora borealis, for two nights running, they observed the outlines of a human face, with beard and sidelocks. Violent arguments broke out over the identity of the bearded sage in the sky, whether or not the face was smiling (or merely suffering from a mild attack of gas), and the meaning of the weird manifestation. And just last week, amid the panic and feathers of a kosher slaughterhouse on Zhitlovsky Avenue, a chicken turned on the shochet as he raised his ritual knife and announced, in Aramaic, the imminent advent of Messiah. According to the *Tog*, the miraculous chicken offered a number of startling predictions, though it neglected to mention the soup in which, having once more fallen silent as God Himself, it afterward featured. Even the most casual study of the record, Landsman thinks, would show that strange times to be a Jew have almost always been, as well, strange times to be a chicken.

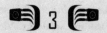 3

In the street the wind shakes rain from the flaps of its overcoat. Landsman tucks himself into the hotel doorway. Two men, one with a cello case strapped to his back, the other cradling a violin or viola, struggle against the weather toward the door of Pearl of Manila across the street. The symphony hall is ten blocks and a world away from this end of Max Nordau Street, but the craving of a Jew for pork, in particular when it has been deep-fried, is a force greater than night or distance or a cold blast off the Gulf of Alaska. Landsman himself is fighting the urge to return to room 505, and his bottle of slivovitz, and his World's Fair souvenir glass.

Instead, he lights a papiros. After a decade of abstinence, Landsman took up smoking again not quite three years ago. His then-wife was pregnant at the time. It was a much-discussed and in some quarters a long-desired pregnancy—her first—but not a planned one. As with many pregnancies that are discussed too long there was a history of ambivalence in the prospective father. At seventeen weeks and a day—the day Landsman bought his first package of Broadways in ten years—they got a bad result. Some but not all of the cells that made up the fetus, code-named Django, had an extra chromosome on the twentieth pair. A mosaicism, it was called. It might cause grave abnormalities. It might have no effect at all. In the available literature, a faithful person could find encouragement, and a faithless one ample reason to despond. Landsman's view of things—ambivalent, despondent, and with no faith in anything—prevailed. A doctor with half a dozen laminaria dilators broke the seal on the life of Django Landsman. Three months later, Landsman and his cigarettes moved out of the house on Tshernovits Island that he and Bina had shared for nearly all the fifteen years of their marriage. It was not that he couldn't live with the guilt. He just couldn't live with it and Bina, too.

An old man, pushing himself like a rickety handcart, weaves a course toward the door of the hotel. A short man, under five feet, dragging a large valise. Landsman observes the long white coat, worn open over a white suit with a waistcoat, and the wide-brimmed white hat pulled down over his ears. A white beard and sidelocks, wispy and thick at the same time. The valise an ancient chimera of stained brocade and scratched hide. The whole right side of the man's body sags five degrees lower than the left, where the suitcase, which must contain the old boy's entire collection of lead ingots, weighs it down. The man stops and raises a finger, as if he has a question to pose of Landsman. The wind toys with the man's whiskers and with the brim of his hat. From his beard, armpits, breath, and skin, the wind plucks a rich smell of stale tobacco and wet flannel and the sweat of a man who lives in the street. Landsman notes the color of the man's antiquated boots, yellowish ivory, like his beard, with sharp toes and buttons running up the sides.

Landsman recalls that he used to see this nut a lot, back when he was arresting Tenenboym for petty theft and possession. The yid was no younger then and is no older now. People used to call him Elijah, because he turned up in all kinds of unlikely spots, with his pushke box and his indefinable air of having something important to say.

"Darling," he says to Landsman now. "This is the Hotel Zamenhof, no?"

His Yiddish sounds a bit exotic to Landsman, flavored with

Dutch maybe. He is bent and frail, but his face, apart from crow's-feet around the blue eyes, looks youthful and unlined. The eyes themselves hold a match flame of eagerness that puzzles Landsman. The prospect of a night at the Zamenhof does not often give rise to such anticipation.

"That's right." Landsman offers Elijah the Prophet a Broadway, and the little man takes two and tucks one into the reliquary of his breast pocket. "Hot and cold water. Licensed shammes right on the premises."

"Are you the manager, sweetness?"

Landsman can't help smiling at that. He steps aside, gesturing toward the door. "The manager's inside," he says.

But the little man just stands there getting rained on, his beard fluttering like a flag of truce. He gazes up at the faceless face of the Zamenhof, gray in the murky streetlight. A narrow pile of dirty white brick and slit windows, three or four blocks off the tawdriest stretch of Monastir Street, the place has all the allure of a dehumidifier. Its neon sign blinks on and off, tormenting the dreams of the losers across the street at the Blackpool.

"The Zamenhof," the old man says, echoing the intermittent letters on the neon sign. "Not the Zamenhof. The Zamenhof."

Now the latke, a rookie named Netsky, comes jogging up, holding on to his round, flat, wide-brimmed patrolman's hat.

"Detective," the latke says, out of breath, and then gives the old man a squint and a nod. "Evening, Grandpa. Right, uh, Detective, sorry, I just got the call, I was hung up for a minute there." Netsky has coffee on his breath and powdered sugar on the right cuff of his blue coat. "Where's the dead yid?"

"In two-oh-eight," Landsman says, opening the door for the latke, then turning back to the old man. "Coming in, Grandpa?"

"No," Elijah says, with a hint of mild emotion that Landsman can't quite read. It might be regret, or relief, or the grim satisfaction of a man with a taste for disappointment. The flicker trapped in the old man's eyes has given way to a film of tears. "I was only curious. Thank you, Officer Landsman."

"It's Detective now," Landsman says, startled that the old man has retrieved his name. "You *remember* me, Grandpa?"

"I remember everything, darling." Elijah reaches into a hip pocket of his bleach yellow coat and takes out his pushke, a wooden casket, about the size of a box meant for index cards, painted black. On the front of the box, Hebrew words are painted: L'ERETZ YISROEL. Cut into the top of the box is a narrow slit for coins or a folded dollar bill. "A small donation?" Elijah says.

The Holy Land has never seemed more remote or unattainable than it does to a Jew of Sitka. It is on the far side of the planet, a wretched place ruled by men united only in their resolve to keep out all but a worn fistful of small-change Jews. For half a century, Arab strongmen and Muslim partisans, Persians and Egyptians, socialists and nationalists and monarchists, pan-Arabists and pan-Islamists, traditionalists and the Party of Ali, have all sunk their teeth into Eretz Yisroel and worried it down to bone and gristle. Jerusalem is a city of blood and slogans painted on the wall, severed heads on telephone poles. Observant Jews around the world have not abandoned their hope to dwell one day in the land of Zion. But Jews have been tossed out of the joint three times now—in 586 BCE, in 70 CE and with savage finality in 1948. It's hard even for the faithful not to feel a sense of discouragement about their chances of once again getting a foot in the door.

Landsman gets out his wallet and pokes a folded twenty into Elijah's pushke. "Lots of luck," he says.

The little man hoists his heavy valise and starts to shuffle away. Landsman reaches out and pulls at Elijah's sleeve, a question formulating in his heart, a child's question about the old wish of his people for a home. Elijah turns with a look of practiced wariness. Maybe Landsman is some kind of troublemaker. Landsman feels the question ebb away like the nicotine in his bloodstream.

"What you got in the bag, Grandpa?" Landsman says. "Looks heavy."

"It's a book."

"One book?"

"It's very big."

"Long story?"

"Very long."

"What's it about?"

"It's about Messiah," Elijah says. "Now please take your hand off of me."

Landsman lets go. The old man straightens his back and raises his head. The clouds on his eyes blow over, and he looks angry, disdainful, and not in the least old.

"Messiah is coming," he says. It isn't quite a warning and yet somehow as a promise of redemption, it lacks a certain warmth.

"That works out well," Landsman says, jerking his thumb toward the hotel lobby. "As of tonight we have a vacancy."

Elijah looks hurt, or maybe just disgusted. He opens the black box and looks inside. He takes out the twenty-dollar bill that Landsman gave him and hands it back. Then he picks up his suitcase, settles his floppy white hat down over his head, and trudges off into the rain.

Landsman crumples the twenty and drops it into his hip pocket. He grinds his papiros under his shoe and goes into the hotel.

"Who's the nut?" Netsky says.

"They call him Elijah. He's harmless," says Tenenboym from behind the steel mesh of the reception window. "You used to see him around sometimes. Always pimping for Messiah." Tenenboym clacks a gold toothpick against his molars. "Listen, Detective, I'm not supposed to say anything. But I might as well tell you. Management is sending out a letter tomorrow."

"I can't wait to hear this," Landsman says.

"The owners sold out to a Kansas City concern."

"They're tossing us."

"Maybe," Tenenboym says. "Maybe not. Nobody's status is clear. But it's not out of the question that you might have to move out."

"Is that what it's going to say in the letter?"

Tenenboym shrugs. "The letter's all written in lawyer."

Landsman puts Netsky the latke on the front door. "Don't tell them what they heard or saw," he reminds him. "And don't give them a hard time, even if they look like they could use one."

Menashe Shpringer, the criminalist working the graveyard shift, blows into the lobby in a black coat and fur hat, with a rattling of rain. In one hand Shpringer carries a dripping umbrella. With the other he tows a chrome caddy to which his black vinyl toolbox and a plastic bin, with holes for handles, are strapped with bungee cord. Shpringer is a fireplug, his bowed legs and simian arms affixed to his neck without apparent benefit of shoulders. His face is mostly jowl and his ridged forehead looks like one of those domed beehives you see representing Industry in medieval woodcuts. The bin is blazoned with the single word EVIDENCE in blue letters.

"Are you leaving town?" Shpringer says. It's not an uncommon greeting these days. A lot of people have left town in the past couple of years, fled the District for the short roster of places that will welcome them, or that have tired of hearing about pogroms secondhand and are hoping to throw one for themselves. Landsman says that as far as he knows, he is not going anywhere. Most of the places that will take Jews require that you have a near relative living there. All of Landsman's nearest relatives are dead or facing Reversion themselves.

"Then let me say goodbye to you now, forever," Shpringer says. "Tomorrow night at this time I will be basking in the warm Saskatchewan sun."

"Saskatoon?" Landsman guesses.

"Thirty below they had today," Shpringer says. "That was the high."

"Look at it this way," Landsman says. "You could be living in this dump."

"The Zamenhof." In his memory, Shpringer pulls Landsman's file, and frowns at its contents. "That's right. Home sweet home, eh?"

"It suits me in my current style of life."

Shpringer smiles a thin smile from which almost every trace of pity has been erased.

"Which way to the dead man?" he says.

 4

First thing Shpringer screws in all the lightbulbs that Lasker loosened. Then he lowers his safety glasses and goes to work. He gives Lasker a manicure and pedicure and looks inside his mouth for a severed finger or a bronze doubloon. He lifts prints with his dust and brush. He takes 317 Polaroids. He takes pictures of the corpse, the room, the perforated pillow, the fingerprints he has raised. He takes a picture of the chessboard.

"One for me," Landsman says.

Shpringer snaps a second shot of the board that the murder obliged Lasker to abandon. Then he hands it to Landsman, an eyebrow raised.

"Valuable clue," Landsman says.

One piece at a time, Shpringer undoes the dead man's Nimzo-Croatian Defense or whatever it is he had going, zipping each chessman into its own baggie.

"How'd you get so dirty?" he says without looking at Landsman.

Landsman notices the bright brown dust clinging to his shoe tops, his cuffs, the knees of his pants. "I was looking in the basement. There's a huge, I don't know, service pipe down there." He feels the blood flow into his cheeks. "I had to check it out."

"A Warsaw tunnel," Shpringer says. "They go all through this part of the Untershtot."

"You don't believe that."

"When the greeners got here after the war. The ones who had been in the ghetto at Warsaw. At Bialystok. The ex-partisans. I guess some of them didn't trust the Americans very much. So they dug tunnels. Just in case they had to fight again. That's the real reason it's called the Untershtot."

"A rumor, Shpringer. An urban myth. It's just a utility pipe."

Shpringer grunts. He bags the bath towel, the hand towel, and a worn tile of soap. He counts the ginger pubic hairs pasted to the toilet seat and then bags each one. "Speaking of rumors," he says, "what do you hear from Felsenfeld?"

Felsenfeld is Inspector Felsenfeld, the squad commander. "What do you mean, what do I hear from him? I just saw him this afternoon," Landsman says. "I didn't *hear* anything from him, the man hasn't uttered three words together in ten years. What kind of question is that? What rumors?"

"Just wondering."

Shpringer is running his fingers in their latex glove across the freckled skin of Lasker's left arm. It bears needle tracks and faint marks where the deceased tied himself off.

"Felsenfeld's hand was on his belly all day," Landsman says, reflecting. "Maybe I heard him say 'reflux.'" Then: "What do you see?"

Shpringer frowns at the flesh above Lasker's elbow, where the tourniquet marks are bunched. "Looks like he used a belt," he says. "Only his belt is too wide to have made these marks." He has already put Lasker's belt, along with two pairs of gray trousers and two blue blazers, into a brown paper bag.

"His works are in the drawer, in a black zip," Landsman says. "I didn't look too close."

Shpringer opens the drawer in Lasker's bedside table and takes out the black toilet kit. He unzips it and then makes a funny sound in his throat. The cover of the kit opens toward Landsman. At first Landsman can't see what has caught Shpringer's interest.

"What do you know about this Lasker?" Shpringer says.

"I'm willing to venture that on occasion he played chess," Landsman says. One of the three books in the room is a creased and broken-backed paperback edition of *Three Hundred Chess Games* by Siegbert Tarrasch. It has a manila pocket pasted to its inside back cover, with a return card that shows it was last borrowed from the central branch of the Sitka Public Library in July 1986. Landsman can't help thinking that he first made love to his future ex-wife in July 1986. Bina was twenty at the time, and Landsman was twenty-three, and it was the height of the northern summer. July 1986 is the date stamped onto the card in the pocket of Landsman's illusions. The other two books are cheap Yiddish thrillers. "Beyond that I know goat shit."

As Shpringer has inferred from the marks on Lasker's arm, the deceased's apparent tourniquet of choice was a leather strap, black, about half an inch wide. Shpringer pulls it out of the zip and holds it up between two fingers as if it might bite. Halfway along the strap hangs a small leather box designed to hold a slip of paper on which a scribe, with ink and a feather, has written four passages from the Torah. Each morning the pious Jew twines one of these doodads along his left arm, ties another to his forehead, and prays for understanding of the kind of God Who obliges somebody to do something like that every damn day of his life. But there is nothing inside the box on Emanuel Lasker's prayer strap. It's just the thing he chose to use to dilate the vein in his arm.

"That's a new one," Shpringer says. "Tying off with tefillin."

"Now that I think about it," Landsman says, "he had the look. Like maybe he used to be black hat. They take on a kind of a—I don't know. They look shorn."

Landsman pulls on a glove and, gripping Lasker's chin, tilts from side to side the dead man's head with its swollen mask of blood vessels. "If he used to wear a beard, then it was a while ago," he says. "Skin tone on his face is even."

He lets go of Lasker's face and steps away from the body. It would not be quite accurate to say that he pegged Lasker for a former black hat. But with the chin of a fat boy, and the air of ruination, Landsman figured Lasker for having once been something more than a sockless junkie in a cheap hotel. He sighs. "What I wouldn't give to be lying on the sunny beaches of Saskatoon."

There are noises in the hallway, and the rattle of metal and straps, and the next moment two workers from the morgue come in with a collapsible gurney. Shpringer tells them to bring the evidence bin and the bags he has filled, and then lumbers out, one wheel of his trolley squeaking as he goes.

"Piece of shit," Landsman informs the morgue boys, meaning the case, not the victim. This judgment does not appear to surprise or come to them as news. Landsman goes back up to his room to rejoin his bottle of slivovitz and the World's Fair shot glass that has captured his affections. He sits down in the chair by the pressboard desk, with a dirty shirt for a seat cushion. He takes the Polaroid out of his pocket and studies the game that Lasker left behind, trying to decide whether the next move was to be White's or Black's, and what would be the next move after that. But there are too many pieces, and it is too difficult to hold the moves in his head, and Landsman doesn't own anything like a chess set on which to lay it all out. After a few minutes he feels himself drifting off to sleep. But no, he isn't going to do that, not when he knows that what awaits him are trite Escher dreams, woozy checkerboards, giant rooks casting phallic shadows.

He takes off his clothes, and steps under the shower, and lies down for half an hour with his eyes wide open, taking memories— of his little sister in her Super Cub, of Bina in the summer of

1986—out of their plastic bags. He studies them as if they are transcriptions, in a dusty book stolen from the library, of bygone checkmates and brilliancies. After half an hour of that useful pursuit, he gets up and puts on a clean shirt and tie, and goes down to Sitka Central to file his report.

5

Landsman learned to hate the game of chess at the hands of his father and his uncle Hertz. The brothers-in-law were boyhood friends back in Lodz, fellow members of the Makkabi Youth Chess Club. Landsman remembers how they used to talk about the day, in the summer of 1939, when the great Tartakower dropped by to put on a demonstration for the boys of the Makkabi. Savielly Tartakower was a Polish citizen, a grandmaster, and a character famous for having said "The blunders are all there on the board, waiting to be made." He came from Paris to report on a tournament for a French chess journal and to visit with the director of the Makkabi Youth Chess Club, an old comrade from his days on the Russian front in the army of Franz Josef. At the director's urging, Tartakower now proposed a game against the club's best young player, Isidor Landsman.

They sat down together, the strapping war veteran in his bespoke suit and harsh good humor, and the stammering fifteen-year-old with a wall eye, a receding hairline, and a mustache that was often mistaken for a sooty thumbprint. Tartakower drew Black, and Landsman's father chose the English Opening. For the first hour, Tartakower's play was inattentive, even autonomic. He left his great chess engine idling and played by the book. Thirty-four moves in, with genial scorn, he offered Landsman's father a draw. Landsman's father needed to piss, his ears were ringing, he was only staving off the inevitable. But he declined. His game by now was based on nothing but feel and desperation. He reacted, he refused exchanges, his sole assets a stubborn nature and a wild sense of the board. After seventy moves and four hours and ten minutes of play, Tartakower, not so genial anymore, repeated his earlier offer. Landsman's father, plagued by tinnitus, about to wet his pants, accepted. In later years Landsman's father sometimes let on that his mind, that queer organ, never quite recovered from the ordeal of this game. But of course there were worse ordeals to come.

"That was not in the least enjoyable," Tartakower is supposed to have told Landsman's father, rising from his chair. Young Hertz Shemets, with his unfailing eye for weakness, spotted a tremor in Tartakower's hand, holding a hastily fetched glass of Tokay. Then Tartakower pointed to Isidor Landsman's skull. "But I'm sure it was preferable to being obliged to live in there."

Not quite two years later, Hertz Shemets, his mother, and his kid sister, Freydl, arrived on Baranof Island, Alaska, with the first wave of Galitzer settlers. He came on the notorious *Diamond*, a World War I–era troop transport that Secretary Ickes ordered taken out of mothballs and rechristened as a left-handed memorial, or so legend has it, to the late Anthony Dimond, the Alaska Territory's nonvoting delegate to the House of Representatives. (Until the fatal intervention on a Washington, D.C., street corner of a drunken, taxi-driving schlemiel named Denny Lanning— eternal hero of the Sitka Jews—Delegate Dimond had been on the verge of getting the Alaskan Settlement Act killed in committee.) Thin, pale, bewildered, Hertz Shemets stepped from the *Diamond*, from the dark and the reek of soup and rusty puddles, to the clean cold spice of Sitka pine. With his family and his people he was numbered, inoculated, deloused, tagged like a migrant bird by the stipulations of the Alaskan Settlement Act of 1940. In a cardboard pocketbook he carried an "Ickes passport," a special emergency visa printed on special flimsy paper with special smeary ink.

There was nowhere else for him to go. It said so, in large type, on the front of an Ickes passport. He would not be permitted to travel to Seattle, or San Francisco, or even Juneau or Ketchikan. All the normal quotas on Jewish immigration to the United States remained in force. Even with the timely death of Dimond, the Act could not be forced up the American body politic without a certain amount of muscle and grease, and restrictions on Jewish movement were part of the deal.

On the heels of Jews from Germany and Austria, the Shemets family was dumped with their fellow Galitzers at Camp Slattery, in a muskeg swamp ten miles from the hard-bitten, half-decrepit town of Sitka, capital of the old Russian Alaska colony. In drafty, tin-roofed huts and barracks, they underwent six months of intensive acclimatization by a crack team of fifteen billion mosquitoes working under contract with the U.S. Interior Department. Hertz was conscripted for a road gang, then assigned to the crew that built the Sitka airfield. He lost two molars when he was smacked by a shovel, working a muck detail deep in a caisson sunk in the mud of Sitka harbor. In later years, whenever you drove with him over the Tshernovits Bridge, he would rub at his jaw, and his hard eyes in his sharp face would take on a wistful air. Freydl was sent to school in a chilly barn whose roof rang with steady rain. Their mother was taught the rudiments of agriculture, the use of plow, fertilizer, and irrigation hose. Brochures and posters held up the short Alaskan growing season as an allegory of the brief duration of her stay. Mrs. Shemets ought to think of the Sitka Settlement as a cellar or potting shed in which, like flower bulbs, she and her children could be put up for the winter, until their home soil thawed enough to allow them to be replanted there. No one imagined that the soil of Europe would be sowed so deeply with salt and ash.

Despite the agricultural palaver, the modest homesteads and farm cooperatives proposed by the Sitka Settlement Corporation never materialized. Japan attacked Pearl Harbor. The Interior Department's attention wandered toward more pressing strategic concerns, such as oil reserves and mining. At the conclusion of their term at "Ickes College," the Shemets family, like most of their fellow refugees, were kicked loose to fend for themselves. Just as Delegate Dimond had predicted, they drifted up to the raw, newly booming town of Sitka. Hertz studied criminal justice at the new Sitka Technical Institute and, on graduating in 1948, was hired as a paralegal by the first big U.S. law firm to open a branch office here. His sister, Freydl, Landsman's mother, was among the earliest Girl Scouts in the settlement.

Nineteen forty-eight: Strange times to be a Jew. In August the defense of Jerusalem collapsed and the outnumbered Jews of the three-month-old republic of Israel were routed, massacred, and driven into the sea. As Hertz was starting his job at Foehn Harmattan & Buran, the House Committee on Territories and Insular Affairs began a long-delayed review of status called for by the Sitka Settlement Act. Like the rest of Congress, like most Americans, the House Committee was sobered by grim revelations of the slaughter of two million Jews in Europe, by the barbarity of the rout of Zionism, by the plight of the refugees of Palestine and Europe. At the same time, they were practical souls. The population of Sitka Settlement had already swollen to two million. In direct violation of the act, Jews had spread up and down the western shore of Baranof Island, out to Kruzof, all the way up to West Chichagof Island. The economy was booming. American Jews were lobbying hard. In the end, Congress granted the Sitka Settlement "interim status" as a federal district. But candidacy for separate statehood was explicitly ruled out. NO JEWLASKA, LAWMAKERS PROMISE, ran the headline in the *Daily Times*. The emphasis was always on the word "interim." In sixty years that status would revert, and the Sitka Jews would be left once again to shift for themselves.

One warm September afternoon not long after, Hertz Shemets was walking down Seward Street, prolonging his lunch break, when he bumped into his old chum from Lodz, Isidor Landsman. Landsman's father had just arrived in Sitka, alone, aboard the *Williwaw*, fresh from a tour of the death and DP camps of Europe. He was twenty-five, bald, and missing most of his teeth. He was six feet tall and weighed 125 pounds. He smelled funny, talked crazy, and had outlived his entire family. He was oblivious to the raucous frontier energy of downtown Sitka, the work crews of young Jewesses in their blue head scarves, singing Negro spirituals with Yiddish lyrics that paraphrased Lincoln and Marx. The lively stench of fish flesh and felled tree and turned earth, the rumble of the dredgers and steam shovels grading mountains and filling in Sitka Sound, none of it seemed to touch him. He walked with his head down, a hunch in his shoulders, as if only burrowing through this world on his inexplicable way from one strange dimension to the next. Nothing penetrated or illuminated the dark tunnel of his passage. But when Isidor Landsman realized that the grinning man, hair slicked, shoes like a couple of Kaiser automobiles, smelling of the grilled-onion cheeseburger he had just consumed at the lunch counter of Woolworth's, was his old friend Hertz Shemets from the Makkabi Youth Chess Club, he lifted his eyes. The eternal kink went out of his shoulder. He opened his mouth and closed it again, speechless with outrage, joy, and wonder. Then he burst into tears.

Hertz took Landsman's father back to Woolworth's, bought him lunch (an egg sandwich, his first milk shake, a decent pickle) and then led him down to Lincoln Street, to the new Hotel Einstein, in whose café the great exiles of Jewish chess met every day to demolish one another without pity or heart. Landsman's father, half demented at this point by fat, sugar, and the lingering ill effects of typhus, mopped up the room. He took on all comers and sent them out of the Einstein so soundly thrashed that one or two of them never forgave him.

Even then he displayed the mournful, agonized style of play that helped ruin the game for Landsman as a child. "Your father played chess," Hertz Shemets once said, "like a man with a toothache, a hemorrhoid, and gas." He sighed, he moaned. He tugged in fits at the patchy remnant of his brown hair, or chased it with his fingers back and forth across his pate like a pastry chef scattering flour on a marble slab. The blunders of his opponents were each a separate cramp in the abdomen. His own moves, however daring, however startling and original and strong, struck him like successive pieces of terrible news, so that he covered his mouth and rolled his eyes at the sight of them.

Uncle Hertz's style was nothing like that. He played calmly, with an air of unconcern, keeping his body at a slight angle to the board, as if expecting very shortly to be served a meal or to take a pretty girl onto his lap. But his eyes saw everything, the way they'd seen the telltale tremor in Tartakower's hand that day at the Makkabi Youth Chess Club. He took in his reversals without alarm and his chances with a faint air of amusement. Smoking Broadways end on end, he watched his old friend squirm and mutter his way through the assembled geniuses of the Einstein. Then, when the room was laid to waste, Hertz made the necessary move. He invited Isidor Landsman home.

In the summer of 1948, the Shemets family lived in a two-room apartment in a brand-new building on a brand-new island. The building was home to two dozen families, all of them Polar Bears, as the first-wave refugees called themselves. The mother slept in the bedroom, Freydl got the sofa, and Hertz made his bed on the floor. By now they were all staunch Alaskan Jews, which meant they were utopians, which meant they saw imperfection everywhere they looked. A barb-tongued and quarrelsome family, in particular Freydl Shemets, who at fourteen already stood five feet eight inches tall and weighed 110 kilograms. She took one look at Landsman's father, hovering uncertainly in the doorway of the apartment, and correctly diagnosed him to be as unreclaimable and inaccessible as the wilderness that she had come to regard as her home. It was love at first sight.

In later years it was tough for Landsman to get much out of his father about what if anything he had seen in Freydl Shemets. She was not a bad-looking girl. Egyptian-eyed, olive-skinned, in her short pants, hiking boots, and the rolled sleeves of her Pendleton shirt, she exuded the old Makkabi movement spirit of *mens sana in corpore sano*. She pitied Isidor Landsman deeply for the loss of his family, for the suffering he had endured in the camps. But she was one of those Polar Bear kids who handled their own feelings of guilt at having escaped the filth, the starvation, the ditches and killing factories by offering survivors a constant stream of advice, information, and criticism disguised as morale boosting. As if the choking, low-hanging black pall of the Destruction could be lifted by one determined kibitzer.

That first night Landsman's father slept, with Hertz, on the floor of the Shemets apartment. The next day Freydl took him shopping for clothes, paying for them out of her own bat mitzvah nest egg. She helped him rent a room from a recent widower who lived in the building. She massaged his scalp with an onion, in the belief that this would cause his hair to renew itself. She fed him calf liver for his tired blood. For the next five years, she nudged and badgered and bullied him until he sat up straight, made eye contact when speaking, learned American, and wore dentures. She married him the day after she turned eighteen, and got a job at the *Sitka Tog*, working her way up through the women's page to features editor. She worked sixty to seventy-five hours a week, five days a week, until her death from cancer, when Landsman was in college. During that time Hertz Shemets impressed the American lawyers at Foehn Harmattan so much that they took up a subscription and pulled the strings they needed to pull to send him to law school in Seattle. He later became the first Jew hired by the Sitka detail of the FBI, its first district director, and eventually, having caught Hoover's eye, ran the Bureau's regional counterintelligence program.

Landsman's father played chess.

Every morning, in rain, snow, or fog, he walked two miles to the Hotel Einstein coffee shop, sat down at an aluminum-topped table in the back, facing the door, and took out a small set of maple and cherry chessmen that had been a present from his brother-in-law. Every night he sat at his bench in the back of the little house on Adler Street where Landsman grew up, in Halibut Point, looking over the eight or nine correspondence games he had going at any one time. He wrote notes for *Chess Review*. He revised a biography of Tartakower that he never quite finished or abandoned. He drew a pension from the German government. And, with the help of his brother-in-law, he taught his son to hate the game he himself loved.

"You don't want to do that," Landsman's father would plead after Landsman released, with bloodless fingers, his knight or pawn to meet the fate that always came as a surprise to Landsman, no matter how much he studied, practiced, or played the game of chess. "Take it from me."

"I do."

"You don't."

But in the service of his own small misery, Landsman could be stubborn, too. Satisfied, burning with shame, he would watch unfold the grim destiny that he had been unable to foresee. And Landsman's father would demolish him, flay him, vivisect him, gazing at his son all the while from behind the sagging porch of his face.

After some years of this sport, Landsman sat down at his mother's typewriter to write his father a letter in which he confessed his loathing for the game of chess, and begged his father not to force him to play anymore. Landsman carried this letter in his satchel for a week, enduring three more bloody defeats, and then mailed it from the Untershtot post office. Two days later, Isidor Landsman killed himself, in room 21 of the Hotel Einstein, by an overdose of Nembutal.

After that Landsman started to have some problems. He wet the bed, got fat, stopped talking. His mother put him in therapy with a remarkably gentle and ineffectual doctor named Melamed. It was not until twenty-three years after his father's death that Landsman rediscovered the fatal letter, in a box that also held a fair copy of the unfinished biography of Tartakower. It turned out that Landsman's father had never even opened the letter from his son, let alone read it. By the time the mailman delivered it, Landsman's father was already dead.

6

Landsman is tripping on the memory of those old chess-playing yids, hunched at the back of the Café Einstein, as he drives out to pick up Berko. It is six-fifteen in the morning, by his watch. By the sky, the empty boulevard, and the stone of dread lying in his belly, it is the dead of night. Sunrise, this close to the arctic circle and the winter solstice, is still at least two hours off.

Landsman is at the wheel of a 1971 Chevrolet Chevelle Super Sport, which he bought ten years ago in an access of nostalgic optimism and has driven until all its secret flaws seem indistinguishable from his own. In the '71 model year, the Chevelle went from two pairs of headlight bulbs to a single pair. Right now one of these bulbs is blown. Landsman gropes his way cyclops-style along the promenade. Ahead of him rise the tower blocks of the Shvartser-Yam, on their artificial spit of land in the middle of Sitka Sound, huddled in the darkness like prisoners rounded up with a powerful hose.

Russian shtarkers developed the Shvartser-Yam during the mid-eighties, on purest quake-bait landfill, in the first heady days of legalized casino gambling. Time-shares, vacation homes, and bachelor pads, that was the idea, with the Grand Yalta casino and its jumping tables at the center of the action. But legal gambling is out now, banned by the Traditional Values Act, and the casino building houses a KosherMart, a Walgreens, and a Big Macher outlet store. The shtarkers went back to bankrolling illegal policy rackets, betting mills, and floating craps games. The swingers and vacationers gave way to a population of upper-lowlifes, Russian immigrants, a smattering of ultra-orthodox Jews, and a bunch of bohemian semiprofessionals who like the atmosphere of ruined festivity that lingers in the neighborhood like a strand of tinsel on the branch of a bare tree.

The Taytsh-Shemets family lives in the Dnyeper, on the twenty-fourth floor. The Dnyeper is round as a stack of pie tins. Many of its residents, spurning fine views of Mount Edgecumbe's collapsed cone, the gleaming Safety Pin, or the lights of the Untershtot, have enclosed their curving balconies with storm windows and louvers in order to gain an extra room. The Taytsh-Shemetses did that when the baby came along: the first baby. Now both little Taytsh-Shemetses sleep out there, stashed away on the balcony like disused skis.

Landsman parks the Super Sport in the spot behind the Dumpsters that he has come to view as his own, though he supposes a man should not come to cherish tender feelings toward a parking place. Simply having a place to put his car that is twenty-four stories down from a standing invitation to breakfast should never pass, in a man's heart, for a homecoming.

He's a few minutes ahead of six-thirty, and though he's pretty sure that everybody is awake in the Taytsh-Shemets household, he decides to take the stairs. The Dnyeper stairwell reeks of sea air, cabbage, cold cement. When he gets to the top, he lights a papiros to reward himself for industry and stands on the Taytsh-Shemets doormat, keeping the mezuzah company. He has one lung coughed up and the other on its way when Ester-Malke Taytsh opens the door. She holds a home pregnancy test stick with a bead, on its business end, of what must be urine. When she notices Landsman noticing it, she coolly makes it disappear into a pocket of her bathrobe.

"You know there's a doorbell, right?" she says through a tangled curtain of hair, brick-brown and too fine for the bob she always sports. It has a way of spilling across her face, especially when she is cracking wise. "I mean, coughing works, too."

She leaves the door open and Landsman standing there on the thick coir mat that says GET LOST. Landsman touches two fingers to the mezuzah on his way in and then gives them a perfunctory kiss. That is what you do if you are a believer, like Berko, or a mocking asshole, like Landsman. He hangs his hat and overcoat on an elk-antler rack by the front door. He follows Ester-Malke's skinny ass, wrapped in her white cotton robe, down the hall and into the kitchen. The kitchen is narrow, laid out galley-style, the stove, sink, and refrigerator down one side, cabinets down the other. At the end a breakfast bar, with two stools, overlooks the living-dining room. Steam curls out of a waffle iron on the counter in cartoon-locomotive puffs. The drip-filter coffee maker hawks and spits like a decrepit Jewish policeman after ten flights of steps.

Landsman sidles up to the stool he favors and stands beside it. From the hip pocket of his tweed blazer he takes a pocket chess set and unwraps it. He bought it at the all-night drugstore on Korczak Platz. "Fat man still in his pajamas?" he says.

"Getting dressed."

"Fat baby?"

"Picking the necktie."

"And the other one, what's his name?" In fact, his name, thanks to a recent vogue for crafting given names from family names, is Feingold Taytsh-Shemets. They call him Goldy. Four years ago Landsman had the honor to hold down Goldy's scrawny legs while an ancient Jew with a knife came after his foreskin. "His Majesty."

In answer, she nods her head toward the living-dining.

"Still sick?" Landsman says.

"Better today."

Landsman goes around the breakfast bar, past the glass-topped dining table, and over to the big white sectional sofa to get a look at what the television is doing to his godson. "Look who it is," he says.

Goldy is wearing his polar-bear jammies, the height of retrospective chic for an Alaskan Jewish kid. Polar bears, snowflakes, igloos, the northern imagery that was so ubiquitous when Landsman was a boy, it's all back in style again. Only this time it seems to be meant ironically. Snowflakes, yes, the Jews found them here, though, thanks to greenhouse gases, there are measurably fewer than in the old days. But no polar bears. No igloos. No reindeer. Mostly just a lot of angry Indians, fog, and rain, and half a century of a sense of mistakenness so keen, worked so deep into the systems of the Jews, that it emerges everywhere, even on their children's pajamas.

"You ready to work today, Goldele?" Landsman says. He lays the back of his hand against the boy's forehead. It feels nice and cool. Goldy's Shnapish the Dog yarmulke hangs crooked, and Landsman smooths it and adjusts the bobby pin that holds it in place. "Ready to fight crime?"

"Sure thing, Uncle."

Landsman reaches out to shake the boy's hand, and without even looking, Goldy slides his dry paw into Landsman's. A minute blue rectangle of light swims on the tear layer of the boy's dark brown eyes. Landsman has watched this program with his godson before, on the educational channel. Like 90 percent of the television they watch, it comes from the south and is shown dubbed into Yiddish. It concerns the adventures of a pair of children with Jewish names who look like they might be part Indian and have no visible parents. They do have a crystalline magical dragon scale that they wish on in order to travel to a land of pastel dragons, each distinguished by its color and its particular brand of imbecility. Little by little, the children spend more and more time with their magical dragon scale until one day they travel off to the land of rainbow idiocy and never return; their bodies are found by the night manager of their cheap flop, each with a bullet in the back of the head. Maybe, Landsman thinks, something gets lost in the translation.

"Still want to be a noz when you grow up?" Landsman says. "Like your dad and your uncle Meyer?"

"Yes," Goldy says without enthusiasm. "You bet I do."

"That's the boy."

They shake hands again. This conversation is the equivalent of Landsman's kissing the mezuzah, the kind of thing that starts out as a joke and ends up as a strap to hang on to.

"You taking up chess?" Ester-Malke says when he walks back into the kitchen.

"God forbid," says Landsman. He climbs up onto his stool and struggles with the tiny pawns and knights and kings of the travel set, setting them up to reflect the board left behind by the so-called Emanuel Lasker. He has a hard time telling the pieces apart, but every time he holds one up to his face to get a good look at it, he drops it.

"Stop looking at me that way," he says to Ester-Malke, just guessing. "I don't like it."

"Damn it, Meyer," she says, watching his hands. "You have the shakes."

"I didn't sleep all night."

"Uh-huh."

The thing about Ester-Malke Taytsh is that before she went back to school, became a social worker, and married Berko, she enjoyed a brief but distinguished career as a South Sitka fuckup. She has a couple of small-bore criminals in her past, a regretted tattoo on her belly, and a bridge in her jaw, a souvenir of the last man to mistreat her. Landsman has known her longer than Berko has, having busted her on a vandalism charge when she was still in high school. Ester-Malke understands how to handle a loser, by intuition and habit, and without any of the reproach she brings to bear on her own wasted youth. She goes to the refrigerator and takes out a bottle of Bruner Adler, pops the top, and hands it to Landsman. He rolls it against his sleepless temples, then takes a long swallow.

"So," he says, feeling better in an instant. "You're late?"

She puts on a half-theatrical expression of guilt, goes for the pregnancy-test stick, then leaves her hand in the pocket, clutching the stick without taking it out. Landsman knows, because she has broached the subject once or twice, that Ester-Malke worries he might envy her and Berko their successful program of breeding and their two fine sons. Landsman does, at times, with bitterness. But when she brings it up, he generally bothers to deny it.

"Shit," he says as a bishop goes skittering across the floor and disappears under the bar counter.

"Was it a black one or a white?"

"Black. A bishop. Shit. It's gone."

Ester-Malke goes to the spice rack, tightens the waistband of her robe, studies her options. "Here," she says. She takes out a jar of chocolate sprinkles, unscrews it, tips one into her palm, and hands it to Landsman. "Use that."

Landsman is kneeling on the ground under the counter. He finds the missing bishop and manages to poke it into its hole at h6. Ester-Malke puts the jar back in the cabinet and returns her right hand to the mystery of her bathrobe pocket.

Landsman eats the chocolate sprinkle. "Berko knows?" he says.

Ester-Malke shakes her head, hiding behind her hair. "It's nothing," she says.

"Officially nothing?"

She shrugs.

"Didn't you look at the test?"

"I'm afraid to."

"You're afraid to what?" says Berko, appearing at the door to the kitchen with young Pinchas Taytsh-Shemets—inevitably, Pinky—tucked into the crook of his right arm. A month ago they made a party for the kid, with a cake and a candle. So, Landsman reckons, that will bring in the third Taytsh-Shemets, if any, at around twenty-one, twenty-two months after the second. And seven months after Reversion. Seven months into the unknown world to come. Another diminutive prisoner of history and fate, another potential Messiah—for Messiah, say the experts, is born into every generation—to fill the sails of Elijah the Prophet's demented caravel of dreams. Ester-Malke's hand emerges from her pocket without the pregnancy test, and she gives Landsman a South Sitka high sign with one arched eyebrow.

"Afraid to hear what I had to eat yesterday," Landsman says. By way of creating a diversion, he takes Lasker's copy of *Three Hundred Chess Games* out of the other hip pocket of his jacket and lays it on the bar beside the chessboard.

"This is about your dead junkie?" Berko says, eyeing the board.

"Emanuel Lasker," Landsman says. "But that was just a name in the registration. We found no kind of ID on him at all. We don't know who he was yet."

"Emanuel Lasker. I feel I know the name." Berko squeezes sideways into the kitchen in his suit pants and shirtsleeves. The pants are heather-gray merino with double pleats, the shirt white on white. At his throat, tied with a handsome knot, hangs a navy necktie patterned with orange blobs. The tie is extra long, the trousers capacious and held up by navy suspenders taxed by the span and the arc of his belly. Under the shirt he wears the fringed four-corner, and a trim blue yarmulke perches on the glossy black furze at the back of his head, but no beard will grow on his chin. There is not a beard to be found on the chins of any of the men in his maternal family, reaching back all the way, no doubt, to the time when Raven created everything (apart from the sun, which he stole). Berko Shemets is observant, but in his own way and for his own reasons. He is a minotaur, and the world of Jews is his labyrinth.

He came to live with the Landsmans in the house on Adler Street on a day in late spring 1981, a shambling giant boy known, in the Sea Monster House of the Raven Moiety of the Longhair Tribe, as Johnny "the Jew" Bear. He stood five feet nine inches in his mukluks that afternoon, thirteen years old and only an inch shorter than Landsman at eighteen. Until that moment no one had ever mentioned this boy to Landsman or his little sister. Now the kid was going to be sleeping in the bedroom that had once served Meyer and Naomi's father as Klein bottle for the infinite loop of his insomnia.

"Who the hell are you?" Landsman asked him as the kid stole sideways into the living room. Twisting a billed cap in his hands, taking everything in with his dark, all-consuming gaze. Hertz and Freydl were standing out on the front walk, screaming at each other. Apparently, Landsman's uncle had neglected to mention to his sister that his son was coming to live at her house.

"My name is Johnny Bear," Berko said. "I'm part of the Shemets Collection."

Hertz Shemets remains a noted expert on Tlingit art and artifacts. At one time this hobby or pastime sent him wandering deeper and farther into the Indianer-Lands than any other Jew of his generation. So, yes, his study of Native culture and his trips into the Indianer-Lands were a beard for his COINTELPRO work during the sixties. But they were not *only* a beard. Hertz Shemets was drawn to the Indian way of life. He learned to gaff a seal with a steel hook, through the eye, and to slaughter and put up a bear, and to enjoy the flavor of candlefish grease as much as that of schmaltz. And he fathered a child on Miss Laurie Jo Bear of Hoonah. When she was killed during the so-called Synagogue Riots, her half-Jew son, an object of torment and scorn among the Raven Moiety, appealed for rescue to the father he barely knew. It was a *zwischenzug*, an unexpected move in the orderly unfolding of a game. It caught Uncle Hertz off guard.

"What are you going to do, turn him away?" he yelled at Landsman's mother. "They're making his life a living hell up there. His mother is dead. Murdered by Jews."

In fact, eleven Native Alaskans were killed in the rioting that followed the bombing of a prayer house that a group of Jews had built on disputed land. There are pockets in these islands where the map drawn by Harold Ickes falters and gives way, dotted stretches of the Line. Most of them are too remote or mountainous to be inhabited, frozen or flooded year-round. But some of these crosshatched patches, choice and level and temperate, have proved irresistible over the years to the Jews in their millions. Jews want livable space. In the seventies some of them, mostly members of small Orthodox sects, began to take it.

The construction of a prayer house at St. Cyril by the splinter from a splinter of a sect from Lisianski was the final outrage for many Natives. It was met with demonstrations, rallies, lawyers, and dark rumblings from Congress over yet another affront to peace and parity by the overweening Jews of the north. Two days before its consecration, somebody—no one ever came forward or was charged—threw a double Molotov through a window, burning the prayer house to its concrete pad. The congregants and their supporters swarmed into the town of St. Cyril, smashing crab traps, breaking the windows of the Alaska Native Brotherhood hall, and setting spectacular fire to a shedful of Roman candles and cherry bombs. The driver of a truckload of angry yids lost control of the wheel and plowed into the grocery store where Laurie Jo worked as a checker, killing her instantly. The Synagogue Riots remain the lowest moment in the bitter and inglorious history of Tlingit-Jewish relations.

"Is that my fault? Is that my problem?" Landsman's mother yelled back. "An Indian living in my house, that is something I do not need!"

The children listened to them for a while, Johnny Bear standing in the doorway, kicking at his duffel bag with the toe of his sneaker.

"Good thing you don't speak Yiddish," Landsman told the younger boy.

"I don't need to, dickwad," said Johnny the Jew. "I been hearing this shit all my life."

After the thing was settled—and it had been settled before Landsman's mother ever started with the yelling—Hertz came in to say goodbye. His son had two inches on him. When he took the boy in his arms for a quick stiff hug, it looked like the side chair was embracing the couch. Then he stepped away.

"I'm sorry, John," he said. He gripped his son by the ears and held on tight. He scanned the boy's face like a telegram. "I want you to know that. I don't want you ever to look at me and think that I'm feeling anything but sorry."

"I want to live with you," said the boy tonelessly.

"So you have mentioned." The words were harsh and the manner callous, but all at once—it shocked the hell out of Landsman—there was a shine of tears in Uncle Hertz's eyes. "I'm well-known, John, as a complete son of a bitch. You'd be worse off with me than living in the street." He looked around his sister's living room, the plastic slipcovers on the furniture, the art like barbed wire, the abstract menorah. "God knows what they'll make of you here."

"A Jew," said Johnny Bear, and it was hard to tell whether he meant it as a boast or a prediction of ruin. "Like you."

"That seems unlikely," Hertz said. "I'd like to see them manage that. Goodbye, John."

He gave Naomi a pat on the head. Just before he went out, he stopped to shake hands with Landsman. "Help your cousin, Meyerle, he's going to need it."

"He looks like he can help himself."

"He does, doesn't he?" said Uncle Hertz. "That at least he gets from me."

Now Ber Shemets, as he came in time to style himself, lives like a Jew, wears a skullcap and four-corner like a Jew. He reasons as a Jew, worships as a Jew, fathers and loves his wife and serves the public as a Jew. He spins theory with his hands, keeps kosher, and sports a penis cut (his father saw to it before abandoning the infant Bear) on the bias. But to look at, he's pure Tlingit. Tartar eyes, dense black hair, broad face built for joy but trained in the craft of sorrow. The Bears are a big people, and Berko stands two meters tall in his socks and weighs in at 110 kilograms. He has a big head, big feet, big belly and hands. Everything about Berko is big except for the baby in his arms, smiling shyly at Landsman with his thatch of black horsehair standing up like magnetized iron filings. Cute as a button, Landsman would be the first to acknowledge, but even after a year, the sight of Pinky still puts a dent in the soft place behind Landsman's sternum. Pinky was born exactly two years after Django's due date—September 22.

"Emanuel Lasker was a famous chess player," Landsman informs Berko, who takes a mug of coffee from Ester-Malke and frowns into the steam. "A German Jew. In the teens and twenties." He spent the hour between five and six at his computer in the desolate squad room, seeing what he could turn up. "A mathematician. Lost to Capablanca, like everybody else back then. The book was in the room. And a chessboard, set up that way."

Berko has heavy eyelids, soulful, bruised-looking, but when he drops them down over those pop eyes, it's like the beam of a flashlight bleeding through a slit, a look so cold and skeptical it can lead innocent men to doubt their own alibis.

"And you feel," he says, with a significant glance at the bottle of beer in Landsman's hand, "that the configuration of pieces on the board, what?" The slit draws narrower, the beam flares brighter. "Encodes the name of his killer?"

"In the alphabet of Atlantis," Landsman says.

"Uh-huh."

"The Jew played chess. And he tied off with tefillin. And somebody killed him with a great deal of care and discretion. I don't know. Maybe there's nothing in the chess angle. I can't get anything out of it. I went through the whole book, but I couldn't figure out which game he was playing. If any. Those diagrams, I don't know, I get a headache looking at them. I get a headache just looking at the board, a curse on it."

Landsman's voice comes out sounding every bit as hollow and hopeless as he feels, which was not his intention at all. Berko looks over the top of Pinky's head at his wife, to see if he really needs to worry about Landsman.

"Tell you what, Meyer. If you put down that beer," Berko says, trying and failing not to sound like a policeman, "I'll let you hold this nice baby. How about that? Look at him. Look at those thighs, come on. You have to squeeze them. Put down the beer, all right? And hold this nice baby for a minute."

"He is a nice baby," Landsman says. He removes another inch of beer from the bottle. Then he puts it down, and shuts up, and takes the baby, and smells him, and does the usual injury to his heart. Pinky smells like yogurt and laundry soap. A hint of his father's bay rum. Landsman carries the baby to the doorway of the kitchen, and tries not to inhale, and watches as Ester-Malke peels a sheet of waffles from the iron. She is using an old Westinghouse with Bakelite handles in the shape of leaves. It can blast out four crisp waffles at a time.

"Buttermilk?" Berko says, studying the chessboard now, stroking a finger along his heavy upper lip.

"What else?" Ester-Malke says.

"Real, or milk with vinegar?"

"We did a double-blind test, Berko." Ester-Malke hands Landsman a plate of waffles in exchange for her younger son, and even though he doesn't feel like eating, Landsman is happy to make the trade. "You can't tell the difference, remember?"

"Well, he can't play chess, either," Landsman says. "But look at him pretending."

"Fuck you, Meyer," Berko says. "Okay, now, seriously, which piece is the battleship?"

The family chess madness had burned out or redirected its

energies by the time Berko came to live with Landsman and his mother. Isidor Landsman had been dead for six years, and Hertz Shemets had transferred his skills at feinting and attack to a much larger chessboard. That meant there was no one to teach Berko the game but Landsman, a duty that Landsman carefully neglected.

"Butter?" Ester-Malke says. She ladles fresh batter into the cells of the waffle iron while Pinky sits on her hip and offers his unsolicited advice.

"No butter."

"Syrup?"

"No syrup."

"You don't really want a waffle, do you, Meyer?" Berko says. He abandons the pretense of studying the board and moves on to the volume by Siegbert Tarrasch as if he will be able to make heads or tails of that.

"Not in all honesty," Landsman says. "But I know that I should."

Ester-Malke eases the lid of the iron down onto the grids of batter. "I'm pregnant," she says in a mild tone.

"What?" Berko says, looking up from the book of orderly surprises. "Fuck!" This word is spoken in American, Berko's preferred language for swearing and harsh talk. He starts working over the stick of imaginary chewing gum that seems to appear in his mouth whenever he's getting ready to blow. "That's great, Es. That's just great. You know? Because there's still one fucking desk drawer in this shit-ass apartment that doesn't have a motherfucking baby in it!"

Then he raises *Three Hundred Chess Games* over his head and prepares, showily, to hurl it across the breakfast bar and into the living-diningroom. This is the Shemets in him coming out. Landsman's mother was also a big one for the hurling of objects in anger, and the histrionic displays of Uncle Hertz, that cool customer, are rare but legendary.

"Evidence," Landsman reminds him. Berko raises the book

higher, and Landsman says, "Evidence, God damn it!" and then
Berko throws it. The book struggles through the air, pages
fluttering, and strikes something jingly, probably the silver spice
box on the glass-topped dining table. The baby sticks out his lower
lip, then sticks it out a little farther, then hesitates, looking from
his mother to his father and back. Then he bursts into desolate
sobs. Berko glares at Pinky as if betrayed. He goes around the bar
to retrieve the mishandled evidence.

"What did Tateh do?" Ester-Malke says to the baby, kissing his
cheek and scowling at the large black-edged hole in the air that
Berko has left behind. "Did bad Detective Super-sperm throw the
silly old book?"

"Good waffle!" Landsman says, setting down his plate
untouched. He raises his voice. "Hey, Berko, I'm, uh, I think I'm
going to wait down in the car." He swipes Ester-Malke's cheek with
his lips. "Tell what's-his-name Uncle Meyerle says goodbye."

Landsman goes out to the elevators, where the wind whistles
down the shafts. The neighbor, Fried, comes out in his long black
coat, his white hair combed back and curling at his collar. Fried
is an opera singer, and the Taytsh-Shemetses feel he looks down
on them. But that is only because Fried has told them he is better
than they are. Sitkaniks generally take care to maintain this view of
their neighbors, in particular of the Natives and all those who dwell
in the south. Fried and Landsman get into the elevator together.
Fried asks Landsman if he has found any dead bodies lately, and
Landsman asks Fried if he has made any dead composers turn over
in their graves lately, and after that, they don't say anything much.
Landsman goes back out to his parking place and gets into the car.
He runs the engine and sits in the heat blowing in off the engine.
With the smell of Pinky on his collar and the cool dry ghost of
Goldy's hand in his, he plays goalkeeper as a squad of unprofitable
regrets mounts a steady attack on his ability to get through a day
without feeling anything. He climbs out and smokes a papiros in
the rain. He turns his eyes north, across the marina, to the looping

aluminum spike on its windswept island. Once more he feels a sharp nostalgia for the fair, for the heroic Jewish engineering of the Safety Pin (officially the Promise of Sanctuary Tower, but nobody calls it that), and for the cleavage of the uniformed lady who used to tear your ticket on the elevator ride to the restaurant at the Safety Pin's tip. Then he gets back in the car. A few minutes later, Berko comes out of the building and rolls like a bass drum into the Super Sport. He has the book and the pocket chess set in one hand, balancing them atop his left thigh.

"Sorry about all that," he says. "What a jerk, huh?"

"No big deal."

"We'll just have to find a bigger place."

"Right."

"Somewhere."

"That's the trick."

"It's a blessing."

"You bet. Mazel tov, Berko."

Landsman's congratulations are so ironic that they are heartfelt, and they are so heartfelt that they can only come off as insincere, and he and his partner sit there for a while, not going anywhere, listening to them congeal.

"Ester-Malke says she's so tired, she doesn't even remember having sex with me," Berko says with a deep sigh.

"Maybe you didn't."

"It's a miracle, you're saying. Like the talking chicken in the butcher shop."

"Uh-huh."

"A sign and a portent."

"One way of looking at it."

"Speaking of signs," Berko says. He opens the Sitka Public Library's long-missing copy of *Three Hundred Chess Games* to its inside back cover and slides the return card from its pasted pocket. Behind the card lies a photograph, a three-by-five color snapshot, glossy with a white border. It is the picture of a literal sign, a rectangle of black plastic into which are stamped three white roman letters, with a stamped white arrow underneath, pointing to the left. The sign dangles on two lengths of slender chain from a dirty white square of acoustic tile.

"PIE," Landsman reads.

"It seems to have fallen out in the course of my vigorous examination of the evidence," Berko says. "I figure it must have been wedged into the card pocket, or with your keen shammes vision, you would have noticed it. Recognize it?"

"Yes," Landsman says. "I know it."

At the airport that serves the raw northern city of Yakovy—the terminus from which you set off, if you are a Jew looking for modest adventure, into the modest bush of the District—tucked away at the far end of the main building, a modest operation offers pie, and only pie, American-style. The place is nothing more than a window that opens onto a kitchen equipped with five gleaming ovens. Next to the window hangs a whiteboard, and every day the proprietors—a couple of hostile Klondikes and their mysterious daughter—write out a list of the day's wares: blackberry, apple rhubarb, peach, banana cream. The pie is good, even famous in a modest way. Anybody who has passed through the Yakovy airfield knows it, and there are rumors of people who will fly in from Juneau or Fairbanks or farther away to eat it. Landsman's late sister was a devotee of the coconut cream in particular.

"So, nu," Berko says. "So what do you think?"

"I knew it," Landsman says. "The minute I walked into the room and saw Lasker lying there, I said to myself, Landsman, this whole case is going to turn on a question of pie."

"So you think it means nothing."

"Nothing means nothing," Landsman says, and all of a sudden he feels choked up, throat swollen, eyes burning with tears. Maybe it's lack of sleep, or too much time spent in the company of his shot glass. Or maybe it's the sudden image of Naomi, leaning against a wall outside that nameless and inexplicable pie shop, scarfing up a slice of coconut cream pie from a paper plate with a plastic fork, eyes closed, lips pursed and streaked with white, grooving on a mouthful of cream, crust and custard in a profound and animal way. "God damn it, Berko. I wish I had some of that pie right now."

"I was thinking the same thing," Berko says.

7

For twenty-seven years Sitka Central has been temporarily housed in eleven modular buildings in a vacant lot behind the old Russian orphanage. Rumor holds that the modulars began life as a Bible college in Slidell, Louisiana. They are windowless, low-ceilinged, flimsy, and cramped. The visitor finds, packed into the Homicide modular, a reception area, an office for each of the two detective inspectors, a shower stall with a toilet and sink, a squad room (four cubicles, four chairs, four telephones, a chalkboard, and a row of mail slots), an interrogation hotbox, and a break room. The break room comes equipped with a coffee brewer and a small refrigerator. The break room has also long housed a thriving colony of spores that, at a point in the remote past, spontaneously evolved the form and appearance of a love seat. But when Landsman and Berko pull into the gravel lot by the Homicide modular, a pair of Filipino custodians are lugging out the monstrous fungus.

"It's moving," Berko says.

People have been threatening for years to get rid of the sofa, but it is a shock to Landsman to see it finally on its way. Enough of a shock that it takes him a second or two to register the woman standing alongside the steps. She is holding a black umbrella and wearing a bright orange parka with a blazing dyed-green ruff of synthetic fur. Her right arm is raised, index finger extended toward the trash bins, like a painting of the angel Michael casting Adam and Eve from the Garden. A lock of corkscrewing red hair has sprung free of the green fur ruff and dangles down over her face. This is a chronic problem for her. When she is kneeling to examine a doubtful stain on the floor of a crime scene, or studying a photograph under a loupe, she has to blow that lock of hair out of the way with a sharp, irritated puff of breath.

Now she is scowling at the Super Sport as Landsman cuts the engine. She lowers her all-banishing hand. From this distance, it looks to Landsman as if the lady is three or four cups the worse for strong coffee, and somebody has already pissed her off once this morning, maybe twice. Landsman was married to her for twelve years, working the same Homicide squad for five. He is sensitive to her moods.

"Tell me you didn't know about this," he says to Berko, cutting the engine.

"I still don't know about it," Berko says. "I'm hoping if I close my eyes for a second and then open them again, it's going to turn out not to be true."

Landsman tries it. "No dice," he says with regret, and gets out of the car. "Give us a minute."

"Please, take all the time you want."

Landsman requires ten seconds to cross the gravel lot. Bina looks happy to see him for a count of three, followed by a two-count of looking anxious and lovely. She plays out the last five seconds by looking ready to mix it up with Landsman, if that's how he wants things to go.

"What the fuck?" Landsman says, hating to disappoint her.

"Two months of ex-wife," Bina says. "After that, it's anybody's guess."

Just after their divorce came through, Bina headed south for a year, enrolling in some kind of leadership training program for women police detectives. On her return, she accepted the lofty post of detective inspector at the Yakovy Homicide Section. There she found stimulus and fulfillment leading investigations into the hypothermia deaths of unemployed salmon fishermen amid the drainage channels of the Venice of Northwest Chichagof Island. Landsman hasn't seen her since his sister's funeral, and he gathers from the pitying look she gives his old chassis that he has gone further downhill in the months since then.

"Aren't you happy to see me, Meyer?" she says. "You don't say anything about my parka?"

"It's extremely orange," Landsman says.

"You need to be visible up there," she says. "In the woods. Or they'll think you're a bear and shoot you."

"It's a nice color on you," Landsman hears himself manage. "Goes with your eyes."

Bina accepts a compliment as if it's a can of soda that she suspects him of having shaken. "So you're saying you're surprised," she says.

"I'm surprised."

"You didn't hear about Felsenfeld?"

"It's Felsenfeld. What would I hear?" He recalls Shpringer having asked him the same question the night before, and now the insight comes to him with a keenness worthy of the man who caught Podolsky the Hospital Killer. "Felsenfeld skipped."

"Turned in his badge two nights ago. Left for Melbourne, Australia, last night. His wife's sister lives there."

"And now I have to work for you?" He knows it can't have been Bina's idea; and the move, even if it's only for two months, is unquestionably a promotion for her. But he can't quite believe that she could permit such a thing—that she would be able to stand it. "That's impossible."

"Anything is possible nowadays," Bina says. "I read it in the newspaper."

All at once the lines of her face are smoothed over, and he sees what a strain it is for her still to be around him, how relieved she is when Berko Shemets walks up.

"Everyone is here!" she says.

When Landsman turns around he finds his partner standing right behind him. Berko owns considerable powers of stealth that, naturally, he attributes to his Indian forebears. Landsman likes to ascribe them to powerful forces of surface tension, the way Berko's enormous snowshoe feet warp the earth.

"Well, well, well," Berko says genially. From the first time that Landsman brought Bina home, she and Berko seemed to share an understanding of, an angle on, a laugh at the expense of Landsman, the funny little sorehead in the last panel of a comic strip with the black lily of an exploded cigar wilting in his puss. She holds out her hand, and they shake.

"Welcome back, Detective Landsman," he says sheepishly.

"Inspector," she says, "and it's Gelbfish. Again."

Berko shuffles carefully through the hand of facts she has just dealt him. "My mistake," he says. "How'd you like Yakovy?"

"It was all right."

"Fun town?"

"I really wouldn't know."

"Meet anybody?"

Bina shakes her head, blushing, then blushing more deeply at the thought that she was blushing. "I just worked," she says. "You know me."

The sodden pink mass of the old sofa disappears around the corner of the modular, and Landsman experiences another moment of insight.

"The Burial Society is coming," he says. He means the transition task force from the U.S. Interior Department, the advance men for Reversion, come to watch over and prepare the corpse for interment in the grave of history. For the past year or so, they have been murmuring their bureaucratic kaddish over every part of the

District bureaucracy, making inventories and recommendations. Laying the foundation, Landsman imagines, so that when anything subsequently goes awry or turns sour, blame can plausibly be laid at the feet of the Jews.

"Gentleman named Spade," she says. "Showing up sometime Monday, Tuesday at the latest."

"*Felsenfeld*," Landsman says with disgust. Typical that the man would slink out three days before a shoymer from the Burial Society is due to come calling. "A black year on him."

Two more custodians come banging out of the trailer, carrying off the divisional pornography library and a life-size cardboard cutout photograph of the president of America, with his cleft chin, his golfer's tan, his air of self-importance, worn lightly, quarterback-style. The detectives like to dress the cardboard president in lacy underpants and pelt him with wadded clots of wet toilet paper.

"Time to measure Sitka Central for a shroud," Berko says, watching it go.

"You don't even begin to understand," Bina says, and Landsman understands at once, from the dark seam in her voice, that she is trying to contain, with effort, a quantum of very bad news. Then Bina says, "Inside, boys," sounding like every other commanding officer Landsman has been obliged to obey. A moment ago the idea of having to serve under his ex-wife even for two months did not seem imaginable, but seeing the way she jerks her head toward the modular and orders them inside gives him reason to hope that his feelings about her, not that he still has any, of course, might turn to the universal gray of discipline.

Following classic refugee tradition the office is as Felsenfeld left it, photographs, half-dead houseplants, bottles of seltzer on the file cabinet next to a family-size tub of antacid chews.

"Sit," Bina says, going around to the rubberized steel desk chair and settling herself into it with careless resolve. She throws off the orange parka, revealing a dust-brown wool pantsuit worn over a white oxford-cloth shirt, an outfit much more in keeping with Landsman's idea of how Bina thinks about clothes. He tries and fails not to observe the way her heavy breasts, each of whose moles and freckles he can still project like constellations against the planetarium dome of his imagination, strain against the placket and pockets of her shirt. He and Berko hang their coats on the hooks behind the door and carry their hats in their hands. They each take one of the remaining chairs. Felsenfeld's wife in her photograph and his children in theirs have not grown any less homely since the last time Landsman looked at them. The salmon and halibut are still astonished to find themselves hanging dead at the end of Felsenfeld's lines.

"Okay, listen, boys," Bina says. She is a woman for belling cats and taking bulls by the horns. "We're all aware of the awkwardness of the situation here. It could be weird enough if I just used to squad with you both. The fact that one of you used to be my husband, and the other one my, uh, cousin, well, shit." The last word is spoken in flawless American, as are the next four. "Know what I'm saying?"

She pauses, seeming to await a response. Landsman turns to Berko. "You were the cousin, right?"

Bina smiles to show Landsman that she doesn't think he's particularly funny. She reaches around behind her and drags over from their place on the file cabinet a pile of pale blue file folders, each of them at least half an inch thick and all of them flagged with a tab of cough-syrup-red plastic. At the sight of it, Landsman's heart sinks, just as it does when by ill chance he happens to meet his own regard in a mirror.

"See these?"

"Yes, Inspector Gelbfish," Berko says, sounding strangely insincere. "I see them."

"Know what they are?"

"I know they can't be our open cases," Landsman says. "All piled up together on your desk."

"One good thing about Yakovy?" Bina says.

They await their chief's report on her travels.

She says, "The rain. Two hundred inches a year. Rains the smart ass right out of people. Even yids."

"That's a lot of rain," Berko says.

"Now, just listen to me. And listen carefully, please, because I will be speaking bullshit. In two months a U.S. Marshal is going to stride into this godforsaken modular with his cut-rate suit and his Sunday-school way of talking and request that I turn over the keys to the freak show that is the B Squad file cabinets, over which, as of this morning, it is my honor to preside." They are talkers, the Gelbfishes, speech makers and reasoners and aces of wheedling. Bina's father nearly talked Landsman out of marrying her. On the night before the wedding. "And really, I say that sincerely. You both know that I have been working my ass off my whole adult life, hoping that one day I'd be fortunate enough to park it in this chair, behind this desk, and try to maintain the grand Sitka Central tradition that every once in a while we catch a murderer and put him in jail. And now here I am. Until the first of January."

"We feel the same way, Bina," Berko says, sounding more sincere this time. "Freak show and all."

Landsman says that it goes double for him.

"I appreciate that," she says. "And I know how bad you feel about . . . this."

She rests her long, freckled hand on the stack of files. If accurately gathered, it will comprise eleven folders, the oldest dating back over two years. There are three other pairs of detectives in the Homicide section, and none of them could boast of such a fine, tall stack of unsolved cases.

"We're close on the Feytel," Berko says. "We're just waiting on the district attorney there. And Pinsky. And the Zilberblat thing. Zilberblat's mother—"

Bina holds up her hand, cutting Berko off. Landsman says

nothing. He is too ashamed to speak. As far as he is concerned, that pile of folders is a monument to his recent decline. That it's not another ten inches taller testifies to the steadfastness his big little cousin Berko has shown in carrying him.

"Stop," Bina says. "Just stop right there. And pay attention, because this is the part where I flash my fluent grasp of bullshit."

She reaches behind her back and takes a sheet of paper from her in-box, as well as another, much thinner blue file that Landsman recognizes at once, since he created it himself at four-thirty that morning. She reaches into the breast pocket of her suit jacket and takes out a pair of half-glasses that Landsman has never seen before. She is getting old, and he is getting old, right on schedule, and yet as time ruins them, they are not, strangely enough, married to each other.

"A policy has been formulated by the wise Jews who oversee our destiny as police officers of the Sitka District," Bina begins. She scans the sheet of paper with an air of agitation, even dismay. "It takes off from the admirable principle that when authority is turned over to the U.S. Marshal for Sitka, it would be a nice thing for everyone, not to mention providing adequate posterior coverage, if there were no active cases outstanding."

"Give me a fucking break, Bina," Berko says in American. He has grasped from the start what Inspector Gelbfish is getting at. It takes Landsman another minute to catch on.

"No cases outstanding," he repeats with idiotic calm.

"This policy," Bina says, "has been given the catchy name of 'effective resolution.' Essentially, what that means is, you are to devote exactly as much time to resolving your outstanding cases as there remain days in your tenure as homicide detectives carrying the District shield. Say roughly nine weeks. You have eleven cases outstanding. You can, you know, divvy it up however you want. However you want to work it, that's fine with me."

"Wrap up?" Berko says. "You mean—"

"You know what I mean, Detective," Bina says. There is no emotion in her voice and no readable expression on her face. "Stick them to whatever sticky people you can find. If they won't stick, use a little glue. The rest of them"—a hint of a catch in her voice— "just black-flag and file in cabinet nine."

Nine is where they keep the cold cases. Filing a case in cabinet nine saves less space but is otherwise the same as lighting it on fire and taking the ashes out for a walk in a gale-force wind.

"Bury them?" Berko says, hoisting it into a question right at the end.

"Put in a good-faith effort, within the limits of this new policy with the musical name, and then, if that fails, put in a bad-faith effort." Bina stares at the domed paperweight on Felsenfeld's desk. Inside the paperweight is a tiny model, a cartoon in cheap plastic, of the Sitka skyline. A jumble of high-rises clustered around the Safety Pin, that lonely digit pointed at the sky as if in accusation. "And then slap a black flag on them."

"You said eleven," Landsman says.

"You noticed that."

"After last night, though, with all due respect, Inspector, and as embarrassing as it is. Well. It's twelve. Not eleven. Twelve open cases for Shemets and Landsman."

Bina picks up the slim blue folder that Landsman gave birth to the night before. "This one?" She opens it and studies, or pretends to study, Landsman's report on the apparent gun murder, at point blank, of the man who called himself Emanuel Lasker. "Yes. Okay. Now I want you to watch how this is done."

She opens the top drawer of Felsenfeld's desk, which, for the next two months, at least, will be hers. She rummages around inside it, grimacing as if the drawer contains a pile of used foam-rubber earplugs, which, last time Landsman looked, was indeed the case. She pulls out a plastic tab for marking a case folder. A black one. She pries loose the red tab that Landsman attached to the Lasker file early that morning, and substitutes the black one in its place, breathing shallowly the way you do when you clean a nasty wound or sponge up something awful from the rug. She ages ten years, it seems to Landsman, in the ten seconds it takes her to make the switch. Then she holds the newly cold case away from her body, tweezing it between two fingers of one hand.

"Effective resolution," she says.

The Noz, as the name implies, is the law enforcement bar, owned by a couple of ex-nozzes, choked with the smoke of noz grievance and gossip. It never closes, and it never runs short of off-duty law enforcement officers to prop up its big oak bar. Just the place, the Noz, if you want to give voice to your outrage over the latest masterwork of bullshit to be handed down by the departmental bigs. So Landsman and Berko steer well clear of the Noz. They walk past the Pearl of Manila, though its Filipino-style Chinese donuts beckon like glittering sugar-dusted tokens of a better existence. They avoid Feter Shnayer, and Karlinsky's, and the Inside Passage, and the Nyu-Yorker Grill. This early in the morning, most of them are closed anyway, and the joints that are open tend to service cops, firefighters, paramedics.

They hunch up their shoulders against the cold and hurry, the big man and the little one, bumping against each other. The breath comes out of their bodies in billows that twine and are absorbed into the greater fog lying over the Untershtot. Fat streamers of fog twist along the streets, smearing headlights and neon, blotting out the harbor, leaving a track of oily silver beads on the lapels of coats and the crowns of hats.

"Nobody goes to the Nyu-Yorker," Berko says. "We ought to be fine there."

"I saw Tabatchnik in there one time."

"I'm pretty sure Tabatchnik would never steal the plans for your secret weapon, Meyer."

Landsman only wishes he were in possession of the plans for some kind of death ray, or mind-control beam, something to shake the corridors of power. Put some genuine fear of God into the Americans. Stave off, just for a year, a decade, a century, the tide of Jewish exile.

They are about to brave the grim Front Page, with its clotted milk and its coffee fresh from a stint as a barium enema at Sitka General, when Landsman sees old Dennis Brennan's khaki ass taking up a tottering stool at the counter. The press pretty well abandoned the Front Page years ago, when the *Blat* went under and the *Tog* moved its offices to a new building out by the airport. But Brennan left Sitka for fortune and glory a while back. He must have just blown back into town pretty recently. It's a safe bet nobody's told him the Front Page is dead.

"Too late," Berko says. "Bastard saw us."

For a moment Landsman isn't sure the bastard did. Brennan's back is to the door, and he's studying the stocks page of the prominent American newspaper whose Sitka bureau he constituted before he got his big break. Landsman takes hold of Berko's coat and starts to tow his partner down the street. He has thought of the perfect place for them to talk, maybe get a bite, without being overheard.

"Detective Shemets. A moment."

"Too late," Landsman concedes.

He turns, and Brennan's there, that large-headed man, hatless and coatless, necktie blown over his shoulder, a penny in his left loafer, bankrupt in the right. Patches on the elbows of his tweed jacket, its color a practical shade of gravy stain. His cheek could use a shave and his pate a fresh coat of wax. Maybe things didn't go so well for Dennis Brennan out in the big time.

"Look at the head on that sheygets, the thing has its own atmosphere," Landsman says. "Thing has ice caps."

"Indeed the man has a very big head."

"Every time I see it, I feel sorry for necks."

"Maybe I should get my hands around his. Give it some support."

Brennan puts up his larval white fingers and blinks his little eyes, the colorless blue of skimmed milk. He works up a practiced rueful smile, but Landsman notes that he keeps a good four feet of Ben Maymon Street between him and Berko.

"A need to repeat the rash threats of yore does not, I assure you, exist, Detective Shemets," the reporter says in his swift and preposterous Yiddish. "Evergreen and ripe with the sap of their original violence they remain."

Brennan studied German in college and learned his Yiddish from some pompous old German at the Institute, and he talks, somebody once remarked, "like a sausage recipe with footnotes." A heavy drinker, unsuited by temperament to long twilight and rain. Throws off a false scent of being stolid and slow on the uptake, in a way common among detectives and reporters. But a shlemiel all the same. No one ever seemed more astonished by the splash Dennis Brennan made in Sitka than Brennan himself.

"That I fear your wrath let us agree beforehand, Detective. And that just now I pretended not to see you walking past this desolate hole whose sole recommendation, apart from the fact that the management has forgotten, in my long absence, the state of my credit, is a total lack of newspaper reporters. I knew, however, that with my luck, such a strategy was likely to return at a later time and bite me upon the ass."

"Nothing is that hungry, Brennan," Landsman says. "You were probably safe."

Brennan looks hurt. A sensitive soul, this macrocephalic gentile, a nurser of slights, resistant to banter and irony. His convoluted style of talking makes everything he says sound like a joke, a fact that only compounds the man's need to be taken seriously.

"Dennis J. Brennan," Berko says. "Working the Sitka beat again?"

"For my sins, Detective Shemets, for my sins."

This goes without saying. Assignment to the Sitka bureau of any of the stateside newspapers or networks that bother to maintain one is a proverbial punishment for incompetence or failure. Brennan's reassignment here must be the mark of some kind of colossal cock-up.

"I thought that was why they sent you *away*, Brennan," Berko says, and now he's the one who isn't joking. His eyes go dead, and he chews that imaginary piece of Doublemint or seal fat or the gristly knob of Brennan's heart. "For your sins."

"The motivation, Detective, for my leaving a cup of terrible coffee and a broken appointment with an informant who, in any case, lacks anything resembling information, to come out here and risk your possible anger."

"Brennan, please, I beg you to speak American," Berko says. "What the fuck do you want?"

"I want a story," Brennan says. "What else? And I know I'll never get one from you unless I try to clear the air. So. For the record." Once again he lashes himself to the tiller of his Flying Dutchman version of the mother tongue. "I lack the intention to undo or to take back anything. Inflict suffering on this grossly enlarged head of mine, please, but I stand behind what I wrote, every word of it, to this day. It was accurate and supported and sourced. And yet I do not mind telling you that the whole sorry affair left a bad taste in my mouth—"

"Was it the taste of your ass?" Landsman suggests brightly. "Maybe you've been biting upon yourself."

Brennan sails madly on. Landsman gets the feeling that the goy has been saving up this spiel for a while now. That maybe he's looking for something more from Berko than a story.

"Certainly it was a good thing for my career, so-called. For a few years. It propelled me out of the boondocks, you should pardon the expression, to L.A., Salt Lake, Kansas City." As he names the stations of his decline, Brennan's voice gets lower and softer. "Spokane. But I know that it was a painful thing for you and your family, Detective. And so, if you would allow me, I would like to offer my apology for the hurt that I caused."

Just after the elections that carried the current administration to its first term in power, Dennis J. Brennan wrote a series of articles for his paper. He presented, in careful and dogged detail, the sordid history of corruption, malfeasance, and unconstitutional skullduggery engaged in by Hertz Shemets, over the course of forty years at the FBI. The COINTELPRO program was shut down, its business was farmed out to other departments, and Uncle Hertz was driven into retirement and disgrace. Landsman, who was shocked by nothing, found it tough to get out of bed for a couple of days after the first article ran. He'd known as well as anyone and better than almost everyone that his uncle was badly flawed both as a man and as an officer of the law. But if you wanted to go looking for the reasons that a kid became a noz, it almost never paid to search anywhere but a branch or two up the family tree. Flaws and all, Uncle Hertz was a hero to Landsman. Smart, tough, unremitting, patient, methodical, sure of his actions. If his willingness to cut corners, his bad temper, his secretiveness did not make him a hero, they definitely made him a noz.

"I'm going to put this very gently, Dennis," Berko says, "because you're all right. You work hard, you're a decent writer, and you're the only guy I know who makes my partner look like a clotheshorse: Fuck you."

Brennan nods. "I figured you might say that," he replies, sadly and in American.

"My father's a fucking hermit," Berko says. "He's a mushroom, he lives under a log with the earwigs and the crawly things. Whatever nefarious shit he was up to, he was only doing what he thought was good for the Jews, and you know what's fucked up about that? He was *right*, because now look at the motherfucking mess we're in without him."

"Jesus, Shemets, I hate to hear that. And I hate to think that a story I wrote had anything to do with—that it led to, in any way—the predicament you yids now find yourself in. . . . Ah, fuck it. Forget it."

"Okay," Landsman says. He grabs hold of Berko's sleeve again. "Come."

"Hey, uh, yeah. So where you guys going? What's up?"

"Just fighting crime," Landsman says. "Same as last time you blew through here."

But now that he's unburdened himself, the hound inside Brennan can smell it on Berko and Landsman. Maybe he could smell it on them from a block away, could see it through the glass, a hitch in Berko's rolling gait, an extra kilo of stoop in Landsman's shoulder. Maybe the whole apology routine has been building to the question he drags up, in his native tongue, naked and plain:

"Who died?"

"A yid in a predicament," Berko tells him. "Dog bites man."

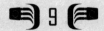

9

They leave Brennan standing outside the Front Page, with his necktie smacking him on the forehead like a remorseful palm, and walk to the corner of Seward and down Peretz, then turn in just past the Palatz Theater, in the lee of Baranof Castle Hill, to a black door, in a black marble facade, with a big picture window painted black.

"You are not serious," Berko says.

"In fifteen years I never saw another shammes at the Vorsht."

"It's nine-thirty in the morning on a Friday, Meyer. There's nobody in there but the rats."

"Not true," Landsman says. He leads Berko around to the side door and lays his knuckles against it, two taps. "I always figured this was the place to plan my misdeeds, if I ever found myself with misdeeds that needed planning."

The heavy steel door swings open with a groan, revealing Mrs. Kalushiner, dressed to go to shul or a job at the bank, in a gray skirt suit and black pumps, with her hair done up in pink foam rollers. In her hand she carries a paper cup filled with a liquid that looks like coffee or maybe prune juice. Mrs. Kalushiner chews tobacco. The cup is her constant if not sole companion.

"You," she says, making a face like she just tasted earwax on her fingertip. Then, in her refined way, she spits into the cup. From force of wise habit, she takes a long look up and down the alley to see what style of trouble they have brought along. She makes a rapid and brutal study of the giant yarmulke-wearing Indian who wants to come into her place of business. In the past, the people Landsman has brought here, at this hour of the day, have all been twitchy, mouse-eyed shtinkers like Benny "Shpilkes" Plotner and Zigmund Landau, the Heifetz of Informers. Nobody ever looked less like a shtinker than Berko Shemets. And with all due respect to the beanie and the fringes, no way would this be a middleman or even a low-echelon street wiseguy, not with that Indian puss. When, after careful consideration, she can't fit Berko into her taxonomy of lowlifes, Mrs. Kalushiner spits into her cup. Then she returns her gaze to Landsman and sighs. By one kind of reckoning, she owes Landsman seventeen favors; by another, she ought to give him a punch in the belly. She steps aside and lets them pass.

The place is as empty as an off-duty downtown bus and smells twice as bad. Somebody came through recently with a bucket of bleach to paint in some high notes over the Vorsht's steady bass line of sweat and urinals. The keen nose can also detect, above or beneath it all, the coat-lining smell of worn dollar bills.

"Sit there," Mrs. Kalushiner says, without indicating where she would like them to sit. The round tables that crowd the stage wear overturned chairs like sets of antlers. Landsman flips two of them, and he and Berko take their seats away from the stage, by the heavily bolted front door. Mrs. Kalushiner wanders into the back room, and the beaded curtain clatters behind her with the sound of loose teeth in a bucket.

"What a doll," Berko says.

"A sweetheart," Landsman agrees. "She only comes in here in the mornings. That way she never has to look at the clientele." The Vorsht is the place where the musicians of Sitka do their drinking, after the theaters and the other clubs close down. Long after midnight they come huddling in, snow on their hats, rain in their cuffs, and pack the little stage, and kill one another with clarinets and fiddles. As usual when angels gather, they draw a following of devils: gangsters, ganefs, and hard-luck women. "She doesn't care for musicians."

"But her husband was a — Oh. I get it."

Nathan Kalushiner, until his death, was the owner of the Vorsht and the king of the C-soprano clarinet. He was a gambler, and a junkie, and a very bad man in many respects, but he could play like there was a dybbuk inside him. Landsman, a music lover, used to look out for the crazy little shkotz and try to extricate him from the ugly situations in which Kalushiner's poor judgment and gnawed-at soul landed him. Then one day Kalushiner disappeared, along with the wife of a well-known Russian shtarker, leaving Mrs. Kalushiner nothing but the Vorsht and the goodwill of its creditors. Parts of Nathan Kalushiner, but not his C-soprano clarinet, later washed up under the docks up at Yakovy.

"And that's the guy's dog?" Berko says, pointing to the stage. At the spot where Kalushiner used to stand and blow every night sits a curly half-terrier mutt, white with brown spots and a black patch around one eye. He's just sitting, ears raised, as if listening to some echoed voice or music in his brain. A length of slack chain connects him to a steel loop mounted on the wall.

"That's Hershel," Landsman says. There's something painful to him about the dog's patient mien, his canine air of calm endurance. Landsman looks away. "Five years he's been standing there."

"Touching."

"I guess. The animal, to be honest, he gives me the willies."

Mrs. Kalushiner reappears, carrying a metal bowl filled with pickled tomatoes and cucumbers, a basket of poppy-seed rolls, and a bowl of sour cream. That's all balanced along her left arm. The right hand, of course, carries the paper spittoon.

"Beautiful pickles," Berko suggests, and when that gets him nowhere, he tries, "Cute dog."

What's touching, thinks Landsman, is the effort that Berko

Shemets is always willing to put into starting a conversation with somebody. The tighter people clam up, the more determined old Berko becomes. That was true of him even as a boy. He had that eagerness to engage with people, especially with his vacuum-packed cousin Meyer.

"A dog is a dog," Mrs. Kalushiner says. She slams down the pickles and sour cream, drops the basket of rolls, and then retreats to the back room with another clash of beads.

"So I need to ask you a favor," Landsman says, his gaze on the dog, who has lowered himself to the stage on his arthritic knees and lies with his head on his forepaws. "And I'm hoping very much that you'll say no."

"Does this favor have anything to do with 'effective resolution'?"

"Are you mocking the concept?"

"Not necessary," Berko says. "The concept mocks itself." He plucks a pickled tomato from the dish, dabs it in the sour cream, then pokes it neatly into his mouth with a forefinger. He screws up his face with pleasure at the resultant sour squirt of pulp and brine. "Bina looks good."

"I thought she looked good."

"A little butch."

"So you always said."

"Bina, Bina." Berko gives his head a bleak shake, one that somehow manages at the same time to look fond. "In her last life, she must have been a weather vane."

"I think you're wrong," Landsman says. "You're right, but you're wrong."

"You're saying Bina is not a careerist."

"I'm not saying that."

"She is, Meyer, and she always has been. That's one of the things I have always most liked about her. Bina is a smart cookie. She is tough. She is political. She is viewed as loyal, and in two directions, up and down, and that is a hard trick to pull off. She is inspector material all around. In any police force, in any country in the world."

"She was first in her class," Landsman says. "At the academy."

"But you scored higher on the entrance exam."

"Why, yes," Landsman says. "I did. Have I mentioned that before?"

"Even U.S. Marshals are smart enough to notice Bina Gelbfish," Berko says. "If she is trying to make sure there's a place for her in Sitka law enforcement after Reversion, I'm not going to blame her for that."

"You make your point," Landsman says. "Only I don't buy it. That isn't why she took this job. Or it's not the only reason."

"Why did she, then?"

Landsman shrugs. "I don't know," he admits. "Maybe she ran out of things to do that make sense."

"I hope not. Or the next thing you know, she'll be getting back together with you."

"God forbid."

"Horrors."

Landsman pretends to spit three times over his shoulder. Then, right as he's wondering if this custom has anything to do with the habit of chewing tobacco, Mrs. Kalushiner comes back, dragging the great leg iron of her life.

"I have hard-boiled eggs," she says menacingly. "I have bagel. I have jellied leg."

"Just a little something to drink, Mrs. K.," Landsman says. "Berko?"

"Burp water," Berko says. "With a twist of lime."

"You want to eat," she tells him. It isn't a guess.

"Why not?" Berko says. "All right, bring me a couple of eggs."

Mrs. Kalushiner turns to Landsman, and he feels Berko's eyes on his, daring him and expecting him to order a slivovitz. Landsman can feel Berko's fatigue, his impatience and irritation with Landsman and his problems. It's about time he pulled himself together, isn't it? Find something worth living his life for, and get on it with it.

"Coca-Cola," Landsman says. "If you please."

This may be the first thing that Landsman or anyone has ever done to surprise the widow of Nathan Kalushiner. She raises one steel-gray eyebrow, then turns away. Berko reaches for one of the pickled cucumbers, shaking off the peppercorns and cloves that stud its freckled green skin. He crunches it between his teeth and frowns happily.

"It takes a sour woman to make a good pickle," he says, and then, as if offhand, teasing, "Sure you don't want another beer?"

Landsman would love a beer. He can taste the bitter caramel of it on the back of his tongue. In the meantime, the one that Ester-Malke gave him has yet to leave his body, but Landsman is getting indications that it has its bags packed and is ready to go. The proposition or appeal that he has determined to make to his partner now strikes him as perhaps the stupidest idea he has ever had, certainly not worth living for. But it will have to do.

"Fuck you," he says, getting up from the table. "I need to take a leak."

In the men's room, Landsman discovers the body of an electric guitarist. From a table at the back of the Vorsht, Landsman has often admired this yid and his playing. He was among the first to import the techniques and attitudes of American and British rock guitarists to the Bulgars and freylekhs of Jewish dance music. He is roughly the same age and background as Landsman, grew up in Halibut Point, and in moments of vainglory, Landsman has compared himself, or rather his detective work, to the intuitive and flashy playing of this man who appears to be dead or passed out in the stall with his money hand in the toilet bowl. The man is wearing a black leather three-piece suit and a red ribbon necktie. His celebrated fingers have been denuded of their rings, leaving ghostly indentations. A wallet lies on the tiled floor, looking empty and distended.

The musician snores once. Landsman employs those intuitive and flashy skills in feeling at the man's carotid for a pulse. It's steady. The air around the musician hums almost to burning with the radiance of alcohol. The wallet seems to have been rifled of its cash and identification. Landsman pats down the musician and finds a pint of Canadian vodka in the left hip pocket of his leather blazer. They got his cash but not his booze. Landsman doesn't want a drink. In fact, he feels a lurch inside him at the idea of pouring this garbage into his belly, some kind of moral muscle that recoils. He chances a quick peek into the cobwebby root cellar of his soul. He can't help noticing that this pulse of revulsion for what is, after all, a popular brand of Canadian vodka seems to have something to do with his ex-wife, with her being back in the Sitka again and looking so strong and juicy and Bina. The daily sight of her is going to be torment, like God torturing Moses with a glimpse of Zion from the top of Mount Pisgah every single day of his life.

Landsman uncaps the bottle of vodka and takes a long stiff pull. It burns like a compound of solvent and lye. Several inches remain in the bottle when he is through, but Landsman himself is filled top to bottom with nothing but the burn of remorse. All the old parallels it once pleased him to draw between the guitarist and himself are turned against him. After a brief but vigorous debate, Landsman decides not to throw the bottle in the trash, where it will be of no use to anyone. He transfers it to the snug hip pocket of his own decline. He drags the musician out of the stall and carefully dries his right hand. Last he takes the piss he came in here to take. The music of Landsman's urine against porcelain and water lures the musician into opening his eyes.

"I'm fine," he tells Landsman from the floor.

"Sure you are, sweetness," Landsman says.

"Just don't call my wife."

"I won't," Landsman assures him, but the yid is already out again. Landsman drags the musician out into the back hallway and leaves him on the floor with a phone book under his head for a pillow. Then he goes back to the table and Berko Shemets and takes a well-behaved sip from his glass of bubbles and syrup.

"Mmm," he says. "Coke."

"So," says Berko. "This favor of yours."

"Yeah," Landsman says. His resurgent confidence in himself and his intentions, the sense of well-being, is clearly an illusion produced by a snort of lousy vodka. He rationalizes this with the thought that from the point of view of, say, God, all human confidence is an illusion and every intention a joke. "Kind of a big one."

Berko knows where Landsman is heading. But Landsman isn't quite ready to go there yet.

"You and Ester-Malke," Landsman says. "You guys applied for residency."

"Is that your big question?"

"No, this is just the buildup."

"We applied for green cards. Everybody in the District has applied for a residency card, unless they're going to Canada or Argentina or wherever. Jesus, Meyer, didn't you?"

"I know I meant to," Landsman says. "Maybe I did. I can't remember."

This is too shocking for Berko to process, and not what Landsman has led them here to say.

"I did, all right?" Landsman says. "I remember now. Sure. Filled out my I-999 and everything."

Berko nods as if he believes Landsman's lie.

"So," Landsman says. "You guys are planning to stick around, then. Stay in Sitka."

"Assuming we can get documented."

"Any reason to think you won't?"

"Just the numbers. They're saying it's going to be under forty percent." Berko shakes his head, which is pretty much the national gesture at the moment when it comes to the question of where the other Sitka Jews are going to go, or what they are going to do, after

Reversion. Actually, no guarantees have been made at all—the 40 percent figure is just another rumor at the end of time—and there are some wild-eyed radicals claiming that the actual number of Jews who will be permitted to remain as legal residents of the newly enlarged state of Alaska when Reversion is finally enforced will be closer to 10 or even 5 percent. These are the same people going around calling for armed resistance, secession, a declaration of independence, and so forth. Landsman has paid very little attention to the controversies and rumors, to the most important question in his local universe.

"The old man?" Landsman says. "Doesn't he have any juice left?"

For forty years—as Denny Brennan's series revealed—Hertz Shemets used his position as local director of the FBI's domestic surveillance program to run his own private game on the Americans. The Bureau first recruited him in the fifties to fight Communists and the Yiddish Left, which, though fractious, was strong, hardened, embittered, suspicious of the Americans, and, in the case of the former Israelis, not especially grateful to be here. Hertz Shemets's brief was to monitor and infiltrate the local Red population; Hertz wiped them out. He fed the socialists to the Communists, and the Stalinists to the Trotskyites, and the Hebrew Zionists to the Yiddish Zionists, and when feeding time was over, he wiped the mouths of those still standing and fed them to each other. Starting in the late sixties, Hertz was turned loose on the nascent radical movement among the Tlingit, and in time he pulled its teeth and claws, too.

But those activities were a front, as Brennan showed, for Hertz's real agenda: to obtain Permanent Status for the District: P.S., or even, in his wildest dreams, statehood. "Enough wandering," Landsman can remember his uncle saying to his father, whose soul retained to the day he died a tinge of romantic Zionism. "Enough with expulsions and migrations and dreaming about next year in the camel lands. It's time for us to take what we can get and stay put."

So every year, it turned out, Uncle Hertz diverted up to half his operating budget to corrupt the people who had authorized it. He bought senators, baited congressional honeypots, and above all romanced rich American Jews whose influence he saw as critical to his plan. Three times Permanent Status bills came up and died, twice in committee, once in a bitter and close battle on the floor. A year after that floor fight, the current president of America ran and won on a platform that showcased the long-overdue enforcement of Reversion, pledging to restore "Alaska for Alaskans, wild and clean." And Dennis Brennan chased Hertz under a log.

"The old man?" Berko says. "Down there on his vest-pocket Indian reservation? With his goat? And a freezer full of moose meat? Yeah, he's a fucking gray eminence in the corridors of power. But anyway, it's looking all right."

"Is it?"

"Ester-Malke and I both already got three-year work permits."

"That's a good sign."

"So they say."

"Naturally, you wouldn't want to do anything to endanger your status."

"No."

"Disobey orders. Piss somebody off. Neglect your express duty."

"Never."

"That's settled, then." Landsman reaches into the pocket of his blazer and takes out the chess set. "Did I ever tell you about the note my father left when he killed himself?"

"I heard it was a poem."

"Call it doggerel," Landsman says. "Six lines of Yiddish verse addressed to an unnamed female."

"Oho."

"No, no. Nothing racy. It was, what, it was an expression of regret for his inadequacy. Chagrin at his failure. An avowal of devotion and respect. A touching statement of gratitude for the comfort she had given him, and above all, for the measure of forgetfulness that her company had brought to him over the long, bitter course of the years."

"You have it memorized."

"I did. But I noticed something about it that bothered me. So then I made myself forget it."

"What did you notice?"

Landsman ignores the question as Mrs. Kalushiner arrives with the eggs, six of them, peeled and arranged on a dish with six round indentations, each the size of an egg's fat bottom. Salt. Pepper. A jar of mustard.

"Maybe if they took the leash off him," Berko says, pointing to Hershel with his thumb, "he would go out for a sandwich or something."

"He likes the leash," Mrs. Kalushiner says. "Without it, he doesn't sleep." She leaves them again.

"That bothers me," Berko says, watching Hershel.

"I know what you mean."

Berko salts an egg and bites it. His teeth leave castellations in the boiled white. "So this poem, then," he says. "The verse."

"So, naturally," Landsman says, "everyone assumed the addressee of my father's verse to be my mother. Starting with my mother."

"She fit the description."

"So it was generally agreed. That is why I never told anybody what I had deduced. In my first official case as a junior shammes."

"Which was?"

"Which was that if you put together the first letters of each of the six lines of the poem, they spelled out a name. Caissa."

"Caissa? What kind of name is that?"

"I believe it is Latin," Landsman says. "Caissa is the goddess of chess players."

He opens the lid of the pocket chess set that he bought at the drugstore on Korczak Platz. The pieces in play remain as he arranged them at the Taytsh-Shemets apartment earlier that morning, as left behind by the man who called himself Emanuel Lasker. Or by his killer, or by pale Caissa, the goddess of chess players, dropping in to bid farewell to another one of her hapless worshippers. Black down to three pawns, a pair of knights, a bishop, and a rook. White holding on to all of his major and minor pieces and a pair of pawns, one of them a move away from promotion. A strange disordered aspect to the situation, as if the game that led up to this move had been a chaotic one.

"If it was anything else, Berko," Landsman says, apologizing with upturned palms. "A deck of cards. A crossword puzzle. A bingo card."

"I get it," Berko says.

"It had to be an unfinished goddamned game of chess."

Berko turns the board around and studies it for a moment or two, then looks up at Landsman. *Now is the time for you to ask me*, he says with those great dark eyes of his.

"So. Like I said. I need to ask you a favor."

"No," Berko says, "you don't."

"You heard the lady. You saw her black-flag it. The thing was a piece of shit to begin with. Bina made it official."

"You don't think so."

"Please, Berko, don't start having respect for my judgment now," Landsman says. "Not after all this work I've put into undermining it."

Berko has been staring at the dog with increasing fixity. Abruptly, he gets up and goes over to the stage. He clomps up the three wooden steps and stands looking down at Hershel. Then he holds out his hand to be sniffed. The dog clambers back into a sitting position and reads with his nose the transcript of the back of Berko's hand, babies and waffles and the interior of a 1971 Super Sport. Berko crouches heavily beside the dog and unhooks the clasp of the leash from the collar. He takes hold of the dog's head in his massive hands and looks into the dog's eyes. "Enough already," he says. "He isn't coming."

The dog regards Berko as if sincerely interested in this bit of news. Then he lurches to his hind legs and hobbles over to the steps and tumbles carefully down them. Toenails clacking, he crosses the concrete floor to the table where Landsman sits and looks up as if for confirmation.

"That's the straight emes, Hershel," Landsman tells the dog. "They used dental records."

The dog appears to consider this; then, much to Landsman's surprise, he walks over to the front door. Berko gives Landsman a look of reprimand: *What did I tell you?* He darts a glance toward the beaded curtain, then slides back the bolt, turns the key, and opens the door. The dog trots right out as if he has pressing business elsewhere.

Berko comes back to the table, looking like he has just liberated a soul from the wheel of karma. "You heard the lady. We have nine weeks," he says. "Give or take. We can afford to waste a day or two looking busy while we poke around into this dead junkie from your flop."

"You are going to have a baby," Landsman says. "There will be five of you."

"I hear what you're saying."

"I'm saying, that's five Taytsh-Shemetses we are going to fuck over if somebody is looking for reasons to deny people their residency cards, as widely reported, and one of those reasons is a recent citation for acting in direct contradiction of orders from a superior officer, not to mention egregious flouting of departmental policy, however idiotic and craven."

Berko blinks and pops another pickled tomato into his mouth. He chews it, and sighs. "I never had a brother or a sister," he says. "All I ever had was cousins. Most of them were Indians, and they didn't want to know me. Two were Jews. One of those Jews, may her name be a blessing, is dead. That leaves me with you."

"I appreciate this, Berko," Landsman says. "I want you to know that."

"Fuck that shit," Berko says in American. "We're going to the Einstein, aren't we?"

"Yeah," Landsman says. "That's where I figured we ought to start."

Before they can stand up or try to settle things with Mrs. Kalushiner, there is a scratching at the front door and then a long, low moan. The sound is human and forlorn, and it makes the hair on Landsman's nape stand erect. He goes to the front door and lets in the dog, who climbs back up onto the stage to the place where he has worn away the paint on the floorboards, and sits, ears raised to catch the sound of a vanished horn, waiting patiently for the leash to be restored.

The north end of Peretz Street is all slab concrete, steel pillars, aluminum-rimmed windows double-glazed against the cold. The buildings in this part of the Untershtot went up in the early fifties, rapidly assembled shelter machines built by survivors, with a kind of noble ugliness. Now they have only the ugliness of age and vacancy. Empty storefronts, papered-over glass. In the windows of 1911, where Landsman's father used to attend meetings of the Edelshtat Society before the storefront gave way to a beauty-supply outlet, a plush kangaroo with a sardonic leer holds a cardboard sign: AUSTRALIA OR BUST. At 1906 the Hotel Einstein looks, as some wag remarked on its opening to the public, like a rat cage stored in a fish tank. It is a favorite venue for the suicides of Sitka. It is also, by custom and charter, the home of the Einstein Chess Club.

A member of the Einstein Chess Club named Melekh Gaystik won the world championship title over the Dutchman Jan Timman at St. Petersburg in 1980. The World's Fair fresh in their memory, Sitkaniks viewed Gaystik's triumph as further proof of their merit and identity as a people. Gaystik was subject to fits of rage, black moods, and bouts of incoherence, but these flaws were overlooked in the general celebration.

One fruit of Gaystik's victory was the gift of the hotel ballroom by the Einstein management, free of rent, to the chess club. Hotel weddings were out of vogue, and management had been trying for years to clear the patzers, with their mutterings and smoke, from the coffee shop. Gaystik provided management the excuse they needed. They sealed off the main doors of the ballroom so that you could enter only through the back, off an alley. They pulled up the fine ashwood parquetry and laid down a demented checkerboard of linoleum in shades of soot, bile, and surgical-scrub green. The modernist chandelier was replaced by banks of fluorescent tubes bolted to the high concrete ceiling. Two months later, the young world champion wandered into the old coffee shop where Landsman's father had once made his mark, sat down in a booth at the back, took out a Colt .38 Detective Special, and shot himself in the mouth. There was a note in his pocket. It said only *I liked things better the way they were before.*

"Emanuel Lasker," the Russian says to the two detectives, looking up from the chessboard, under an old neon clock that advertises the defunct newspaper, the *Blat*. He is a skeletal man, his skin thin, pink, and peeling. He wears a pointed black beard. His eyes are close-set and the color of cold seawater. "Emanuel Lasker." The Russian's shoulders hunch, and he ducks his head, and his rib cage swells and narrows. It looks like laughter, but no sound comes out. "I wish that he does come around here." Like that of most Russian immigrants, the man's Yiddish is experimental and brusque. He reminds Landsman of somebody, though Landsman can't say whom. "I give him such a kick to his ass for him."

"You ever look at his games?" the Russian's opponent wants to know. He is a young man with pudding cheeks and rimless glasses and a complexion tinged with green, like the white of a dollar bill. The lenses of his glasses ice over as he aims them at Landsman. "You ever look at his games, Detective?"

"Just to make this clear," Landsman says, "that isn't the Lasker we have in mind."

"This man was only using the name as an alias," Berko says. "Otherwise we'd be looking for a man who's already been dead sixty years."

"You look at Lasker's games today," the young man continues, "there's too much complexity. He makes everything too hard."

"Only it seems complexity to you, Velvel," says the Russian, "for the reason of how much you are simple."

The shammeses have interrupted their game in its dense middle stages with the Russian, playing White, holding an unassailable knight outpost. The men are still caught up in their game, the way a pair of mountains gets caught up in a whiteout. Their natural impulse is to treat the detectives with the abstract contempt they reserve for all kibitzers. Landsman wonders if he and Berko ought to wait until the players have finished and then try again. But there are other games in progress, other players to question. Around the old ballroom, legs scratch the linoleum like fingernails on a chalkboard. Chessmen click like the cylinder turning in Melekh Gaystik's .38. The men—there are no women here—play by means of steadily hectoring their opponents with self-aspersions, chilly laughter, whistling, harumphs.

"As long as we're making things clear," Berko says, "this man who called himself Emanuel Lasker, but was not the noted world champion born in Prussia in 1868, has died, and we are investigating that death. In our capacity as homicide detectives, which we mentioned but without, it seems, making much of an impression."

"A Jew with blond hair," the Russian says.

"And freckles," Velvel says.

"You see," the Russian says. "We pay close attention." He snatches up one of his rooks the way you pluck at a stray hair on somebody's collar. Together his fingers and the rook take their trip down the file and break the bad news to the Black's remaining bishop with a tap.

Velvel speaks Russian now, with a Yiddish accent, offering

his wishes for the resumption of friendly relations between his opponent's mother and a well-endowed stallion.

"I am orphan," the Russian says.

He sits back in his chair as if expecting his opponent to require some time to recover from the loss of his bishop. He knots his arms around his chest and jams his hands into his armpits. It is the gesture of a man who wants to smoke a papiros in a room where the habit has been forbidden. Landsman wonders what his father would have done with himself if the Einstein Chess Club had banned smoking while he was alive. The man could go through a whole pack of Broadways in a single game.

"Blond," the Russian says, the very soul of helpfulness. "Freckles. What else, please?"

Landsman shuffles through his scanty hand of details, trying to decide which one to play. "A student of the game, we're guessing. Up on his chess history. He had a book by Siegbert Tarrasch in his room. And then there's the alias he was using."

"So astute," the Russian says without bothering to sound sincere. "A couple of top-dollar shammeses."

The remark does not so much rankle Landsman as nudge him half a wisecrack closer to remembering this bony Russian with the peeling skin. "At one time, possibly," he continues more slowly, groping for the memory, watching the Russian, "the deceased was a pious Jew. A black hat."

The Russian tugs his hands out from under his arms. He sits forward in his chair. The ice on his Baltic eyes seems to thaw all at once. "He was smack addict?" His tone barely qualifies as a question, and when Landsman doesn't immediately deny the charge, he says, "Frank." He pronounces the name American-style, with a long, sharp vowel and a shadowless *R*. "Ah, no."

"Frank," Velvel agrees.

"I—" The Russian slumps, knees spread, hands dangling at his sides. "Detectives, can I tell you one thing?" he says. "Truly, sometimes I hate this lamentable excuse for a world."

"Tell us about Frank," Berko says. "You liked him."

The Russian hoists his shoulders, his eyes iced over again. "I do not like anyone," he says. "But when Frank comes in here, at least I do not run screaming out the door. He is funny. Not handsome man. But handsome voice. Serious voice. Like the man who plays serious music on the radio. At three o'clock in the morning, you know, talking about Shostakovich. He says things in serious voice, it's funny. Everything he says, always it's a little bit criticism. Cut of your hair, how ugly your pants, how Velvel jumps every time a person mentions his wife."

"True enough," Velvel says. "I do."

"Always teasing you, but, I don't know why, it don't piss you off."

"It was— You felt like he was harder on himself," Velvel says.

"When you play him, even though he wins every time, you feel you play better against him than with the assholes in this club," the Russian says. "Frank is never asshole."

"Meyer," says Berko, soft. He flies the flags of his eyebrows in the direction of the next table. They have an audience.

Landsman turns. Two men confront each other over a game in its early stages. One wears the modern jacket and pants and full beard of a Lubavitcher Jew. His beard is dense and black as if shaded in with a soft pencil. A steady hand has pinned a black velour skullcap trimmed with black silk to the black tangle of his hair. His navy overcoat and blue fedora hang from a hook set into the mirrored wall behind him. The lining of his coat and the label of his hat are reflected in the glass. Exhaustion stains the underlids of his eyes: fervent eyes, bovine and sad. His opponent is a Bobover in a long robe, britches, white hose, and slippers. His skin is as pale as a page of commentary. His hat perches on his lap, a black cake on a black dish. His skullcap lies flat as a sewn pocket against the back of his cropped head. To the eye not disillusioned by police work, they might appear to be as lost as any pair of Einstein patzers in the diffused radiance of their game. Landsman would be willing to bet a hundred dollars, however, that neither of them even knows whose move it is. They have been listening to every word at the neighboring table; they are listening now.

Berko walks over to the table on the other side of the Russian and Velvel. It's unoccupied. He picks up a bentwood chair with a ripped cane seat and swings it around to a spot between the table of the black hats and the table where the Russian is breaking Velvel down. He sits down in that grand fat-man way he has, spreading his legs, tossing the flaps of his overcoat behind him, as if he is going to make a fine meal of them all. He takes off his own homburg, palming it by the crown. His Indian hair stands thick and lustrous, threaded lately with silver. Gray hair makes Berko look wiser and kinder, an effect that, though he is relatively wise and fairly kind, he will not hesitate to abuse. The bentwood chair grows alarmed at the scope and contour of Berko's buttocks.

"Hi!" Berko says to the black hats. He rubs his palms together, then spreads them across his thighs. All the man needs is a napkin to tuck into his collar, a fork, and a knife. "How are you?"

With the art and determination of the very worst actors, the black hats look up, surprised.

"We don't want any trouble," the Lubavitcher says.

"My favorite phrase in the Yiddish language," Berko says sincerely. "Now, how about we get you in on this discussion? Tell us about Frank."

"We did not know him," the Lubavitcher says. "Frank who?"

The Bobover says nothing.

"Friend Bobover," Landsman says gently. "Your name."

"My name is Saltiel Lapidus," the Bobover says. His eyes are girlish and shy. He folds his fingers in his lap, on top of his hat. "And I know nothing about anything."

"You played with this Frank? You knew him?"

Saltiel Lapidus gives his head a hasty shake. "No."

"Yes," the Lubavitcher says. "He was known to us."

Lapidus glares at his friend, and the Lubavitcher looks away.

Landsman reads the story. Chess is permitted to the pious Jew, even—alone among games—on the Sabbath. But the Einstein Chess Club is a resolutely secular institution. The Lubavitcher dragged the Bobover into this profane temple on a Friday morning with Sabbath coming and both of them having better things to do. He said everything would be fine, what harm could come of it? And now see.

Landsman is curious, even touched. A friendship across sectarian lines is not a common phenomenon, in his experience. In the past, it has struck him that, apart from homosexuals, only chess players have found a reliable way to bridge, intensely but without fatal violence, the gulf that separates any given pair of men.

"I have seen him here," the Lubavitcher declares, his eyes on his friend, as if to show him they have nothing to fear. "This so-called Frank. Maybe I played him one or two times. In my opinion, he was a highly talented player."

"Compared to you, Fishkin," the Russian says, "a monkey is Raúl Capablanca."

"You," Landsman says to the Russian, his voice level, playing a hunch. "You knew he was a heroin addict. How?"

"Detective Landsman," the Russian says, half reproachful. "You do not recognize me?"

It felt like a hunch. But it was only a mislaid memory.

"Vassily Shitnovitzer," Landsman says. It has not been so long—a dozen years—since he arrested a young Russian of that name for conspiracy to sell heroin. A recent immigrant, a former convict swept clear of the chaos that followed the collapse of the Third Russian Republic. A man with broken Yiddish, this heroin dealer, and pale eyes set too close together. "And you knew me all this time."

"You are handsome fellow. Hard to forget," Shitnovitzer says. "Also snappy dresser."

"Shitnovitzer spent a long time in Butyrka," Landsman tells

Berko, meaning the notorious Moscow prison. "Nice guy. Use to sell junk from the kitchen of the coffee shop here."

"You sold heroin to Frank?" Berko says to Shitnovitzer.

"I am retired," Vassily Shitnovitzer says, shaking his head. "Sixty-four federal months in Ellensburg, Washington. Worse than Butyrka. Never again I don't touch that stuff, Detectives, and even if I do, believe me, I don't go near Frank. I am crazy, but I am not lunatic."

Landsman feels the bump and the skid as the tires lock. They have just hit something.

"Why not?" Berko says, kindly and wise. "Why does selling smack to Frank make you not just a criminal but a lunatic, Mr. Shitnovitzer?"

There is a small, decisive clink, a bit hollow, like false teeth clapping together. Velvel tips over his king.

"I resign," says Velvel. He takes off his glasses, slips them into his pocket, and stands up. He forgot an appointment. He's late for work. His mother is calling him on the ultrasonic frequency reserved by the government for Jewish mothers in the event of lunch.

"Sit down," Berko says without turning around. The kid sits down.

A cramp has seized Shitnovitzer's intestines; that's how it looks to Landsman.

"Bad mazel," he says finally.

"Bad mazel," Landsman repeats, letting his doubt and his disappointment show.

"Like a coat. A hat of bad mazel on his head. So much bad mazel, you don't want to touch him or share oxygen nearby."

"I saw him playing five games at once," Velvel offers. "For a hundred dollars. He won them all. Then I saw him vomiting in the alley."

"Detectives, please," Saltiel Lapidus says in a pained voice. "We have nothing to do with this. We know nothing about this man. Heroin. Vomiting in alleys. Please, we're already uncomfortable enough."

"Embarrassed," the Lubavitcher suggests.

"*Sorry*," Lapidus concludes. "And we have nothing to say. So, please, may we go?"

"Sure thing," Berko says. "Take off. Just write down your names and contact information for us before you go."

He takes out his so-called notebook, a small, fat sheaf of paper held together with an extra-large paper clip. At any given moment it might be found to contain business cards, tides tables, to-do lists, chronological listings of English kings, theories scrawled at three in the morning, five-dollar bills, jotted recipes, folded cocktail napkins with the layout of a South Sitka alley in which a hooker was killed. He shuffles through his notebook until he arrives at a blank scrap of index card, which he hands to Fishkin the Lubavitcher. He holds out his stub of pencil, but, no thank you, Fishkin has a pen of his own. He writes down his name and address and the number of his Shoyfer, then passes it to Lapidus, who does the same.

"Only," Fishkin says, "don't call us. Don't come to our homes. I beg you. We don't have anything to say. There's nothing about that Jew that we can tell you."

Every noz in the District learns to respect the silence of the black hat. It is a refusal to answer that can spread and gather and deepen until, like a fog, it fills the streets of an entire black-hat neighborhood. Black hats wield skillful attorneys, and political clout, and boisterous newspapers, and can enfold a hapless inspector or even a commissioner in a great black-hatted stink that doesn't go away until the witness or suspect is kicked loose or the charges are dropped. Landsman would need the full weight of the department behind him, and at the very least his skipper's approval, before he could invite Lapidus and Fishkin into the hotbox of the homicide modular.

He risks a glance at Berko, who risks a slight shake of the head.

"Go," Landsman says.

Lapidus lurches to his feet like a man defeated by his bowels. The business of coat and galoshes is undertaken with a show of battered dignity. He returns the iron lid of his hat by half-inches to his head, the way you ease down a manhole cover. With a grieving eye, he watches Fishkin sweep his unplayed morning into a hinged wooden box. Side by side, the black hats conduct themselves among the tables, past the other players, who look up to watch them go. Just before they reach the doors, the left leg of Saltiel Lapidus comes unstrung at its tuning key. He sags, gives way, and reaches to steady himself with a hand on the shoulder of his friend. The floor under his feet is bare and smooth. As far as Landsman can tell, there is nothing to catch the toe.

"I never saw such a sad Bobover," he observes. "Jew was on the verge of tears."

"You want to push him again?"

"Just an inch or two."

"That's all you get with them anyway," Berko says.

They hurry past the patzers: a seedy violinist from the Sitka Odeon; a chiropodist, you see his picture on bus benches. Berko bursts through the doors after Lapidus and Fishkin. Landsman is about to follow when something wistful tugs at his memory, a whiff of some brand of aftershave that nobody wears anymore, the jangling chorus of a song that was moderately popular one August twenty-five summers ago. Landsman turns to the table nearest the door.

An old man sits clenched like a fist around a chessboard, facing an empty chair. He has the pieces set up on their opening squares and has drawn or assigned himself White. Waiting for his opponent to show. Shining skull edged with tufts of grayish hair like pocket lint. The lower part of his face hidden by the cant of his head. Visible to Landsman are the hollows of his temples, his halo of dandruff, the bony bridge of his nose, the grooves on his brow like a grid left in raw pie crust by the tines of a fork. And the furious hunch of his shoulders, gripping the problem of the chessboard, planning his brilliant campaign. They were broad shoulders at one time, the shoulders of a hero or a mover of pianos.

"Mr. Litvak," Landsman says.

Litvak selects his king's knight the way a painter chooses a brush. His hands remain agile and ropy. He daubs an arcing stroke toward the center of the board; he always favored the hypermodern style of play. At the sight of the Réti Opening and Litvak's hands, Landsman is flooded, almost knocked down, by the old dread of chess, by the tedium, the irritation, the shame of those days spent breaking his father's heart over the chessboards in the Einstein coffee shop.

He says louder, "Alter Litvak."

Litvak looks up, puzzled and myopic. He was a man for a fistfight, barrel-chested, a hunter, a fisherman, a soldier. When he reached for a chessman, you saw the flash of the lightning bolt on his big gold Army Ranger ring. Now he looks shrunken, depleted, the king in the story reduced by the curse of eternal life to a cricket in the ashes of the hearth. Only the vaulting nose remains as testament to the former grandeur of his face. Looking at the wreckage of the man, Landsman thinks that if his father had not taken his own life, he would in all likelihood be dead nevertheless.

Litvak makes an impatient or petitioning gesture with his hand. He takes from his breast pocket a marbled black notepad and a fat fountain pen. He wears his beard neatly trimmed, as ever. A houndstooth blazer, tasseled boat shoes, a display handkerchief, a scarf strung through his lapels. The man has not lost his sporting air. In the pleats of his throat is a shining scar, a whitish comma tinged with pink. As he writes in the pad with his big Waterman, Litvak's breath comes through his great fleshy nose in patient gusts. The scratch of the nib is all that remains to him for a voice. He passes the pad to Landsman. His script is steady and clear.

Do I know you

His gaze sharpens, and he cocks his head to one side, sizing Landsman up, reading the wrinkled suit, the porkpie hat, the face like Hershel the dog's, knowing Landsman without recognizing him. He takes back the pad and appends one word to his question.

Do I know you Detective

"Meyer Landsman," Landsman says, handing the old man a business card. "You knew my father. I used to come here with him from time to time. Back when the club was in the coffee shop."

The red-rimmed eyes widen. Wonder mingles with horror as Mr. Litvak intensifies his study of Landsman, searching for some proof of this unlikely claim. He turns a page in his pad and pronounces his findings in the matter.

Impossible No way Meyerle Landsman could be such a lumpy old sack of onions

"Afraid so," Landsman says.

What are you doing here terrible chess player

"I was only a kid," Landsman says, horrified to detect a creak of self-pity in his tone. What an awful place, what wretched men, what a cruel and pointless game. "Mr. Litvak, you don't happen to know a man, I gather he plays here sometimes, a Jew maybe they call him Frank?"

Yes I know him has he done something wrong

"How well do you know him?"

Not as well as I would like

"Do you know where he lives, Mr. Litvak? Have you seen him recently?"

Months pls say you are not a homicide det.

"Again," Landsman says, "I'm afraid so."

The old man blinks. If he is shocked or saddened by the inference, you can't read it anywhere in his face or body language. But then a man not in control of his emotions would never get very far with the Réti Opening. Maybe there is a hint of shakiness in the word he writes next in his pad.

Overdose?

"Gunshot," Landsman says.

The door to the club creaks open, and a couple of patzers come in from the alley looking gray and cold. A gaunt scarecrow barely out of his teens, with a trimmed golden beard and a suit that's too small for him, and a short, chubby man, dark and curly-bearded, in a suit that's much too large. Their crew cuts look patchy, as if self-inflicted, and they wear matching black crocheted yarmulkes. They hesitate a moment in the doorway, abashed, looking at Mr. Litvak as if they expect to be scolded.

The old man speaks then, inhaling the words, his voice a dinosaurian ghost. It's an awful sound, a malfunction of the windpipe. A moment after it fades, Landsman realizes that he said, "My grandnephews."

Litvak waves them in and passes Landsman's card to the chubby one.

"Nice to meet you, Detective," the chubby one says with the hint of an accent, maybe Australian. He takes the empty chair, glances at the board, and smartly brings out his own king's knight. "Sorry, Uncle Alter. That one was late, as usual."

The skinny one hangs back with his hand on the open door of the club.

"Landsman!" Berko calls from the alley, where he has Fishkin and Lapidus corralled beside the Dumpster. It appears to Landsman that Lapidus is bawling like a child. "What the hell?"

"Right there," Landsman says. "I have to go, Mr. Litvak." For an instant he handles the bones, horn, and leather of the old man's hand. "Where can I reach you if I need to talk to you some more?"

Litvak writes out an address and tears the leaf from his pad.

"Madagascar?" Landsman says, reading the name of some unimaginable street in Tananarive. "That's a new one." At the sight of that faraway address, at the thought of that house on rue Jean Bart, Landsman feels a profound ebb in his will to pursue the matter of the dead yid in 208. What difference will it make if he catches the killer? A year from now, Jews will be Africans, and this old ballroom will be filled with tea-dancing gentiles, and every case that ever was opened or closed by a Sitka policeman will have been filed in cabinet nine. "When are you leaving?"

"Next week," says the chubby great-nephew, sounding doubtful.

The old man emits another horrible reptilian croak, one that nobody understands. He writes, then slides the notepad across to his great-nephew.

"'Man makes plans,'" the kid reads. "'And God laughs.'"

Sometimes when the younger black hats are caught by the police, they turn haughty and angry and demand their rights as American subjects. And sometimes they break down and cry. Men tend to cry, in Landsman's experience, when they have been living for a long time with a sense of rightness and safety, and then they realize that all along, just under their boots, lay the abyss. That is part of the policeman's job, to jerk back the pretty carpet that covers over the deep jagged hole in the floor. Landsman wonders if that's how it is with Saltiel Lapidus. Tears stream down his cheeks. A glinting thread of mucus dangles from his right nostril.

"Mr. Lapidus is feeling a little sad," Berko says. "But he won't say why."

Landsman feels around in the pocket of his overcoat for a package of Kleenex and finds one miraculous sheet. Lapidus hesitates, then takes it and blows his nose with feeling.

"I swear to you, I didn't know the man," Lapidus says. "I don't know where he lived, who he was. I don't know anything. I swear on my life. We played chess a few times. He always won."

"You're just grieving for the sake of humanity, then," Landsman says, trying to keep the sarcasm out of his tone.

"Exactly right," Lapidus says, and then he balls the tissue in his fist and tosses that crumpled flower into the gutter.

"Are you going to take us in?" Fishkin demands. "Because if you are, then I want to call a lawyer. And if you're not, then you have to let us go."

"A black-hat lawyer," Berko says, and it's a kind of moan or plea directed toward Landsman. "Woe is me."

"Get going, then," Landsman says.

Berko gives them a nod. The two men crunch off through the filthy slush of the alley.

"So, nu, I'm irritated," Berko says. "I admit this one is starting to irritate me."

Landsman nods and scratches at the stubble of his chin in a way that is meant to signify deep ratiocination, but his heart and thoughts are hung up in the memory of chess games that he lost to men who were already old thirty years ago.

"Did you see that old guy in there?" he says. "By the door. Alter Litvak. Been hanging around the Einstein for years. Used to play my father. Your father, too."

"I've heard the name." Berko looks back at the steel fire door that is the Einstein Club's grand entrance. "War hero. Cuba."

"The man has no voice, he has to write everything down. I asked him where I could find him if I needed to talk to him, and he wrote that he was going to Madagascar."

"That's a new one."

"That's what I said."

"Did he know our Frank?"

"Not well, he said."

"Nobody knew our Frank," Berko says. "But everybody is very sad that he died." He buttons his coat over his belly, turns up his collar, settles his hat more firmly on his head. "Even you."

"Fuck you," Landsman says. "The yid was nothing to me."

"Maybe he was a Russian? That might explain the chess. And your pal Vassily's behavior. Maybe Lebed or Moskowits is behind the hit."

"If he's Russian, it doesn't explain what the two black hats were so afraid of," Landsman says. "Those two don't know from Moskowits. Russian shtarkers, a gangland hit, it just doesn't mean that much to your average Bobover." He gives his chin another few pulls and then makes up his mind. He looks up at the strip of radiant gray sky that stretches along the top of the narrow alley behind the Hotel Einstein. "I wonder what time sunset is tonight."

"Why? We're going to poke a stick into the Harkavy, Meyer? I don't think Bina will care much for that, we start stirring up the black hats down there."

"You don't, eh?" Landsman smiles. He takes the valet ticket from his pocket. "Then we'd better steer clear of the Harkavy."

"Uh-oh. You have that smile."

"You don't like this smile?"

"Only I've noticed what comes after is usually a question that you plan to answer yourself."

"How about this one. What kind of a yid, Berko, tell me this, what kind of a yid can make a prison-hard Russian sociopath want to crap in his pants, and bring tears to the eyes of the most pious black hat in Sitka?"

"I know you want me to say a Verbover," Berko says. After Berko passed out of the academy, his first billet was the Fifth Precinct, the Harkavy, where the Verbovers landed, along with most of their fellow black hats, after the 1948 arrival of the ninth Verbover rebbe, father-in-law of the present model, with the pitiful remnant of his court. It was a classic ghetto assignment, trying to help and protect people who disdain and despise you and the authority you represent. It ended when the young half-

Indian latke took a bullet in the shoulder, two inches from his heart, in the Shavuos Massacre at Goldblatt's Dairy Restaurant. "I know that's who you want me to say."

This is how Berko once explained to Landsman the sacred gang known as the Chasids of Verbov: They started out, back in the Ukraine, black hats like all the other black hats, scorning and keeping their distance from the trash and hoo-hah of the secular world, inside their imaginary ghetto wall of ritual and faith. Then the entire sect was burned in the fires of the Destruction, down to a hard, dense core of something blacker than any hat. What was left of the ninth Verbover rebbe emerged from those fires with eleven disciples and, among his family, only the sixth of his eight daughters. He rose into the air like a charred scrap of paper and blew to this narrow strip between the Baranof Mountains and the end of the world. And here he found a way to remake the old-style black-hat detachment. He carried its logic to its logical end, the way evil geniuses do in cheap novels. He built a criminal empire that profited on the meaningless tohubohu beyond the theoretical walls, on beings so flawed, corrupted, and hopeless of redemption that only cosmic courtesy led the Verbovers even to consider them human at all.

"I had the same thought, of course," Berko confesses. "Which I immediately suppressed." He claps his big hands over his face and leaves them there for a moment before dragging them slowly down, pulling at his cheeks until they stretch past his chin like the jowl flaps of a bulldog. "Woe is me, Meyer, you want us to go out to Verbov Island?"

"Fuck, no," Landsman says in American. "Truth, Berko. I hate that place. If we have to go to an island, I'd much rather go to Madagascar."

They stand there in the alley behind the Einstein, thinking through the numerous arguments against and the few that can be made in favor of pissing off the most powerful underworld characters north of the 55th parallel. They attempt to generate alternate explanations for the squirrelly behavior of the patzers in the Einstein.

"We'd better see Itzik Zimbalist," Berko says finally. "Anybody else out there, it's going to be as useful as talking to a dog. And a dog already broke my heart once today."

12

The street grid here on the island is still Sitka's, ruled and numbered, but apart from that, you are gone, sweetness: star-shot, teleported, spun clear through the wormhole to the planet of the Jews. Friday afternoon on Verbov Island, and Landsman's Chevelle Super Sport surfs the wave of black hats along Avenue 225. The hats in question are felt numbers, with high, dented crowns and mile-wide brims, the kind favored by overseers in plantation melodramas. The women sport head scarves and glossy wigs spun from the hair of the poor Jewesses of Morocco and Mesopotamia. Their coats and long dresses are the finest rags of Paris and New York, their shoes the flower of Italy. Boys careen down the sidewalks on in-line roller skates in a slipstream of scarves and sidelocks, flashing the orange linings of their unzipped parkas. Girls hobbled by long skirts go along braided arm in arm, raucous chains of Verbover girls vehement and clannish as schools of philosophy. The sky has turned steely, the wind has died, and the air crackles with the alchemy of children and the promise of snow.

"Look at this place," Landsman says. "It's hopping."

"Not one empty storefront."

"And more of these no-good yids than ever."

Landsman stops for a red at NW Twenty-eighth Street. Outside a corner store, by a study hall, Torah bachelors loiter, Scripture grifters, unmatchable luftmenshen and garden-variety hoodlums. When they notice Landsman's car, with its reek of plainclothesman hubris and its inflammatory double-S on the grille, they leave off yelling at one another and give Landsman the Bessarabian fish-eye. He is on their turf. He goes clean-shaven and does not tremble before God. He is not a Verbover Jew and therefore is not really a Jew at all. And if he is not a Jew, then he is nothing.

"Look at those assholes looking," Landsman says. "I don't like it."

"Meyer."

The truth is, black-hat Jews make Landsman angry, and they always have. He finds that it is a pleasurable anger, rich with layers of envy, condescension, resentment, and pity. He puts the car in gear and shoves open his door.

"Meyer. No."

Landsman steps around the open door of the Super Sport. He feels the women watching. He smells the sudden fear on the breath of the men around him, like caries of the teeth. He hears the laughter of the chickens that have not yet met their fates, the hum of the air compressors keeping the carp alive in their tanks. He's glowing like a needle that you heat to kill a tick.

"So, nu," he says to the yids on the corner. "Which one of you buffaloes wants a ride in my sweet nozmobile?"

A yid steps forward, a fair-skinned slab, low and wide, with a lumpy forehead and a forked yellow beard. "I suggest you return to your vehicle, Officer," he says softly, reasonably. "And go on where you're going."

Landsman grins. "Is that what you suggest?" he says.

The other street-corner men step forward now, filling in the space all around the bruiser with the lightning beard. There must be twenty of them, more than Landsman believed at first. Landsman's glow gutters, flickers like a lightbulb going bad.

"I'll put it another way," says the blond bruiser, a bulge at his hip drawing the attention of his fingers. "Get back in the car."

Landsman pulls at his chin. Madness, he thinks. Chasing a theoretical lead in a nonexistent case, you lose your temper for no reason. The next thing you know, you have caused an incident among a branch of black hats with clout, money, and a stockpile of Manchurian and surplus Russian firearms recently estimated by police intelligence, in a confidential report, to be adequate to the needs of a guerrilla insurgency in a small Central American republic. Madness, the reliable madness of Landsman.

"How about you come over here and make me?" Landsman says.

That's when Berko opens his door and displays his ancestral Bear bulk in the street. His profile is regal, worthy of a coin or a carved mountainside. And he carries in his right hand the uncanniest hammer any Jew or gentile is ever likely to see. It's a replica of the one that Chief Katlian is reported to have swung during the Russian-Tlingit war of 1804, which the Russians lost. Berko fashioned it for the purpose of intimidating yids when he was thirteen and new to their labyrinth, and it has not failed its purpose yet, which is why Berko keeps it in the backseat of Landsman's car. The head is a thirty-five-pound block of meteorite iron that Hertz Shemets dug up at an old Russian site near Yakovy. The handle was carved with a Sears hunting knife from a forty-ounce baseball bat. Interlocking black ravens and red sea monsters writhe along the shaft, grinning big-toothed grins. Their pigmentation used up fourteen Flair pens. A pair of raven feathers dangles on a leather thong from the top of the shaft. This detail may not be historically accurate, but it works on the yiddish mind to savage effect, saying:

Indianer.

The word gets handed up and down the stalls and storefronts. Sitka Jews rarely see or speak to Indians, except in federal court or in the small Jewish towns along the Line. It takes very little imagination for these Verbovers to picture Berko and his hammer engaged in the wholesale spattering of paleface brainpans. Then they catch sight of Berko's yarmulke, and a flutter of fine white fringe at his waist from his ritual four-corner, and you can feel all that giddy xenophobia drain off the crowd, leaving a residue of racist vertigo. That's how it goes for Berko Shemets in the District of Sitka when he breaks out the hammer and goes Indian. Fifty years of movie scalpings and whistling arrows and burning Conestogas have their effect on people's minds. And then sheer incongruity does the rest.

"Berko Shemets," says the man with the forked beard, blinking, as big slow feathers of snow begin to fall on his shoulders and hat. "What's up, yid?"

"Dovid Sussman," Berko says, lowering the hammer. "I thought it was you."

Onto his cousin he trains his big minotaur eyes full of long suffering and reproach. It was not Berko's idea to come to Verbov Island. It was not Berko's idea to pursue the Lasker case after they had been told to lay off. It was not Berko's idea to flee in shame to a cheap Untershtot flophouse where mystery junkies get capped by the goddess of chess.

"A sweet Sabbath to you, Sussman," Berko says, tossing the hammer into the back of Landsman's car. When it hits the floor, the springs inside the bucket seats ring like bells.

"A sweet Sabbath to you, too, Detective," Sussman says. The other yids echo the greeting, a bit unsure. Then they turn away and resume their back-and-forth over a fine point of pot koshering or VIN erasure.

When they get in the car, Berko slams the door and says, "I *hate* doing that."

They drive down Avenue 225, and every face turns to look at the Indian Jew in the blue Chevrolet.

"So much for asking a few discreet questions," Berko says bitterly. "One day, Meyer, so help me, I'm going to use my head knocker on you."

"Maybe you should," Landsman says. "Maybe I would welcome it as therapy."

They crawl west on Avenue 225 toward the shop of Itzik Zimbalist. Courts and cul-de-sacs, single-family neo-Ukrainians and condominium units, steep-roofed clapboard structures painted somber colors and built right out to the property lines. The houses jostle and shoulder one another the way black hats do in synagogue.

"Not a single for-sale sign," Landsman observes. "Laundry on every line. All the other sects have been packing up the Torahs and the hatboxes. The Harkavy's half a ghost town. But not the Verbovers. Either they're totally oblivious to Reversion, or they know something we don't."

"They're Verbovers," Berko says. "Which way would you bet?"

"You're saying the rebbe put the fix in. Green cards for everyone." Landsman considers this possibility. He knows, of course, that a criminal organization like the Verbover ring can't flourish without the ready services of bagmen and secret lobbyists, without regular applications of grease and body English to the works of government. The Verbovers, with their Talmudic grasp of systems, their deep pockets, and the impenetrable face they present to the outer world have broken or rigged many mechanisms of control. But to have figured a way to gaff the entire INS like a Coke machine with a dollar on a string?

"Nobody has that much weight," Landsman says. "Not even the Verbover rebbe."

Berko ducks his head and gives his shoulders a half-shrug, as if he doesn't want to say anything more lest terrible forces be unleashed, scourges and plagues and holy tornadoes.

"Just because you don't believe in miracles," he says.

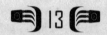

13

Zimbalist, the boundary maven, that learned old fart, he's ready when a rumor of Indians in a blue hunk of Michigan muscle comes rumbling up to his front door. Zimbalist's shop is a stone building with a zinc roof and big doors on rollers, at the wide end of a cobbled platz. The platz starts narrow at one end and broadens out like the nose of a cartoon Jew. Half a dozen crooked lanes tumble into it, following paths first laid down by long-vanished Ukrainian goats or aurochs, past housefronts that are faithful copies of lost Ukrainian originals. A Disney shtetl, bright and clean as a freshly forged birth certificate. An artful jumble of mud-brown and mustard-yellow houses, wood and plaster with thatched roofs. Across from Zimbalist's shop, at the narrow end of the platz, stands the house of Heskel Shpilman, tenth in the dynastic line from the original rebbe of Verbov, himself a famous worker of miracles. Three neat white cubes of spotless stucco, with mansard roofs of blue slate tile and tall windows, shuttered and narrow. An exact copy of the original home, back in Verbov, of the present rebbe's wife's grandfather, the eighth Verbover rebbe, right down to the nickel-plated bathtub in the upstairs washroom. Even before they turned to money laundering, smuggling, and graft, Verbover rebbes distinguished themselves from the competition by the splendor of their waistcoats, the French silver on their Sabbath table, the soft Italian boots on their feet.

The boundary maven is small, frail, slope-shouldered, call him seventy-five but looking ten years older. Patchy cinder-gray hair worn too long, sunken dark eyes, and pale skin tinged yellow like a celery heart. He wears a zip cardigan with collar flaps and a pair of old plastic sandals, navy blue, over white socks with a hole for the left big toe and its horn. His herringbone trousers are stained with egg yolk, acid, tar, epoxy fixative, sealing wax, green paint, mastodon blood. The maven's face is bony, mostly nose and chin, evolved for noticing, probing, cutting straight to gaps, breaches, and lapses. His full ashy beard flutters in the wind like bird fluff caught on a barbed-wire fence. In a hundred years of helplessness, this would be the last face that Landsman would ever turn to hoping for aid or information, but Berko knows more about black-hat life than Landsman ever will.

Standing next to Zimbalist, in front of the arched stone door of the shop, a beardless young bachelor holds an umbrella to keep the snow off the old fart's head. The black cake of the kid's hat is already dusted with a quarter inch of frosting. Zimbalist gives him the attention you give a tree in a pot.

"You're fatter than ever," he says by way of greeting as Berko swaggers toward him, some ghost of the weight of the war hammer lingering in his gait. "Big as a sofa."

"Professor Zimbalist," Berko says, swinging that invisible mallet. "You look like something that fell out of a used vacuum-cleaner bag."

"Eight years you don't bother me."

"Yeah, I thought I'd give you a break."

"That's nice. Too bad every other Jew in this accursed potato paring of a District kept right on banging me a kettle all day long." He turns to the bachelor with the umbrella. "Tea. Glasses. Jam."

The bachelor murmurs an Aramaic allusion to abject obedience quoted from the *Tractate on the Hierarchy of Dogs, Cats, and Mice,* opens the door for the boundary maven, and they go in. It's one vast, echoing room, divided by theory into a garage, a workshop, and an office that's lined with steel map cabinets, framed testimonials, and all the black-spined volumes of the endless, bottomless Law. The big rolling doors are there to let the vans go in and out. Three vans, judging from the trey of oil stains on the smooth cement floor.

Landsman gets paid—and lives—to notice what normal people miss, but it seems to him that until he walked into Zimbalist the boundary maven's shop, he hasn't given enough attention to string. String, twine, rope, cord, tape, filament, lanyard, hawser, and cable; polypropylene, hemp, rubber, rubberized copper, Kevlar, steel, silk, flax, braided velvet. The boundary maven has vast stretches of the Talmud by heart. Topography, geography, geodesy, geometry, trigonometry, they're a reflex, like sighting along the barrel of a gun. But the boundary maven lives and dies by the quality of his string. Most of it—you can measure it in miles, or in vershts, or in hands, like a boundary maven—is coiled neatly on spools hung from the wall or stacked neatly, by size, on metal spindles. But a lot of it is heaped here and there in crazes and tangles. Brambles, hair combings, huge thorny elf knots of string and wire, blowing around the shop like tumbleweeds.

"This is my partner, Professor, Detective Landsman," Berko says. "You want somebody to bang you a kettle, let me tell you."

"A pain in the ass like you?"

"Don't get me started."

Landsman and the professor shake hands.

"I know this one," the boundary maven says, coming in close to get a better look at Landsman, giving him the squint-eye as if he's one of the maven's ten thousand boundary maps. "That caught the maniac Podolsky. That sent Hyman Tsharny to prison."

Landsman stiffens and shakes out the foil sheet of his blast shield, ready for an earful. Hyman Tsharny, a Verbover dollar washer with a string of video stores, hired two Filipino shlossers—

contract killers—to help him cement a tricky business deal. But Landsman's best informer is Benito Taganes, the Filipino-style Chinese donut king. Benito's information led Landsman to the roadhouse by the airfield where the hapless shlossers were waiting for a plane, and their testimony put Tsharny away, despite the best efforts of the thickest courtroom kevlar that Verbover money could buy. Hyman Tsharny is still the only Verbover ever to be convicted and sentenced on criminal charges in the District.

"Look at him." Zimbalist's face breaks open at the bottom. His teeth are like the pipes of an organ made of bones. His laugh sounds like a handful of rusty forks and nail heads clattering on the ground. "He thinks I give a shit about these people, may their loins be as withered as their souls." The maven stops laughing. "What, you thought I was one of them?"

It feels like the deadliest question Landsman has ever been asked. "No, Professor," he says. Landsman also had some doubt that Zimbalist was really a professor, but there in the office, above the head of the bachelor struggling with the electric kettle, are the framed credentials and certificates from the Yeshiva of Warsaw (1939), the Polish Free State (1950), and Bronfman Manual and Technical (1955). Also those testimonials, *haskamos*, and affidavits, each in its sober black frame, one from what looks to be every rabbi in the District, two-bit and big-time, from Yakovy to Sitka. Landsman makes a show of giving Zimbalist another once-over, but it's obvious just from the big yarmulke covering the eczema at the back of his skull, with its fancy embroidery of silver thread, that the boundary maven isn't a Verbover. "I wouldn't make that mistake."

"No? What about marrying one of them, like I did? Would you make that mistake?"

"When it comes to marriage I like to let other people make the mistakes," Landsman says. "My ex-wife, for example."

Zimbalist waves them over, past the stout oak map table, to a couple of broken ladder-back chairs beside a massive rolltop desk. The bachelor can't get out of his way fast enough, and the boundary maven grabs him by the ear.

"What are you doing?" He seizes the kid's hand. "Look at those fingernails! Feh!" He drops the hand as if it's a piece of bad fish. "Go, get out of here, get on the radio. Find out where those idiots are and what's taking so long."

He pours water into a pot and throws in a fistful of loose tea that looks suspiciously like shredded string. "One eruv they have to patrol. One! I have twelve men working for me, there's not a single one of them who couldn't get lost trying to find his foot-fingers at the far end of his socks."

Landsman has put a lot of work into the avoidance of having to understand concepts like that of the eruv, but he knows that it's a typical Jewish ritual dodge, a scam run on God, that controlling motherfucker. It has something to do with pretending that telephone poles are doorposts, and that the wires are lintels. You can tie off an area using poles and strings and call it an eruv, then pretend on the Sabbath that this eruv you've drawn—in the case of Zimbalist and his crew, it's pretty much the whole District— is your house. That way you can get around the Sabbath ban on carrying in a public place, and walk to shul with a couple of Alka-Seltzers in your pocket, and it isn't a sin. Given enough string and enough poles, and with a little creative use of existing walls, fences, cliffs, and rivers, you could tie a circle around pretty much any place and call it an eruv.

But somebody has to lay down those lines, survey the territory, maintain the strings and the poles, and guard the integrity of the make-believe walls and doors against weather, vandalism, bears, and the telephone company. That's where the boundary maven comes in. He has the whole strings-and-poles market cornered. The Verbovers took him up first, and with their strong-arm tactics behind him, one by one the Satmar, Bobov, Lubavitch, Ger, and all the other black-hat sects have come to rely on his services and his expertise. When a question arises as to whether or not some particular stretch of sidewalk or lakefront or open field is contained within an eruv, Zimbalist, though not a rabbi, is the one to whom all the rabbis defer. On his maps and his crews and his spools of polypropylene baling twine depends the state of the souls of every pious Jew in the District. By some accounts, he's the most powerful yid in town. And that's why he's allowed to sit down behind his big oak desk with its seventy-two pigeonholes, smack in the middle of Verbov Island, and drink a glass of tea with the man who collared Hyman Tsharny.

"What's the matter with you?" he says to Berko, easing himself with a rubbery squeak onto an inflatable donut cushion. He takes a package of Broadways from a cigarette clip on his desk. "Why are you going around scaring everybody with that hammer of yours?"

"My partner was disappointed by the welcome we received," Berko says.

"It lacked that Sabbath glow," Landsman says, lighting a papiros of his own. "In my opinion."

Zimbalist slides a three-cornered copper ashtray across the desk. On the side of the ashtray, it says KRASNY'S TOBACCO AND STATIONERY, which is where Isidor Landsman used to go for his monthly copy of *Chess Review*. Krasny's, with its lending library and encyclopedic humidor and annual poetry prize, was crushed by American chain stores years ago, and at the sight of this homely ashtray, the squeeze box of Landsman's heart gives a nostalgic wheeze.

"Two years of my life I gave those people," Berko says. "You'd think some of them could remember me. Am I that easy to forget?"

"Let me tell you something, Detective." With another squeak of the rubber donut, Zimbalist is up again and pouring tea into three filthy glasses. "The way they breed around here, those people you saw in the street today aren't the ones you knew eight years ago, those are their grandchildren. Nowadays they're born pregnant."

He hands them each a steaming glass, too hot to hold. It scalds the tips of Landsman's fingers. It smells like grass, rose hips, maybe a hint of string.

"They keep on making new Jews," Berko says, stirring a spoonful of jam into his glass. "Nobody is making places to put them."

"That is the truth," Zimbalist says as his bony ass hits the donut. He grimaces. "Strange times to be a Jew."

"Not around here, apparently," says Landsman. "Strictly life as usual on Verbov Island. A stolen BMW in every driveway and a talking chicken in every pot."

"These people don't worry until the rebbe tells them to worry," Zimbalist says.

"Maybe they don't have anything to worry about," Berko says. "Maybe the rebbe already took care of the problem."

"I wouldn't know."

"I don't believe that for a second."

"So don't believe it."

One of the garage doors goes sliding back on its wheels, and a white van pulls in, a bright mask of snow on its windshield. Four men in yellow coveralls pile out of the van, their noses red, their beards tied up in black nets. They start blowing their noses and stamping their feet, and Zimbalist has to go over and yell at them for a while. It turns out there was a problem near the reservoir in Sholem-Aleykhem Park, some idiot at Municipal put up a handball wall, right smack in the middle of a make-believe doorway between two light poles. They all tramp over to the map table in the middle of the office. While Zimbalist gets down the appropriate chart and unrolls it, the crew members take turns nodding and flexing their scowling muscles at Landsman and Berko. After that the crew just ignores them.

"They say the maven has a string map for every city where ten Jewish men ever bumped noses," Berko says to Landsman. "Clear on back to Jericho."

"I started that rumor myself," Zimbalist says, keeping his eyes on the chart. He tracks down the site, and one of the boys sketches in the handball wall with the stub of a pencil. Zimbalist quickly plots out a workaround that will hold through sundown tomorrow, a salient in the great imaginary wall of the eruv. He sends his boys back down to the Harkavy to run some plastic pipe up the sides of a couple of nearby phone poles, so that the Satmars who live on the east side of Sholem-Aleykhem Park can take their dogs out for a walk without endangering their souls.

"I'm sorry," he says, coming back around the desk. He winces. "I don't enjoy the act of sitting anymore. Now, what can I do for you? I doubt very much that you came here with a question about *reshus harabim*."

"We're working a homicide, Professor Zimbalist," Landsman says. "And we have reason to believe the deceased may have been a Verbover, or had ties to the Verbovers, at least at one time."

"Ties," the maven says, giving them a glimpse of those pipe-organ stalactites of his. "I suppose I know something about those."

"He was living in a hotel on Max Nordau Street under the name of Emanuel Lasker."

"Lasker? Like the chess player?" There's a crease in the parchment of Zimbalist's yellow forehead, and deep in the eye sockets, a scrape of flint and steel: surprise, puzzlement, a memory kindling. "I used to follow the game," he explains. "A long time ago."

"So did I," Landsman says. "So did our dead guy, right up to the end. Next to the body, there was a game all set up. He was reading Siegbert Tarrasch. And he was familiar to the regulars at the Einstein Chess Club. They knew him as Frank."

"Frank," the boundary maven says, giving it a Yankee twang. "Frank, Frank, Frank. That was his first name? It's a common Jewish last name, but a first name, no. You know for a fact he was a Jew, this Frank?"

Berko and Landsman exchange a quick look. They don't know anything for sure. The phylacteries in the nightstand could have

been a plant or a memento, something left behind by a prior
occupant of room 208. Nobody at the Einstein Club claimed to
have seen Frank the dead junkie in shul, rocking in the grip of the
Standing Prayer.

"We have reason to believe," Berko repeats calmly, "that he
may at one time have been a Verbover Jew."

"What kind of reason?"

"There were a couple of likely telephone poles," Landsman
says. "We tied a string between them."

He reaches into his pocket and takes out an envelope. He passes
one of Shpringer's death Polaroids across the desk to Zimbalist,
who holds it at arm's length, long enough to form the idea that
it's a picture of a corpse. He takes a deep breath and purses his
lips, getting ready to lay on them a solid professorial consideration
of the evidence at hand. A picture of a dead man, it's a break,
to be honest, in the routine of a boundary maven's life. Then he
looks at the picture, and in the instant before he regains absolute
control of his features Landsman sees Zimbalist take a swift punch
in the belly. The wind departs his lungs, and the blood drains from
his face. In his eyes, the steady maven flicker of intelligence is
snuffed out. For a second Landsman is looking at a Polaroid of a
dead boundary maven. Then the lights come back on in the old
fart's face. Berko and Landsman wait a little, and then a little more,
and Landsman understands that the boundary maven is fighting as
hard as he can to maintain that control, to hold on to the chance of
making his next words *Detectives, I have never seen that man before in my
life*, and having it sound plausible, inevitable, true.

"Who was he, Professor Zimbalist?" Berko says at last.

Zimbalist sets the photograph down on the desk and looks at
it some more, not bothering about what his eyes or his lips might
be doing.

"Oy, that boy," he says. "That sweet, sweet boy."

He takes a handkerchief from the pocket of his zippered
cardigan and blots the tears from his cheeks and barks once. It's

a horrible sound. Landsman picks up the maven's glass of tea and pours it into his own. From his hip pocket, he takes the bottle of vodka he impounded in the men's room of the Vorsht that morning. He pours two fingers into the glass of tea and then holds the cup out to the old fart.

Zimbalist takes the vodka without a word and knocks it down in one shot. Then he returns the handkerchief to its pocket and gives Landsman his photograph.

"I taught that boy to play chess," he says. "When that man was a boy, I mean. Before he grew up. I'm sorry, I'm not making sense." He goes for another Broadway, but he has already smoked them all. It takes him a while to figure this out. He sits there, poking around in the foil with a hooked finger, as if he's going for the peanut in a package of Cracker Jack. Landsman fixes him up with a smoke. "Thanks, Landsman. Thank you."

But then he doesn't say anything, he just sits there watching the papiros burn down. He peers out from his cavernous eyeholes at Berko, then steals a cardplayer peek at Landsman. He's recovering from the shock now. Trying to map the situation, the lines he cannot cross, the doorways that he mustn't step through on peril of his soul. The hairy, mottled crab of his hand flicks one of its legs toward the telephone on his desk. In another minute, the truth and darkness of life will once again have been remanded to the custody of lawyers.

The garage door creaks and rumbles, and with a moan of gratitude, Zimbalist starts to pop up again, but this time Berko beats him to his feet. He drops a heavy hand on the old man's shoulder.

"Sit down, Professor," he says. "I beg you. Take it slow if you have to, but please, sit your ass down on that donut." He leaves the hand where it is, giving Zimbalist a gentle squeeze, and nods toward the garage. "Meyer."

Landsman crosses the workshop to the garage and hauls out his shield. He walks directly into the path of the van as if the shield really is a badge that can stop a two-ton Chevy. The driver hits the brakes, and the howl of tires echoes against the cold stone walls of the garage. The driver rolls down his window. He has the full Zimbalist crew equipage: beard in a net, yellow coverall, well developed scowl.

"What gives, Detective?" he wants to know.

"Go take a drive," Landsman says. "We're talking." He reaches over to the dispatch panel and grabs hold of the skulking bachelor by the collar of his long coat. Dangles the kid like a puppy around to the passenger side of the van and drags open the side door, then tenderly shoves the bachelor into the van. "And take this little pisher with you."

"Boss?" the driver calls over to the boundary maven. After a moment Zimbalist nods and waves the driver away.

"But where should I go?" the driver says to Landsman.

"I don't know," Landsman says. He drags the van's door shut and shoves it home. "Go buy me a nice present."

Landsman pounds on the hood of the van, and it rolls back out into the storm of white lines being knit like strings of the boundary maven across the replica housefronts and the blazing gray sky. Landsman pulls the garage door into place and throws the latch.

"Nu, how about you start over?" he says to Zimbalist when he sits down again in the ladder back chair. He crosses his legs and lights another papiros for each of them. "We have plenty of time."

"Come on, Professor," Berko says. "You know the victim since he's a boy, right? All those memories have got to be going around and around in your head right now. As bad as you feel, it's going to feel better if you just start talking."

"It isn't that," the boundary maven says. "It's—It isn't that." He takes the lit papiros from Landsman, and this time he smokes most of it before he starts to talk. He is a learned yid, and he likes to have his thoughts in order.

"His name is Menachem," he begins. "Mendel. He is, or was, thirty-eight, a year older than you, Detective Shemets, but he had the same birthday, August fifteenth, isn't that right? Eh? I thought so. You see? *This* is the map cabinet." He taps his hairless dome. "Maps of Jericho, Detective Shemets, Jericho and Tyre."

Tapping the map cabinet gets a little out of control, and he knocks the yarmulke off his head. When he grabs at it, ash cascades all down his sweater.

"Mendele's IQ was measured at one-seventy," he continues. "By the time he was eight or nine, he could read Hebrew, Aramaic, Judeo-Spanish, Latin, Greek. The most difficult texts, the thorniest tangles of logic and argument. By then Mendele was already a much better chess player than I could ever hope to be. He had a remarkable memory for recorded games; he had only to read a transcript once, and after that, he could reproduce it on a board or in his head, move by move, without a mistake. When he was older and they didn't let him play so much anymore, he would work through famous games in his head. He must have known three, four hundred games by heart."

"That's what they used to say about Melekh Gaystik," Landsman says. "He had that kind of mind for the game."

"Melekh Gaystik," Zimbalist says. "Gaystik was a freak. It was not human, the way Gaystik played. He had a mind like some kind of bug, the only thing he knew to do was eat you. He was rude. Filthy. Mean. Mendele wasn't like that at all. He made toys for his sisters, dolls out of clothespins and felt, a house from a box of oatmeal. Always glue on his fingers, a clothespin in his pocket with a face on it. I would give him twine for the hair. Eight little sisters hanging off him all the time. A pet duck that used to follow him around like a dog." Zimbalist's thin brown lips hitch themselves up at the corners. "Believe it or not, I once arranged for a match to be played between Mendel and Melekh Gaystik. You could do such things—Gaystik was always broke and in debt, and he would have played against a half-drunk bear if the money was right. The boy was twelve at the time, Gaystik twenty-six. It was the year before he won the championship at Petersburg. They played three games in the back of my shop, which at that time—you remember, Detective—was on Ringelblum Avenue. I offered Gaystik five thousand dollars to play against Mendele. The boy won the first and the third. The second game he had Black and played Gaystik to a draw. Yes, Gaystik was only too happy to keep the match a secret."

"Why?" Landsman wants to know. "Why did the games have to be kept secret?"

"Because this boy," the boundary maven says. "The one who died in a hotel room on Max Nordau Street. Not a nice hotel, I imagine."

"A fleabag," Landsman says.

"He was shooting heroin into his arm?"

Landsman nods, and after a hard second or two, Zimbalist nods, too.

"Yes. Of course. Nu. The reason why I was obliged to arrange the games in secret was that this boy had been forbidden to play chess with outsiders. Somehow or other, I never learned how, Mendele's father got wind of the match against Gaystik. It was a near thing for me. In spite of the fact that my wife was a relative of the father, I almost lost his *haskama*, which at that time was the foundation of my business. I built this whole operation on that endorsement."

"The father. You're not saying—it was Heskel Shpilman," Berko says. "The man there in the picture is the son of the Verbover rebbe."

Landsman notices how quiet it is on Verbov Island, in the snow, inside a stone barn, with dark coming on, as the profane week and the world that profaned it prepare to be plunged into the flame of two matched candles.

"That's right," Zimbalist says at last. "Mendel Shpilman. The only son. He had a twin brother who was born dead. Later, that was interpreted as a sign."

Landsman says, "A sign of what? That he would be a prodigy? That he would turn out to be a junkie living in a cheap Untershtot flop?"

"Not that," says Zimbalist. "That nobody imagined."

"They said . . . they used to say . . ." Berko begins. He screws up his face, as if he knows what he'll say next is going to irk Landsman or give him cause for scorn. He unscrews his brown eyes, lets it pass. He can't bring himself to repeat it. "Mendel Shpilman. Dear God. I heard some stories."

"A lot of stories," Zimbalist says. "Nothing but stories till he was twenty years old."

"What kind of stories?" Landsman says, duly irked. "Stories about what? Tell me already, damn you."

14

So Zimbalist tells them a Mendel story.

A certain woman, he says, was dying of cancer at Sitka General Hospital. A woman of his acquaintance, call her. This was back in 1973. The woman was twice a widow, her first husband a gambler shot by shtarkers in Germany before the war, her second a string monkey in Zimbalist's employ who got tangled in a live power line. It was through supporting the widow of his dead worker with cash and favors that Zimbalist got to know her. It's not impossible that they fell in love. They were both past the age of foolish passion, so they were passionate without being fools. She was a dark, lean woman already in the habit of controlling her appetites. They kept their affair a secret from everyone, not least Mrs. Zimbalist.

To visit his lady friend in the hospital when she took ill, Zimbalist resorted to subterfuge, stealth, and the bribing of orderlies. He slept on a towel on the floor of the ward, curled between her bed and the wall. In the half-dark, when his mistress called out from the distances of morphine, he would spill water between her cracked lips and cool her forehead with a damp cloth. The clock on the hospital wall hummed to itself, got antsy, kept snapping off pieces of the night with its minute hand. In the morning Zimbalist would creep back to his shop on Ringelblum Avenue—he told his wife he was sleeping there because his snoring was so bad—and wait for the boy.

Almost every morning after worship and study, Mendel Shpilman would come and play chess. Chess was permitted, even though the Verbover rabbinate and the larger community of the pious viewed it as a waste of the boy's time. The older Mendel got—the more dazzling his feats of scholarship, the brighter his reputation for acumen beyond his years—the more painful this waste appeared. It was not just Mendel's memory, the agile reasoning, the grasp of precedent, history, law. No, even as a kid, Mendel Shpilman seemed to intuit the messy human flow that both powered the Law and required its elaborate system of drains and sluices. Fear, doubt, lust, dishonesty, broken vows, murder and love, uncertainty about the intentions of God and men, little Mendel saw all of that not only in the Aramaic abstract but when it appeared in his father's study, clothed in the dark serge and juicy mother tongue of everyday life. If conflicts ever arose in the boy's mind, doubts about the relevance of the Law that he was learning in the Verbover court at the feet of a bunch of king-size ganefs and crooks, they never showed. Not when he was a kid who believed, and not when the day came that he turned his back on it all. He had the kind of mind that could hold and consider contradictory propositions without losing its balance.

It was because the Shpilmans were so proud of his excellence as a Jewish son and scholar that they tolerated the side of Mendel's character that loved only to play. Mendel was always getting up elaborate pranks and hoaxes, staging plays that featured his sisters, his aunts, the duck. Some people thought the greatest miracle Mendel ever performed was to persuade his formidable father, year after year, to take the part of Queen Vashti in the Purimshpiel. The sight of that somber emperor, that mountain of dignity, that fearsome bulk mincing around in high-heeled shoes! A blond wig! Lipstick and rouge, bangles and spangles! It might have been the most horrible feat of female impersonation Jewry ever produced. People loved it. And they loved Mendel for making it happen each year. But it was just another proof of the love that Heskel Shpilman had for his boy. And it was the same loving indulgence that permitted Mendel to waste an hour every day at chess, with the proviso that his opponent be chosen from the community of Verbov.

Mendel chose the boundary maven, the lone outsider in their midst. It was a small display of rebellion or perversity that some, in later years, would have occasion to revisit. But in the Verbov orbit, only Zimbalist had even a prayer of beating Mendel.

"How is she?" Mendel said to Zimbalist one morning after the lady friend had been dying at Sitka General for two months and was nearly gone.

Zimbalist experienced a shock at the question—nothing to compare to the fate of the widow's second husband, of course, but enough to stop his heart for a beat or two. He remembers every game that he and Mendel Shpilman ever played against each other, he says, except for this one; of this game he can manage to recall a solitary move. Zimbalist's wife was a Shpilman, a cousin to this boy. Zimbalist's livelihood, his honor, perhaps even his life, demanded that the secret of his adultery be kept. He was absolutely certain that so far it had been. Through his wires and strings, the boundary maven felt every whisper and rumor the way a spider hears in its feet the thrashings of a fly. There was no way word of it could have reached Mendel Shpilman without Zimbalist hearing about it first.

He said, "How is who?"

The boy stared at him. Mendel was not a handsome kid. He had a perpetual flush, close-set eyes, a second and hints of a third chin without clear benefit of a first. But the eyes, though too small and too near the bridge of his nose, were dense and fitful with color, like the spots on a butterfly wing, blue, green, gold. Pity, mockery, forgiveness. No judgment. No reproach.

"Never mind," Mendel said gently. Then he moved his queen's bishop, returning it to its original position on the board.

The move had no purpose that Zimbalist, pondering it, could see. At one moment fantastic schools of chess seemed to be contained or implied by it. The next it appeared to be only what, in all likelihood, it was: a kind of retraction.

Zimbalist struggled for the next hour to understand that move, and for the strength to resist confiding to a ten-year-old whose universe was bounded by the study house, the shul, and the door to his mother's kitchen, the sorrow and dark rapture of Zimbalist's love for the dying widow, how some secret thirst of his own was quenched every time he dribbled cool water through her peeling lips.

They played through the remainder of their hour without further conversation. But when it was time for the boy to go, he turned in the doorway of the shop on Ringelblum Avenue and took hold of Zimbalist's sleeve. He hesitated as if reluctant or embarrassed. Or maybe he was feeling afraid. Then he got a hard pinched expression on his face that Zimbalist recognized as the internalized voice of the rebbe, reminding his son of his duty to serve the community.

"When you see her tonight," Mendel said, "tell her that I send her my blessing. Tell her I say hello."

"I will," Zimbalist said, or remembers saying.

"Tell her from me that all will be well."

The little monkey face, the sad mouth, the eyes saying that for as much as he knew you and loved you, he might still be pulling your leg.

"Oh, I will," Zimbalist said, and then he broke down in hiccuping sobs. The boy took a clean handkerchief from his pocket and gave it to Zimbalist. Patiently, he held the boundary maven's hand. His fingers were soft, a bit sticky. On the inside of his wrist, his younger sister Reyzl had scrawled her name in red ink. When Zimbalist regained his composure, Mendel let go of his hand and stuffed the damp handkerchief into his pocket.

"See you tomorrow," he said.

That night, when Zimbalist crept onto the ward, just before he spread his towel on the floor, he spooned the boy's blessing into the ear of his unconscious mistress. He did it without hope and with very little in the way of faith. In the dark of five A.M., Zimbalist's lady friend woke him and told him to go home and eat breakfast with his wife. It was the first coherent thing she had said in weeks.

"Did you give her my blessing?" Mendel asked him when they sat down to play later that morning.

"I did."

"Where is she?"

"At Sitka General."

"With other people? On a ward?"

Zimbalist nodded.

"And you gave my blessing to the other people, too?"

The idea had never occurred to Zimbalist. "I didn't say anything to them," he said. "I don't know them."

"There was more than enough blessing to go around," Mendel informed him. "Tell them. Give it to them tonight."

But that night, when Zimbalist went to visit his lady friend, she had been moved to another ward, one where nobody was in danger of death, and somehow or other, Zimbalist forgot the boy's reminder. Two weeks later, the woman's doctors sent her home, shaking their heads in puzzlement. Two weeks after that, an X ray showed no trace of the cancer in her body.

By then she and Zimbalist had broken off their affair by mutual agreement, and he slept every night in the marital bed. The daily meetings with Mendel in the back of the shop on Ringelblum Avenue continued for a while, but Zimbalist found that he had lost his pleasure in them. The apparent miracle of the cancer cure forever altered his relations with Mendel Shpilman. Zimbalist could not shake a sense of vertigo that came over him every time Mendel looked at him with his close-set eyes, flecked with pity and gold. The boundary maven's faith in faithlessness had been shaken by a simple question—*How is she?*—by a dozen words of blessing, by a simple bishop move that seemed to imply a chess beyond the chess that Zimbalist knew.

It was as repayment for the miracle that Zimbalist had arranged the secret match between Mendel and Melekh Gaystik, king of the Café Einstein and future champion of the world. Three games in the back room of a shop on Ringelblum Avenue, with the boy winning two out of three. When this act of subterfuge was uncovered—and not the other; no one else ever learned of the affair—the visits between Zimbalist and Mendel Shpilman were broken off. After that, he and Mendel never shared another hour at the board.

"That's what comes from giving out blessings," says Zimbalist the boundary maven. "But it took Mendel Shpilman a long time to figure that out."

15

"You met this ganef," Landsman half asks Berko as they hump along behind the boundary maven through the Sabbath snow to the rebbe's door. For the journey across the platz, Zimbalist washed his face and armpits in a sink at the back of the shop. He wet a comb and raked all seventeen of his hairs into a moire across the top of his head. Then he put on a brown corduroy sport coat, an orange down vest, black galoshes, and over everything, a belted bearskin coat trailing a smell of mothballs like a muffler twenty feet long. From a moose antler by the door, the maven took a football or miniature ottoman made of wolverine fur and set it on top of his head. Now he waddles along ahead of the detectives, reeking of naphthalene, looking like a small bear urged by cruel masters to perform demeaning feats. Under an hour before dark, and the snow falling is like pieces of broken daylight. The Sitka sky is dull silver plate and tarnishing fast.

"Yeah, I met him," Berko says. "They brought me in to see him right after I started working the Fifth Precinct. They had a ceremony in his office, over the study hall on South Ansky Street. He pinned something to the crown of my latke, a gold leaf. After that he used to send me a nice basket of fruit at Purim. Delivered right to my house, even though I never gave out my home address.

Every year pears and oranges until we moved out to the Shvartser-Yam."

"I hear he's kind of on the large side."

"He's cute. Cute as a fucking button."

"That stuff the maven was just telling us about Mendel. The wonders and miracles. Berko, you believe any of that?"

"You know it's not about believing for me, Meyer. It never has been."

"But do you—I'm curious—do you really feel like you're waiting for Messiah?"

Berko shrugs, uninterested in the question, keeping his eyes on the track of the black galoshes in the snow. "It's Messiah," he says. "What else can you do but wait?"

"And then when he comes, what? Peace on earth?"

"Peace, prosperity. Plenty to eat. Nobody sick or lonely. Nobody selling anything. I don't know."

"And Palestine? When Messiah comes, all the Jews move back there? To the promised land? Fur hats and all?"

"I heard Messiah cut a deal with the beavers," Berko says. "No more fur."

Under the glow of a big iron gas lamp mounted, by an iron bracket, to the front of the rebbe's house, a loose knot of men is killing the last of the week. Hangers-on, the rebbe-struck, an outright simpleton or two. And the usual impromptu mess of would-be Swiss Guards who make the job tougher for the biks holding up either side of the front door. Everybody's telling everybody else to go home and bless the light with their families, leave the rebbe to eat his Sabbath dinner in peace already. Nobody's quite leaving, nobody's quite sticking around. They swap authentic lies about recent miracles and portents, new Canadian immigration scams, and forty new versions of the story of the Indian with the hammer, how he recited the Alenu while dancing an Indian patch tanz.

When they hear the crunch and chiming of Zimbalist's galoshes coming toward them across the platz, they leave off making their noises, one by one, like a calliope running out of steam. Fifty years Zimbalist has been living in their midst and he's still, by some tangle of choice and necessity, an outsider. He's a wizard, a juju man, with his fingers on the strings that ring the District, and his palms cupping the brackish water of their souls every Sabbath. Perched at the tops of the boundary maven's poles, his crews can see into every window, they can listen in on every telephone call. Or at least that is what these men have heard.

"Coming through, please," the maven says, heading for the front steps with their pretty railings of curlicued wrought iron. "Friend Belsky, move aside."

The men make way as if Zimbalist is running toward a water bucket holding something on fire. Before they can quite close up the gap, they see Landsman and Berko coming their way and throw down a silence so heavy that Landsman can feel it pressing on the sides of his head. He can hear the snow fizzing and the sizzle each snowflake makes as it hits the top of the gas lamp. The men put on an exhibition of hard looks and innocent looks and looks so blank they threaten to vacuum all the air from Landsman's lungs. Somebody says, "I don't see any hammer."

Detectives Landsman and Shemets wish them the joy of the Sabbath. Then they turn their attention to the biks by the door, a couple of thickset, red-haired, pop-eyed boys with pug noses and dense woolly beards the rusty gold of brisket gravy. Two red Rudashevskys, biks from a long line of biks, bred for simplicity, density, power, and lightness of foot.

"Professor Zimbalist," says the Rudashevsky to the left of the door. "A good Sabbath to you."

"And to you, Friend Rudashevsky. I regret to disturb your watch on this peaceful afternoon." The boundary maven settles the furry ottoman more snugly on his head. Off to a flowery start, but when he goes to open the drawer of his face, no more coin falls out. Landsman reaches into his hip pocket. Zimbalist is just standing there, his arms hanging slack, maybe thinking it's all his fault, that it was chess that bent the boy from the God-directed angle of his glory, and now Zimbalist has to go in there and tell the father the sorry ending of the tale. So Landsman brushes up against Zimbalist's shoulder, with his fingers around the cold smooth neck of the pint of Canadian vodka in his pocket. He taps the bottle against Zimbalist's bony claw until the old fart catches on and palms it.

"Nu, Yossele, it's Detective Shemets," Berko says, taking over the operation, squinting up into the scattering gaslight with a hand over his eyes. The gang of men behind them begins to murmur, sensing now the quick unfolding of something bad and marvelous. The wind jerks the snowflakes back and forth on its hundred hooks. "What's up, yid?"

"Detective," says the Rudashevsky to the right, maybe Yossele's brother, maybe his cousin. Maybe both at once. "We heard you were in the neighborhood."

"This is Detective Landsman, my partner. Could you please tell Rabbi Shpilman that we'd like to have a moment of his time? Please believe, we wouldn't disturb him at this hour if it wasn't so important."

Black hats, even Verbovers, don't usually challenge the right or authority of policemen to conduct police business in the Harkavy or on Verbov Island. They don't cooperate, but they usually don't interfere. On the other hand, to enter the home of exile's strongest rabbi, at the very brink of the holiest moment of the week, for that you need a good reason. You need to be coming to tell him, for example, that his only son is dead.

"A moment of the rebbe's time?" says a Rudashevsky.

"If you had a million dollars, please don't mind my saying so, with all due respect, Detective Shemets," says the other, broader of shoulder and hairier of knuckle than Yossele, laying a hand over his heart, "it wouldn't be worth so much as that."

Landsman turns to Berko. "Have you got that kind of money on you?"

Berko jabs Landsman in the side with an elbow. Landsman never walked a black-hat beat in his latke days, groping his way along a murky sea bottom of blank looks and silences that could crush a submarine. Landsman doesn't know how to show the proper respect.

"Come, Yossele. Shmerl, sweetness," Berko croons. "I need to get home to my table. Let us in."

Yossele tugs on his brisket-colored chin muffler. Then the other begins to speak in a low, steady undertone. The bik is wearing, hidden by one of his looping auburn sidelocks, a headset-style microphone and earpiece.

"I am to inquire respectfully," the bik says after a moment, the force of the order flowing across his features, softening them as it stiffens his diction, "what business brings the distinguished officers of the law to the rebbe's home so late this Friday afternoon."

"Idiots!" Zimbalist says, a slug of vodka in him, careering up the steps like a fool of a bear on a unicycle. He grabs the lapels of Yossele Rudashevsky's coat and dances with them, left and right, anger and grief. "They're here about Mendele!"

The men standing around in front of the Shpilman house have been muttering and commenting and critiquing the performance, but they shut up. Life wheezes in and out of their lungs, rattles in the snot of their noses. The heat of the lantern vaporizes the snow. The air seems to shatter like a world of tiny windows with a tinkling sound. And Landsman feels something that makes him want to put a hand to the back of his neck. He is a dealer in entropy and a disbeliever by trade and inclination. To Landsman, heaven is kitsch, God a word, and the soul, at most, the charge on your battery. But in the three-second lull that follows Zimbalist's crying out the name of the rebbe's lost son, Landsman has the feeling that something comes fluttering among them. Dipping down over the crowd of men, brushing them with its wing. Maybe it's just the knowledge, leaping from man to man, of why these two homicide detectives must have come at this hour. Or maybe it's the old power to conjure of a name in which their fondest hope once resided. Or maybe Landsman just needs a good night's sleep in a hotel with no dead Jews in it.

Yossele turns to Shmerl, the dough of his forehead kneaded, holding on to Zimbalist with the brainless tenderness of a brutal man. Shmerl speaks another few syllables into the heart of the Verbover rebbe's house. He looks east, west. He checks with the mandolin man on the roof; there is always a man on the roof with a semiautomatic mandolin. Then he eases open the paneled door. Yossele sets old Zimbalist down with a jingling of galoshes clasps and pats him on the cheek. "If you please, Detectives," he says.

You come into a wainscoted hall, a door at the far end, on the left a wooden stair leading up to the second floor. The stairs and risers, the wainscot, even the floorboards are all cut from big slabs of some kind of pine, knotty and butter-colored. Along the wall opposite the stairway runs a low bench, also knotty pine, covered in a purple velvet cushion, worn to a shine in patches and bearing six round indentations made by years of Verbover buttocks.

"The esteemed detectives will please wait here," Shmerl says.

He and Yossele return to their posts, leaving Landsman and Berko under the steady but indifferent scrutiny of a third hulking Rudashevsky who lounges against the baluster at the bottom of the stairs.

"Sit, Professor," says the indoor Rudashevsky.

"Thank you," he says. "But I don't care to sit."

"You all right, Professor?" Berko says, laying a hand on the maven's arm.

"A handball court," Zimbalist says as if in reply to the question. "Who plays handball anymore?"

Something in the pocket of Zimbalist's coat catches Berko's eye. Landsman takes a sudden interest in a small wooden rack affixed to the wall by the door, well stocked with two slick, colorful brochures. One is entitled "Who Is the Verbover Rebbe?" and it informs him that they are standing in the formal or ceremonial entrance of the house, and that the family comes and goes and does its living at the other end, just like in the house of the president of America. The other brochure they're giving away is called "Five Great Truths and Five Big Lies About Verbover Hasidism."

"I saw the movie," Berko says, reading over Landsman's shoulder.

The stair creaks. The Rudashevsky mumbles, as if announcing a change in the dinner menu, "Rabbi Baronshteyn."

Landsman knows Baronshteyn only by reputation. Another boy wonder, with a law degree in addition to his rabbi's smikha, he married one of the rebbe's eight daughters. He is never photographed, and he never leaves Verbov Island, unless you believe the stories of his sneaking into some South Sitka roach motel in the dead of night to exact personal retribution on a policy-game skimmer, or on some shlosser who mishandled a hit.

"Detective Shemets, Detective Landsman. I am Aryeh Baronshteyn, the rebbe's gabay."

Landsman is surprised by how young he is, thirty at the outside. High, narrow forehead, black eyes hard as a couple of stones left on a grave marker. He has concealed his girlish mouth in the manly bloom of a King Solomon beard, fitted with careful streaks of gray to suggest maturity. The sidelocks hang limp and orderly. He has the air of a self-denier, but his clothes betray the old Verbover love of flash. His calves are plump and muscular in their silk garters and white hose. He keeps his long feet encased in brushed black velveteen slippers. The frock coat looks fresh from the bespoke needle of Moses and Sons on Asch Street. Only the plain knit skullcap has a modest air. Underneath it, his brush-cut hair glints like the business end of a paint-stripping rotor. His face displays no trace of wariness, but Landsman can see where wariness has been carefully erased.

"Reb Baronshteyn," Berko murmurs, taking off his hat. Landsman does likewise.

Baronshteyn keeps his hands in the pockets of his frock coat, a satin number with velour lapels and pocket flaps. He's making an attempt to look at his ease, but some men just don't know how to stand around with their hands in their pockets and look natural.

"What do you want here?" he says. He mimes a glance at his watch, poking it from the cuff of his milled cotton shirt just long enough for them to read the name of Patek Philippe on its face. "It's very late."

"We're here to talk to Rebbe Shpilman, Rabbi," Landsman says. "If your time is so precious, then we surely don't want to waste it by talking to you."

"It isn't my time that I fear to have you waste, Detective Landsman. And I can tell you right now that if you attempt to display, in this house, the disrespectful attitude and disgraceful behavior for which you are notorious, then you will not remain in this house. Is that clear?"

"I think you have me mixed up with the other Detective Meyer Landsman," Landsman says. "I'm the one who's just doing his job."

"Then you are here as part of a murder investigation? May I ask in what way it concerns the rebbe?"

"We really do need to talk to the rebbe," Berko says. "If he tells us he'd like to have you present, you're welcome to stay. But with all due respect, Rabbi, we're not here to answer your questions. And we aren't here to waste anybody's time."

"In addition to being his adviser, Detective, I am the rebbe's attorney. You know that."

"We're aware of that, sir."

"My office is across the platz," Baronshteyn says, going to the front door and holding it open like a gracious doorman. Snow pours down past the open doorway, glowing in the gaslight like an endless jackpot of coins. "I'm sure I will be able to answer whatever questions you have."

"Baronshteyn, you puppy. Get out of their way."

Zimbalist is on his feet now, hat collapsing over one ear, in his vast mangy coat and his miasma of mothballs and grief.

"Professor Zimbalist." Baronshteyn's tone is one of warning, but his eye grows keen as he takes in the ruin of the boundary maven. He may never have seen Zimbalist in proximity to an emotion. The spectacle clearly interests him. "Have a care."

"You tried to take his place. Well, now you have it. How does it feel?" Zimbalist totters a step closer to the gabay. There must be all kinds of cords and tripwires crisscrossing the space between them. But for once the boundary maven seems to have mislaid his string map. "He's more alive even now than you will ever be, you smelt, you waxworks."

He crashes past Berko and Landsman, reaching for the banister or the gabay's throat. Baronshteyn doesn't flinch. Berko grabs hold of the belt at the waist of the bearskin coat and drags Zimbalist back.

"*Who* is?" says Baronshteyn. "Who are you talking about?" He looks at Landsman. "Detective, did something happen to Mendel Shpilman?"

Landsman will review the performance later with Berko, but his first impression is that Baronshteyn sounds surprised by the possibility.

"Professor," Berko says. "We appreciate the help. Thank you." He zips up Zimbalist's sweater and buttons his jacket. He tucks one side of the bearskin coat over the other and knots the belt tightly at the waist. "Now, please, go home. Yossele, Shmerl, somebody walk the professor home before his wife gets worried and calls the police."

Yossele takes Zimbalist by the arm, and they start down the steps.

Berko shuts the door against the cold. "Take us to the rebbe, counselor," he says. "Now."

16

Rabbi Heskel Shpilman is a deformed mountain, a giant ruined dessert, a cartoon house with the windows shut and the sink left running. A little kid lumped him together, a mob of kids, blind orphans who never laid eyes on a man. They clumped the dough of his arms and legs to the dough of his body, then jammed his head down on top. A millionaire could cover a Rolls-Royce with the fine black silk-and-velvet expanse of the rebbe's frock coat and trousers. It would require the brain strength of the eighteen greatest sages in history to reason through the arguments against and in favor of classifying the rebbe's massive bottom as either a creature of the deep, a man-made structure, or an unavoidable act of God. If he stands up, or if he sits down, it doesn't make any difference in what you see.

"I suggest we dispense with the pleasantries," the rebbe says.

His voice comes pitched high, droll, the voice of the well-proportioned, scholarly man he must have been once. Landsman has heard that it's a glandular disorder. He has heard that the Verbover rebbe, for all his bulk, maintains the diet of a martyr, broth and roots and a daily crust of bread. But Landsman prefers to see the man as distended with the gas of violence and corruption.

His belly filled with bones and shoes and the hearts of men, half digested in the acid of his Law.

"Sit down and tell me what you came here to say."

"We can do that, rebbe," Berko says.

They each take a chair in front of the rebbe's desk. The office is pure Austro-Hungarian empire. Behemoths of mahogany, ebony and bird's-eye maple crowd the walls, ornate as cathedrals. In the corner by the door stands the famous Verbover Clock, a survivor of the old home back in Ukraine. Looted when Russia fell, then shipped back to Germany, it survived the dropping of the atomic bomb on Berlin in 1946 and all the confusions of the time that followed. It runs counterclockwise, reverse-numbered with the first twelve letters of the Hebrew alphabet. Its recovery was a turning point in the fortunes of the Verbover court and marked the start of Heskel Shpilman's ascent. Baronshteyn takes up a position behind and to the right of the rebbe, at a lectern where he can keep one eye on the street, one eye on whatever volume is being combed for precedents and justifications, and one eye, a lidless inner eye, on the man who is the center of his existence.

Landsman clears his throat. He is the primary, and this is his job to do. He steals another glance at the Verbover Clock. There are seven minutes remaining in this sorry excuse for a week.

"Before you begin, Detectives," says Aryeh Baronshteyn, "let me state for the record that I am here in my capacity as attorney to Rabbi Shpilman. Rebbe, if you have any doubt about whether you ought to answer a question put to you by the detectives, please refrain from answering, and allow me to ask them to clarify or rephrase it."

"This isn't an interrogation, Rabbi Baronshteyn," Berko says.

"You are welcome here, more than welcome, Aryeh," the rebbe says. "Indeed, I insist that you be present. But as my gabay and my son-in-law. Not as my lawyer. For this I don't need a lawyer."

"If I may, dear Rebbe. These men are homicide detectives. You are the Verbover rebbe. If you don't need a lawyer, then nobody needs a lawyer. And believe me, everybody needs a lawyer." Baronshteyn slides a pad of yellow paper from the interior of the lectern, where he no doubt keeps his vials of curare and his necklaces of severed human ears. He unscrews the cap of a fountain pen. "I will at least take notes. On," he deadpans, "a legal pad."

The Verbover rebbe contemplates Landsman from deep inside the redoubt of his flesh. He has light eyes, somewhere between green and gold. They're nothing like the pebbles abandoned by mourners on Baronshteyn's tombstone puss. Fatherly eyes that suffer and forgive and find amusement. They know what Landsman has lost, what he has squandered and let slip from his grasp through doubt, faithlessness, and the pursuit of being tough. They understand the furious wobble that throws off the trajectory of Landsman's good intentions. They comprehend the love affair that Landsman has with violence, his wild willingness to put his body out there on the street to break and to be broken. Until this minute Landsman didn't grasp what he and every noz in the District, and the Russian shtarkers and small-time wiseguys, and the FBI and the IRS and the ATF, were up against. He never understood how the other sects could tolerate and even defer to the presence of these pious gangsters in their black-hat midst. You could lead men with a pair of eyes like that. You could send them to the very lip of whatever abyss you chose.

"Tell me why you are here, Detective Landsman," the rebbe says.

Through the door of the outer office comes the muffled jangle of a telephone. There is no phone on the desk and none in sight. The rebbe works some feat of semaphore with half an eyebrow and a minor muscle of the eye. Baronshteyn puts down his pen. The ringing swells and dwindles as Baronshteyn slips the black missive of his body through the slot of the office door. A moment later, Landsman hears him answer. The words are unclear, the tone curt, maybe even harsh.

The rebbe catches Landsman trying to eavesdrop and puts his eyebrow muscles to more strenuous use.

"Right," says Landsman. "It's like this. It so happens, Rabbi Shpilman, that I live in the Zamenhof. It's a hotel, not a good one, down on Max Nordau Street. Last night the manager knocked on my door and asked me would I mind coming down to have a look at another guest in the hotel. The manager had been worried about this guest. He was afraid the Jew might have overdosed. And so he had let himself into the room. It turned out that the man was dead. He was registered under an assumed name. He had no identification. But there were a few hints of this and that in his room. And today my partner and I followed up on one of those hints, and it led us here. To you. We believe—we are all but certain—that the dead man was your son."

Baronshteyn sidles back into the room as Landsman is giving the news. His face has been wiped, as if with a soft cloth, of all prints or smudges of emotion.

"All but certain," the rebbe says dully, nothing moving in his face but the lights in his eyes. "I see. All but certain. Hints of this and that."

"We have a picture," Landsman says. Once again he produces like a grim magician Shpringer's photograph of the dead Jew in 208. He starts to pass it to the rebbe but consideration, a sudden flutter of sympathy, stops his hand.

"Perhaps it would be best," says Baronshteyn, "if I—"

"No," the rebbe says.

Shpilman takes the photograph from Landsman and, with both hands, brings it very close to his face, straight up into the precinct of his right eyeball. He's only nearsighted, but there is something vampiric in the gesture, as if he's trying to drain a vital liquor from the photograph with the lamprey mouth of his eye. He measures it from top to bottom and end to end. His expression never alters. Then he lowers the photograph to the clutter of his desk and clucks his tongue once. Baronshteyn steps forward to take a look at the picture, but the rebbe waves him off and says, "It's him."

Landsman, his instruments dialed up to full gain, widest aperture, is tuned to catch some faint radiation of regret or satisfaction that might escape the singularities at the heart of Baronshteyn's eyes. And it's there; a brief tracer arc of particles lights them up. But what Landsman detects in that instant, to his surprise, is disappointment. For an instant Aryeh Baronshteyn looks like a man who just drew an ace of spades and is contemplating the fan of useless diamonds in his hand. He exhales a short breath, half a sigh, and walks slowly back to his lectern.

"Shot," the rebbe says.

"Once," says Landsman.

"By whom, please?"

"Well, we don't know that."

"Any witnesses?"

"Not so far."

"Motive?"

Landsman says no, then turns to Berko for confirmation, and Berko gives his head a somber shake.

"*Shot.*" The Rebbe shakes his head as if marveling: *How do you like that?* With no discernible change in his voice or manner, he says, "You are well, Detective Shemets?"

"I can't complain, Rabbi Shpilman."

"Your wife and children? Healthy and strong?"

"They could be worse."

"Two sons, I believe, one an infant."

"Right, as usual."

The massive cheeks tremble in assent or satisfaction. The rebbe murmurs a conventional blessing on the heads of Berko's little boys. Then his gaze rolls in Landsman's direction, and when it locks on him, Landsman feels a stab of panic. The rebbe knows everything. He knows about the mosaic chromosome and the boy Landsman sacrificed to preserve hard-earned illusions about the tendency of life to get things wrong. And now he's going to offer a blessing for Django, too. But the rebbe says nothing, and the gears in the Verbover Clock grind away. Berko glances at his wristwatch; time to get home to the candles and the wine. To his blessed boys, who could be worse. To Ester-Malke, with the braided loaf of another child tucked somewhere in her belly. He and Landsman have no dispensation to be here past sundown, investigating a case that officially no longer exists. No one's life is at stake. There is nothing to be done to save any of them, not the yids in this room, not the yid, poor thing, who brought them here.

"Rabbi Shpilman?"

"Yes, Detective Landsman?"

"Are you all right?"

"Do I seem 'all right' to you, Detective Landsman?"

"I've only just had the honor of meeting you," Landsman says carefully, more in deference to Berko's sensibilities than to the rabbi or his office. "But to be honest, you seem all right."

"In a way that appears suspicious? That seems to inculpate me, perhaps?"

"Rebbe, please, no jokes," Baronshteyn says.

"As to that," Landsman says, ignoring the mouthpiece, "I wouldn't venture an opinion."

"My son has been dead to me for many years, Detective. Many years. I tore my clothes and said kaddish and lit a candle for his loss long ago." The words themselves trade in anger and bitterness, but his tone is breathtakingly void of emotion. "What you found in the Zamenhof Hotel—was it the Zamenhof?—what you found there, if it is him, that was only a husk. The kernel was long since cut out and spoiled."

"A husk," Landsman says. "I see."

He knows what a hard thing it can be to have fathered a heroin addict. He has seen this kind of coldness before. But something rankles him about these yids who tear their lapels and sit shiva for living children. It seems to Landsman to make a mockery of both the living and the dead.

"Now, all right. From what I have heard," Landsman continues, "and I certainly don't claim to understand it, your son—as a boy— he showed certain, well, indications, or . . . that he might be . . . I'm not sure I have this right. The Tzaddik Ha-Dor, is that it? If the conditions were right, if the Jews of this generation were worthy, then he might reveal himself as, uh, as Messiah."

"It's ridiculous, nu, Detective Landsman," the rebbe says. "The very idea makes you smile."

"Not at all," Landsman says. "But if your son was Messiah, then I guess we're all in trouble. Because right now he's lying in a drawer down in the basement of Sitka General."

"Meyer," Berko says.

"With all due respect," Landsman puts in.

The rebbe doesn't answer at first, and when he finally speaks, it is with evident care. "We are taught by the Baal Shem Tov, of blessed memory, that a man with the potential to be Messiah is born into every generation. This is the Tzaddik Ha-Dor. Now, Mendel. Mendele, Mendele."

He closes his eyes. He might be remembering. He might be fighting back tears. He opens them. They're dry, and he remembers.

"Mendel had a remarkable nature as a boy. I'm not talking about miracles. Miracles are a burden for a tzaddik, not the proof of one. Miracles prove nothing except to those whose faith is bought very cheap, sir. There was something *in* Mendele. There was a fire. This is a cold, dark place, Detectives. A gray, wet place. Mendele gave off light and warmth. You wanted to stand close to him. To warm your hands, to melt the ice on your beard. To banish the darkness for a minute or two. But then when you left Mendele, you *stayed* warm, and it seemed like there was a little more light, maybe one candle's worth, in the world. And that was when you realized the fire was inside of you all the time. And that was the miracle. Just that." He strokes his beard, pulling on it, as if trying to think of something he might have missed. "Nothing else."

"When was the last time you saw him?" Berko says.

"Twenty-three years ago," the rebbe says without hesitation. "On the twentieth of Elul. No one in this house has spoken to or seen him since then."

"Not even his mother?"

The question shocks them all, even Landsman, the yid who asked it.

"Do you suppose, Detective Landsman, that my wife would ever attempt to subvert my authority with respect to this or any other matter?"

"I suppose everything, Rabbi Shpilman," Landsman says. "I don't mean anything by it."

"Have you come here with any notions," Baronshteyn says, "about who might have killed Mendel?"

"Actually—" Landsman begins.

"Actually," the Verbover rebbe says, cutting Landsman off. He plucks a sheet of paper from the chaos of his desk, tractates, promulgations, and bans, classified documents, adding machine tapes, surveillance reports on the habits of marked men. There's a second or two of tromboning as he brings the paper within focusing range. The flesh of his right arm sloshes in the wineskin of his sleeve. "These particular homicide detectives are not supposed to be investigating this matter at all. Am I wrong?"

He sets down the paper, and Landsman has to wonder how he ever could have seen anything in the rebbe's eyes but ten thousand miles of frozen sea. Landsman is shocked, knocked overboard into that cold water. To keep himself afloat, he clings to the ballast of his cynicism. Did the order to black-flag the Lasker case come straight from Verbov Island? Has Shpilman known all along that his son is dead, murdered in room 208 of the Hotel Zamenhof? Did he himself order the killing? Are the business and directives of the Homicide Section of Sitka Central routinely submitted for his inspection? These might make interesting questions if Landsman could get his heart out of his mouth and ask them.

"What did he do?" Landsman says at last. "Exactly why was he dead to you already? What did he know? What, while we're on the subject, do *you* know, Rebbe? Rabbi Baronshteyn? I know you people have the fix in. I don't know what kind of deal you've worked for yourselves. But looking around this fine island of yours, I can see, you should excuse the expression, that you are carrying a lot of serious weight."

"Meyer," Berko says, a warning in it.

"Don't you come back here, Landsman," the rebbe says. "Don't ever bother anyone in this household, or any of the folk on this island. Stay away from Zimbalist. And stay away from me. If I hear that you have so much as asked one of my people to light your cigarette, I will have you and your shield. Is that clear?"

"With all due respect—" Landsman begins.

"An empty formula in your case, surely."

"Nevertheless," Landsman says, recovering himself. "If I had a dollar for every time some shtarker with a glandular problem tried to scare me off a case, with all due respect, I wouldn't have to sit here listening to threats from a man who can't even manage to shed a tear for the son I'm sure he helped into an early grave. Whether he died twenty-three years ago or last night."

"Please do not mistake me for some two-bit Hirshbeyn Avenue wiseguy," the rebbe says. "I am not threatening you."

"No? What are you, blessing me?"

"I'm looking at you, Detective Landsman. I understand that like my son, poor thing, you may not have been provided by the Holy Name with the most admirable of fathers."

"Rav Heskel!" Baronshteyn cries.

But the rabbi ignores his gabay and moves on before Landsman can ask him what the hell he thinks he knows about poor old Isidor.

"I can see that at one time, again like Mendel, you may have been something very much more than you are today. You may have been a fine shammes. But I doubt that you have ever qualified as a great sage."

"On the contrary," Landsman says.

"So. Please believe me when I tell you that you need to find another use for the time that remains to you."

Inside the Verbover Clock, an old system of hammers and chimes takes up a melody, older still, that welcomes to every Jewish home and house of prayer the bride of the end of the week.

"We're out of time," says Baronshteyn. "Gentlemen."

The detectives stand, and the men wish one another the joy of the Sabbath. Then the detectives put on their hats and turn for the door.

"We'll need someone to identify the body," Berko says.

"Unless you want us to put him out by the curb," Landsman says.

"We will send someone tomorrow," the rebbe says. He turns in his chair, showing them his back. He bows his head, then reaches for a pair of canes hanging from a hook on the wall behind him. The canes have silver heads, chased with gold. He stabs them into the carpet and then, with the wheeze of antique machinery, hoists himself to his feet. "After the Sabbath."

Baronshteyn follows them back down the stairs to the Rudashevsky by the door. Over their heads, the floorboards of the study utter a grievous creak. They hear the sharp taps and rain-barrel slosh of the rebbe's tread. The family will have gathered in the back part of the house, waiting for him to come and bless them all.

Baronshteyn opens the front door of the replica house. Shmerl and Yossele step into the hall, snow on their hats and shoulders, snow in their wintry gray eyes. The brothers or cousins or cousin-brothers form the points of a triangle with the indoor version, a three-fingered fist of solid Rudashevsky closing around Landsman and Berko.

Baronshteyn shoves his narrow face in close to Landsman's. Landsman lids his nostrils against a smell of tomato seeds, tobacco, sour cream.

"This is a little island," Baronshteyn says. "But there are a thousand places on it where a noz, even a decorated shammes, could get lost and never come out. So be careful, Detectives, all right? And a good Sabbath to you both."

17

Look at Landsman, one shirttail hanging out, snow-dusted porkpie knocked to the left, coat hooked to a thumb over his shoulder. Hanging on to a sky-blue cafeteria ticket as if it's the strap keeping him on his feet. His cheek needs the razor. His back is killing him. For reasons he doesn't understand—or maybe for no reason—he hasn't had a drink of alcohol since nine-thirty in the morning. Standing in the chrome-and-tile desolation of the Polar-Shtern Kafeteria at nine o'clock on a Friday night, in a snowstorm, he's the loneliest Jew in the Sitka District. He can feel the shifting of something dark and irresistible inside him, a hundred tons of black mud on a hillside, gathering its skirts to go sliding. The thought of food, even a golden ingot of the noodle pudding that is the crown jewel of the Polar-Shtern Kafeteria, makes him queasy. But he hasn't eaten all day.

In fact, Landsman knows that he is not, by a long shot, the loneliest Jew in the Sitka District. He scorns himself for even entertaining the notion. The presence of self-pity in his thoughts is proof that he is circling the bung hole, spiraling inward and down, down, down. To resist this Coriolis motion, Landsman relies on three techniques. One is work, but work is now officially a joke. One is alcohol, which makes the drop come faster and go deeper and last longer but helps him not to care. The third is to have a bite. So he carries his blue ticket and his tray to the big Litvak lady behind the glass counter, with the hair net and the polyethylene gloves and the metal spoon, and forks it over.

"The cheese blintzes, please," he says, not wanting cheese blintzes or even bothering to see if they are on the menu tonight. "How are you, Mrs. Nemintziner?"

Mrs. Nemintziner gentles three tight blintzes onto a white plate with a blue stripe on the rim. To ornament the evening meals of the lonely souls of Sitka, she has prepared several dozen slices of pickled crab apple on lettuce leaves. She tricks out Landsman's dinner with one of these corsages. Then she punches his ticket and slings his plate at him. "How should I be?" she says.

Landsman acknowledges that the answer to this question is beyond him. He carries his tray of blintzes filled with cottage cheese to the coffee urns and drains off a mug's worth. He hands over his punched ticket and his cash to the cashier, then wanders across the wasteland of the dining area, past two of his rivals for the title of loneliest Jew. He heads for the table he prefers, by the front windows, where he can keep an eye on the street. At the next table, somebody left a half-eaten plate of corned beef and boiled potatoes and a half-empty glass of what appears to be black-cherry soda. The abandoned meal, and the stained crumple of the napkin fill Landsman with a mild nausea of misgiving. But this is his table, and it is a fact that a noz likes to be able to keep an eye on the street. Landsman sits down, tucks his napkin into his collar, cuts apart a cheese blintz, and puts some into his mouth. He chews. He swallows. Good boy.

One of his rivals in the Polar-Shtern tonight is a bottom-rung bet runner named Penguin Simkowitz who mishandled a lot of somebody's money a few years back and was beaten so badly by shtarkers that it addled his brain and speech. The other, working over a plate of herring in cream, Landsman doesn't know. But the yid's left eye socket is concealed behind a tan adhesive bandage.

The left lens of his eyeglasses is missing. His hair is restricted to three downy gray patches at the front of his head. He cut his cheek shaving. When this man silently begins to weep into his plate of herring, Landsman tips over his king.

Then he sees Buchbinder, that archaeologist of delusion. A dentist, he was driven by his talent with pliers and the lost-wax mold, in classic dentist manner to take up some after-hours form of miniature madness such as jewelry making or dollhouse parquetry. But then, as happens sometimes to dentists, Buchbinder got a little carried away. The deepest, oldest madness of the Jews took hold of him. He started to turn out re-creations of the cutlery and getups employed by the ancient Koyenim, the high priests of Yahweh. To scale at first but soon full-size. Blood buckets, gobbet forks, ash shovels, all of it as required by Leviticus for the old holy barbecues in Jerusalem. He used to keep a museum, maybe it's still there, up at the tired end of Ibn Ezra Street. A storefront in the building where Buchbinder pulled the teeth of lowlife Jews. In the display window the Temple of Solomon, built from cardboard, buried under a sandstorm of dust, ornamented with cherubim and dead flies. The place got vandalized a lot by the neighborhood junkies. You used to get a call, working the Untershtot beat, come in there at three in the morning to find Buchbinder weeping among the broken showcases, a turd floating in some gilded copper censer of the high priest.

When Buchbinder sees Landsman, his eyes narrow with suspicion or myopia. Returning from the men's room to his plate of corned beef and his cherry soda, working over the buttons of his fly with the absent air of a man in the grip of a startling but useless inference about the world. Buchbinder is a stout man, a German, enveloped in a cardigan with raglan sleeves and a knit sash. Between the arc of the man's belly and the knotted sash are hints of past strife, but an understanding appears to have been reached. Tweed trousers, on his feet a pair of hiking sneakers.

His hair and beard, dark blond with flecks of gray and silver. A metal clasp grips a crewel work yarmulke to the back of his head. He tosses a smile in Landsman's direction like a man dropping a quarter in a cripple's cup, fishes some closely printed tome from his hip pocket, and resumes his meal. He rocks back and forth while he reads and chews.

"Still running that museum of yours, Doctor?" Landsman says.

Buchbinder looks up, puzzled, trying to place this irritating stranger with the blintzes.

"It's Landsman. Sitka Central. Maybe you remember, I used to—"

"Oh, yes," he says with a tight smile. "How are you? We are an institute, not a museum, but that is all right."

"Sorry."

"No harm has been done," he says, his supple Yiddish fitted with a stiffening wire of the German accent to which he and his fellow yekkes, even after sixty years, stubbornly cling. "It is a common mistake."

It can't be all *that* common, Landsman thinks, but he says, "Still up there on Ibn Ezra?"

"No," says Dr. Buchbinder. He wipes a streak of brown mustard from his lips with his napkin. "No, sir, I have closed it down. Officially and permanently."

His manner is grandiloquent, even celebratory, which strikes Landsman as odd, given the content of his declaration.

"Tough neighborhood," Landsman suggests.

"Oh, they were animals," Buchbinder says with the same cheeriness. "I can't tell you how many times they broke my heart." He stuffs a last forkful of corned beef into his mouth and subjects it to proper handling by his teeth. "But I doubt they'll trouble me in my new location."

"And where is that?"

Buchbinder smiles, dabs at his beard, then pushes back from the table. He raises an eyebrow, keeping the big surprise to himself a moment longer.

"Where else?" he says at last. "Jerusalem."

"Wow," Landsman says, keeping the straightest face he's got. He has never seen the regulations for admission of Jews to Jerusalem, but he's fairly certain that not being an obsessed religious lunatic is at the top of the list. "Jerusalem, eh? That's a long way."

"Yes, it is."

"Lock, stock, and barrel?"

"The whole operation."

"Know anyone there?"

There are still Jews living in Jerusalem, as there always have been. A few. They were there long before the Zionists started showing up, their trunks packed with Hebrew dictionaries, agricultural manuals, and plenty of trouble for everyone.

"Not really," Buchbinder says. "Apart from—well." He pauses and lowers his voice. "Messiah."

"Well, that's a good start," Landsman says. "I hear he's in with the best people there."

Buchbinder nods, untouchable in the sugar-cube sanctuary of his dream. "Lock, stock, and barrel," he says. He returns his book to his jacket pocket and stuffs himself and the sweater into an old blue anorak. "Good night, Landsman."

"Good night, Dr. Buchbinder. Put in a good word for me with Messiah."

"Oh," he says, "there's no need of that."

"No need or no point?"

Abruptly, the merry eyes turn as steely as the disc of a dentist's mirror. They assay Landsman's condition with the insight of twenty-five years spent searching tirelessly for points of weakness and rot. Just for a moment Landsman doubts the man's insanity.

"That's up to you," Buchbinder says. "Isn't it?"

As Buchbinder pushes out of the Polar-Shtern, he stops to hold the door for a blazing orange parka carried on a gust of slanting snow. Bina is dragging that old overstuffed cowhide tote of hers slung over one shoulder. From it a clutch of documents protrudes, highlighted in yellow, stapled and paper-clipped and flagged with strips of colored tape. She throws back the hood of her parka. She has pushed up her hair, and pinned it up, and left it to fend for itself at the back of her head. Its color is a wistful shade that Landsman remembers observing in only one other place in his life, and that was deep in the grooves of the first pumpkin he ever beheld, a big dark red-orange brute. She lugs her tote over to the ticket lady. When she comes through the turnstile on her way to the stacks of cafeteria trays, Landsman will come directly into her line of sight.

At once Landsman makes the mature decision to pretend that he has not seen Bina. He looks out the plate windows at Khalyastre Street. The depth of snowfall he estimates at close to six inches. Three separate trails of footprints snake in and out of one another, the edges of each print blurring as it fills with fallen snow. Across the street, handbills pasted to the boarded windows of Krasny's Tobacco and Stationery advertise the performance, last night at

the Vorsht, of the guitarist who got rolled in the toilet for his
finger rings and cash. From the phone pole at the corner, a craze of
wires runs out in all directions, mapping the walls and doorways of
this great imaginary ghetto of the Jews. The involuntary processes
of Landsman's shammes mind record the details of the scene. But
his conscious thoughts are focused on the moment when Bina will
see him sitting there, alone at his table, chewing on a blintz, and
call his name.

This moment takes its sweet time showing up. Landsman risks
a second look. Bina already has her dinner on a tray and is waiting
for her change with her back to Landsman. She saw him; she must
have seen him. That is when the great fissure oozes open, the
hillside gives way, and the wall of black mud comes rolling down.
Landsman and Bina were married to each other for twelve years and
together for five before that. Each was the other's first lover, first
betrayer, first refuge, first roommate, first audience, first person to
turn to when something— even the marriage itself—went wrong.
For half their lives, they tangled their histories, bodies, phobias,
theories, recipes, libraries, record collections. They mounted
spectacular arguments, nose-to-nose, hands flying, spittle flying,
throwing things, kicking things, breaking things, rolling around
on the ground grabbing up fistfuls of each other's hair. The next
day he would bear the red moons of Bina's nails in his cheeks and
on the meat of his chest, and she wore his purple fingerprints like
an armlet. For something like seven years of their lives together
they fucked almost every day. Angry, loving, sick, well, cold, hot,
half asleep. They went at it on every manner of bed, couch, and
cushion. On futons and towels and old shower curtains, in the back
of a pickup truck, behind a Dumpster, on top of a water tower,
inside a rack of coats at a Hands of Esau dinner. They even fucked
each other— once— on the giant fungus in the break room.

After Bina came over from Narcotics, they worked the same shift
in Homicide for four solid years. Landsman partnered with Zelly

Boybriker, and then Berko, and Bina had poor old Morris Handler. But one day the same sly angel who had brought them together in the first place arranged a confluence of leaves taken and injuries to Morris Handler that left Landsman and Bina partners, for the one and only time, on the Grinshteyn case. Together they endured that visitation of failure, failing every day for hours, failing in their bed at night, failing in the streets of Sitka. The murdered girl, Ariela, and the broken Grinshteyns, mother and father, ugly and ruined and hating each other and the hole they were left holding on to: He and Bina had shared that, too. And then there was Django, who took form and impetus from the failure of the Grinshteyn case, from that hole shaped like a plump little girl. Bina and Landsman were twisted together, a braided pair of chromosomes with a mystery flaw. And now? Now each of them pretends not to see the other and looks away.

Landsman looks away.

The footprints in the snow have become shallow as an angel's. Across the street a small, bent man leans into the wind, dragging a heavy suitcase past the boarded windows of Krasny's. The wide white brim of his hat flaps like the wings of a bird. Landsman watches the progress of Elijah the Prophet through the snowstorm and plans his own death. This is a fourth strategy he has evolved to cheer himself when he's going down the drain. But of course he has to be careful not to overdo it.

Landsman, the son and paternal grandson of suicides, has seen human beings dispatch themselves in every possible way, from the inept to the efficient. He knows how it should and should not be performed. Bridge leaps and dives from hotel windows: picturesque but iffy. Stairwell leaps: unreliable, an impulse decision, too much like an accidental death. Slashing wrists, with or without the popular but unnecessary bathtub variation: harder than it seems, tinged with a girlish love of theater. Ritual disembowelment with a samurai sword: hard work, requires a second, and would smack, in a yid, of affectation. Landsman has never seen it done that way, but he knew a noz once who claimed that he had. Landsman's grandfather threw himself under the wheels of a streetcar in Lodz, which showed a degree of determination that Landsman has always admired. His father employed thirty 100 mg tablets of Nembutal, washed down with a glass of caraway vodka, a method that has much to recommend it. Add a plastic bag over the head, capacious and free of holes, and you have yourself something neat, quiet, and reliable.

But when he envisions taking his own life, Landsman likes to do it with a handgun, like Melekh Gaystik, the champion of the world. His own chopped Model 39 is more than enough sholem for the job. If you know where to put the muzzle (just inside the angle of the mentum) and how to steer your shot (20 degrees off the vertical, toward the lizard core of the brain), it's fast and reliable. Messy, but Landsman doesn't have any qualms, for some reason, about leaving behind a mess.

"Since when do you like blintzes?"

He jumps at the sound of her voice. His knee bangs the table leg, and coffee splashes the plate glass in an exit-wound spatter.

"Hey, Skipper," he says in American. He scrabbles for a napkin, but he took only one from the dispenser by the trays. The coffee is running everywhere. He grabs random scraps of paper from his jacket pocket and blots at the spreading spill.

"Anybody sitting here?" She balances the tray in one hand and fights off her swollen briefcase with the other. She's wearing a particular expression that he knows well. Eyebrows arched, slight foretaste of a smile. It's the face she puts on before she walks into a hotel ballroom to mingle with a bunch of male law enforcement, or enters a grocery store in the Harkavy wearing a skirt that doesn't cover her knees. It's a face that says, *I'm not looking for trouble here. I just came in for a pack of gum.* She drops the bag and sits before he has a chance to reply.

"Please," he says, pulling his own plate back to make room. Bina hands him some more napkins, and he takes care of the mess. He dumps the clump of soggy paper on a neighboring table. "I don't know why I ordered them. You're right, cheese blintzes, feh."

Bina lays down a napkin with a knife, fork, and spoon. She takes two plates from the tray and sets them side by side: a scoop of tuna salad on one of Mrs. Nemintziner's lettuce leaves, and a glinting golden square of noodle pudding. She reaches down into her bulging tote bag and pulls out a small plastic box with a hinged lid. It contains a round pill box with a threaded lid from which she tips out a vitamin pill, a fish-oil pill, and the enzyme tablet that lets her stomach digest milk. Inside the hinged plastic box she also carries packets of salt, pepper, horseradish, and hand-wipes, a doll size bottle of Tabasco sauce, chlorine pills for treating drinking water, Pepto-Bismol chews, and God knows what else. If you go to a concert, Bina has opera glasses. If you need to sit on the grass, she whips out a towel. Ant traps, a corkscrew, candles and matches, a dog muzzle, a penknife, a tiny aerosol can of freon, a magnifying glass—Landsman has seen everything come out of that overstuffed cowhide at one time or another.

You have to look to Jews like Bina Gelbfish, Landsman thinks, to explain the wide range and persistence of the race. Jews who carry their homes in an old cowhide bag, on the back of a camel, in the bubble of air at the center of their brains. Jews who land on their feet, hit the ground running, ride out the vicissitudes, and make the best of what falls to hand, from Egypt to Babylon, from Minsk Gubernya to the District of Sitka. Methodical, organized, persistent, resourceful, prepared. Berko is right: Bina would flourish in any precinct house in the world. A mere redrawing of borders, a change in governments, those things can never faze a Jewess with a good supply of hand wipes in her bag.

"Tuna salad," Landsman observes, thinking of how she stopped eating tuna when she found out she was pregnant with Django.

"Yeah, I try to ingest as much mercury as I can," Bina says, reading the memory on his face. She swallows the enzyme tablet. "Mercury's kind of my thing nowadays."

Landsman jerks a thumb toward Mrs. Nemintziner, standing ready with her spoon.

"You ought to order the baked thermometer."

"I would," she says, "but they only had rectal."

"See Penguin?"

"Penguin Simkowitz? Where?" She looks around, turning from the waist, and Landsman seizes the opportunity to peer into her shirt. He can see the freckled top of her left breast, the lace edge of her bra cup, the dark indication of her nipple against the cup. The desire floods him to run his hand inside her shirt, to hold her breast, to climb into the soft hollow there and curl up and fall asleep. When she turns back, she catches him in his dream of cleavage. Landsman feels a burn in his cheeks. "Huh," she says.

"How was your day?" Landsman says, as if it's the most natural question he could ask.

"Let's make a deal," she says, and her tone ices over. She buttons the top button of her blouse. "How about we sit here, you and I, and eat our dinners together, and we don't say one damned word about my day. How does that sound to you, Meyer?"

"I think that sounds all right," he says.

"Good."

She spoons up a mouthful of tuna salad. He catches the glint of her gold-rimmed bicuspid and thinks of the day she came home with it, looped on nitrous oxide and inviting him to put his tongue into her mouth and see how it felt. After the first bite of tuna salad, Bina gets serious. She shovels in ten or eleven more spoonfuls, chewing and swallowing with abandon. Her breath comes through her nostrils in avid jets. Her eyes are fixed on the intercourse of her plate and spoon. A girl with a healthy appetite, that was his mother's first recorded statement on the subject of Bina Gelbfish twenty years ago. Like most of his mother's compliments, it was convertible to an insult when needed. But Landsman trusts only a woman who eats like a man. When there is nothing left but a mayonnaise slick on the lettuce leaf, Bina wipes her mouth on her napkin and lets out a deep sigh of satiety.

"Nu, what should we talk about, then? Not your day, either."

"Definitely not."

"What does that leave us?"

"In my case," Landsman says, "not very much."

"Some things never change." She pushes away the empty plate and calls forward the noodle pudding to meet its fate. It makes him happier than he has been in years just to see her giving that kugel the eye.

"I still like to talk about my car," he says.

"You know I don't care for love poetry."

"Definitely let's not talk about Reversion."

"Agreed. And I do not want to hear about the talking chicken, or the kreplach shaped like the head of Maimonides, or any of that other miraculous shit."

He wonders what Bina would make of the story that Zimbalist told them today about the man lying in a drawer in the basement of Sitka General.

"Nothing about Jews at all, let's stipulate," Landsman says.

"Stipulated, Meyer, I am heartily sick of Jews."

"And not Alaska."

"God, no."

"No politics. Nothing about Russia, or Manchuria, or Germany, or the Arabs."

"I am heartily sick of the Arabs, too."

"How about the noodle pudding, then?" Landsman says.

"Good," she says. "Only, please, Meyer, eat a little, it makes my heart ache to look at you, my God, you're so thin. Here, you have to have a bite of this. I don't know what they do to it, somebody told me they put a little ginger. Let me tell you, up in Yakovy, a good kugel is something you dream about."

She cuts him a piece of noodle pudding and starts to poke it right into his mouth with her fork. Something like a cold hand grabs hold of his guts at the sight of the kugel coming his way. He averts his face. The fork stops in mid-trajectory. Bina dumps the wedge of egg custard and noodle, jeweled with sultanas, onto his plate beside the unmolested blintzes.

"Anyway, you should try it," she says. She takes a couple of bites herself, then lays down her fork. "I guess that's all there is to say about noodle pudding."

Landsman sips his coffee, and Bina swallows her remaining pills with a glass of water.

"Nu," she says.

"Okay, then," says Landsman.

If he lets her go, he will never lie in the hollow of her breast, asleep. He will never sleep again without the help of a handful of Nembutal or the good offices of his chopped M-39.

Bina pushes back from the table and pulls on her parka. She returns the plastic box to the leather case, then shoulders it with a groan. "Good night, Meyer."

"Where are you staying?"

"With my parents," she says in the tone you might use to pronounce a death sentence on the planet.

"Oy vey."

"Tell me about it. Just until I find a place. Anyway, it can't be worse than the Hotel Zamenhof."

She zips up her coat and then stands there for a long few seconds, submitting him to her shammes inspection. Her gaze is not as comprehensive as his—she misses the details sometimes—but the things that she does see, she can link up quickly in her mind to the things that she knows about women and men, victims and murderers. She can shape them with confidence into narratives that hold together and make sense. She does not solve cases so much as tell the stories of them.

"Look at you. You are like a house falling down."

"I know," Landsman says, feeling his chest tighten.

"I heard you were bad, but I thought they were just trying to cheer me up."

He laughs and wipes his cheek with the sleeve of his jacket.

"What's this?" she says. With the nails of her thumb and forefinger, she tweezes a crumpled, coffee-stained wad of paper from the mass of napkins that Landsman dumped onto the neighboring table. Landsman makes a grab at it, but Bina's too fast for him, and she always was. She pulls apart the wad and stretches it flat.

"'Five Great Truths and Five Big Lies About Verbover Hasidism,'" she says. Her eyebrows reach for each other across the bridge of her nose. "You thinking of turning black hat on me?"

He doesn't answer quickly enough, and she gathers what there is to be gathered from his face and his silence and what she knows about him, which is basically everything.

"What are you up to, Meyer?" she says. All at once she looks as weary and spent as he feels. "No. Never mind. I'm too fucking tired." She crumples the Verbover brochure back up, and throws it at his head.

"We said we weren't going to talk about it," Landsman says.

"Yeah, well, we said a lot of things," she says. "You and I."

She half turns, getting a purchase on the shoulder strap of the bag in which she lives her life. "I want to see you tomorrow in my office."

"Hmm. Right. Only the thing is," Landsman says, "I'm just coming off a twelve-day shift."

This statement, while correct, makes no apparent impression on Bina. She might not have heard him, or he might not be speaking an Indo-European language.

"I'll see you tomorrow," he says. "Unless I blow my brains out tonight."

"I said no love poetry," Bina says. She gathers up a tumbling coil of her dark-pumpkin hair and shoves it into a toothed clip above and behind her right ear. "Brains or no brains. Be in my office at nine."

Landsman watches her walk across the dining area to the doors of the Polar-Shtern Kafeteria. He bets himself a dollar that she won't look back at him before she puts up her hood and steps out into the snow. But he's a charitable man, and it was a sucker bet, and so he never bothers to collect.

19

When the telephone wakes him at six the next morning, Landsman is sitting in the wing chair, in his white underpants, with a tender hold on the grip of his M-39.

Tenenboym is just going off duty. "You asked," he says, and then he hangs up.

Landsman doesn't remember putting in for a wake-up call. He doesn't remember polishing off the bottle of slivovitz that stands empty on the scratched urethane surface of the oak-veneer tabletop, next to the wing chair. He doesn't remember eating the noodle pudding whose remaining third now huddles in a corner of a plastic clamshell container beside the bottle of slivovitz. From the position of the shards of painted glass on the floor, he can reconstruct having hurled his 1977 Sitka World's Fair shot glass against the radiator. Maybe he was feeling frustrated over being unable to make any progress with the pocket chess set that lies facedown under the bed, its minute chessmen sprinkled liberally around the room. But he has no memory of the throw itself, or of shattering glass. He might have been drinking a toast to something or someone, with the radiator standing in for a fireplace. He doesn't remember. But nothing about the squalid scenery of room 505 can be said to surprise him, least of all the loaded sholem in his hand.

He checks the firing pin safety and returns the gun to its holster, slung across the back of the wing chair. Then he goes over to the wall and drags the pull-down bed from its notch. He peels back the covers and climbs in. The linens are clean, and they smell of the steam press and of the dust in the hole in the wall. Dimly, Landsman recalls conceiving a romantic project, sometime around midnight the night before, to show up for work early, see what forensics and ballistics have made of the Shpilman case, maybe even go out to the islands, the Russian neighborhoods, and try to nudge the patzer ex-con Vassily Shitnovitzer. Do what he can, give it his best shot, before Bina takes a pair of pliers to his teeth and claws at nine. He smiles ruefully at the headstrong young bravo he was last midnight. A six A.M. wake up call.

He pulls the covers up over his head and closes his eyes. Unbidden, the configuration of pawns and pieces lays itself out on a chessboard in his mind, the Black king hemmed in but unchecked at the center of the board, the White pawn on the b file about to become something better. There is no longer any need for the pocket set; to his horror, he has the thing by heart. He tries to drive it from his mind, to expunge it, to sweep aside the pieces and fill in all the white checkers with black. An all-black board, uncorrupted by pieces or players, gambits or endgames, tempo or tactics or material advantage, black as the Baranof Mountains.

He is still lying there, all the white squares of his mind blotted out, in his underpants and socks, when there's a knock at the door. He sits up, facing the wall, his heart a drum banging in his temples, the sheets pulled down tight over him like he's a kid hoping to spook somebody. He's been lying on his stomach, maybe for a while. He remembers hearing, from the bottom of a tomb of black mud, in a lightless cave a mile beneath the surface of the earth, the distant vibrations of his Shoyfer, and sometime after that, the soft chirping of the phone on the oak-veneer table. But he was buried so deep under the mud that even if the telephones had been mere telephones in a dream, he would not have had the strength or the inclination to answer them. His pillow is drenched in a foul brew of drunk-sweat, panic, and saliva. He looks at his watch. It's ten-twenty.

"Meyer?"

Landsman falls back onto the bed, upside down and tangled in the sheets. "I quit," he says. "Bina, I resign."

Bina doesn't say anything right away. Landsman hopes she has accepted his resignation—which is superfluous anyway—and returned to the modular, and the man from the Burial Society, and her transition from Jewish policewoman to an officer of the law of the great state of Alaska. Once he is sure she has gone, Landsman will arrange for the maid who changes the bedding and towels once a week to come in and shoot him. Then all she has to do to bury him is return the pull-down bed to its notch in the wall. His claustrophobia, his fear of the dark, will no longer trouble him.

A moment later, he hears the teeth of a key in a lock, and the door of room 505 swings open. Bina creeps in the way you creep into a sickroom, a cardiac ward, expecting a shock, reminders of mortality, grim truths about the body.

"Jesus fucking Christ," she says with that flawless hardpan accent of hers. It is an expression that always strikes Landsman as curious, or at least as something that he would pay money to see.

She wades through pieces of Landsman's gray suit and a bath towel and stands at the foot of the bed. Her eyes take in the pink wallpaper patterned with garlands in burgundy flock, the green plush carpet with its random motif of burn spots and mystery stains, the broken glass, the empty bottle, the peeling and chipped veneer of the pressboard furniture. Watching her with his head at the foot of the pull-down bed, Landsman enjoys the look of horror on her face, mostly because if he doesn't, then he will have to feel ashamed.

"How do you say 'shit heap' in Esperanto?" Bina says. She goes over to the veneer table and looks down at the last bedraggled curls of noodle pudding lying in the grease-streaked clamshell.

"At least you ate something."

She turns the wing chair around to face the bed, then lowers her tote to the ground. She studies the seat of the chair. From her face, he can see that she's wondering if she ought to go after the seat of the chair with something caustic or antibacterial out of her magic bag. At last she lowers herself into the wing chair, a little at a time. She's dressed in a gray pantsuit, some kind of slick stuff with an iridescent under-sheen of black. Under the jacket she wears a silk shell in celadon green. Her face is bare except for two streaks of brick lip rouge on her mouth. At this hour of the day, her morning effort to control her tangled hair with pins and clips has not yet begun to fail. If she slept well last night, in the narrow bed in her old room, on the top floor of a two-family house on Japonski Island, with old Mr. Oysher and his prosthetic leg bumping around downstairs, it doesn't show in the hollows and shadows of her face. Her eyebrows are all involved with each other again. Her rouged lips have narrowed to a brick-red seam two millimeters wide.

"So how's your morning going, Inspector?"

"I don't like waiting," she says. "And I especially don't like waiting for you."

"Maybe you didn't hear me," Landsman says. "I quit."

"It's funny, but you repeating that particular bit of idiocy does surprisingly little to improve my mood."

"I can't work for you, Bina. Come on. That's just insane. It's exactly the kind of insanity I would expect from the department right now. If things are that bad, if that's what it comes to, then forget it. I'm sick of all this play-out-the-string jazz. So, nu, I quit. What do you need me for? Slap black flags on all our cases. Open, closed. Who gives a damn? It's just a bunch of dead yids anyway."

"I went through the stack again," she says. He notes that after all these years, she has retained her thrilling power to ignore him and his bouts of blackness. "I didn't see anything in any of them that looked like it was going to tie in with the Verbovers." She reaches into her briefcase and takes out a pack of Broadways, shakes one loose, and fits it to her lips. She says the next eight words in an offhand way that he immediately suspects. "Except for maybe that junkie you found downstairs."

"You black-flagged that one," Landsman replies with a policeman's perfect disingenuousness. "You're smoking again, too?"

"Tobacco, mercury." She brushes back a coil of hair and lights her papiros, blows smoke. "Playing out the string."

"Let me have one."

She passes him the Broadway and he sits ups, winding himself in a careful toga of bed linens. She looks him over in his splendor as she lights a second papiros. She notes the gray hair around his nipples, the progress of flab at his waist, his bony knees.

"Sleeping in socks and underwear," she says. "Always a bad sign with you."

"I guess I have the cafard," he says. "I guess it kind of hit me last night."

"Last night?"

"Last year?"

She looks around for something to use as an ashtray. "Did you and Berko go out to Verbov Island yesterday," she says, "to poke around this Lasker thing?"

There's really no point in lying to her. But Landsman has been disobeying orders far too long to start telling the truth about it now.

"You didn't get a call?" he says.

"A call? From Verbov Island? On a Saturday morning? Who there's going to call me on a Saturday morning?" Her eyes get shrewd, tight at the corners. "And what are they going to tell me when they do?"

"I'm sorry," Landsman says. "Excuse me. I can't hold it anymore."

He gets up, stands right up in his underwear with a sheet hanging off him. He pads around the pull-down bed to the tiny bathroom with its sink and its steel mirror and its shower head. There's no curtain, just a drain in the middle of the floor. He closes the door and urinates for a long time, with genuine pleasure. Setting the burning papiros on the edge of the toilet tank, he gives his face some brisk business with soap and a washcloth. There's a wool bathrobe, white with red, green, yellow, and black stripes in an Indian pattern, on a hook behind the bathroom door. He ties it around himself. He puts the papiros back into his mouth and looks at himself in the scratched rectangle of polished steel that's mounted above the sink. What he sees there affords him no surprises or unknown depths. He flushes the toilet and goes back into the room.

"Bina," he says, "I did not know this man. He was put in my way. I was given the opportunity to know him, I suppose, but I declined it. If this man and I had gotten to know each other, possibly we would have become pals. Maybe not. He had his thing with heroin, and that was probably enough for him. It usually is. But whether I knew him or not, and whether we could have grown old together holding hands on a sofa down in the lobby, is neither here nor there. Somebody came into this hotel, my hotel, and shot that man in the back of the head while he was off in dreamland. And that bothers me. Set aside whatever general objections I might have worked up over the years to the underlying concept of homicide. Forget about right and wrong, law and order, police procedure, departmental policy, Reversion, Jews and Indians. This dump is my house. For the next two months, or however long it turns out to be, I live here. All these hard-lucks paying rent on a pull-down bed and a sheet of steel bolted to the bathroom wall, for better or worse, they're my people now. I can't honestly say I like them very much. Some of them are all right. Most of them are pretty bad. But I'll be damned if I'm going to let somebody walk in here and put a bullet in their heads."

Bina has boiled up two cups of instant coffee. She hands one to Landsman. "Black and sweet," she says. "Right?"

"Bina."

"You're on your own. The black flag stays put. You get caught, you get in a jam, you get your knees broken by Rudashevskys, I don't know anything about it." She goes over to her bag and takes out an accordion file thick with folders. She puts it on the veneer table. "The forensic is only a partial. Shpringer sort of left it hanging. Blood and hair. Latents. It isn't much. The ballistics are still out."

"Bina, thank you. Bina, listen, this guy. His name wasn't Lasker. This guy—"

She puts a hand to his mouth. She has not touched him in three years. It probably would be too much to say that he feels the darkness lift at the touch of her fingertips against his lips. But it shivers, and light bleeds in among the cracks.

"I don't know anything about it," she says. She removes her hand. She takes a sip of instant coffee and makes a face. "Feh."

She puts down the cup, picks up her bag, and goes to the door. She stops and looks back at Landsman, standing there in the bathrobe that she bought for him on his birthday when he turned thirty-five.

"You have some nerve," she says. "I can't believe you and Berko went out there."

"We had to tell him his son was dead."

"His *son*."

"Mendel Shpilman. The rebbe's only son."

Bina opens her mouth, then closes it. Not astonished so much as engaged, sinking her terrier teeth into the information, gnawing on the bloody joint of it. Landsman can see that she likes the way it gives against the sharp grip of her jaw. But her eyes take on a weariness that Landsman recognizes. Bina will never lose her detective's appetite for people's stories, Landsman thinks, of puzzling her way back through them from the final burst of violence to the first mistake. But sometimes a shammes gets a little tired of that hunger.

"And what did the rebbe say?" She lets go of the doorknob with an air of genuine regret.

"He seemed a little bitter."

"Did he seem surprised?"

"Not especially, but I don't know what you can make of that. I take it the kid had been heading down the chute for a long time. Do I think Shpilman would have fed his own son a bullet? In theory, sure. That goes double for Baronshteyn."

Her bag hits the floor like a body. She stands and works her shoulder in a small aching circle. He could offer to massage it for her, but wisely, he refrains.

"I suppose I can expect a phone call," she says. "From Baronshteyn. As soon as there are three stars in the sky."

"Well, I wouldn't listen too carefully when he tries to tell you how broken up he is that Mendel Shpilman is out of the picture. Everybody loves it when the prodigal returns, except for the guy that's been sleeping in his pajamas." Landsman takes a sip of the coffee, dreadfully bitter and sweet.

"The prodigal."

"He was some kind of a miracle kid. At chess, at Torah, at languages. I heard a story today about him healing a woman's cancer, not that I really believe that, but. I guess there were a lot of stories going around about him inside the black-hat world. That he might be the Tzaddik Ha-Dor—you know what that is?"

"Sort of. Yes. Anyway, I know what the words mean," Bina says. Her father, Guryeh Gelbfish, is a learned man in the traditional sense, and he squandered a certain portion of his learning on his only child, a girl. "The righteous man of this generation."

"So the story is that these guys, these tzaddiks, they have been showing up for work, one per generation, for the past couple of thousand years, right? Cooling their heels. Waiting for the time to be right, or the world to be right, or, some people say, for the time to be wrong and the world to be as wrong as it can be. Some of them we know about. Most of them kept a pretty low profile. I guess the idea is that the Tzaddik Ha-Dor could be anyone."

"He is despised and rejected of men," Bina says, or rather, recites. "A man of sorrows and acquainted with grief."

"That's what I'm saying," says Landsman. "Anyone. A bum. A scholar. A junkie. Even a shammes."

"I guess it could be," Bina says. She works it out in her mind, the road from wonder-working prodigy of the Verbovers to murdered junkie in a flophouse on Max Nordau Street. The story adds up in a way that appears to sadden her. "Anyway, I'm glad it isn't me."

"You don't want to redeem the world anymore?"

"Did I used to want to redeem the world?"

"I think that you did, yes."

She considers it, rubbing the side of her nose with a finger, trying to remember. "I guess I got over it," she says, but Landsman doesn't buy that. Bina never stopped wanting to redeem the world. She just let the world she was trying to redeem get smaller and smaller until, at one point, it could be bounded in the hat of a hopeless policeman. "It's all talking chickens to me now."

She should probably exit on that line, but she stands around for another fifteen seconds of unredeemed time, leaning against the door, watching Landsman fiddle with the frayed ends of his bathrobe sash.

"What are you going to tell Baronshteyn when he calls?" Landsman says.

"That you were totally out of line, and I'll see that you come up for a board. I may have to lift your shield. I'll try to fight it, but with this shoymer from the Burial Society coming—Spade, a curse on him—I don't have a lot of room to maneuver. And neither do you."

"Okay, you warned me," Landsman says. "I have been warned."

"So what are you going to do?"

"Now? Now I want to put a touch on the mother. Shpilman said nobody ever heard from Mendel or spoke to him. But for some reason, I'm not inclined to take his word for it."

"Batsheva Shpilman. That is going to be a tough touch," Bina says. "Especially for a man."

"True," Landsman says with a display of wistfulness.

"No," Bina says. "No, Meyer. Forget it. You are on your own."

"She'll be at the funeral. All you need to do is—"

"All I need to do," Bina says, "is stay out of the way of shoymers, watch my ass, and get through the next two months without setting fire to it."

"I'd be happy to watch your ass for you," Landsman says, just for old times' sake.

"Get dressed," Bina says. "And do yourself a favor? Clean this shit up. Look at this dump. I can't believe you're living like this. Sweet God, aren't you ashamed of yourself?"

Once Bina Gelbfish believed in Meyer Landsman. Or she believed, from the moment she met him, that there was a sense in that meeting, that some detectable intention lay behind their marriage. They were twisted like a pair of chromosomes, of course they were, but where Landsman saw in that twisting together only a tangle, a chance snarling of lines, Bina saw the hand of the Maker of Knots. And for her faith, Landsman repaid her with his faith in Nothing itself.

"Only every time I see your face," Landsman says.

20

Landsman cadges half a dozen papiroses from the weekend manager, Krankheit, then kills an hour setting fire to three of them while the reports on the dead man in 208 render up their pitiful account of proteins and grease marks and dust. As Bina said, there's nothing new in any of it. The killer seems to have been a professional, a shlosser of skill who left no trace of his passage. The dead man's fingerprints match those on record for a Menachem-Mendel Shpilman, arrested seven times on drug charges over the past ten years, under a variety of aliases, including Wilhelm Steinitz, Aron Nimzovitch, and Richard Réti. So much, and no more, is clear.

Landsman contemplates sending down for a pint, but he takes a hot shower instead. Alcohol has failed him, the thought of food turns his stomach, and let's face it, if he was ever really going to kill himself, he would have done so long before now. So, all right, work is a joke; it remains work. And that is the true content of the accordion file that Bina brought him, her message to him across the divide of departmental policy and marital estrangement and careers rolling in opposite directions: *Just keep at it.*

Landsman frees his last clean suit from its plastic sack, shaves his chin, works up a lustrous nap in his porkpie hat with his hat brush. He is off duty today, but duty means nothing, today means nothing, nothing means anything but a clean suit, three fresh Broadways, the wobble of the hangover just behind his eyes, the murmur of the brush against the whiskey-brown felt of his hat. And, all right, maybe a trace in his hotel room of the smell of Bina, of the sour collar of her shirt, her verbena soap, the marjoram smell of her armpit. He rides down in the elevator feeling as if he has stepped out from under the onrushing shadow of a plummeting piano, some kind of jazzy clangor in his ear. The knot of his gold-and-green rep necktie presses its thumb against his larynx like a scruple pressing against a guilty conscience, a reminder that he is alive. His hat is as glossy as a seal.

Max Nordau Street has not been plowed; the road crews of Sitka, slashed to skeletons, concentrate on the arterials and the highway. Landsman leaves the Super Sport with the garageman after retrieving his rubber overshoes from the trunk. Then he stomps his way carefully through the foot-deep drifts to Mabuhay Donuts on Monastir Street.

The Filipino-style Chinese donut, or shtekeleh, is the great contribution of the District of Sitka to the food lovers of the world. In its present form, it cannot be found in the Philippines. No Chinese trencherman would recognize it as the fruit of his native fry kettles. Like the storm god Yahweh of Sumeria, the shtekeleh was not invented by the Jews, but the world would sport neither God nor the shtekeleh without Jews and their desires. A panatela of fried dough not quite sweet, not quite salty, rolled in sugar, crisp-skinned, tender inside, and honeycombed with air pockets. You sink it in your paper cup of milky tea and close your eyes, and for ten fat seconds, you seem to glimpse the possibility of finer things.

The hidden master of the Filipino-style Chinese donut is Benito Taganes, proprietor and king of the bubbling vats at Mabuhay. Mabuhay, dark, cramped, invisible from the street, stays open all night long. It drains the bars and cafés after hours, concentrates the wicked and the guilty along its chipped Formica counter, and thrums with the gossip of criminals, policemen, shtarkers and shlemiels, whores and night owls. With the fat applauding in the fryers, the exhaust fans roaring, and the boom box blasting the heartsick *kundimans* of Benito's Manila childhood, the clientele makes free with their secrets. A golden mist of kosher oil hangs in the air and baffles the senses. Who could overhear with ears full of KosherFry and the wailing of Diomedes Maturan? But Benito Taganes overhears, and he remembers. Benito could draw you a family tree for Alexei Lebed, the chieftain of the Russian mob, only on it you would find not grandparents and nieces but bagmen, bump-offs, and offshore bank accounts. He could sing you a *kundiman* of wives who remain loyal to their imprisoned husbands and husbands doing time because their wives dropped dimes on them. He knows who's keeping the head of Furry Markov in his garage, and which narcotics inspector is on the payroll of Anatoly Moskowits the Wild Beast. Only nobody knows that he knows but Meyer Landsman.

"A donut, Reb Taganes," Landsman says when he comes stomping in from the alley, shivering the crust of snow from his overshoes. The Sitka Saturday afternoon lies dead as a failed messiah in its winding rag of snow. There was nobody on the sidewalk, hardly a car in the street. But here inside Mabuhay Donuts, three or four floaters, solitaries, and drunks between benders lean against the sparkly resin counter, sucking the tea from their shtekelehs and working the calculations of their next big mistakes.

"Only one?" Benito says. He is a squat, thick man with skin the color of the milky tea he serves, his cheeks pitted like a pair of dark moons. Though his hair is black, he's past seventy. As a young man he was the flyweight champion of Luzon, and with his thick fingers and the tattooed salamis of his forearms he gets taken for a tough customer, which serves the needs of his business. His big caramel eyes betray him, so he keeps them hooded and downcast. But Landsman has looked into them. To run a shtinker, you have to see the broken heart inside the deadest pan. "Look like you should to eat a couple, maybe ~~three~~, Detective."

Benito elbows ~~aside~~ the nephew or cousin he's got working the fry basket, and snake-charms a rope of raw dough into the fat. A few minutes later, Landsman is holding a tight paper packet of heaven in his hand.

"I have that information you wanted on Olivia's sister's daughter," Landsman says around a warm sugary mouthful.

Benito draws a cup of tea for Landsman and then nods toward the alley. He pulls on his anorak and they go out. Benito takes a ring of keys from his belt loop and works open an iron door two doors down from Mabuhay Donuts. This is where Benito keeps his lover, Olivia, in three small, tidy rooms with a Warhol portrait of Dietrich and a bitter smell of vitamins and rotten gardenia. Olivia's not there. The lady has been in and out of the hospital lately, dying in chapters, with a cliff-hanger at the end of every one. Benito waves Landsman into a red leather armchair piped in white. Of course, Landsman has no information for Benito about any of Olivia's sisters' daughters. Olivia is not really a lady, either, but Landsman is also the only one who knows that about Benito Taganes the donut king. Years ago, a serial rapist named Kohn forced himself on Miss Olivia Lagdameo and found out her secret. Kohn's *second* big surprise that night was the chance appearance of Patrolman Landsman. What Landsman did to Kohn's face left the momzer talking with a slur for the rest of his life. So it's a mixture of gratitude and shame, and not money, that drives the flow of information from Benito to the man who saved Olivia.

"Ever hear anything about the son of Heskel Shpilman?" Landsman says, setting down the donuts and the cup of tea. "Kid named Mendel?"

Benito stands, hands clasped behind his back, like a boy called on to recite a poem at school. "Over the years," he says. "A thing or two. Junkie, no?"

Landsman arcs one fuzzy eyebrow a quarter of an inch. You don't answer a shtinker's questions, especially not the rhetorical ones.

"Mendel Shpilman," Benito decides. "Seen him around maybe a few time. Funny guy. Talk a little Tagalog. Sing a little Filipino song. What happen, he not dead?"

Still Landsman doesn't say anything, but he likes Benny Taganes, and running him always feels a little rude. To cover the silence, he picks up the shtekeleh and takes a bite. It's still warm, and there's a hint of vanilla, and the crust crunches between his teeth like a caramel glaze on a pot of custard. As it goes into Landsman's mouth, Benito watches with the appraising coldness of an orchestra conductor auditioning a flutist.

"That's good, Benny."

"Don't insult me, Detective, I beg you."

"Sorry."

"I know it's good."

"The best."

"Nothing in your life even comes close."

This is so easily true that the sentiment brings a sting of tears to Landsman's eyes, and to cover that, he eats another donut.

"Somebody was looking for the yid," Benito says in his rough and fluent Yiddish. "Two, three months back. A couple somebodies."

"You saw them?"

Benito shrugs. His tactics and operations he keeps a mystery from Landsman, the cousins and nephews and the network of sub-shtinkers he employs.

"Somebody saw them," he says. "It might have been me."

"Were they black hats?"

Benito considers the question for a long moment, and Landsman can see it troubles him in a way that's somehow scientific, almost pleasurable. He gives his head a slow, certain shake. "No black hats," he says. "But beards."

"Beards? You mean, what, they were religious types?"

"Little yarmulkes. Neat beards. Young men."

"Russians? Accents?"

"If I heard about these young men, then the one who told me didn't say nothing about accents. If I saw them myself, then I'm sorry, I don't remember. Hey, what's the matter, what for you don't write this down, Detective?"

Early on in their collaboration, Landsman made a show of taking Benito's information very seriously. Now he fishes out his notebook and scratches a line or two, just to keep the donut king happy. He's not sure what to make of them, these two or three neat young Jews, religious but not black hat.

"And they were asking what, exactly, please?" he says.

"Whereabouts. Information."

"Did they get it?"

"Not at Mabuhay Donuts. Not from a Taganes."

Benito's Shoyfer rings, and he snaps it open and lays it against his ear. All the hardness goes out of the lines around his mouth. His face matches his eyes now, soft, brimming with feeling. He rattles on tenderly in Tagalog. Landsman catches the lowing sound of his own last name.

"How's Olivia?" Landsman asks as Benito closes his phone and ladles a yard of cold plaster into the mold of his face.

"She can't eat," Benito says. "No more shtekelehs."

"That's a shame."

They're through. Landsman gets up, slips the notebook back into his hip pocket, and feeds himself the last bite. He feels stronger and happier than he has in weeks or perhaps months. There is something in the death of Mendel Shpilman, a story to grab hold of, and it's shaking the dust and spiders off him. Or else it's the donut. They head for the door, but Benito puts a hand on Landsman's arm.

"Why you don't ask me anything else, Detective?"

"What would you like me to ask you?" Landsman frowns, then lights doubtfully on a question. "You heard something today, maybe? Something out of Verbov Island?" It's hard to imagine but not inconceivable that word of Verbover displeasure over Landsman's visit to the rebbe already would have reached Benito's ears.

"Verbov Island? No, another thing. You still looking for the Zilberblat?"

Viktor Zilberblat is one of the eleven outstanding cases that Landsman and Berko are supposed to be resolving effectively. Zilberblat was stabbed to death last March outside of the Hofbrau tavern in the Nachtasyl, the old German quarter, a few blocks from here. The knife was small and dull, and the murder had an unstudied air.

"Somebody see the brother," Benito Taganes says. "Rafi. Sneaking around."

Nobody was sorry to see Viktor go, least of all his brother, Rafael. Viktor had abused Rafael, cheated him, humiliated him, and made free with his cash and his woman. After Viktor died, Rafael left town, whereabouts unknown. The evidence linking Rafael to the knife is inconclusive at best. Two semireliable witnesses put him forty miles away from the Nachtasyl for two hours on either side of the likely time of his brother's murder. But Rafi Zilberblat has a long and monotonous police record, and he will do very nicely, Landsman reflects, given the lowered standard of proof that the new policy implies.

"Sneaking where?" Landsman says. The information is like a hot black mouthful of coffee. He can feel himself coiling around Rafael Zilberblat's freedom like a hundred-pound snake.

"That Big Macher store, it's gone now, up at Granite Creek. Somebody see him sneaking in and out of there. Carrying things. A can of propane. Maybe he living inside the empty store."

"Thanks, Benny," Landsman says. "I'll check it out."

Landsman starts to let himself out of the apartment. Benito

Taganes takes hold of his sleeve. He smooths the collar of Landsman's overcoat with a paternal hand. He brushes away the crumbs of cinnamon sugar.

"Your wife," he says. "Here again?"

"In all her glory."

"Nice lady. Benny says hello."

"I'll tell her to drop by."

"No, you don't tell her nothing." Benito grins. "Now she your boss."

"She was always my boss," Landsman says. "Now it's just official."

The grin winks out, and Landsman averts his gaze from the spectacle of Benito Taganes's grieving eyes. Benito's wife is a voiceless and shadowy little woman, but Miss Olivia in her heyday conducted herself like the boss of half the world.

"Better for you," Benito says. "You need."

 21

Landsman straps an extra clip to his belt and drives out to the north end, past Halibut Point, where the city sputters and the water reaches across the land like the arm of a policeman. Just off the Ickes Highway, the wreck of a shopping center marks the end of the dream of Jewish Sitka. The push to fill every space from here to Yakovy with the Jews of the world gave out in this parking lot. There was no Permanent Status, no influx of new jewflesh from the bitter corners and dark alleys of Diaspora. The planned housing developments remain lines on blue paper, encumbering some steel drawer.

The Granite Creek Big Macher outlet died about two years ago. Its doors are chained and along its windowless flank where Yiddish and Roman characters once spelled out the name of the store, there is only a cryptic series of holes, domino pips, a braille of failure.

Landsman leaves his car at the median and hikes across the giant frozen blank of the parking lot toward the front door. The snow is not as deep here as in the streets of the central city. The sky is high and pale gray, with darker gray tiger stripes. Landsman huffs through his nostrils as he marches toward the glass doors, their handles pinioned like arms with a dangling length of blue rubberized chain. Landsman has this idea that he's going to knock on those doors with his shield held high and his attitude vibrating like a force field, and that slinking whippet of a man, Rafi Zilberblat, is going to step sheepish and blinking into the snow-dazzling day.

The first bullet blackens the air alongside Landsman's right ear like a fat humming fly. He doesn't even know it's a bullet until he hears, or remembers hearing, a muffled burst and then a clamor of the glass. By then he's falling on his belly in the snow, flattening himself on the ground, where the next bullet finds the back of his head and burns it like a trail of gasoline touched by a match. Landsman drags out his sholem, but there is a cobweb in his head or over his face, and a paralysis of regret affects him. His plan was no plan at all, and now it has gone bad. He has no backup. Nobody knows where he is but Benito Taganes, with his molasses gaze and his all but universal silence. Landsman is going to die in a desolate parking lot at the margin of the world. He closes his eyes. He opens them, and the cobweb is denser and sparkling with some kind of dew. Footsteps in the snow, more than one person. Landsman raises his gun and takes aim through the sparkling strands of whatever is going wrong in his brain. He fires.

There is a cry of pain, feminine, a whuff of breath, and then the lady wishes a cancer upon Landsman's testicles. Snow packs Landsman's ears and melts into the collar of his coat and down his neck. Somebody snatches at Landsman's gun and tries to drag him to his feet. Popcorn on the breath. The bandage over Landsman's eyes stretches thin as he lurches upright. He can see the mustachioed snout of Rafi Zilberblat, and by the doors of the Big Macher, a plump bottle blonde lying on her back, her life pumping from her belly into the steaming red snow. And a couple of guns, one of them in Zilberblat's hand, pointed at Landsman's head. At the glint of the automatic, the cobweb of Landsman's regrets and self-recriminations goes away. The smell of popcorn, coming from inside the abandoned store, alters his perception of the smell of blood and brings out the sweetness of it. Landsman ducks and lets go of his Smith & Wesson.

THE YIDDISH POLICEMEN'S UNION   181

Zilberblat was yanking so hard on the gun that when Landsman unclenches, the other man goes tumbling backward into the snow. Landsman scrambles on top of Zilberblat. He's just acting now, without a thought in his head. He yanks his sholem loose and turns it around, and the world pulls the trigger on all its guns. Zilberblat grows a horn of blood from the crown of his head. The cobwebs are now in Landsman's ears. He can hear only the breath at the back of his throat and his own blood pulsing.

For an instant a strange peace opens like an umbrella inside Landsman as he straddles the man he just killed, knees burning in the snow. He retains the presence of mind to recognize that this tranquillity is not necessarily a good sign. Then the doubts begin to crowd in around the knowledge of the mess he has made, bystanders gathering around a suicide leaper. Landsman staggers to his feet. He sees the gore on his coat, the tatters of brain, a tooth.

Two dead humans in the snow. The smell of popcorn, a buttery stink of feet, overwhelms him.

While he is busy heaving up his guts into the snow, another man wanders out of the Big Macher store. A young man with a rat snout and a loping gait. Landsman retains the wit to mark him as a Zilberblat. This Zilberblat has his arms raised and a wild look on his face. His hands are empty. But when he sees Landsman bleeding and sick on all fours, he abandons his project of surrender. He picks up the automatic lying on the ground by the ruin of his brother. Landsman careens to his feet, and the trail of fire at the back of his head flares up. He feels the ground give way, and then there is a roaring blackness.

After he dies, he wakes up lying facedown in the snow. He can't feel snow on his cheek. The wild ringing in his ears is gone. He humps himself up to a sitting position. The blood from the back of his head has scattered rhododendrons in the snow. The man and the woman he shot have not moved, but there is no sign of the young Zilberblat who did or did not shoot and kill him. With a sudden clarity of thought and a mounting suspicion that he has forgotten to die, Landsman pats himself down. His watch, wallet, car keys, cell phone, gun, and badge are gone. He looks for his car parked in the distance, along the frontage road. When he sees that his Super Sport is gone, he knows that he is still alive, because only life could offer such a bitter vista.

"Another fucking Zilberblat," he says. "And they're all like that."

He is cold. He considers entering the Big Macher, but the stench of popcorn keeps him away. He turns from the yawning doors and lifts his eyes toward the high hill and beyond it the mountains, black with trees. Then he sits down in the snow. After a while, he lies down. It's snug and comfortable, and there's a smell of cool dust, and he closes his eyes and falls asleep, folded up into his nice dark little hole in the wall of the Hotel Zamenhof, and for once in his life, the claustrophobia doesn't trouble him, not a bit.

22

Landsman is holding a baby boy. The baby cries, for no very grave reason. His wailing constricts Landsman's heart in a pleasurable way. Landsman feels relieved to discover that he has a fat handsome baby who smells of waffles and soap. He squeezes the puffy feet, gauges the weight of the little grandfather in his arms, at once negligible and vast. He turns to Bina to tell her the good news: It was all a mistake. Here is their boy. But there is no Bina to tell, only the memory in Landsman's nostrils of rain on her hair. And then he wakes up and realizes that the crying baby is Pinky Shemets, having his diaper changed or registering a protest over something or other. Landsman blinks, and the world intrudes in the form of a batik wall covering, and he is hollowed out, as if it's the first time, by the loss of his son.

Landsman is lying on Berko and Ester-Malke's bed, on his side, facing the wall with its dyed linen scene of Balinese gardens and savage birds. Someone has undressed him, leaving him in his underpants. He sits up. The skin at the back of his head prickles, and then a cord of pain goes taut. Landsman pats the site of his injury. A bandage meets his fingers, a crinkly oblong of gauze and tape. Surrounding it, a queer hairless patch of scalp. Memories fall on top of one another with a slapping sound like crime-scene photographs fresh from Dr. Shpringer's death camera. A jocular emergency room tech, an X ray, an injection of morphine, a looming swab dipped in Betadine. Before that, the light from a streetlamp striping the white vinyl ceiling of an ambulance. And before that. Before the ride in the ambulance. Purple slush. Steam from the spilled contents of a human gut. A hornet at his ear. A red jet bursting from the forehead of Rafi Zilberblat. A cipher of holes in a blank expanse of plaster. Landsman backs away from the memory of what happened in the Big Macher parking lot, so quickly that he bumps right into the pang of losing Django Landsman in his dream.

"Woe is me," Landsman says. He wipes his eyes. He would give up a gland, a minor organ, for a papiros.

The bedroom door opens, and Berko comes in, carrying an almost-full pack of Broadways.

"Have I ever told you that I love you?" Landsman says, knowing full well that he never has.

"You never have, thank God," Berko says. "I got these from the neighbor, the Fried woman. I told her it was a police seizure."

"I am insanely grateful."

"I note the adverb."

Berko notes also that Landsman has been crying; one eyebrow shoots up, hangs suspended, drifts down like a tablecloth settling onto a table.

"Baby okay?" Landsman says.

"Teeth." Berko takes a coat hanger from a hook on the back of the bedroom door. On the hanger are Landsman's clothes, neat and brushed. Berko feels around in the hip pocket of Landsman's blazer and produces a matchbook. Then he comes and stands by the bed and holds out the papiroses and matches.

"I can't honestly claim," says Landsman, "that I know what I'm doing here."

"It was Ester-Malke's idea. Knowing how you feel about hospitals. They said you didn't need to stay."

"Have a seat."

There is no chair in the room. Landsman slides over, and Berko sits down on the edge of the bed, causing alarm among the bedsprings.

"It's really okay if I smoke?"

"Not really, no. Go stand by the window."

Landsman tips himself out of the bed. When he rolls up the bamboo shade on the window, he is surprised to see that it's pouring rain. The smell of rain blows in through the two inches the window has been cranked open, explaining the fragrance of Bina's hair in his dream. Landsman looks down to the parking lot of the apartment building and observes that the snow has melted and been washed away. The light feels all wrong, too.

"What time is it?"

"Four-thirty . . . two," Berko says without checking his watch.

"What day is it?"

"Sunday."

Landsman cranks open the window all the way and hooks his left buttock over the sill. Rain falls on his aching head. He lights his papiros and takes a long drag and tries to decide if he's disturbed by this information. "Long time since I did that," he says. "Slept through a whole day."

"You must have needed it," Berko observes blandly. A sideways look in Landsman's direction. "Ester-Malke's the one who took your pants off, by the way. Just so you know."

Landsman flicks ash out of the window. "I was shot."

"Grazed. They said it's more like a kind of burn. They didn't need to stitch it."

"There were three of them. Rafael Zilberblat. A pisher I made for his brother. And some chicken. The brother took my car, my wallet. My badge and my sholem. Left me there."

"So it was reconstructed."

"I wanted to call for help, but the little ratface Jew took my Shoyfer, too."

The mention of Landsman's phone makes Berko smile.

"What?" Landsman says.

"So, your pisher's tooling along. North on the Ickes, headed for Yakovy, Fairbanks, Irkutsk."

"Uh-huh."

"Your phone rings. Your pisher answers it."

"And it's you?"

"Bina."

"I like it."

"Two minutes on the phone with the Zilberblat, she has his whereabouts, his description, the name of his dog when he was eleven. A couple of latkes pick him up five minutes later outside Krestov. Your car is fine. Your wallet still had cash in it."

Landsman affects to take an interest in the way that fire turns cured tobacco to flakes of ash. "And my badge and gun?" he says.

"Ah."

"Ah."

"Your badge and your gun are now in the hands of your commanding officer."

"Does she intend to return them?"

Berko reaches over and smooths the indentation that Landsman left in the surface of his bed.

"It was strictly line of duty," Landsman says, his tone sounding whiny even to his own ear. "I got a tip on Rafi Zilberblat." He shrugs and runs his fingers along the bandage at the back of his head. "I just wanted to talk to the yid."

"You should have called me first."

"I didn't want to bother you on a Saturday."

It's no excuse, and it comes out even lamer than Landsman hoped.

"Nu, I'm an idiot," Landsman admits. "And a bad policeman, too."

"Rule number one."

THE YIDDISH POLICEMEN'S UNION   187

"I know. I just felt like doing something right then. I didn't think it was going to go the way that it went."

"In any case," Berko says. "The pisher. The little brother. Calls himself Willy Zilberblat. He confessed on his late brother's behalf. Says indeed Rafi killed Viktor. With half a pair of scissors."

"How about that."

"All other things being equal, I would say Bina has reason to be happy with you on that one. You resolved it very effectively."

"*Half* a pair of scissors."

"How's that for resourceful?"

"Frugal, even."

"And the chicken you handled so roughly—that was you, too?"

"It was me."

"Nicely done, Meyer." There is no sarcasm in Berko's tone or face. "You put a pill in Yacheved Flederman."

"I did not."

"You had yourself quite a day."

"The nurse?"

"Our colleagues on the B Squad are delighted with you."

"That killed that old geezer, what's his name, Herman Pozner?"

"It was their only open case from last year. They thought she was in Mexico."

"Fuck me," Landsman says in American.

"Tabatchnik and Karpas already put in a good word for you with Bina, as I understand."

Landsman grinds the papiros out against the side of the building, then flicks the butt into the rain. Tabatchnik and Karpas are really kicking the asses of Landsman and Shemets; it's not even close.

"Even when I have good luck," he says, "it's bad luck." He sighs. "Has there been anything out of Verbov Island?"

"Not a peep."

"Nothing in the papers?"

"Not in the *Licht* or the *Rut*." These are the leading black-hat dailies. "No rumors that I've heard. Nobody's talking about it. Nothing. Total silence."

Landsman gets up off the windowsill and goes to the phone on the table beside the bed. He dials a number he memorized years ago, asks a question, gets an answer, hangs up. "The Verbovers picked up Mendel Shpilman's body late last night."

The telephone in Landsman's hand startles, chirping like a robot bird. He passes it to Berko.

"He seems fine," Berko says after a moment. "Yes, I imagine that he will need some rest. All right." He lowers the handset and stares at it, covering the mouthpiece with the pad of his thumb. "Your ex-wife."

"I hear you're fine," Bina tells Landsman when he gets on the phone.

"So they tell me," Landsman says.

"Take some time," she suggests. "Give yourself a break."

The import takes a second to register, her tone is so gentle and unruffled.

"You would not," he says. "Bina, please tell me this is not true."

"Two dead people. By your gun. No witnesses but a kid who didn't see what happened. It's automatic. Suspension with pay, pending a review by the board."

"They were shooting guns at me. I had a reliable tip, I approached with my gun in my holster, I was polite as a mouse. And they started shooting at me."

"And of course you'll get the chance to tell your story. In the meantime, I'm going to keep your shield and your gun in this nice pink plastic Hello Kitty zipper bag that Willy Zilberblat was carrying them around in, okay? And you just try to get yourself all nice and better, all right?"

"This thing could take weeks to sort out," Landsman says. "By the time I'm back on duty, there might not *be* a Sitka Central. There are no grounds for a suspension here, and you know it. Under the circumstances, you can keep me on active duty while the review goes forward, and still be running this case totally by the book."

"There are books," Bina says. "And there are books."

"Don't be cryptic," he says, and then in American, "What the fuck?"

For a long couple of seconds, Bina doesn't reply.

"I had a call from Chief Inspector Vayngartner. Last night. Not long," she says, "after dark."

"I see."

"He tells me *he* just had a call. On his *home* phone, this is. And I guess the esteemed gentleman on the other end of the line was maybe a little upset about certain behaviors that Detective Meyer Landsman might have been exhibiting in this gentleman's neighborhood on Friday afternoon. Creating public disturbances. Showing grave disrespect for the locals. Operating without authority or approval."

"And Vayngartner replied?"

"He said you were a good detective, but you were known to have certain problems."

And there, Landsman, is the line for your headstone.

"So what did you tell Vayngartner?" he says. "When he called to ruin your Saturday night."

"My Saturday night. My Saturday night is like a microwave burrito. Very tough to ruin something that starts out so bad to begin with. As it happens, I told Chief Inspector Vayngartner how you had just been shot."

"And he said?"

"He said that in light of this fresh evidence, he might have to reconsider long-held atheistic beliefs. And that I should do whatever I could to make sure you were comfortable, and that for the next little time, you got plenty of rest. So that's what I'm doing. You're suspended, with full pay, until further notice."

"Bina. Bina, please. You know how I am."

"I do."

"If I can't work— You can't—"

"I have to." The temperature of her voice drops so quickly that ice crystals tinkle on the line. "You know how much of a choice I have in a situation like this."

"You mean when gangsters pull strings to keep a murder investigation from going forward? That the kind of situation you mean?"

"I answer to the chief inspector," Bina explains, as if she's talking to a donkey. She knows perfectly well that there is nothing Landsman hates more than being treated like he's stupid. "And you answer to me."

"I wish you hadn't called my phone," Landsman says after a moment. "Better you should just have let me die."

"Don't be melodramatic," Bina says. "Oh, and you're welcome."

"And what am I supposed to do now, besides be grateful for having my balls cut off?"

"That's up to you, Detective. Maybe you could try thinking about the future for a change."

"The future," Landsman says. "You mean, what, like flying cars? Hotels on the moon?"

"I mean *your* future."

"You want to go to the moon with me, Bina? I hear they still take Jews."

"Goodbye, Meyer."

She hangs up. Landsman cuts the connection on his end and stands there for a minute with Berko watching him from the bed. Landsman feels a last surge of anger and enthusiasm blow through him, like a clot of dust being cleared from a pipe. Then he's empty.

He sits down on the bed. He gets in under the covers and turns his face back to the Balinese scene on the wall and closes his eyes.

"Uh, Meyer?" Berko says. But Landsman doesn't answer. "You planning to stay in my bed a whole lot longer?"

Landsman sees no percentage in answering the question. After a minute Berko bounces himself off the mattress and onto his feet. Landsman can feel him studying the situation, appraising the depth of black water that separates the two partners, trying to make the right call.

"For what it's worth," Berko says finally, "Bina also came to see you in the ER."

Landsman finds he has no memory of this visit at all. It's gone, like the squeeze of a baby's foot against his palm.

"You were doped up pretty good," Berko says. "Talking many kinds of shit."

"Did I embarrass myself with her?" Landsman manages to ask in a tiny voice.

"Yes," Berko says, "I fear that you did."

Then he withdraws from his own bedroom and leaves Landsman there to puzzle out the question, if he can muster the strength, of how much further he can sink.

Landsman can hear them talking about him in the hushed tones reserved for madmen, assholes, and unwanted guests. All through the rest of the afternoon, as they eat their dinner. Through the uproar of bath and ass-powdering and a bedtime story that requires Berko Shemets to honk like a goose. Landsman lies on his side with a burning seam at the back of his skull and drifts in and out of consciousness of the smell of rain at the window, the murmuring and clamor of the family in the other room. Every hour that passes, another hundredweight of sand is poured in through a tiny hole in Landsman's soul. First he can't lift his head off the mattress. Then he can't seem to open his eyes. After his eyes are closed, what happens is never quite sleep, and the thoughts that plague him, though atrocious, are never quite dreams.

Sometime in the middle of the night, Goldy careers into the room. His tread is heavy and lumbering, a baby monster's. He doesn't just climb into the bed, he roils the blankets the way a wire whisk roils a batter. Its like he's fleeing something, panicked, but when Landsman speaks, asks him what's wrong, the boy doesn't answer. His eyes are closed, and his heart beats steadily and low. Whatever he was running from, he found shelter from it in his parents' bed. The kid is sound asleep. He smells like a piece of cut apple that's starting to turn. He digs his toes into the small of Landsman's back with care and without mercy. He grinds his teeth. The sound of it is like dull shears on a sheet of tin.

After an hour of this kind of treatment, around four-thirty, the baby starts to scream, way out on his balcony. Landsman can hear Ester-Malke trying to comfort him. Ordinarily, she would bring him into her bed, but that's not an option tonight, and it takes her a long time to settle the little grandfather down. By the time Ester-Malke wanders into the bedroom with the baby in her arms, he's snuffling and quieter and almost asleep. Ester-Malke dumps Pinky between his brother and Landsman and walks out.

Reunited in their parents' bed, the Shemets boys set up a whistling and rumbling and a blatting of inner valves that would shame the grand pipe organ of Temple Emanu-El. The boys execute a series of maneuvers, a kung fu of slumber, that drives Landsman to the very limit of the bed. They chop at Landsman, stab him with their toes, grunt and mutter. They masticate the fiber of their dreams. Around dawn, something very bad happens in the baby's diaper. It's the worst night that Landsman has ever spent on a mattress, and that is saying a good deal.

The coffeemaker begins its expectorations around seven. A few thousand molecules of coffee vapor tumble into the bedroom and worry the hairs inside Landsman's beak. He hears the shuffle of slippers against the carpet in the hall. He fights long and hard against the impulse to acknowledge that Ester-Malke is standing there, in the doorway of her bedroom, ruing him and every fit of charity toward him that's ever seized her. He doesn't care. Why should he care? At last Landsman realizes that in his struggle not to care about anything lie the paradoxical seeds of defeat: So, all right, he cares. He opens one eye. Ester-Malke leans against the doorjamb, hugging herself, surveying the scene of destruction in a place that once was her bed. Whatever the name of the emotion inspired in a mother by the sight of filial cuteness, it competes in her expression with horror and dismay at the spectacle of Landsman in his underpants.

"I need you out of my bed," she whispers. "Soon and in a way that's lasting."

"All right," says Landsman. Taking stock of his wounds, his aches, the prevailing direction of his moods, he sits up. For all the torment of the night, he feels oddly settled. More present, somehow, in his limbs and skin and senses. Somehow, maybe, a little more real. He has not shared a bed with another human being in over two years. He wonders if that is a practice he ought not to have foregone. He takes his clothes from the door and puts them on. Carrying his socks and belt, he follows Ester-Malke back down the hall.

"Though the couch has its points," Ester-Malke continues. "For example, it features no babies or four-year-olds."

"You have a serious toenail problem among your youth," Landsman says. "Also something, I think it might be a sea otter, died and is rotting in the little one's diaper."

In the kitchen she pours them each a cup of coffee. Then she goes to the door and retrieves the *Tog* from the mat that says GET LOST. Landsman sits on his stool at the counter and stares into the murk of the living room where the bulk of his partner rears up from the floor like an island. The couch is a wreck of blankets.

Landsman is about to tell Ester-Malke *I don't deserve friends like you* when she comes back into the kitchen, reading the paper, and says, "No wonder you needed so much sleep." She bumps into the doorway. Something good or terrible or unbelievable is described on the front page.

Landsman reaches for his reading glasses in the pocket of his jacket. They are cracked at the nosepiece, each lens severed from its mate. It's truly a pair of glasses, two monocles on their stems. Ester-Malke gets the electrician's tape, yellow as a hazard warning, from the drawer under the phone. She binds up the glasses and passes them back to Landsman. The gob of tape is as thick as a filbert. It draws the gaze even of the wearer, leaving him cross-eyed.

"I'll bet that looks really good," he says, taking up the newspaper.

Two big stories lead off the news in this morning's *Tog*. One is an account of an apparent shoot-out, leaving two dead, in the deserted parking lot of a Big Macher outlet store. The principals were a lone homicide detective, Meyer Landsman, forty-two, and two suspects long sought by Sitka law enforcement in connection with a pair of apparently unrelated murders. The other story is headlined:

"BOY TZADDIK" FOUND DEAD IN SITKA HOTEL

The accompanying text whips up a tissue of miracles, evasions, and outright lies about the life and death of Menachem-Mendel Shpilman, late Thursday night, at the Hotel Zamenhof on Max Nordau Street. According to the medical examiner's office—the examining doctor himself having moved to Canada—the preliminary finding on cause of death is something known in fairy tales as "drug-related misadventure." "Though little known to the world outside," the *Tog*'s man writes,

> in the closed world of the pious, Mr. Shpilman
> was viewed, for the better part of his early life,
> as a prodigy, a wonder, and a holy teacher, indeed,
> as possibly the long-promised Redeemer. The old
> Shpilman home on S. Ansky Street in the Harkavy
> was often thronged with visitors and supplicants

during Mr. Shpilman's childhood, with the devout
and the curious traveling from as far as Buenos
Aires and Beirut to meet the talented boy who
was born on the fateful ninth day of the month of
Av. Many hoped and even arranged to be present
on one of a number of occasions when rumors
flew that he was about to "declare his kingdom."
But Mr. Shpilman never made any declarations.
Twenty-three years ago, on the day projected for
his marriage to a daughter of the Shtrakenzer
rebbe, he all but disappeared, and during the long
ignominy of Mr. Shpilman's recent life, the early
promise had largely been forgotten.

The chaff from the ME's office is the only item in the story
resembling an explanation of the death. Hotel management and
the Central Division are said to have declined comment. At the
end of the article, Landsman learns that there will be no synagogue
service, just the burial itself, at the old Montefiore cemetery, to be
presided over by the father of the deceased.

"Berko said he disowned him," Ester-Malke says, reading over
Landsman's shoulder. "He said the old man wanted nothing to do
with the kid. I guess he changed his mind."

Reading the article, Landsman suffers a cramp of envy toward
Mendel Shpilman, tempered by pity. Landsman struggled for many
years under the weight of fatherly expectations, but he has no
idea how it might feel to fulfill or exceed them. Isidor Landsman,
he knows, would have loved to father a son as gifted as Mendel.
Landsman can't help thinking that if he had been able to play chess
like Mendel Shpilman, maybe his father would have felt he had
something to live for, a small messiah to redeem him. Landsman
thinks of the letter that he sent his father, hoping to gain his freedom
from the burden of that life and those expectations. He considers
the years he spent believing that he caused Isidor Landsman a fatal

grief. How much guilt did Mendel Shpilman feel? Had he believed what was said of him, in his gift or wild calling? In the attempt to free himself from that burden, did Mendel feel that he must turn his back not only on his father but on all the Jews in the world?

"I don't think Rabbi Shpilman ever changes his mind," Landsman says. "I think somebody would have to change it for him."

"Who would that be?"

"If I had to guess? I'm thinking that maybe it was the mother."

"Good for her. Trust a mother not to let them toss her son out like an empty bottle."

"Trust a mother," Landsman says. He studies the photograph in the *Tog* of Mendel Shpilman at fifteen, beard patchy, sidelocks flying, coolly presiding over a conference of young Talmudists who seethed and sulked around him. "The Tzaddik Ha-Dor, in Better Days," reads the caption.

"What are you thinking about, Meyer?" Ester-Malke says, striking a note of doubt.

"The future," Landsman says.

23

A mob of black-hat Jews chugs its way, a freight train of grief, from the gates of the cemetery—the house of life, they call it—up a hillside toward a hole cut into the mud. A pine box slick with rain pitches and tosses on the surf of weeping men. Satmars hold umbrellas over the heads of Verbovers. Gerers and Shtrakenzers and Viznitzers link arms with the boldness of schoolgirls on a lark. Rivalries, grudges, sectarian disputes, mutual excommunications, they've been laid aside for a day so that everyone can mourn with due passion a yid who was forgotten by them until last Friday night. Not even a yid—the shell of a yid, thinned to transparency around the hard void of a twenty-year junk habit. Every generation loses the messiah it has failed to deserve. Now the pious of the Sitka District have pinpointed the site of their collective unworthiness and gathered in the rain to lay it in the ground.

Around the grave site, black clumps of fir trees sway like grieving Chasids. Beyond the cemetery walls, hats and black umbrellas shelter thousands of the unworthiest of the unworthy against the rain. Deep structures of obligation and credit have determined which are permitted to enter the gates of the house of life and which must stand outside kibitzing, with rain soaking into their hose. These deep structures, in turn, have drawn the attention of detectives from Burglary, Contraband, and Fraud. Landsman picks out Skolsky, Burwitz, Feld, and Globus, always with his shirttail hanging out, perched on the roof of a gray Ford Victoria. It's not every day that the entire Verbover hierarchy comes out and stands around on a hillside, posed in relation to one another like circles on a prosecutor's flow chart. On the roof of a Wal-Mart a quarter mile away, three Americans in blue windbreakers point their telephoto lenses and the trembling pistil of a condenser microphone. A stout blue cord of latkes and motorcycle units has been stitched through the crowd to keep it from coming undone. The press is here, too, cameramen and reporters from Channel 1, from the local papers, crews from the NBC affiliate over in Juneau and a cable news channel. Dennis Brennan, without the sense or maybe enough felt in the world to cover that big head of his against the rain. Then you have the half-believing, and the half-observant, and the modern Orthodox, and the merely credulous, and the skeptical, and the curious, and a healthy delegation from the Einstein Chess Club.

Landsman can see them all from the vantage of his powerlessness and his exile, reunited with his Super Sport on a barren hilltop across Mizmor Boulevard from the house of life. He's parked in a cul-de-sac some developer laid out, paved, then saddled with the name of Tikvah Street, the Hebrew word denoting hope and connoting to the Yiddish ear on this grim afternoon at the end of time seventeen flavors of irony. The hoped-for houses were never built. Wooden stakes tied with orange flags and nylon cord map out a miniature Zion in the mud around the cul-de-sac, a ghostly eruv of failure. Landsman is flying solo, sober as a carp in a bathtub, clutching a pair of binoculars in his clammy grip. The need for a drink is like a missing tooth. He can't keep his mind off it, and yet there's something pleasurable in probing the gap. Or maybe the ache of something missing is just the hole left behind when Bina lifted his badge.

Landsman waits out the funeral in his car, studying it through the good Zeiss lenses and running down the car battery with a

CBC radio documentary about the blues singer Robert Johnson, whose singing voice sounds as broken and reedy as a Jew saying kaddish in the rain. Landsman has a carton of Broadways, and he burns them wildly, trying to drive from the Super Sport's interior a lingering odor of Willy Zilberblat. It's a foul smell, like a pot of water in which two days ago somebody boiled noodles. Berko tried to persuade Landsman that he was imagining this residue of the little Zilberblat's brief tenure inside Landsman's life. But Landsman is happy for the excuse to fumigate with cigarettes, which don't kill the urge for a drink but somehow dull its bite.

Berko also tried to persuade Landsman to wait a day or two on the matter of Mendel Shpilman's death by misadventure. As they rode down in the elevator from the apartment, he dared Landsman to look him straight in the eye and tell him that Landsman's plan for this damp Monday afternoon did not consist of showing up, shorn of his badge and his gun, to hurl impertinent questions at the grieving queen of gangsters as she departed from the house of life and the remains of her only son.

"You can't get near her," Berko insisted as he followed Landsman out of the elevator and across the lobby to the door of the Dnyeper. Berko was in his elephantine pajamas. Pieces of a suit were spilling out of his arms. He had his shoes hooked over two fingers, his belt around his neck. From the breast pocket of his mustard pajamas with their white pinstripe the points of two slices of toast protruded like a pocket square. "And even if you can, you still can't."

He was making a nice policeman-like distinction between the things that balls could accomplish and those that the breakers of balls would never permit.

"They will stiff-arm you," Berko said. "They will shake out your pants for the small change. They will bring you up on charges."

Landsman could not refute the point. Batsheva Shpilman rarely set foot beyond the boundary of her deep and tiny world. But when she did, it was likely to be in a heavy thicket of iron and lawyers. "No badge, no backing, no warrant, no investigation, looking half crazy with egg on your suit, you bother the lady, you could get shot, with only minor aftereffects for the shooters."

Berko trailed Landsman out of the building, dancing into his socks and shoes, down to the bus stop at the corner.

"You're saying don't do it, Berko," Landsman said, "or just don't do it without *you*? You think I'll let you piss away whatever shot you and Ester-Malke have to get through to the other end of Reversion? You're crazy. I've done you a lot of disservices and caused you a lot of trouble over the years, but I hope I'm not that much of an ass. And if you're saying you don't think I should do it *period*, well . . . "

Landsman stopped marching. The full weight of good sense behind this second argument struck him.

"I don't know what I'm saying, Meyer. I'm just saying, fuck." Berko got this look sometimes, more when he was a boy, a shine of sincerity on the whites of his eyes. Landsman had to look away. He turned his face to the wind blowing in off the Sound. "I'm saying at least don't take the bus, all right? Let me drive you down to the impound yard, at least."

There was a distant rumble, a screech of air brakes. The 61B Harkavy appeared farther down the promenade, kicking up a shimmering curtain of rain.

"At least this," Berko said. He hoisted his suit jacket by the collar. He held it out as if he wanted Landsman to put it on. "In the pocket. Take it."

Landsman weighs the sholem in his hand now—a cute little Beretta .22 with a plastic grip—poisons himself on nicotine, tries to understand the lamentations of this black Delta yid, Mr. Johnson. After a period that he doesn't bother to note or measure, call it an hour, the long dark train, discharged of its goods, starts back down the hill toward the gates. At the head of it, puffing slowly, head erect, broad-brimmed hat running rain, comes the locomotive bulk of the tenth Verbover rebbe. Behind him come the string of daughters, seven or twelve of them, and their husbands and children, and then Landsman sits up and dials in a crisp Zeiss image of Batsheva Shpilman. He's been expecting some kind of witchy amalgam of Mrs. Macbeth and American first lady: Marilyn Monroe Kennedy in her pink pillbox hat, with mesmeric spirals for eyes. But as Batsheva Shpilman comes into clear view, right before she falls below the line of mourners jamming the cemetery gates, Landsman remarks a small, bony frame, an old-lady halt in her tread. Her face is concealed behind a black veil. Her clothes are unremarkable, a vehicle for blackness.

As the Shpilmans approach the gates, the line of uniformed nozzes gathers into a tight knot, driving the crowd back. Landsman slips the gun into his hip pocket, switches off the radio, and gets out of the car. The rain has slowed to a steady fine mesh. He begins to lope down the hill toward Mizmor Boulevard. Over the last hour the crowd has swollen, bunching up around the cemetery gates. Jiggling, shifting, prone to sudden mass lurches, animated by the Brownian motion of collective woe. The uniformed latkes are working hard, trying to clear a path between the family and the big black four-by-fours of the funeral cortege.

Landsman scrapes and stumbles, shredding weeds, gathering clots of mud on his shoes. As he exerts himself on the slippery hillside, his injuries start to bother him. He wonders if the doctors missed a broken rib. At one point he loses his footing and slides, his heels cutting ten-foot gouges in the mud, and ends by falling on his ass. He's too superstitious not to see this as a bad omen, but when you're a pessimist, all omens are bad.

The truth is that he has no plan at all, not even the graceless and rudimentary one that Berko envisioned. Landsman has been a noz for eighteen years, a detective for thirteen, spent the last seven working homicide, a top man, a prince of policemen. He has never been nobody before, a crazy little Jew with a question and a gun. He doesn't know how one proceeds under the circumstances, except with the certainty, pressed to the heart like a keepsake of love, that in the end nothing really matters.

Mizmor Boulevard is a parking lot, mourners and spectators in a haze of diesel fumes. Landsman threads a course among the bumpers and fenders and then plunges into the mass of people jammed onto the parkway strip. Boys and young men, hoping for a better view, have climbed up into the branches of a row of luckless European larches that never quite took root along the median. The yids around Landsman get out of his way, and when they don't get out of his way, Landsman gives them a hint with the bones of his shoulder.

They smell of lamentation, these yids, long underwear, tobacco smoke on wet overcoats, mud. They're praying like they're going to faint, fainting like it's a kind of observance. Weeping women cling to each other and break open their throats. They aren't mourning Mendel Shpilman, they can't be. It's something else they feel has gone out of the world, the shadow of a shadow, the hope of a hope. This half-island they have come to love as home is being taken from them. They are like goldfish in a bag, about to be dumped back into the big black lake of Diaspora. But that's too much to think about. So instead, they lament the loss of a lucky break they never got, a chance that was no chance at all, a king who was never going to come in the first place, even without a jacketed slug in the brainpan. Landsman puts his shoulder to them and mutters, "Pardon me."

He makes for one great beast of a limousine, a custom twenty-foot stretch four-by-four. The journey from the top of the hill, down the hillside, across the boulevard, through the umbrellas and beards and Jewish ululations to the side of the big-ass limousine has a kind of jumpy, handheld quality in his imagination as he lives it. Amateur footage of an assassination attempt in progress. But Landsman hasn't come to shoot anybody. He just wants to talk to the lady, get her attention, catch her eye. He just wants to ask her one question. Which question, nu, that he doesn't know.

In the end somebody beats him to it: in fact, a dozen men.

The reporters have tunneled their way through the black hats like Landsman, digging with their scapulae and elbows. When the diminutive woman in the black veil totters through the gates on the arm of her son-in-law, they haul out the questions they have brought. They unpocket them like stones and throw them all at once. They vandalize the woman with questions. She pays no attention; her head never turns, the veil never trembles or parts. Baronshteyn guides the dead man's mother to the hulk of the limo. The chauffeur climbs down from the stretch four-by-four's passenger seat. He's a jockey-shaped Filipino with a scar on his chin like a second smile. He runs to open the door for his employer. Landsman is still a couple of hundred feet away. He isn't going to make it in time to ask her a question, or to do anything at all.

A growl, a feral rolling in the throat, low and half human, a rumble of warning or dark admonition: one of the black hats standing by the cars has taken a reporter's question amiss. Or maybe he's taken them all amiss, along with the style in which they were tendered. Landsman sees the angry black hat, wide, blond, tieless, his shirttails untucked, and recognizes him as Dovid Sussman, the yid whom Berko Shemets teased out on Verbov Island. A bruiser with a bulge at the hinge of his jaw and another under his left arm. Sussman throws an arm around the neck of Dennis Brennan, poor thing, gets him in a choke hold. Lecturing Brennan with his teeth at his ear, Sussman drags the reporter back, out of the path of the family as they come through the gates.

That's when one of the latkes steps in to intervene, which, after all, is what he's there for. But because he's scared—the kid looks scared—maybe he's too free with his truncheon when it comes to the bones of Dovid Sussman's head. There's a sick snap, and then Sussman turns to liquid and pours himself onto the ground at the latke's feet.

For an instant the crowd, the afternoon, the whole wide world of Jews breathes in and forgets to breathe out again. After that it's madness, a Jewish riot, at once violent and verbal, fat with intemperate accusations and implacable curses. Skin diseases are called down, damnations and hemorrhages. Yelling, surging black hats, sticks and fists, shouting and screaming, beards fluttering like crusader flags, swearing, the smell of churning mud, of blood and ironed trousers. Two men carry a banner stretched between poles, bidding farewell to their lost prince Menachem; somebody grabs one pole and somebody else grabs another. The banner tears loose and gets sucked into the gears of the crowd. The poles are put to work on the jaws and craniums of policemen. The word FAREWELL painstakingly painted on the banner gets torn free and spat out. It sails into the air over the heads of the mourners and the policemen, the gangsters and the pious, the living and the dead.

Landsman loses track of the rebbe, but he sees a bunch of Rudashevskys pile the mother, Batsheva, into the back of the four-by-four. The chauffeur grabs the driver's-side door and kicks up into his seat like a gymnast. The Rudashevskys pound on the side of the car, saying, "*go go go.*" Landsman, still groping in his pockets for the shining coin of one good question, watches, and watching, he notices a suite of small things. The Filipino chauffeur is rattled. He doesn't fasten his shoulder strap. He doesn't give a good solid cattle-clearing blast on his horn. And the stem of the lock at the top of the door panel never drops. The chauffeur simply throws the long black four-by-four into gear and rolls forward, gaining too much speed for such a crowded area.

Landsman steps back as the four-by-four shoulders its way toward him. A strand of mourners detaches itself from the greater black braid and drags along behind Batsheva Shpilman's four-by-four. A slipstream of sorrow. For an instant the mourners hanging on to the car serve to block the Rudashevskys' view of the four-by-four, and of anyone fool enough to try to climb inside it. Landsman nods, catching the rhythm of the crowd's madness and his own. He watches for his moment and wiggles his fingers. When the car rumbles by, he yanks open the rear door.

Instantly, the power of the engine is translated into a sense of panic in his legs. It's like a proof of the physics of his foolishness, the inescapable momentum of his own bad luck. As he gets dragged along beside the car for fifteen feet or so, he finds time to wonder if this was how the end came for his sister, a quick demonstration of gravity and mass. His wrists strain their cables. Then he gets a knee up into the limousine's interior and tumbles in.

24

A dark cavern lit with blue diodes. Cool, dry, fragrant with some kind of lemon deodorizer. Landsman senses in himself a trace of that smell, a lemony hint of boundless hope and energy. This may have been the stupidest thing he's ever done, but it needed to be done, and the feeling of having done it, for this instant, is the answer to the only question he knows how to ask.

"There's ginger ale," says the queen of Verbov Island. She's folded like a throw rug, coiled in a shadowy back corner of the interior. Her dress is drab but cut of fine stuff, and the lining of her raincoat betrays a fashionable logo. "Drink it, I don't care to."

But Landsman gives his attention to the rear-facing seat, up by the chauffeur, and the likeliest source of trouble. Sitting there is six feet, maybe two hundred pounds, of female in a black sharkskin suit with a white-on-white collarless shirt. This formidable person's eyes are gray and hard. They remind Landsman of the backs of two dull spoons. She wears a white earpiece wormed around the flange of her left ear, and her tomato-gravy hair is cut short as a man's.

"I didn't know they made lady Rudashevskys," Landsman says, crouched on his toes in the wide space between the front- and rear-facing benches.

"That is Shprintzl," says his hostess in the back of the car. Then Batsheva Shpilman lifts her veil. The body is frail, perhaps even gaunt, but it can't be with age, because the fine-featured face, though hollow, is smooth, a pleasure to look at. She has wide-set eyes of a blue that wavers between heartbreaking and fatal. Her mouth is unpainted but full and red. The nostrils in her long, straight nose arch like a pair of wings. Her face is so strong and lovely, and her frame so wasted, that it's disturbing to look at her. Her head sits atop her veined throat like an alien parasite, preying on her body. "I want you to be sure to notice that she hasn't killed you yet."

"Thank you, Shprintzl," Landsman says.

"No problem," Shprintzl Rudashevsky says in American, in a voice like an onion rolling in a bucket.

Batsheva Shpilman points to the opposite end of the backseat. Her hand is gloved in black velvet, buttoned at the cuff with three black seed pearls. Landsman takes the suggestion and gets up off the floor. The seat is very comfortable. He can feel the cold sweat of an imaginary highball against his fingertips.

"Also, she hasn't contacted any of her brothers or cousins in the other cars, even though, as you see, she's wired right to them."

"Tight-knit bunch, the Rudashevskys," Landsman says, but he understands what she wants him to understand: "You wanted to talk to me."

"Did I?" she says, and her lips contemplate but decide against lifting at one corner. "You're the one who barged into my car."

"Oh, is this a car? My mistake, I thought it was the Sixty-one bus."

Shprintzl Rudashevsky's wide face takes on a philosophical, even mystic, blankness. She looks like she's wetting her pants and enjoying the warmth. "They're asking about you, darling," she says to the older woman with a nurselike tenderness. "They want to know if you're all right."

"Tell them I'm fine, Shprintzeleh. Tell them we're on our way home." She turns her soft eyes toward Landsman. "We'll drop you at your hotel. I want to see it." They're a color he's never seen, her eyes, a blue you would find in bird plumage or a stained-glass window. "Will that suit you, Detective Landsman?"

Landsman says that will suit him fine. While Shprintzl Rudashevsky murmurs into a concealed microphone, her employer lowers the partition and gives instructions to the chauffeur that will take them to the corner of Max Nordau and Berlevi.

"You look thirsty, Detective," she says, raising the partition again. "You're sure you won't have a ginger ale? Shprintzeleh, get the gentleman a glass ginger ale."

"Thank you, ma'am, I'm not thirsty."

Batsheva Shpilman's eyes widen, narrow, widen again. She's taking inventory of him, checking it against what she knows or has heard. Her gaze is quick and unsparing. She would probably make a fine detective. "Not for ginger ale," she says.

They turn onto Lincoln and roll along the shoreline, past Oysshtelung Island and the broken promise of the Safety Pin, headed toward the Untershtot. In nine minutes they will arrive at the Hotel Zamenhof. Those eyes of hers drown him in a jar of ether. They stick him with pins to a corkboard.

"Sure, all right, why not?" Landsman says.

Shprintzl Rudashevsky fixes him a cold bottle of ginger ale. Landsman holds it to his temples, then takes a swallow, fighting it down with a sensation of medicinal virtue.

"I haven't sat this close to a strange man in forty-five years, Detective," Batsheva Shpilman says. "It's very wrong. I should be ashamed."

"Particularly given your choice of male companions," Landsman says.

"Do you mind?" She lowers the black moire, and her face is gone from the conversation. "I'll feel more comfortable."

"Suit yourself."

"Nu," she says. The veil puffs out with her breath. "All right. Yes, I wanted to talk to you."

"I wanted to talk to you, too."

"Why? Do you think that I killed my son?"

"No, ma'am, I don't. But I was hoping you might know who did."

"So!" she declares, a low thrill in her voice, as if she has caught Landsman out. "He was murdered."

"Uh, well, yes, he was, ma'am. Didn't— What did your husband tell you?"

"What my husband tells me," she says, making it sound rhetorical, like the title of a very slim tract. "You're married, Detective?"

"I was."

"The marriage failed?"

"I guess that's the best way to put it." He reflects for a moment. "I guess that's really the only way."

"My marriage is a complete success," she says without a trace of boastfulness or pride. "Do you understand what that means?"

"No, ma'am," Landsman says. "I'm not sure that I do."

"In every marriage, there are things," she begins. She shakes her head once, and the veil trembles. "One of my grandsons was at my house today, before the funeral. Nine years old. I put the television for him in the sewing room, you're not supposed to, but what does it matter, the little shkotz was bored. I sat with him ten minutes, watching. It was that cartoon program, the wolf that chases the blue rooster."

Landsman says that he knows it.

"Then you know," she says, "how that wolf can run in the middle of the air. He knows how to fly, but only so long as he still thinks he's touching the ground. As soon as he looks down, and sees where he is, and understands what's going on, then he falls and smashes into the ground."

"I've seen that bit," Landsman says.

"That's how it is in a successful marriage," says the rabbi's wife. "I have spent the last fifty years running in the middle of the air. Not looking down. Outside of what God requires, I never talk to my husband. Or vice versa."

"My parents had it worked out the same way," Landsman says. He wonders if he and Bina might have lasted longer if they had given this traditional route a try. "Only they didn't much trouble themselves over God's requirements."

"I heard about Mendel's death from my son-in-law, Aryeh. And that man never tells me anything but lies."

Landsman hears someone jumping up and down on a leather valise. It turns out to be the sound of Shprintzl Rudashevsky's laughter.

"Go on," Mrs. Shpilman says. "Please. Tell me."

"Go on. Nu. Your son was shot. In a way that— Well, to be frank, ma'am, he was executed." Landsman is glad for the veil when he pronounces that word. "Who by, that we can't say. We've learned that some men, two or three men, were looking for Mendel, asking around. These men might not have been very nice. That was a few months back. We know he was using heroin when he died. So, at the end, he felt nothing. No pain, I mean."

"Nothing, you mean," she corrects him. Two blots, blacker than black silk, spread across the veil. "Go on."

"I'm sorry, ma'am. About your son. I should have said that right off."

"I was relieved that you didn't."

"We think that whoever did this to him was better than amateur. But look, I admit it, since Friday morning we're getting more or less nowhere with our investigation of your son's death."

"You keep saying 'we,'" she says. "Meaning, naturally, Sitka Central."

Now he wishes he could see her eyes. Because he gets the

distinct idea that she is toying with him. That she knows he has no right or authority at his back.

"Not exactly," Landsman says.

"The Homicide division."

"No."

"You and your partner."

"Again, no."

"Well, then, maybe I'm confused," she says. "Who is this 'we' getting nowhere investigating my son's death?"

"At this point? I, hmm, it's sort of a theoretical inquiry."

"I see."

"By an independent entity."

"My son-in-law," she says, "claims that you have been suspended because you came by the island. Came by my house. You insulted my husband. You blamed him for being a bad father to Mendel. Aryeh told me that your badge has been taken away."

Landsman rolls the cool shaft of the ginger ale glass along his forehead. "Yes, well. This entity I'm talking about," he says. "So maybe they don't give out with badges."

"Only with theories."

"That's right."

"Such as?"

"Such as. All right, here's one: You were in occasional, maybe even regular, communication with Mendel. You heard from him. You knew where he was. He called you up every once in a while. He sent you postcards. Maybe you even saw him from time to time, on the sly. This secret ride home that you and Friend Rudashevsky are so kindly providing me, for example, it sort of gives me ideas in that direction."

"I have not seen my son, my Mendel, in over twenty years," she says. "Now I never will again."

"But why, Mrs. Shpilman? What happened? Why did he leave the Verbovers? What did he do? Was there a break? An argument?"

She doesn't answer for a minute, like she's fighting the long habit of saying nothing to anyone, let alone to a secular policeman, about Mendel. Or maybe she's fighting the mounting sense of pleasure she will take, in spite of herself, in remembering her son aloud.

"Such a match I made for him," she says.

25

A thousand guests, some from as far away as Miami Beach and Buenos Aires. Seven catering trailers and a Volvo truck stuffed with food and wine. Gifts, swag, and tributes in heaps to rival the Baranof Range. Three days of fasting and prayer. The entire Muzikant family of klezmorim, enough for half a symphony orchestra. Every last Rudashevsky, even the great-grandfather, half drunk and shooting off an ancient Nagant revolver into the air. For a week leading up to the day, a line of people in the hall, out the door, around the corner, and two blocks down Ringelblum Avenue, hoping for a blessing from the bridegroom king. All day and night a noise around the house like a mob in search of a revolution.

An hour before the wedding they were still there, waiting for him, hats and slick umbrellas in the street. He was not likely, this late, to see them or hear their pleas and sob stories. But you never knew. It was always Mendel's nature to make the unpredictable move.

She was at the window, peering through the curtains at the petitioners, when the girl came to say that Mendel was gone and that two ladies were here to see her. Mrs. Shpilman's bedroom overlooked the side yard, but she could see between the neighboring houses through to the corner: hats and umbrellas, slick with rain. Jews shouldered together, soaked in longing for a glimpse of Mendel.

Wedding day, funeral day.

"Gone," she said. She did not turn from the window. She had the sensation of mingled futility and fulfillment one feels in dreams. There was no point in asking the question, and yet it was the only thing she was able to say. "Gone where?"

"Nobody know, missus. Nobody see him since last night."

"Last night"

"This morning."

Last night she had presided at a forshpiel for the daughter of the Shtrakenzer rebbe. A brilliant match. A bride of talent and accomplishment, beautiful, with a fiery streak that Mendel's sisters lacked but which his mother knew her son admired in her. Of course, the Shtrakenzer bride, though perfect, was not suitable; Mrs. Shpilman knew that. Long before the maid came to say that nobody could find Mendel, that he had disappeared sometime in the course of the night, Mrs. Shpilman had known that no degree of accomplishment, beauty, or fire in a girl would ever suit her son. But there was always a shortfall, wasn't there? Between the match that the Holy One, blessed be He, envisioned and the reality of the situation under the chuppah. Between commandment and observance, heaven and earth, husband and wife, Zion and Jew. They called that shortfall "the world." Only when Messiah came would the breach be closed, all separations, distinctions, and distances collapsed. Until then, thanks be unto His Name, sparks, bright sparks, might leap across the gap, as between electric poles. And we must be grateful for their momentary light.

That was how she had planned, at least, to put it to Mendel, should he ever seek her counsel on the matter of his betrothal to the daughter of the Shtrakenzer rebbe.

"Your husband pretty angry," said the girl, Betty, a Filipina, like all the girls.

"What did he say?"

"He didn't say anything, missus. That how I know he's angry. Sending out lot of people looking every place. Calling the mayor."

Mrs. Shpilman turned from the window, the phrase *They were obliged to call off the wedding* metastasizing in her abdomen. Betty was gathering up wads of tissue paper from the Turkey carpet.

"What ladies?" Mrs. Shpilman said. "Who are they? Are they Verbovers?"

"One maybe. Other not. Only say they hoping to talk to you."

"Where are they?"

"Downstairs in your office. One lady all in black clothes, veil on her face. Look like maybe her husband just die."

Mrs. Shpilman can't remember anymore when the first hopeless men and terminal cases started to come around looking for Mendel. Possibly they came in secret at first, to the back door, encouraged by reports from one or the other of the housemaids. There was a maid whose womb had been made barren by a botched operation in Cebu when she was a girl. Mendel took one of those dolls he made his sisters from felt and a clothespin, pinned a crayoned blessing between its wooden legs, and slipped it into her pocket. Ten months after that, Remedios gave birth to a son. There was Dov-Ber Gursky, their driver, secretly ten thousand dollars in the wrong with a Russian finger-breaker. Mendel handed Gursky a five-dollar bill, unbidden, and said he hoped it might help. Two days later, a lawyer in St. Louis wrote to inform Gursky that he had just inherited half a million from an uncle he never knew. By the time of Mendel's bar mitzvah, the sick and dying, the bereft, the parents of damned children, they were getting to be a real pain in the neck. Coming around at any hour of the day or night. Wailing and begging. Mrs. Shpilman had taken steps to protect Mendel, setting hours and conditions. But the boy had a gift. And it was in the nature of a gift that it be endlessly given.

"I can't see them now," Mrs. Shpilman said, sitting down on her narrow bed, with its white candlewick bedspread and the pillows she had embroidered before Mendel was born. "These ladies of yours." Sometimes when they could not get to Mendel, the women would come to her, to the rebbetzin, and she would bless them as well as she could, with the little wherewithal she brought to the task. "I have to finish dressing. The wedding is in one hour, Betty. One hour! They'll find him."

She had been waiting for him to betray her for years, ever since she had first understood that he was what he was. Such a frightening word to a mother, with its implication of fragile bones, vulnerability to predators, nothing to protect the bird but its feathers. And flight. Of course flight. She had understood this about him long before he understood it himself. Breathed it in from the soft nape of his infant neck. Read it like a hidden text in the fuzzy knobs of his knees in short pants. A touch of girlishness in the way he lowered his eyes when others praised him. And then, as he got older, she could not fail to note, though he tried to conceal it, the way he grew uncomfortable, tongue-tied, seeming to bank his fire when a Rudashevsky or certain of his male cousins came into the room.

All through the making of the match, the betrothal, the planning for the wedding, she had been studying Mendele for signs of apprehension or unwillingness. But he remained true to his duty and her plans. Sarcastic at times, yes, even irreverent, mocking her for her steadfast belief that the Holy Name, blessed be He, spends His time like an old housewife making matches among the souls of the not-yet-born. Once he had snatched up a scrap of white tulle her daughters had left in the parlor, covered his head with it, and offered in a voice that was an uncanny imitation of his betrothed's an inventory of the physical shortcomings of Mendel Shpilman. Everyone laughed, but in her heart was a little bird flutter of dread. Apart from that moment, he appeared to remain as he had been, unstinting in his devotion to the 613 commandments, to the study of Torah and Talmud, to his parents, to the faithful for whom he was their star. Surely, even now, Mendel would be found.

She rolled up her stockings, put on her dress, straightened her slip. She put on the wig that she'd had made especially for the wedding at a cost of three thousand dollars. It was a masterpiece, ash blond with hints of red and gold, done up in braids like her own hair when she was a young woman. It was not until she had settled that shining snood of money onto her cropped pate that she began to panic.

On a deal table sat a black telephone with no dial. If she picked it up, an identical phone would ring in her husband's office. In ten years of living in this house, she had used it only three times, once in pain and twice in anger. Over the phone hung a framed photograph of her grandfather, the eighth rebbe, her grandmother, and her mother at the age of five or six, posed under a pasteboard willow, along the banks of a painted stream. Black clothes, the dreamy cloud of her grandfather's beard, over all the radiant ash of time that settled on the dead in old photos. Missing from the group was her mother's brother, whose name was a kind of curse so potent it must never be spoken. His apostasy, though notorious, remained unknown to her. All she understood was that it had begun with a hidden book called *The Mysterious Island*, discovered in a drawer, and culminated with a report of her uncle having been spotted on a street in Warsaw, beardless and wearing a straw boater more scandalous than any French novel.

She placed her hand on the receiver of the phone with no dial. Panic in her organs, panic in her teeth.

"I wouldn't answer if I could," her husband said from right behind her. "If you have to break the Sabbath, at least don't waste the sin."

Though he was not then so lunar as he became in later years, the sight of her husband standing in her bedroom was a cause for wonder, the advent of a second moon in the sky. He took a look around at the needlepoint chairs, the green valance, the white-satin blank of her bed, her bottles and jars. She saw him struggle to keep a mocking smile on his lips. But the expression he managed was something at once avid and repelled. It reminded her of the smile with which her husband had once received an embassy from some far-off court in Ethiopia or Yemen, a sloe-eyed rabbi in a gaudy kaftan. That impossible black rabbi with his outlandish Torah, the realm of women: They were divine whims, convolutions of God's thought, that it was almost a heresy to imagine or try to understand.

The longer he stood there, the less amused and the more lost he seemed to become. Finally, she was moved to pity. He did not belong here. It was a measure of the spreading stain of wrongness on this day that he had traveled so far on his embassy to this land of tasseled cushions and rosewater.

"Sit," she said. "Please."

Grateful, slow, he endangered a chair. "He will be found," he said, his voice soft and threatening.

She didn't like the look of him. Knowing that otherwise he might strike people as gross, he was ordinarily a man of tidy habits. But his hose were crooked now, his shirt misbuttoned. His cheeks were mottled with fatigue, and his whiskers strayed like he had been yanking at them.

"Excuse me, darling," she said. She opened the door to her dressing room and went inside. She despised the dark colors favored by Verbover women of her generation. The room into which she retreated was hung with indigo, deep purple, heliotrope. At a small vanity chair with a fringed skirt, she sat down. She reached out with a stockinged toe and closed the door, leaving a one-inch gap. "I hope you don't mind. It's better this way."

"He will be found," her husband repeated, more matter-of-fact now, trying to reassure her and not himself.

"He'd better be," she said. "So I can kill him."

"Calm yourself."

"I say that very calmly. Is he drunk? Was there drinking?"

"He was fasting. He was fine. Such a teaching he made us last night on Parshat Chayei Sarah. It was electric. A stopped heart would have begun beating again. But when he finished, there were tears on his face. He said he needed air. No one has seen him since."

"I'll kill him," she said.

There was no reply from the bedroom, only the rasp of breath, steady, implacable. She regretted the threat. It was rhetoric on her lips, but in his mind, that library in a bonepit, it took on a dangerous color of agency.

"Do you know, by any chance, where he is?" her husband said after a pause, and there was danger in the lightness of his tone.

"How would I know that?"

"He talks to you. He comes to see you here."

"Never."

"I know he does."

"How could you know that? Unless you have turned the maids into spies."

His silence confirmed the scope of her household's corruption. She felt a glorious seizure of resolve never to leave her dressing room again.

"I didn't come here to find an argument or to reproach you. On the contrary, I hoped that I might borrow a cup of your usual calm prudence. Now that I am here, I feel compelled, against my judgment as a rabbi and as a man, but with the full support of my understanding as a father, to reproach you."

"For what?"

"His aberration. The freakish streak. The twist in his soul. That is your fault. A son like that is the fruit of his mother's tree."

"Go to the window," she told him. "Look through the drape. See those poor suitors and fools and broken yids come to receive a blessing that you, you would never, in your power, in your learning, would never be able to bestow, honestly. Not that such an inability has ever hampered you, in the past, from offering it."

"I can bless in other ways."

"Look at them!"

"You look at them. Come out of that closet and look."

"I've seen them," she said through her teeth. "And they *all* have a twist in the soul."

"But they hide it. Out of modesty and humility and the fear of God, they clothe it. God commands us to cover our heads in His presence. Not to stand bareheaded."

She heard the scrape and creak of his chair leg and the shuffle of his feet in their slippers. She heard the wrecked joint of his left hip crack and snap. He grunted in pain.

"That is all I ask of Mendel," he continued. "What a man may think, what he feels, these have no interest, no relevance to me, or to God. It doesn't matter to the wind whether a flag is red or it's blue."

"Or pink."

There was another silence. This one carried a lighter charge somehow, as if he was coming to a conclusion or remembering how it might have felt at one time to find amusement in her little joke.

"I will find him," he said. "I will sit him down and tell him what I know. Explain to him that as long as he obeys God and His commandments and gives righteously, there is a place for him here. That I will not turn my back to him first. That the choice lies with him to abandon us."

"Can a man be a Tzaddik Ha-Dor but live hidden from himself and everyone around him?"

"A Tzaddik Ha-Dor is always hidden. That's a mark of his nature. Maybe I should explain that to him. Tell him that these— feelings—he experiences and struggles against are, in a way, the proof of his fitness to rule."

"Maybe he isn't running away from marriage to this girl," she said. "Maybe that isn't what frightens him. What he can't live with." The sentence she had never spoken to her husband took up its usual station at the tip of her tongue. She had been composing and refining and abandoning elements of it in her mind for the past forty years, like the stanzas of a poem written by a prisoner denied the use of paper and pen. "Maybe there is another kind of self-deception he can't reconcile himself to living with."

"He has no choice," her husband said. "Even if he has fallen into unbelief. Even if in staying here, he risks hypocrisy or cant. A man with his talents, his gifts, cannot be allowed to move and work and hazard his fortune out there in that unclean world. He would be a danger to everyone. In particular to himself."

"That wasn't the self-deception I meant. I meant the kind that—that Verbovers all engage in."

Silence then, ominous, neither heavy nor light, the vast silence of a dirigible before the static spark.

"I'm not aware," he said, "of any others that confront him."

She let her sentence drop; she had been running in the air for too long by then to look down for more than a second.

"So he must be held here, then," she said. "With or without his consent."

"Believe me, my dear. And do not mistake me. The alternative would be something far worse."

She reeled a moment, then rushed from her dressing room to see what was in his eyes when he threatened the life of his own son, as she construed it, for the sin of being what God had pleased to make him. But, silent as a dirigible, he had sailed. Instead, she found only Betty, back to renew the visitors' appeal. Betty was a good servant, but she had the Filipino knack for taking intense pleasure in scandal. She had a hard time concealing her delight in the news she brought.

"One lady, missus, say she bringing a message from Mendel," Betty said. "Say, sorry, he's not coming home. No wedding today!"

"He's coming home," Mrs. Shpilman said, fighting the wish to slap Betty's face. "Mendel would never . . ." She stopped herself before she could say the words: *Mendel would never leave without saying goodbye.*

The woman bearing a message from her son was not a Verbover. She was a modern Jewess, dressed modestly out of respect for the neighborhood in a long patterned skirt and a stylish dark cloak. Ten or fifteen years older than Mrs. Shpilman. A dark-eyed, dark-haired woman who at one time must have been very beautiful. She jumped up from the wing chair by the window when Mrs. Shpilman came in, and gave her name as Brukh. Her friend was a plump thing, pious by the look of her, perhaps Satmar, in a long black dress with black stockings and a broad-brimmed hat pulled down over an inferior shaydl. Her stockings bagged, and the rhinestone buckle on her hatband, poor thing, was coming unglued. The veil bunched at the upper left in a way that struck Mrs. Shpilman as piteous. Looking at this bereft creature, she forgot for a moment the awful news that had brought the two women to her house. A blessing welled up inside of her with a force so urgent she could barely contain it. She wanted to take the shabby woman in her arms and kiss her in a way that lasted, that burned sadness away. She wondered if that was how it felt to be Mendel all the time.

"What is this nonsense?" she said. "Sit down."

"I'm very sorry, Mrs. Shpilman," said the Brukh woman, resuming her seat, perched on the edge as if to show that she did not plan to stay.

"Have you seen Mendel?"

"Yes."

"And where is he?"

"He's staying with a friend. He won't be there for long."

"He's coming back."

"No. No, I'm sorry, Mrs. Shpilman. But you will be able to reach Mendel through this person. Whenever you need to. Wherever he goes."

"What person, tell me? Who is this friend?"

"If I tell you, you have to promise to keep the information to yourself. Otherwise, Mendel says"—she glanced at her friend as if hoping for some moral support to get past the next seven words—"you will never hear from him again."

"But my dear, I never *want* to hear from him again," Mrs. Shpilman said. "So there's really no point in telling me where he is, is there?"

"I suppose not."

"Only that if you don't tell me where he is, and no nonsense, I will have you sent over to Rudashevsky's Garage and let them get the information out of you the way they like to do it."

"Oh, now, I'm not afraid of you," said the Brukh woman with an astonishing hint of a smile in her voice.

"No? And why is that?"

"Because Mendel told me not to be."

She could feel the reassurance, catch the echo of it in the Brukh woman's voice and manner. An air of teasing, of the playfulness that Mendel imposed on all of his dealings with his mother, and with his dread father, too. Mrs. Shpilman had always thought of it as a devil inside of him, but now she saw that it might be simply a means of survival, protection. Feathers for the little bird.

"He's a fine one to talk about not being afraid. Running away from his duty and his family like this. Why doesn't he work some of that magic of his on himself? Tell me that. Drag his pitiful, cowardly self back here and spare his family a world of disgrace and embarrassment, not to mention a beautiful, innocent girl."

"He would if he could," the Brukh woman said, and the widow beside her, who had said nothing, heaved a sigh. "I really do believe that, Mrs. Shpilman."

"And why can't he? Tell me that."

"You know."

"I don't know anything."

But she did know. Apparently, so did these two strange women who had come to watch her cry. Mrs. Shpilman dropped into a white-

painted Louis XIV chair with a needlepoint cushion, heedless of
creases that this sudden plunge made in the silk of her dress. She
covered her face with her hands and cried. For the shame and the
indignity. For the ruination of months, and years, of planning
and hopes and discussion, the endless embassies and back-and-
forth between the courts of Verbov and Shtrakenz. But mostly,
she confesses, she cried for herself. Because she had determined
with her customary resolve that she would never see her only,
beloved, rotten son again.

What a selfish woman! It was only later that she thought to
spare a moment's regret for the world that Mendel would never
redeem.

After Mrs. Shpilman had been crying for a minute or two, the
frumpy widow rose from the other wing chair and came to stand
beside her.

"Please," she said in a heavy voice, and put a plump hand on
Mrs. Shpilman's arm, a hand whose knuckles were covered in fine
golden hair. It was hard to believe that only twenty years ago, Mrs.
Shpilman had been able to fit the entire thing into her mouth.

"You're playing games," Mrs. Shpilman said, once she had
regained the power of rational thought. In the wake of the initial
shock, which stopped her heart, she felt a strange sense of relief.
If Mendel was nine layers deep, then eight of those layers were
pure goodness. Goodness far better than she and her husband,
hard people who had survived and prospered in a hard world, could
have engendered from their own flesh without some kind of divine
intercession. But the innermost layer, the ninth layer of Mendel
Shpilman, was and always had been a devil, a shkotz that liked to
give heart attacks to his mother. "You're playing games!"

"No."

He lifted the veil and let her see the pain, the uncertainty. She
saw that he feared he was making a grave mistake. She recognized as
her own the determination with which he was willing to make it.

"No, Mama," Mendel said. "I came to say goodbye." Then, reading the expression on her face, with a shaky smile: "And no, I'm not a transvestite."

"Aren't you?"

"No!"

"You look like a transvestite to me."

"A noted expert."

"I want you out of this house." But she only wanted him to stay, hidden on her side of the house, dressed in that frumpy rag, her baby, her princeling, her devilish boy.

"I'm going."

"I never want to see you again. I don't want to call you, I don't want you to call me. I don't want to know where you are."

She had only to summon her husband, and Mendel would stay. In some way that was no more unthinkable than the underlying facts of her comfortable life, they would make him stay.

"All right, Mama," he said.

"Don't call me that."

"All right, Mrs. Shpilman," he said, and in his mouth it sounded affectionate, familiar. She started to cry again. "But just so you know. I'm staying with a friend."

Was there a lover? Was it possible for him to have led a life so secret?

"A 'friend'?" she said.

"An old friend. He's just helping me. Mrs. Brukh here is helping me, too."

"Mendel saved my life," said Mrs. Brukh. "Once upon a time."

"Big deal," said Mrs. Shpilman. "So he saved your life. A lot of good it did him."

"Mrs. Shpilman," said Mendel. He took her hands and clasped them tightly between his own warm palms. His skin burned two degrees hotter than everyone else's. When you took his temperature, the thermometer read 100.6.

"Get your hands off me," she managed to say. "Now."

He kissed her on the top of the head, and even through the layer of alien hair, the imprint of that kiss seemed to linger. Then he let go of her hands, lowered his veil, and lumbered out of the room, hose sagging, with the Brukh woman hurrying out behind him.

Mrs. Shpilman sat in the Louis XIV chair for a long time, hours, years. A coldness filled her, an icy disgust for Creation, for God and His misbegotten works. At first the horror she felt seemed to bear upon her son and the sin that he was refusing to surrender, but then it turned into a horror for herself. She considered the crimes and hurts that had been committed to her benefit, and all of that evil only a drop of water in a great black sea. An awful place, this sea, this gulf between the Intention and the Act that people called "the world." Mendel's flight was not a refusal to surrender; it was a surrender. The Tzaddik Ha-Dor was tendering his resignation. He could not be what that world and its Jews, in the rain with their heartaches and their umbrellas, wanted him to be, what his mother and father wanted him to be. He could not even be what he wanted himself to be. She hoped—sitting there, she prayed—that one day, at least, he might find a way to be what he was.

As soon as the prayer flew upward from her heart, she missed her son. She longed for her son. She reproached herself bitterly for having sent Mendel away without first finding out where he was staying, where he would go, how she could see him or hear his voice from time to time. Then she opened the hands he had enfolded a last time in his, and found, curled in her right palm, a tiny length of string.

26

Yes," she says, "I heard from him. From time to time. I don't want this to sound cynical, Detective, but it was usually when he was in trouble or needed money. Circumstances that, in Mendel's case, may his name be for a blessing, tended to coincide."

"When was the last time?"

"Earlier this year. Last spring. Yes, I remember it was the day before Erev Pesach."

"So, April. Around—"

The lady Rudashevsky takes out a fancy Shoyfer Mazik, starts pressing buttons, and comes up with the date of the day preceding the first evening of Passover. Landsman remarks, a little startled, that it was also the last full day of his sister's life.

"Where was he calling from?"

"Maybe a hospital. I don't know. I could hear a public address, a loudspeaker, in the background. Mendel said he was going to disappear. That he had to disappear for a while, that he wouldn't be able to call. He asked me to send money to a box down in Povorotny that he sometimes used."

"Did he sound afraid?"

The veil trembles like a theater curtain, secret motions taking place on its other side. She nods slowly.

"Did he say why he needed to disappear? Did he say somebody was after him?"

"I don't think so. No. Just that he needed money and he was going to disappear."

"And that's it."

"As far as I— No. Yes. I asked him if he was eating. He sometimes— They forget to eat."

"I know it."

"And he told me, 'Don't worry,' he says, 'I just ate a whole big piece of cherry pie.'"

"Pie," Landsman says. "Cherry pie."

"Does that mean something to you?"

"You never know," he says, but he can feel his rib cage ringing under the mallet of his heart. "Mrs. Shpilman, you said you heard a loudspeaker. Do you think he might have been calling from an airport?"

"Now that you mention it, yes."

The car slows and stops. Landsman sits forward and looks out through the smoked glass. They're in front of the Hotel Zamenhof. Mrs. Shpilman drops her window with a button, and the gray afternoon blows into the car. She raises the veil and peers up at the face of the hotel. She stares at it for a long time. A pair of seedy men, alcoholics, one of whom Landsman once prevented from accidentally urinating into the other's trouser cuff, stagger out of the hotel's lobby slung against each other, a human lean-to thrown up against the rain. They put on a vaudeville with a sheet of newspaper and the wind, then lurch off into the night, a couple of tattered moths. The queen of Verbov Island lowers the veil again and puts her window up. Landsman can feel the reproachful questions burning through the black tissue. How can he stand to live in such a dump? Why didn't he do a better job of protecting her son?

"Who told you that I lived here?" he thinks to ask her. "Your son-in-law?"

"No, he didn't mention it. I heard about it from the other Detective Landsman. The one you used to be married to."

"She told you about me?"

"She telephoned today. Once, many years ago, we had some trouble with a man who was hurting women. A very bad man, a sick man. This was back in the Harkavy, on S. Ansky Street. The women who had been hurt didn't want to talk to the police. Your ex-wife was very helpful to me then, and I'm still in her debt. She is a good woman. A good policewoman."

"No doubt about it."

"She suggested to me that if you happened to come around, I wouldn't be entirely mistaken in putting some confidence in you."

"That was nice of her," Landsman says with perfect sincerity.

"She spoke more highly of you than I would have imagined."

"Like you said, ma'am. She's a good woman."

"But you left her anyway."

"Not because she was a good woman."

"Because you were a bad man?"

"I think I was," Landsman says. "She was too polite to say so."

"It has been many years," Mrs. Shpilman says. "But as I recall, politeness was not a great strength of that Jewess." She pushes the button that unlocks the door. Landsman opens the door and climbs down from the back of the limousine. "At any rate, I'm glad that I hadn't seen this dreadful hotel before now, or I never would have let you anywhere near me."

"It's not much," Landsman says, rain pattering the brim of his hat. "But it's home."

"No, it isn't," Batsheva Shpilman says. "But I'm sure it makes it easier for you to think so."

27

"Γhe Yiddish Policemen's Union,'" says the pie man.

He peers at Landsman across the steel counter of his shop, crossing his arms to show that he is wise to the stratagems of Jews. He narrows his eyes as if he's trying to spot a typographical error on the face of a counterfeit Rolex. Landsman's American is just good enough to make him sound suspect.

"That's right," Landsman says. He wishes there weren't a corner missing from his membership card in the Sitka chapter of the Hands of Esau, the international fraternal organization of Jewish policemen. It has a six-point shield in one corner. Its text is printed in Yiddish. It carries no authority or weight, not even with Landsman, a member in good standing for twenty years. "We're all over the world."

"That doesn't surprise me one bit," the pie man says with a show of asperity. "But, mister, I only serve pie."

"Are you eating pie or aren't you?" says the pie man's wife. Like her husband, she is ample and pale. Her hair is the colorless color of a sheet of foil under a wan light. The daughter is in the back among the berries and the crusts. To the bush pilots, hunters, rescue crews, and other regulars who frequent the airfield at Yakovy, it's considered a piece of luck to spot the pie man's daughter. Landsman hasn't seen her for years. "If you don't want any pie, there is no earthly reason to be wasting your time at this window. People behind you have planes to catch."

She takes the card from her husband and hands it back to Landsman. He does not blame her for her rudeness. The Yakovy airfield is a key station on the northern route of the world's shysters, charlatans, grift doctors, and real estate hacks. Poachers, smugglers, wayward Russians. Drug mules, Native criminals, Yankee hard cases. The Yakovy jurisdiction has never quite been defined. Jews, Indians, and Klondikes all make their claims. Her pie has greater moral character than half her clientele. The pie lady has no reason to trust or to coddle Landsman, with his gimcrack card and a shaved patch on the back of his head. Still, her rudeness gives him a sharp pang of regret for the loss of his badge. If Landsman had a badge, he would say, *The people behind me can go fuck themselves, lady, and you can give yourself a nice thick boysenberry high colonic*. Instead, he makes a show of considering the individuals gathered in a moderately long line behind him. Fisherman, kayakers, small businessmen, some corporate types.

Each of them comes up with a noise or bit of eyebrow semaphore to show that he is eager for pie and losing patience with Landsman and his dog-eared credentials.

"I will have a piece of the apple crumble," Landsman says. "Of which I have fond memories."

"The crumble is my favorite," says the wife, softening a little. She sends her husband to the back counter with a nod. The crumble is there on a gleaming pedestal, a fresh one, uncut. "Coffee?"

"Yes, please."

"À la mode?"

"No, thanks." Landsman slides the photograph of Mendel Shpilman across the counter. "What about you? Ever seen him?"

The woman eyes the photo with each hand tucked carefully

into the opposite armpit. Landsman gauges that she recognizes
Shpilman right away. Then she turns to take from her husband a
paper plate laden with a slice of crumble. She sets it on a tray with
a small Styrofoam cup of coffee and a plastic fork rolled up in a
paper napkin.

"Two-fifty," she says. "Go sit by the bear."

The bear was shot by yids of the sixties. Doctors, from the
look of them, in ski caps and Pendletons. They brim with the
odd, bespectacled manliness of that golden period in the history
of the District of Sitka. A card, typed in Yiddish and American,
is pinned to the wall underneath the photograph of the fatal five
men. It says that the bear, shot near Lisianski, was a 3.7-meter,
four-hundred-kilo brown. Only its skeleton is preserved inside
the glass case beside which Landsman sits down with his slice of
apple crumble and his cup of coffee. He has sat here many times
in the past, contemplating this terrible ivory xylophone over a
piece of pie. Most recently, he sat here with his sister, maybe a
year before she died. He was working the Gorsetmacher case. She
had just dropped off a party of fishermen coming in from the
bush.

Landsman thinks about Naomi. It is a luxury, like a slice of pie.
It is as dangerous and welcome as a drink. He invents dialogue for
Naomi, the words with which she might mock and ridicule him
if she were here. For his sanguinary roll in the snow with those
Zilberblat idiots. For drinking ginger ale with a pious old lady
in the back of that hypertrophied four-by-four. For thinking he
could outlast his drinking problem and stay hyped long enough
to find the killer of Mendel Shpilman. For the loss of his badge.
For lacking the necessary outrage about Reversion, for having no
stance toward it. Naomi claimed that she hated Jews for their meek
submission to fate, for the trust they put in God or the gentiles.
But then Naomi had a stance toward everything. She policed and
maintained her stances; buffed and curated them. She would also,

Landsman thinks, have criticized his choice not to take his pie à la mode.

"The Yiddish Policemen's Union," says the pie man's daughter, sitting down on the bench beside Landsman. She has taken off her apron and washed her hands. Above the elbows, her freckled arms are dusted with flour. There is flour in her blond eyebrows. She wears her hair tied back in a black elastic. She is a hauntingly plain woman with watery blue eyes, about Landsman's age. She gives off a smell of butter, tobacco, and a sour tang of dough that he finds weirdly erotic. She lights a menthol cigarette and sends a jet of smoke toward him. "That's a new one."

She tucks the cigarette into her mouth and holds out her hand to take the membership card. She pretends not to struggle with its text. "I can read Yiddish, you know," she says finally. "It's not like it's fucking Aztec or whatever."

"I really am a policeman," Landsman says. "I'm just making a private inquiry today. That is why I don't use the badge."

"Show me the picture," she says. Landsman hands her the mug shot of Mendel Shpilman. She nods, and the carapace of her weariness splits along a momentary seam.

"Miss, you knew him?"

She hands back the mug shot. Shakes her head, makes a dismissive frown. "What happened to him?" she says.

"He was murdered," Landsman says. "Shot in the head."

"That's harsh," she says. "Oh, Jesus."

Landsman takes a fresh package of tissues from the pocket of his overcoat and passes them to her. She blows her nose and then balls up the tissue in her fist.

"How did you know him?" Landsman says.

"I gave him a ride," she says. "One time. That's it."

"To where?"

"A motel down on Route Three. I liked him. He was funny. He was sweet. Kind of homely. Kind of a mess. He told me he had a, you know, a problem. With drugs. But that he was trying to get better. He seemed— He just had this way about him."

"Comforting?"

"Mm. No. He was just, uh, really, I don't know. Really *there*. For like an hour, I thought I was in love with him."

"But you weren't really?"

"I guess I never really got the chance to find out."

"Did you have sex with him?"

"You're a cop, all right," she says. "A 'noz,' isn't that it?"

"That's right."

"No, I didn't have sex with him. I wanted to. I invited myself into the motel room with him. I guess I kind of, like, you know. Threw myself at him. That's no reflection on him. Like I said, he was super nice and all, but he was a mess. His teeth. Anyway, I guess he picked up on it."

"Picked up on what?"

"That I— I have a little bit of a problem, too. When I get around men. That's why I don't really basically get around them a lot. Don't get any ideas, I don't like you at all."

"No, ma'am."

"I did therapy, twelve-step. I got born again. The only thing that really helped was baking pies."

"No wonder they're so good."

"Ha."

"He didn't take you up on your offer."

"He wouldn't. He was very sweet. He buttoned up my shirt. I felt like a little girl. Then he gave me something. Something he said that I could keep."

"What was that?"

She lowers her gaze, and blood colors her face so deeply, Landsman can almost hear the hum of it. Her next words come out thick and whispery.

"His blessing," she says. Then, more clearly, "He said he was giving me his blessing."

"I'm fairly certain he was gay," Landsman says. "By the way."

"I know," she says. "He told me. He didn't use that word. He didn't really use any word, or if he did, I don't remember it. I think what he said, it was that he didn't care to *bother with it* anymore. He said heroin was simpler and more reliable. Heroin and checkers."

"Chess. He played chess."

"Whatever. I still got his blessing, right?"

She seems to need the answer to this question to be yes.

"Yes," Landsman says.

"Funny little Jew. The freaky thing is, I don't know. It kind of like, worked."

"What worked?"

"The blessing. I mean, I have a boyfriend now. A real one. We're totally dating, it's very strange."

"I'm happy for you both," Landsman says, feeling a stab of envy of her, of all these people who were lucky enough to have Mendel Shpilman lay a blessing on them. He thinks of all the times he must have walked right past Mendel, all the chances that he missed. "So, you're saying, when you gave him the ride to the motel, it was just a, well, a pickup. It was just because you—you were planning to, you know."

"Jump his bones? No." She steps on the cigarette with the toe of her sheepskin boot. "It was a favor. For a friend of mine. Driving him, I mean. She knew the guy. Frank, she called him. She flew him in here from somewhere. She was a pilot. She asked me to give him a lift, help him find a place to stay. Someplace low to the ground, she said. So, whatever, I said I would."

"Naomi," Landsman says. "That was your friend?"

"Uh-huh. You knew her?"

"I know how much she liked pie," Landsman says. "This Frank, he was a client of hers?"

"I guess so. I don't really know. I didn't ask. But they flew in here together. He must have hired her. You could probably find that out with that fancy card you're carrying."

Landsman feels a numbness enter his limbs, a welcome numbness, a sense of doom that is indistinguishable from peacefulness, like the bite of a predator snake that prefers to swallow its victims alive and tranquil. The pie man's daughter inclines her head toward the untouched slice of apple crumble on the paper plate, taking up the empty space between them on the bench.

"You are *so* hurting my feelings," she says.

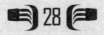 28

In every picture of them taken during a long stretch of their childhood, Landsman is posed with his arm slung around his sister's shoulders. In the early ones, the top of her head reaches to just above his belly. In the last such picture, there is a phantom mustache on Landsman's upper lip, and he has the advantage of an inch, maybe two. The first time you spotted the trend in the pictures, it seemed cute: a big brother looking out for his kid sister. Seven or eight pictures in, the protective gesture took on a menacing air. After a dozen, you started to worry about those Landsman kids. Huddled together, bravely smiling for the camera, like deserving children in the adoption column of a newspaper.

"Orphaned by tragedy," Naomi said one night, turning the pages of an old album. The pages were waxed board covered with a crinkly sheet of polyurethane to hold the photos down. The layer of plastic gave the family depicted in the album a preserved quality, as if it had been bagged like evidence. "Two lovable moppets looking for a home."

"Only Freydl wasn't dead yet," Landsman said, knowing he was handing her a fat straight-line. Their mother had died after a brief, bitter struggle against cancer, having lived just long enough for Naomi to break her heart by dropping out of college.

Naomi said, "Now you tell me."

Lately, when he looks at these pictures, Landsman sees himself as trying to hold his sister down, to keep her from flying off and crashing into a mountain.

Naomi was a tough kid, so much tougher than Landsman ever needed to be. She was two years younger, close enough for everything Landsman did or said to constitute a mark that must be surpassed or a theory to disprove. She was boyish as a girl and mannish as a woman. When some drunken fool asked if she was a lesbian, she would say, "In everything but sexual preference."

It was from an early boyfriend that she had caught the itch to fly. Landsman never asked her what the attraction was, why she had worked so long and hard to get her commercial license and crash the homoidiotic world of male bush pilots. She was not one for pointless speculation, his dashing sister. But as Landsman understands it, the wings of an airplane are engaged in a constant battle with the air that envelops them, denting and baffling and warping it, bending and staving it off. Fighting it the way a salmon fights against the current of the river in which it's going to die. Like a salmon—that aquatic Zionist, forever dreaming of its fatal home—Naomi used up her strength and energy in struggle.

Not that this effort ever showed in her forthright manner, her cocky bearing, her smile. She had the Errol Flynn style of keeping a straight face only when she was joking, and grinning like a jackpot winner whenever things got rough. Slap a pencil mustache on the Jewess, and you could have sent her swinging from the rigging of a three-master, sword in hand. She was not complicated, Landsman's little sister, and in that respect, she was unique among the women of his acquaintance.

"She was a fucking loon," says the air traffic manager of the Flight Service Station at the Yakovy airport. He's Larry Spiro, a skinny, stoop-shouldered Jew from Short Hills, New Jersey. A mexican, as the Sitka Jews call their southern cousins; mexicans call the Sitka Jews icebergers, or "the frozen Chosen." Spiro's thick

eyeglasses correct for astigmatism, and behind them, his eyes have
a skeptical wobble. Wiry gray hair stands out all over his head, like
beams of outrage in a newspaper cartoon. He wears a white oxford
shirt with his monogram on the pocket and a red necktie striped
with gold. Slowly, anticipating the shot of whiskey in front of him,
he pushes back his sleeves. His teeth are the color of the collar of
his shirt.

"Christ." Like most mexicans working in the District, Spiro
clings fiercely to American. For an East Coast Jew, the District of
Sitka constitutes the exile of exiles, Hatzeplatz, the back half acre
of nowhere. To speak American for a Jew like Spiro is to keep himself
living in the real world, to promise himself that he's going back soon.
He smiles. "I never saw a woman get into so much trouble."

They are sitting in the lounge of Ernie's Skagway Bar and Grill,
in the low aluminum slab that was the terminal building back when
this was just an airfield at the edge of the bush. They are in a booth
at the rear, waiting for their steaks. Ernie's Skagway is regarded by
many as offering the only decent steak dinner between Anchorage
and Vancouver. Ernie flies them in from Canada every day, bloody
and packed in ice. The decor is minimal as a snack bar's, vinyl and
laminate and steel. The plates are plastic, the napkins crinkly as the
paper on a doctor's table. You order your food at a counter and sit
down with a number on a spindle. The waitresses are renowned for
their advanced age, ill humor, and physical resemblance to the cabs
of long-haul trucks. All the atmosphere in the place is the product
of its liquor license and its clientele: pilots, hunters and fishermen,
and the usual Yakovy mix of shtarkers and sub rosa operators. On
a Friday night in season, you can buy or sell anything from moose
meat to ketamine, and hear some of the most arrant lies ever put
to language.

At six o'clock on a Monday evening, it's mostly airport staff and
a few loose pilots holding up the bar. Quiet Jews, hard workers, men
in knit neckties, and one American bush pilot, half fluent in Yiddish,
making the claim that he once flew three hundred miles without

realizing he was upside down. The bar itself is an incongruous behemoth, oak, mock Victorian, salvaged from the failure of a cowboy-themed American steak house franchise down in Sitka.

"Trouble," Landsman says. "Right up to the end."

Spiro frowns. He was the manager on duty at Yakovy when Naomi's plane flew into Mount Dunkelblum. There was nothing Spiro could have done to prevent the crash, but the subject is painful to him. He zips open his nylon briefcase and pulls out a thick blue folder. It contains a thick document clipped with a heavy clip and several loose sheets.

"I glanced at the summary again," he says in a somber tone. "The weather was decent. Her plane was a little overdue for service. Her final communication was routine."

"Mm," says Landsman.

"Were you looking for something new?" Spiro's tone is not quite pitying but prepared to turn that way if necessary.

"I don't know, Spiro. I'm just looking."

Landsman takes the folder, and pages quickly through the thick document—a copy of the FAA investigator's final determination—then sets it aside and picks up one of the loose sheets underneath.

"That's the flight plan you were asking about. For the morning before the crash."

Landsman studies the form, which affirms the intention of pilot Naomi Landsman to fly her Piper Super Cub from Peril Strait, Alaska, to Yakovy, D.S., carrying one passenger. The form looks like a computer printout, its blanks neatly filled in twelve-point Times Roman.

"So she phoned this one in, is that it?" Landsman checks the time stamp. "That morning at five-thirty."

"She used the automated system, yes. Most people do."

"Peril Strait," Landsman says. "That's where? Out by Tenakee, right?"

"South of there."

"So, we're talking about a what—a two-hour flight from there to here?"

"More or less."

"I guess she was feeling optimistic," Landsman says. "She put her arrival time at a quarter past six. Forty-five minutes from the time the thing was filed."

Spiro has the kind of mind that is drawn to and repelled by anomaly. He takes the folder from Landsman and turns it around. He pages through the stack of documents that he collected and copied after agreeing to let Landsman buy him a steak.

"She *did* arrive at a quarter past six," he says. "It's noted right here in the AFSS log. Six-seventeen."

"So either— Let me get this straight. Either she made the two-hour hop from Peril Strait to Yakovy in less than forty-five minutes," Landsman says, "or else . . . Or else she changed her flight plan to come to Yakovy, when she was already en route and heading someplace else."

The steaks come; the waitress takes away their number on its pole and leaves their thick slabs of Canadian beef. They smell good and they look good. Spiro ignores them. He has forgotten his drink. He sifts through the pile of pages.

"Okay, here's the day before. She flew from Sitka to Peril Strait with three passengers. She took off at four and closed out her flight plan at six-thirty. Okay, so then it's dark when they get there. She's planning to stay overnight. Then the next morning . . ." Spiro stops. "Huh."

"What?"

"Here's— I'm guessing this was her *original* flight plan. Looks like she was planning to go back to *Sitka* the next morning. Originally. Not to come here to Yakovy."

"With how many passengers?"

"None."

"After she's been flying a while, supposedly headed for Sitka, and alone but actually with a mystery passenger on board, she suddenly switches her destination to Yakovy."

"That's how it looks."

"Peril Strait," Landsman says. "What's in Peril Strait?"

"What's anywhere? Moose, bears. Deer. Fish. Anything a Jew wants to kill."

"I don't think so," Landsman says. "I don't think this was a fishing trip."

Spiro frowns, then gets up and goes over to the bar. He sidles up to the American pilot, and they converse. The pilot looks wary, perhaps constitutionally so. But he nods and follows Spiro back to the booth.

"Rocky Kitka," Spiro says. "Detective Landsman." Then he sits down and takes care of his steak.

Kitka has on black leather jeans and a matching vest worn over his bare skin, which is covered from wrists to throat to the waistband of his pants in Native-themed tattooing. Big-toothed whales and beavers and, down his left biceps, a snake or an eel with a sly expression in its eye.

"You're a pilot?" Landsman says.

"No, I'm a policeman." He laughs with a touching sincerity at his own display of wit.

"Peril Strait," Landsman says. "You've been there?"

Kitka shakes his head, but Landsman disbelieves him at once.

"Know anything about the place?"

"Just the way it looks from the sky."

"Kitka," Landsman says. "That's a Native name."

"My father's Tlingit. My mother's Scotch-Irish and German and Swedish. Pretty much everything in there but Jew."

"Lot of Natives at Peril Strait?"

"Nothing but." Kitka says it with simple authority, then recalls his claim not to know anything about Peril Strait, and his eyes slide away from Landsman's, lighting on the steak. He looks extremely hungry.

"No white people?"

"One or two, maybe, tucked away back in the coves."

"And Jews?" Landsman says.

Kitka gets a hard look in his eye, a protective look. "Like I said. I just know it to fly past."

"I'm making a little investigation," Landsman says. "It turns out there might be something over there to interest a Jew from Sitka."

"That's *Alaska* over there," Kitka says. "A Jewish cop, with all due respect, he can ask questions all day long in that neighborhood, isn't nobody has to answer them."

Landsman slides over in the booth. "Come on, sweetness," he says in Yiddish. "Stop looking at it. It's yours. I didn't touch it."

"You aren't going to eat it?"

"I have no appetite, I don't know why."

"It's the New York, isn't it? I love the New York."

Kitka sits down, and Landsman slides the plate toward him. He drinks his cup of coffee and watches the two men destroy their dinners. Kitka looks much happier when he's done, less wary, less fearful of being set up.

"Shit, that is good meat," he says. He takes a long swallow of ice water from a red plastic schooner. He looks at Spiro, then away, then back at Landsman, then away again. He stares into the water glass. "Price of a meal," he says bitterly. Then: "They got some kind of honor ranch. I hear. For religious Jews that get hooked on drugs and whatnot. I guess even those beards of yours, they get into the drugs and the drinking and the petty crime."

"That makes sense, they'd want to put it someplace out of the way," Spiro says. "There's a lot of shame involved."

"I don't know," Landsman says. "It's not easy to get permission to start a Jewish business of any kind on the other side of the Line. Not even a do-good business like that."

"Like I said," Kitka says. "I just heard a few things. Probably it's bullshit."

"Weird," says Spiro. He's in the world of the dossier again, flipping back and forth among the pages.

Landsman says, "Tell me what's weird."

"Well, I'm looking through all this, and you know what I don't see? I don't see her flight plan for—for the fatal one. Yakovy back to Sitka." He takes out his Shoyfer and hits two keys and waits. "I know she filed one. I remember seeing it. Bella? Spiro. Are you busy? Uh-huh. Okay. Listen. Can you check something for me? I need you to pull a flight plan from the system." He gives the on-duty manager Naomi's name and the date and time of her final flight. "Can you run that? Yeah."

"Did you know my sister, Mr. Kitka?" Landsman says.

"You might say that," Kitka says. "She kicked my ass one time."

"Join the club," Landsman says.

"That can't be," Spiro says, his voice tight. "Could you check again?"

Now no one says anything. They just watch Spiro listening to Bella at the other end of the line.

"Something's not right, Bella," Spiro says finally. "I'm coming back over there."

He hangs up, looking as if his fine steak has begun to disagree with him.

"What is it?" Landsman says. "What's the matter?"

"She can't find the flight plan in the system." He stands up and gathers together the scattered pages of Naomi's file. "But I know that can't be right, because it's referenced by number right here in the crash report." He stops. "Or not."

Again he bats back and forth the pages of the thick clipped sheaf of close-typed pages that comprise the results of the FAA investigation into Naomi's fatal encounter with the northwest slope of Mount Dunkelblum.

"Somebody's been in this file," he says at last, unwillingly at first, his mouth a slit. As the conclusion spreads through his mind, he relaxes into it. Goes slack. "Somebody with weight."

"Weight," Landsman says. "The kind of weight it takes, for example, to get permission to build a Jewish rehab center on BIA land?"

"Too much weight for me," Spiro says. He slams the cover of the file shut, stuffs it under his arm. "I can't be here with you anymore, Landsman. I'm sorry. Thanks for the steak dinner."

After he goes, Landsman takes out his cell phone and dials a number in the Alaskan area code. When the woman on the other end answers, he says, "Wilfred Dick."

"Holy Jesus," Kitka says. "Look out."

But Landsman gets only a desk sergeant.

"The inspector ain't here," the sergeant says. "What's this about?"

"Maybe you heard something, I don't know, about some honor ranch out at Peril Strait?" Landsman says. "Doctors with beards?"

"Beth Tikkun?" says the sergeant, as if it's an American girl whose last name rhymes with "chicken". "I know it."

This knowledge, his tone implies, has not brought him happiness and is not likely to do so anytime soon.

"I might want to pay a little visit there," Landsman says. "Say tomorrow. Think that would be okay?"

The sergeant cannot seem to find an adequate reply to this apparently simple question. "Tomorrow," he says at last.

"Yes, I thought I would fly out there. Have a look around the grounds."

"Huh."

"What's the matter, Sergeant? This Beth Tikkun place, is it on the up-and-up?"

"That calls for an opinion," the sergeant says. "Inspector Dick don't let us have those. I'll be sure to tell him you called."

"You have an airplane, Rocky?" Landsman says, killing the call with his middle finger.

"I lost it," Kitka says. "In a poker game. That's how come I'm working for a Jew owner."

"No offense."

"That's right," Kitka says. "No offense."

"So, let's say I wanted to pay a visit to this temple of healing out there at Peril Strait."

"I got a pickup tomorrow, actually," Kitka says. "Over to Freshwater Bay. I might be able to bend a little to the right on the way over there. But I'm not going to hang around with the meter running." He grins a beaver-tooth grin. "And it's going to cost you a hell of a lot more than a steak dinner."

29

A badge of grass, a green brooch pinned at the collarbone of a mountain to a vast black cloak of fir trees. At the center of the clearing, a handful of buildings clad in brown shakes radiate from a circular fountain, linked by paths and separated by quilted patches of lawn and gravel. A pitch at the far end, chalked for soccer, ringed by an oval track. The place has the feel of a boarding school, a backwoods academy for wayward young wealth. Half a dozen men circle the track in shorts and hooded sweatshirts. Others sit or lie prone in the center of the field, stretching before exercise, legs and arms, angles on the ground. An alphabet of men scattered on a green page. When the plane dips a wing over the playing field, the hoods of the sweatshirts train on its fuselage like the muzzles of antiaircraft cannon. From the sky it is hard to be sure, but in Landsman's judgment, the men move and stand and stretch their pale long legs like youthful types in excellent health. Another fellow comes out of the folds of the forest in a dark coverall. He follows the arc of the Cessna, right arm crooked at the elbow and pressed against his face, making the call: *We have company*. Beyond the woods, Landsman catches a flicker of distant green, a roof, a scattering of white clumps that might be piles of snow.

Kitka muscles the plane around with a shuddering and a rattling and a groan, and then they fall out of the sky all at once, then a little at a time, and hit the water with a final smack. Maybe it was Landsman doing the groaning.

"I never thought I'd say this," Kitka says as the Lycoming engine drops into idle and they can hear themselves think. "But six hundred dollars don't seem like quite enough."

Half an hour out of Yakovy, Landsman decided to spice up their journey with a judicious application of vomit. The plane was harrowed by the smell of twenty years of rotting moose flesh, and Landsman by remorse at having broken his vow, taken after Naomi's death, to repudiate travel by very small airplane. Still, the display of airsickness remains an achievement, given how little Landsman has eaten in the past several days.

"I am sorry, Rocky," Landsman says, trying to lift his voice up out of his socks. "I guess I wasn't ready to fly again yet."

Landsman's last trip by air was undertaken with his sister in her Super Cub, to no ill effect. But that was a good airplane, and Naomi was a skilled pilot, and the weather was fine, and Landsman was drunk. This time he risked the skies in a bitter condition of sobriety. Three pots of bad motel coffee forked his nervous system. He flew at the joint mercy of a stiff chop blowing in from the Yukon and a bad pilot, one whose caution made him reckless and whose self-doubt made him bold. Landsman swayed in the canvas webbing of the weary old 206 that the management of Turkel Regional Airways has seen fit to entrust to Rocky Kitka. The plane rumbled and juddered and shook. All the pins and bolts came loose from Landsman's skeleton, and his head got turned around backward, and his arms fell off, and his eyeball rolled under the cabin heater. Somewhere over the Moore Mountains, Landsman's vow backed up on him.

Kitka throws open the door and leaps with the mooring line onto the floatplane dock. Landsman staggers out of the cabin onto the graying cedar planks. He stands blinking, reeling, breathing deep lungfuls of the local air with its scouring smell of pine needle and sea wrack. He straightens his tie and settles his hat on his head.

Peril Strait is a jumble of boats, a fuel pump, a row of weathered houses in the colors of a rusted-out engine. The houses huddle on their pilings like skinny-legged ladies. A mangy stretch of boardwalk noses among the houses before wandering over to the boat slips to lie down. It all seems to be held together by a craze of hawser, tangles of fishing line, scraps of purse seine strung with crusted floats. The whole village might be nothing but driftwood and wire, flotsam from the drowning of a far-off town.

The floatplane dock appears to have no physical connection to the boardwalk or the village of Peril Strait. It is solid, well built, new-looking, white concrete and gray-painted beams. It boasts of engineering and the logistical needs of men with money. At the shore end, it terminates in a steel gate. Beyond the gate, a winding metal stair has been whipstitched up the hillside to a clearing at the top. Alongside the stairs, a perpendicular railway cuts straight uphill, with a railed platform to elevate what cannot go by stair. A small metal sign bolted to the railing of the dock reads BETH TIKKUN RETREAT CENTER in Yiddish and American, and beneath this, in American, PRIVATE PROPERTY. Landsman fixes his gaze on the Yiddish characters. They look out of place and homely in this wild corner of Baranof Island, a gathering of lurching little Yiddish policemen in black suits and fedoras.

Kitka fills his Stetson with water from a tap mounted against a post of the dock, and splashes down the inside of his plane, one hatful of nonpotable water after another. Landsman is mortified to have made this job necessary, but Kitka and vomit appear to be old acquaintances, and the man never quite loses his smile. With the edge of a plasticized spotter's guide to Alaskan whales and fishes, Kitka squeegees out of the cabin door a compound of vomitus and seawater. He rinses off the spotter's guide, gives it a shake. Then he stands in the doorway, hanging from the arch by one hand, and looks down at Landsman on the dock. The sea slaps against the pontoons of the Cessna and against the pilings. The wind blowing down from the Stikine River hums in Landsman's ear. It stirs the brim of his hat. Over in the village, a woman's voice rises, ragged, bawling out her child or her man. There follows the parodic barking of a dog.

"Guess they know you're coming," Kitka says. "Folks up top there." His smile turns sheepish, narrowing almost to a pout. "I guess we kind of made sure of that."

"I already paid somebody a surprise visit this week; it didn't work out so good," Landsman says. He unpockets the Beretta, pops the clip, checks the magazine. "I doubt they can really be surprised."

"You know who they are?" Kitka says, his eyes on the sholem.

"No," Landsman says. "I don't. Do you?"

"Seriously, bro," Kitka says, "if I did, I would tell you. Even though you puked up my plane."

"Whoever they are," Landsman says, driving home the clip, "I think they might have killed my little sister."

Kitka mulls this statement as if searching it for weak points or loopholes. "I have to be in Freshwater by ten," he says with a show of regret.

"No," Landsman says. "I understand."

"Otherwise, bro, I would totally back you up."

"Hey, come on. What are you saying? This isn't your problem."

"Yeah, but I mean, Naomi. She was a fucking piece of work, though."

"Tell me about it."

"Actually, she never really liked me all that much."

"She could run hot and cold," Landsman says, dropping the gun back into the hip pocket of his jacket. "Sometimes."

"All right, then," Kitka says, kicking a splash of water out of his airplane with the toe of one Roper boot. "Hey, listen. You take care."

"I don't really know how to do that," Landsman admits.

"You had that in common, then," says Kitka. "You and your sister."

Landsman clatters down the dock and tries the knob on the steel gate just for fun. Then he tosses his satchel to the other side of the gate and clambers up and over the grille after it. As he goes over the top of the gate, his foot gets caught in the bars of the grille. His shoe falls off. He tumbles and spills down to the other side, landing with a meaty thud. He bites his tongue, and there's a salt spurt of blood. He dusts himself off and glances back at the dock to make sure Kitka got all of that. Landsman waves to show that he's all right. After a moment Kitka waves back. He closes the door of the plane. The engine snaps awake. The propeller vanishes into the dark sheen of its own revolution.

Landsman starts the long climb to the top of the stairs. If anything, he's in worse shape now than he was when he tried to conquer the stairway in the Shemetses' apartment building on Friday morning. Last night he lay awake on the stiff gritty packet of a motel mattress. Two days ago he was shot at and beaten in the snow. He aches. He wheezes. There's some kind of mystery pain in his rib and another in his left knee. He has to stop once, halfway up, to smoke a hortatory cigarette. He turns to watch the Cessna wobble and hum its way into the low morning clouds, abandoning Landsman to what feels, right then, like a lonely fate.

Landsman hangs from the railing, high above the deserted beach and the village. Down below, on the crooked boardwalk, some people have emerged from their houses to watch him climb. He waves to them, and they obligingly wave back. He steps on the end of his papiros and resumes his steady upward trudge. He has the rush of the waters in the inlet for company, the distant chuckling of crows. Then these sounds fade. He hears only his breathing, the chiming of his soles against the metal treads of the stairway, the creaking strap of his satchel.

At the top, a whitewashed flagpole flies two flags. One is the flag of the United States of America. The other is a modest white number blazoned with a pale blue Star of David. The flagpole stands in a ring of whitewashed stones encircled by a concrete apron. At the base of the flagpole, a small metal plaque reads FLAGPOLE ERECTED THROUGH THE GENEROSITY OF BARRY AND RHONDA GREENBAUM BEVERLY HILLS CALIFORNIA. A walkway leads from the circular apron to the largest of the buildings that Landsman saw from the air. The others are no more than cracker boxes clad in cedar shake, but this one makes a gesture in the direction of style. Its roof is pitched and clad in ribbed steel, painted dark green. Its windows are fitted with transoms and mullions. A deep porch wraps the building on three sides, its pillars the trunks of fir trees, still wearing their bark. At the center of the porch, a wide set of steps leads up from the concrete walk.

Two men stand on the uppermost porch step, watching Landsman come toward them. Both have heavy beards but no sidelocks. No hose, no black hats. The one to the left is young, thirty at the outside. He's tall, even looming, with a forehead like a concrete bunker and an underslung jaw. His beard is unruly, prone to black ringlets, with a whorl of bare skin on each cheek. His big hands dangle at his sides, pulsing like a couple of cephalopods. He wears a black suit with a generous drape and a dark rep tie. Landsman reads the twitch of longing in the big man's fingers and tries to mark the vest for the presence of a gun. As Landsman gets closer, the big man's eyes cool to a lightless black.

The other man is about Landsman's age, height, and build. He's gone softer around the middle than Landsman, and he leans on a cane formed with a curve from some dark, glossy wood. His beard is charcoal streaked with ash, trimmed, almost debonair. He wears a tweed suit complete with vest, and he puffs a thoughtful pipe.

He seems content if not delighted to see Landsman coming his way, curious, a doctor anticipating mild anomaly or a wrinkle in the usual presentation. His shoes are moccasin loafers, laced with leather thong.

Landsman stops at the bottom step of the porch and hitches up his satchel. A woodpecker rattles its cup of dice. For a moment that and the hisses of pine needles are the only sounds. They might be the only three men in all of southeastern Alaska. But Landsman can feel other eyes watching him through the partings of window curtains, through gun sights, periscopes, and peepholes. He can feel the interrupted life of the place, morning exercise, the rinsing of coffee cups. He can smell eggs scorched in butter, toasted bread.

"I don't know how to tell you this," says the tall man with the patchy beard. His voice seems to spend too long bouncing around in his chest before it emerges. The words come out thick, poured with a slow ladle. "But your ride just left without you."

"Am I going somewhere?" Landsman says.

"You aren't staying here, my friend," says the man in the tweed suit. As soon as he says the word "friend" all friendliness seems to drain from his manner.

"But I have a reservation," Landsman says, watching the big man's restless hands. "I'm younger than I look."

The sound like the bones in their bucket, somewhere in the woods.

"Okay, I'm no kid, and I don't have a reservation, but I do have a substance abuse problem," Landsman says. "Surely that counts for something."

"Mister—" says the man in the tweed suit, coming down one step. Landsman can smell the bitter shag he smokes.

"Listen," Landsman says, "I heard about the good work you people are doing here, all right? I've tried everything. I know it's crazy, but I'm at the end of my rope, and I don't have anywhere else to go."

The man in the tweed suit looks back at the tall man at the top of the steps. They don't seem to have any idea who Landsman is or what to make of him. All the fun of the past several days, in particular the torturous hop from Yakovy, seems to have rubbed off some of the noz from Landsman's aura. He hopes and fears that he looks only like a loser, dragging his bad luck in a satchel over one arm.

"I need help," he says, and to his surprise, his eyes get hot with tears. "I'm in a bad way." His voice breaks. "I'm prepared to admit that."

"What's your name?" says the tall man slowly. His eyes are warm without amity. They pity Landsman without taking much of an interest in him.

"Felnboyger," Landsman tries, dragging out the name from some ancient arrest report. "Lev Felnboyger."

"Does anyone know you're here, Mr. Felnboyger?"

"Only my wife. And the pilot, of course."

Landsman sees that the two men know each other well enough to engage in a furious argument without speaking or moving anything but their eyes.

"I'm Dr. Roboy," says the tall man at last. He swings one of his hands toward Landsman, like the payload of a crane at the end of its cable. Landsman wants to get out of its way, but he takes hold of its cool dry bulk. "Please, Mr. Felnboyger, come inside."

He follows them across the sanded fir planks of the porch. High in the rafters of the porch, he spots a wasp's nest, and he watches it for a sign of life, but it seems as deserted as every other structure on this hilltop.

They come into an empty lobby furnished, with a podiatrist's flair, in soft beige oblongs of foam. Drab low-pile carpet, egg-carton gray. On the walls hang trademark-trite scenes of Sitka life, salmon boats and Yeshiva bachelors, café society on Monastir Street, a swinging klezmer that might be a stylized Nathan Kalushiner. Again Landsman has the uneasy sensation that it has all been installed and hung that morning. There is no flake of ash in the ashtrays. The rack of informational brochures is well stocked with copies of "Drug Dependency: Who Needs It!" and "Life: To Rent or to Own?" On the wall, a thermostat sighs as if suffering from the tedium. The room smells of fresh carpet and extinguished pipe. Over the door to a carpeted hallway, an adhesive plaque reads LOBBY FURNISHINGS COURTESY OF BONNIE AND RONALD LEDERER BOCA RATON FLORIDA.

"Have a seat, please," Dr. Roboy says in his thick black syrup of a voice. "Fligler?"

The man in the tweed suit goes back to the French doors, opens the left panel, and checks the throw bolts at the top and bottom. Then he closes the panel, locks it, and pockets the key. He walks back past Landsman, brushing against him with a padded tweed shoulder.

"Fligler," Landsman says, taking hold of the smaller man's arm gently. "You a doctor, too?"

Fligler shakes off Landsman's hand. He produces a book of matches from his pocket. "You bet," he says without sincerity or conviction. With the fingers of his right hand, he peels back a match from the matchbook, scrapes it into flame, and touches it to the bowl of his pipe, all in a single continuous motion. While his right hand is busy entertaining Landsman with this minor feat, his left hand plunges into the pocket of Landsman's jacket and comes away with the .22.

"There's your problem right there," he says, holding the gun up where everyone can see it. "Watch the doctor, now."

Landsman watches dutifully as Fligler raises the gun, considering it with a keen medical eye. But then the next minute a door slams somewhere inside Landsman's head, and after that he gets distracted—for half a second—by the drone of a thousand wasps flying in through the porch of his left ear.

 30

Landsman comes to on his back, looking up at a row of iron kettles. They dangle with precision on sturdy hooks from a rack three feet above his head. In Landsman's nostrils, a nostalgic smell of camp kitchen, cooking gas and dish soap, scorched onion, hard water, a faint stink of tackle box. Metal like a chill of foreboding against his nape. He's stretched out on a long stainless-steel counter, hands cuffed behind his back, jammed up against his sacrum. Barefoot, drooling, ready to be plucked and stuffed in the body cavity with lemon and maybe a nice sprig of sage.

"I heard some crazy rumors about you," Landsman says. "Cannibalism I never heard."

"I wouldn't eat you, Landsman," affirms Baronshteyn. "Not if I was the hungriest man in Alaska and they served you to me with a silver fork. I don't much care for pickles." He's sitting on a high stool to Landsman's left, arms crossed under the skirts of his lush black beard.

He's out of uniform in a pair of new blue dungarees, flannel shirt tucked in at the waist and buttoned almost to the top. A fat hide belt with a heavy buckle and black ranger boots. The shirt too big for his frame, the trousers stiff as plate iron. Except for the skullcap, Baronshteyn looks like a skinny kid done up as a lumberjack for a school play, bogus beard and all. With his boot heels hooked on the rail of the stool, the cuffs of his trousers hike to betray a few hose-pale inches of thin shank.

"Who is this yid?" says the gaunt giant, Roboy. Landsman cranes his neck and takes in the doctor, if he is a doctor, perched on a steel stool of his own down by Landsman's feet. Bags under his eyes like smears of graphite. Beside him stands Nurse Fligler, cane hooked over one arm, watching a papiros die in the custody of his right hand, the left hand tucked ominously into the hip pocket of his tweed jacket. "Why do you know him?"

A panoply of knives, cleavers, choppers, and other tools is ranged along a magnetic rack on the kitchen wall within easy grasp of the industrious chef or shlosser.

"This yid is a shammes named Landsman."

"This is a policeman?" Roboy says. He looks like he just bit into a bonbon filled with some acrid paste. "He carries no badge. Fligler, the man had a badge?"

"I found no badge or other form of law enforcement labeling," Fligler says.

"That is because I had his badge taken away from him," Baronshteyn says. "Isn't that right, Detective?"

"I'll ask the questions here," Landsman says, squirming to find a more comfortable way of lying on top of his own cuffed hands. "If you don't mind."

"It doesn't matter if he has a badge or doesn't," Fligler opines. "Out here a Jewish badge means goat shit."

"I don't care for that kind of language, Friend Fligler," Baronshteyn says. "As I believe I have mentioned before."

"You have, but I can never hear it enough," Fligler says.

Baronshteyn regards Fligler. In the pits of his skull hidden glands secrete their venom. "Friend Fligler here was all for shooting you and dumping your body in the woods," he says amiably to Landsman, keeping his eyes on the man with the gun in his pocket.

"Way out in the woods," Fligler says. "See what comes along and gnaws on your carcass."

"That your treatment plan, Doc?" Landsman says, craning his head around to try to make eye contact with Roboy. "No wonder Mendel Shpilman checked out of here so quick last spring."

They feed on the meat of this remark, gauging its flavor and vitamin content. Baronshteyn allows a modicum of reproach to flow into his poisonous gaze. *You had the yid,* says the look that he flicks at Dr. Roboy. *And you let him get away.*

Baronshteyn leans close, craning in from his stool, and speaks, with that menacing tenderness of his. His breath is stale and acrid. Cheese rinds, bread heels, grounds at the bottom of a cup. "What are you doing, Friend Landsman," he says, "way out here where you don't belong?"

Baronshteyn looks genuinely puzzled. The Jew desires to be informed. This may, Landsman thinks, be the only desire the man ever permits himself to feel.

"I could ask you the same thing," Landsman says, thinking that maybe Baronshteyn has nothing to do with this place, is only a visitor, like Landsman. Maybe he is working the same trail, retracing the recent trajectory of Mendel Shpilman, trying to find the spot where the rebbe's son crossed the shadow that killed him. "What is this place, a boarding school for wayward Verbovers? Who are these characters? You missed a belt loop, by the way."

Baronshteyn's fingers stray toward his waist, then he sits back and makes a face that resembles a smile. "Who knows you're here?" he says. "Besides the flyer?"

Landsman feels a stab of dread for Rocky Kitka, flying upside down through life for hundreds of miles without knowing it. Landsman doesn't know very much about these yids of Peril Strait, but it seems fairly clear that they can be awfully tough on a bush pilot.

"What flyer?" he says.

"I think we have to assume the worst," Dr. Roboy says. "This facility is clearly compromised."

"You have been spending too much time with those people," Baronshteyn says. "You are starting to talk like them." Without taking his eyes off Landsman, he unbuckles his belt and feeds it through the loop that he missed. "You may be right, Roboy." He cinches the belt tight with a distinct air of self-punishment. "But I would be willing to bet that Landsman told nobody. Not even that fat Indian partner of his. Landsman is out on a limb, and he knows it. He has no support. No jurisdiction, no standing, not even a badge. He wouldn't tell anyone he was going to the Indianer-Lands, because he would be afraid they would try to talk him out of it. Or worse, forbid him to go. They would tell him that his judgment has been impaired by his desire to avenge his sister's death."

Roboy wrings his eyebrows over his nose like a pair of fretful hands. "His sister?" he says. "Who's his sister?"

"Am I right, Landsman?"

"I wish I could reassure you, Baronshteyn. But I wrote out a complete account of everything I know about you and this operation."

"Is that right?"

"The phony youth treatment facility."

"I see," Baronshteyn says with mock gravity. "The phony youth treatment facility. Quite a shocking tale."

"A front for your partnership with Roboy and Fligler and their powerful friends." Landsman's heart thrashes with the wildness of his guessing. He's wondering why any Jews would need or want such a large facility out here and how they could manage to persuade the Natives to let them build it. Could they have bought themselves a piece of the Indianer-Lands to build a new McShtetl? Or was this going to be the transfer point for a human-smuggling operation, some kind of Verbover airlift out of Alaska made without benefit of visas or passports? "The fact that you killed Mendel Shpilman and my sister to keep them from talking about what you were doing here. Then used your government connections through Roboy and Fligler to cover up the crash."

"You wrote all this down, did you?"

"Yes, and sent it to my lawyer, to be opened in the case that I should suddenly, for example, vanish from the face of the earth."

"Your lawyer."

"That's right."

"And what lawyer would that be?"

"Sender Slonim."

"Sender Slonim, I see," Baronshteyn says, nodding as if fully persuaded by Landsman's claim. "A good Jew but a bad lawyer." He slides down from the stool, and the thud of his boots puts a period to his examination of the prisoner. "I'm satisfied. Friend Fligler."

There is a *snik* and the scrape of a sole against linoleum, and the next thing Landsman knows, a shadow looms at his right eye. The space between the steel tip and Landsman's cornea can be measured in the flicker of an eyelash. Landsman jerks his head away, but at the other end of the knife, Fligler grabs hold of Landsman's ear and yanks. Landsman curls up into a ball and tries to roll down from the counter. Fligler smacks Landsman's bandaged wound with the head of his cane, and a jagged star bursts across the back of Landsman's eyes. While he's busy ringing like a bell of pain, Fligler turns Landsman onto his belly. He climbs on top of him and jerks his head back and lays the knife against his throat.

"I may not have a badge," Landsman says with difficulty. He addresses himself to Dr. Roboy, whom he senses to be the least resolute yid in the room. "But I'm still a noz. You people kill me, it's a world of trouble for whatever you have going here."

"Probably not," Fligler says.

"Not in all likelihood," Baronshteyn agrees. "None of you yids is even going to *be* a policeman two months from now."

The thin string of carbon and iron atoms that is the

consequential feature of the knife blade burns one degree hotter against Landsman's windpipe.

"Fligler . . ." Roboy says, wiping his mouth with one giant hand.

"Please, Fligler," Landsman says. "Cut my throat. I'll thank you for it. Go on, you pussy."

From the other side of the kitchen door comes a churn of agitated male voices. A pair of feet scrapes the floor, about to knock, and hesitates. Nothing happens.

"What is it?" Roboy says bitterly.

"A word, Doctor," says a voice, young, American, speaking American.

"Don't do anything," Roboy says. "Just wait."

Just before the door swings shut behind Roboy, Landsman hears a voice begin to speak, a rush of angular syllables that do not register on his brain as anything but throaty noise.

Fligler settles his weight more securely into the small of Landsman's back. There follows the small awkwardness of strangers in an elevator. Baronshteyn consults his fine Swiss watch.

"How much of it did I have right?" Landsman says. "Just so I know."

"Ha," Fligler says. "I could laugh."

"Roboy is a trained rehabilitation therapist," Baronshteyn says with a show of tolerant patience, sounding remarkably like Bina when speaking to one of the five billion people, Landsman among them, whom she considers to be on balance an idiot. "They were genuinely trying to help the rebbe's son. Mendel's presence here was entirely voluntary. When he made the decision to leave, there was nothing they could do to stop him."

"I'm sure the news broke your heart," Landsman says.

"And what do you mean by that?"

"I suppose a cleaned-up Mendel Shpilman was no threat to you? To your status as heir apparent?"

"Oy," Baronshteyn says. "What you don't know."

The kitchen door opens and Roboy slips back inside, eyebrows arched. Before the door bangs shut, Landsman catches a glimpse of two young men, bearded and dressed in ill-fitting dark suits. Big boys, one with the black snail of an earphone curled in the shell of his ear. On the outside of the door a small plaque reads KITCHEN EQUIPPED THROUGH THE GENEROSITY OF MR. AND MRS. LANCE PEARLSTEIN PIKESVILLE MD.

"Eight minutes," Roboy says. "Ten at the most."

"Someone coming?" Landsman says. "Who is it? Heskel Shpilman? Or does he even know you're here, Baronshteyn? Did you come to cut a deal with these people? Are they moving in on Verbover action? What did they want with Mendel? Were you going to use him to force the rebbe's hand?"

"Sounds to me as though you need to read that letter of yours again," Baronshteyn observes. "Or get Sender Slonim to tell you what it says."

Landsman can hear people moving around, chair legs screeching against a wooden floor. In the distance, the whirr and click of an electric motor, a golf cart zipping away.

"We cannot do this now," Roboy says, coming close to Landsman, looming over him. His dense beard flocks his entire face from the cheekbones down, flourishing in his nostrils, winding in fine tendrils from the flaps of his ears. "The last thing he wants is any hint of a mess. Okay, Detective." His slow voice turns syrupy, abruptly warmer. A perfunctory affection suffuses it, and Landsman stiffens, awaiting the bad thing that this surely betokens, which proves to be only a stick in the arm, quick and expert.

In the dreamy seconds that precede his loss of consciousness, the guttural language that Landsman heard Roboy speaking plays like a recording in his ear, and he makes a dazzling leap into impossible understanding, like the sudden consciousness in a dream of one's having invented a great theory or written a fine poem that in the morning turns out to be gobbledygook. They are talking, those Jews on the other side of the door, about roses and frankincense. They are standing in a desert wind under the date palms, and Landsman is there, in flowing robes that keep out the biblical sun, speaking Hebrew, and they are all friends and brothers together, and the mountains skip like rams, and the hills like little lambs.

31

Landsman wakes from a dream of feeding his right ear to the propeller blades of a Cessna 206. He stirs under a clammy blanket, electric but unplugged, in a room not much larger than the cot he's stretched across. He touches a cautious finger to the side of his head. Where Fligler originally sapped him, the flesh is swollen and moist. Landsman's left shoulder is killing him, too.

In a narrow window opposite the cot, metal-slat blinds leak the disappointed gray of a November afternoon in southeastern Alaska. It's not light oozing through so much as a residue of light, a day haunted by the memory of the sun.

Landsman tries to sit up and discovers that his shoulder hurts so much because somebody has been kind enough to handcuff his left wrist to a steel leg of the cot frame. With his arm jerked up over his head, Landsman practiced some kind of brutal chiropractic on his shoulder in the thrashing and tossing of sleep. The same kind soul who chained him was thoughtful enough to remove his trousers, shirt, and jacket, reducing him once again to a man in his underpants.

He sits up on his haunches at the head of the cot. Then he eases himself backward off the mattress so that he can squat with his left arm hanging at a more natural angle, his shackled hand resting against the floor. The floor is yellow linoleum, the color of the inside of a used cigarette filter, and as cold as an ME's stethoscope. It features an extensive collection of dust lemmings and dust wigs and a winged smear of black-fly grease. The walls are cinder block painted a thick, glossy shade of dentifrice blue. On the wall beside Landsman's head, a familiar hand has penned a tiny message for Landsman in the mortar line between two cinder blocks: THIS DETAINMENT CELL COURTESY OF THE GENEROSITY OF NEAL AND RISA NUDELMAN SHORT HILLS NEW JERSEY. He wants to laugh, but the sight of his sister's droll alphabet in this place raises the hair on the back of his neck.

Apart from the bed, the only other furnishing, in the corner by the door, is a metal wastebasket. The wastebasket is a thing for children, blue and yellow with a cartoon dog cavorting in a field of daisies. Landsman stares at it for a long time, thinking about nothing, thinking about children's garbage and dogs in cartoons. The obscure unease that Pluto has always inspired, a dog owned by a mouse, daily confronted with the mutational horror of Goofy. An invisible gas clouds his thoughts, exhaust from a bus left parked with its engine running in the middle of his brain.

Landsman crouches by the cot for another minute or so, collecting himself like a beggar chasing scattered dimes along the sidewalk. Then he drags the cot to the door and sits down on it. In a way that is both methodical and wild, he begins to kick at the door with his bare heels. It's a hollow steel door, and it makes a thunderous sound when kicked that's pleasant for a moment, but then the pleasure palls. Next Landsman tries loud and repeated cries of "Help me, I cut myself and I'm bleeding!" He yells until he is hoarse and kicks until his feet throb. At last he gets tired of kicking and yelling. He needs to urinate. Badly. He looks at the trash can and then at the door. It might be the traces of the drug in his system, or the hatred he feels for that tiny room in which his sister passed her last night on earth, and for the men who chained him still in underwear to it. Maybe all his enraged yelling has engendered an actual rage. But the idea of being obliged to piss into a Shnapish the Dog wastebasket makes Landsman angry.

He drags the bed over to the window, and shoves the blinds rattling to one side. The windowpane is pebbled glass. Ripples of a green and gray world set in a heavy steel frame. At one time—maybe until very recently—there was a latch, but his thoughtful hosts have removed it. Now there is only one way to get the window open. Landsman goes for the wastebasket, dragging the cot back and forth behind him like a handy symbol. He raises the wastebasket, takes aim, and hurls it against the pebbled glass of the tall window. It bounces off and flies back at Landsman, striking him squarely in the forehead. A moment later, he tastes blood for the second time that day as it trickles down his cheek to the corner of his lips.

"Shnapish, you bastard," he says.

He shoves the cot all the way over against the long wall and then, working with his free hand, tips the mattress off the cot frame. He stands the mattress against the opposite wall. He grabs hold of the cot frame on either side and, lifting from the knees, heaves it up off the ground. He stands there a moment, holding the rickety frame parallel to his body. He wavers under the sudden weight, which is not great but taxes his strength all the same. He takes a step backward, lowers his head, and drives the cot frame through the window. Green lawn and fog blow into Landsman's dazzled vision. Trees, crows, hovering hornets of broken glass, the gun-barrel-gray waters of the strait, a bright white floatplane trimmed in red. Then the cot frame jerks free of Landsman's grasp and leaps through gaping glass fangs out into the morning.

As a kid in school, Landsman received good marks in physics. Newtonian mechanics, bodies at rest and in motion, actions and reactions, gravity and mass. He found more sense in physics than in anything else they ever tried to teach him. An idea like momentum, for example, the tendency of a body in motion to stay in motion. So maybe Landsman should not be quite so surprised when the cot frame does not content itself with shattering the window. There is a sharp, joint-popping tug on the bones of his shoulder, and he is seized again by the nameless emotion he felt when he tried to climb aboard Mrs. Shpilman's moving limousine: the sudden awareness, like an inverse satori, that he has made a grave if not fatal error.

This is Landsman's luck: He lands in a pile of snow. It's a furtive, die-hard patch tucked deep into the shadow on the north side of the barracks. The only snow visible in the entire compound, and Landsman falls right into it. His jaws snap together, making each tooth ring out with its own pure tone as the impact of his ass against the ground conducts its Newtonian business with the rest of his skeleton.

He lifts his head up out of the snow. Cold air flows over the back of his neck. For the first time since taking wing, he remarks on the fact that he is freezing. He stands up, his jaw still chiming. Snow streaks his back like welts raised by a wire lash. He lurches and staggers to the left under the weight of the cot frame. It offers to help him sit down again in the snow. Sink into it, plunge his sore head into the cold, clean pile of snow. Close his eyes. Relax.

Just then he hears a soft scrape of soles coming from around the corner of the building, a pair of erasers rubbing away the marks of their own passage. A flawed gait, the extra hop and shuffle of a man with a limp. Landsman takes hold of the cot frame and hoists it, then backs up against the shingled side of the barracks. When he sees one hiking boot, the tweed cuff of Fligler's trouser leg, he thrusts the cot frame out. As Fligler rounds the corner, the steel edge of the cot frame catches him full in the face. A red hand of blood spreads its fingers across Fligler's cheeks and forehead. His cane flies up in the air and strikes the pavement with a marimba note. The cot frame, as if shy without its best friend, drags Landsman along with it, onto Fligler, in a heap. The smell of Fligler's blood fills Landsman's nostrils. Landsman scrambles to his feet, grabbing with his free hand for the sholem in Fligler's slack fingers.

He raises the automatic, contemplating shooting the man on the ground with a certain black willingness. Then he glances toward the main house, five hundred feet away. Several dark shapes are moving behind the French doors on this side. The door flies open, and the hole-mouthed pans of big young yids in suits fill the doorway. Landsman envies them their youthful capacity for wonder but still raises the gun in their direction. They duck and pull back, and in their parting, a tall, slim, fair-haired man stands revealed. The new arrival, fresh from the hold of his bright white floatplane. The hair is really something, like a flare of sunlight on a sheet of steel. Penguins on his sweater, baggy corduroy pants. For an instant the man in the penguin sweater frowns at Landsman, looking confused. Then somebody drags him back from the doorway as Landsman tries to take aim.

The cuff digs into Landsman's wrist, sharp enough to abrade the flesh. He changes his aim, pointing the gun at his own left arm. He squeezes off a single careful shot, and the handcuff slides free, a bangle at his wrist. Landsman lowers the bed frame to the ground with an air of mild regret, as if it's the body of a bumbling but loyal family retainer who has served the Landsmans well. Then he takes off into the woods toward a gap in the trees. There must be at least twenty young healthy Jews running after him, shouting, cursing, giving orders. For the first minute he expects to see the branching lightning of a bullet in his brain and to go down underneath the slow roll of its thunder. But there is nothing; they must have been given orders not to shoot.

The last thing he wants is any hint of a mess.

Landsman finds himself running along a dirt road, neat and well maintained, marked with red reflectors on metal stakes. He remembers the distant patch of green that he caught sight of from the air, beyond the forest, dotted with piles of snow. He figures this path must lead there. It must lead, at any rate, somewhere.

Landsman runs through the woods. The dirt track is thick with fallen needles that muffle the thud of his bare heels. He can almost see the heat departing his body, shimmering waves of it that trail along behind. He has a taste at the back of his mouth that's like the memory of the smell of Fligler's blood. The links on the broken chain dangle from the handcuff, tinkling. Somewhere a woodpecker is knocking out its brains against the side of a tree. Landsman's own brain is working too hard, trying to figure these men and their business. The crippled professor type whose TEC-9 Landsman is packing. The doctor with the concrete forehead. The deserted barracks room. The honor ranch that was no such thing. The strapping lads cooling their heels on the property. The golden man in the penguin sweater who will not tolerate a mess.

Meanwhile, another segment of his brain is busy trying to gauge the air temperature— call it 37, 38 degrees F—and from there to calculate or recall some table he might have seen once that gave the time it takes hypothermia to kill a Jewish policeman in his underpants. But the ruling cells of that great ruined organ, addled and drugged, are telling him only to run and keep on running.

The woods give out abruptly, and he's standing in front of a machine shed, molded gray panels of steel, no windows, with a rippled plastic roof. A scrotal pair of propane tanks huddles against the side of the building. The wind is sharper here, and Landsman feels it like a flow of boiling water over his flesh. He runs around to the other side of the shed. It stands at the edge of a barren expanse of straw-covered ground. Way in the distance, a band of green grass dissolves into the rolling fog. A gravel track leads away from the shed, along the bare field of straw. Fifty yards farther along, the track forks. One fork runs to the east, toward that band of green. The other runs on straight and disappears into a dark stand of trees. Landsman turns back to the shed. A big door on rollers. Landsman drags it thundering to one side. Disassembled refrigeration equipment, cryptic pieces of machines, one wall covered in an Arabic written in lengths of black rubber hose. And, right by the door, one of those three-wheeled electric carts called Zumzums (the District's number two export, after Shoyfer-brand cellular telephones). This one is tricked out with a flatbed, the bed lined with a sheet of mud-streaked black rubber. Landsman climbs up behind the wheel. As cold as his ass already is, as cold as the wind is blowing down from the Yukon, the vinyl seat of that Zumzum is even colder. Landsman thumbs its starter switch. He steps on the pedal, and with a thunk and a whirr of differential gears, he's off. He rumbles up to the fork in the road and hesitates between the woods and that tranquil band of green grass, vanishing like a promise of peacefulness into the fog. Then he smashes down the pedal.

Just before he plunges into the stand of trees, Landsman looks back over his shoulder, and sees the yids of Peril Strait coming after him in a big black Ford Caudillo, splashing gravel as it rounds the corner of the supply shed. Landsman has no idea where it came from or, for that matter, how it got here; he didn't see any cars at all from the air. It's five hundred meters behind the Zumzum and gaining easily.

In the woods, gravel gives way to a rough track of packed earth that slips among handsome Sitka spruces, high and secretive. As Landsman whirrs along, he catches sight between the trees of a high chain-link fence topped by gay glinting curls of razor wire. The steel mesh fence is woven with slats of green plastic. In places a gap appears in the green weave of the fence. Through these gaps, Landsman glimpses another steel shed, a clearing, posts, crossbeams, interlaced cables. A huge frame stretched with a web of cargo net, distended coils of barbed wire, rope swings. It might be an athletic facility, some kind of therapeutic playground for patients in recovery. Sure, and the people in the Caudillo might just be bringing him his pants.

The black car is under two hundred yards from him now. The passenger in its front seat rolls down his window and climbs out to sit on the top of his door, steadying himself with one hand on the roof rack. The other hand, Landsman observes, is busy getting ready to fire a handgun. It's a fair, bearded young man in a black suit, cropped hair, a sober tie like Roboy's. He takes his time with the shot, reckoning the ever-dwindling distance. A flash blooms around his hand, and the back of the Zumzum explodes with a crack and a spray of fiberglass slivers. Landsman lets out a cry and takes his foot off the accelerator pedal. So much for not making a mess.

He bumps along on momentum for another five or ten feet and then comes to a stop. The young man hanging out of the Caudillo's window raises his firing arm and judges the effect of his shot. The jagged hole in the fiberglass body of the Zumzum is probably disappointing to the poor kid. But he has to be happy about the fact that his moving target has just become stationary. His next shot is going to be a lot easier. The kid lowers his arm again with a patient slowness that is almost ostentatious, almost cruel. In his care and his parsimonious attitude toward bullets, Landsman senses the hallmark of rigorous training and an athlete's grasp of eternity.

Surrender unfurls across Landsman's heart like the shadow of a flag. There is no way he can outrace the Caudillo, not in a shot-up Zumzum that on a good day tops out around fifteen miles per hour. A warm blanket, maybe a hot cup of tea: These strike him as adequate recompense for failure. The Caudillo comes charging toward him and then sloshes to a halt in a spray of fallen needles. Three of its doors swing open and three men climb out, lumbering young yids in ill-fitting suits and meteor-black shoes, steering their automatic pistols toward Landsman. The guns seem to thrum in their hands as if they contain wild life or gyroscopes. The gunmen can barely restrain them. Hard boys, neckties flying, their beards trimmed neat along the jawline, their skullcaps small crocheted saucers.

The rear door on the near side remains firmly shut, but behind it Landsman makes out the outline of a fourth man. The hard boys close on Landsman in their matching suits, with their earnest haircuts.

Landsman stands up and turns around with his hands in the

air. "You're clones, right?" he says as the three hard boys surround him. "At the end of the picture, it always turns out to be clones."

"Shut up," says the nearest hard boy, speaking American, and Landsman is about to assent when he hears a sound like something both fibrous and doughy being slowly torn in two. In the time it takes him to observe in the eyes of the hard boys that they hear it, too, the sound sharpens and rises to a steady chopping, a sheet of paper caught in the blades of a fan. The sound grows louder and more layered. The hacking cough of an old man. A heavy wrench clanging against a cold cement floor. The flatulence of a burst balloon streaking across the living room and knocking over a lamp. Through the trees a light appears, stitching and staggering like a bumblebee, and suddenly, Landsman knows it for what it is.

"Dick," he says simply and not without wonder, and a shudder shakes him deep down to his bones. The light is an old six-volt lamp, no more powerful than a large flashlight, flickering and wan in the gloom of the spruce forest. The engine that drives the light toward the party of Jews is a V-Twin, custom-manufactured. You can hear the springs of the front forks as they register every jolt in the road.

"Fuck him," mutters one of the hard boys. "And his fucking Matchbox motorcycle."

Landsman has heard different stories about Inspector Willie Dick and his motorcycle. Some say that it was made for a full-grown Bombay millionaire of smaller than average stature, others that it was originally presented as a thirteenth birthday gift to the Prince of Wales, and still others that it once belonged to a daredevil freak in a circus down in Texas or Alabama or some exotic place like that. At first glance, it is a stock 1961 Royal Enfield Crusader, gunmetal gray in the sunlight, its stunning chromium trim carefully restored. You have to get up next to it, or see it alongside a normal-sized motorcycle, to realize that it is built to two-thirds scale. Willie Dick, though full-grown and thirty-seven years old, is only four feet seven inches tall.

Dick rumbles past the Zumzum, squeaks to a stop, kills the elderly British engine. He climbs off the bike and comes swaggering over to Landsman.

"What the fuck?" he says, pulling off his gloves, black leather gauntlets of the sort that might be worn by Max von Sydow playing Erwin Rommel. His voice is always surprisingly rich and deep, given the boyishness of his frame. He describes a slow circuit of appraisal around the flower of Jewish law enforcement. "Detective Meyer Landsman!" He turns to the hard boys and makes a study of their hardness. "Gentlemen."

"Inspector Dick," says the one who told Landsman to shut up. The boy has a jailhouse air, honed and stealthy, a toothbrush sharpened to a shiv. "What brings you to our neck of the woods?"

"With all due respect, Mr. Gold—it is Gold, right? yeah—this is *my* motherfucking neck of the woods." Dick steps out from the group centered around Landsman. He stares in to get a look at the shadow watching from behind the closed door of the Caudillo. Landsman can't be certain, but whoever's there doesn't look big enough to be Roboy or the golden man in the penguin sweater. A hunched little shadow, furtive and watchful. "I was here before you, and I'll be here a long time after you yids are gone."

Detective Inspector Wilfred Dick is a full-blood Tlingit, descended from the Chief Dick who inflicted the last recorded fatality in the history of Russian-Tlingit relations, shooting and killing a marooned, half-starved Russian submariner he caught raiding his crab traps at Stag Bay in 1948. Willie Dick is married, with nine children by his first and only wife, whom Landsman has never seen. Naturally, she is reputed to be a giantess. In 1993 or '94 Dick successfully completed the Iditarod dog-sled race, coming in ninth among forty-seven finishers. He has a Ph.D. in criminology from Gonzaga University in Spokane, Washington. Dick's first act as an adult male of his tribe was to travel, in an old Boston whaler, from the Dick village at Stag Bay to Tribal Police central headquarters in Angoon, in order to persuade the superintendent to set aside, in his case, the minimum height requirements for Tribal Police officers. The stories of how this was accomplished are slanderous, salacious, hard to believe, or some combination of the three. Willie Dick has all the usual bad qualities of very small, very intelligent men: vanity, arrogance, overcompetitiveness, a long memory for injuries and slights. He is also honest, dogged, and fearless, and he owes Landsman a favor; Dick has a long memory for favors, too.

"I'm trying to imagine what you mad Hebrews are up to, and every one of my theories is more fucked up than the last one," he says.

"This man is a patient here," says Gold. "He was trying to check out a little early, is all."

"So you were going to shoot him," Dick says. "That's some badass fucking therapy, you guys. Damn! Strict Freudian, huh?"

He turns back to Landsman and looks him up and down. Dick's dark face is handsome, in a way, the avid eyes operating from the cover of a sage forehead, the chin dimpled, the nose straight and regular. The last time Landsman saw him, Dick kept having to take a pair of reading glasses out of his shirt pocket and put them on. Now he has given in to senescence and adopted a slick black-and-brushed-steel pair of Italian spectacles, the kind worn in thoughtful interviews by aging British rock guitarists. He is dressed in stiff black jeans, black cowboy boots, and a red-and-black-plaid shirt with an open collar. Over his shoulders he wears, as usual, a short cloak, held in place with a braided rawhide thong, made from the skin of a bear he hunted and killed himself. He is an affected creature, Willie Dick—he smokes black cigarettes—but he is a fine homicide detective.

"Jesus Christ, Landsman. You look like a fucking fetal pig I saw one time pickled in a jar."

He unties the braided thong with the fingers of one hand and shrugs out of the cloak. Then he tosses it to Landsman.

For an instant it's as cold as steel against Landsman's body, then wonderfully warm. Dick keeps the grin of mockery in place but, for Landsman's benefit— only Landsman can see it—extinguishes every last trace of humor from his eyes.

"I spoke to that ex-wife of yours," he says in a near-whisper, the voice he uses to threaten suspects and intimidate witnesses. "After I got your message. You have less fucking right to be here than a fucking eyeless African molerat." He raises his voice nearly to the point of staginess. "Detective Landsman, what did I tell you I was going to do to your Jewish ass the next time I caught you running around Indian country without benefit of clothing?"

"I d-don't remember," Landsman says, seized by a violent tremor of gratitude and exposure. "You s-said so many things."

Dick walks over to the Caudillo, and knocks on the closed door like he wants to come in. The door opens, and Dick stands behind it and converses in a low voice with whoever is sitting inside, keeping warm. After a moment Dick comes back and tells Gold, "Man in charge wants to speak to you."

Gold goes around the open door to talk to the man in charge. When he comes back, he looks like his sinuses have been pulled out through his ears and he blames Landsman for it. He nods once to Dick.

"Detective Landsman," Dick says. "I'm very much fucking afraid that you are under arrest."

32

In the emergency room at the Indian hospital in St. Cyril, the Indian doctor looks Landsman over and pronounces him fit to be jailed. The doctor's name is Rau, and he's from Madras, and he's heard all of the jokes before. He's handsome in the Sal Mineo style, big obsidian eyes and a mouth like a cake-icing rose. Mild frostbite, he tells Landsman, nothing serious, though one hour and forty-seven minutes after his rescue, Landsman still can't seem to suppress the temblors that rise from inner faults to shake his body. Cold to the honeycomb of his bones.

"Where's the big dog with the little thing of brandy around his neck?" Landsman says after the doctor tells him he can take off the blanket and put on the jailhouse clothes that lie in a neat stack beside the sink. "When does he show up?"

"Do you enjoy brandy?" Dr. Rau says, as if he's reading from a phrase book, as if he has not the slightest interest either in his question or in any answer that Landsman might ever produce. Landsman tags it at once as a classic interrogator's tone, so cold that it leaves a burn. Dr. Rau's gaze remains resolutely fixed on an empty corner of the room. "Is that something you feel you need?"

"Who said anything about needing?" Landsman says, fumbling

with the button fly of some worn twill trousers. Cotton work shirt, laceless canvas sneaks. They want to dress him like a wino, or a beach bum, or some other kind of loser who turns up naked at your intake desk, homeless, no visible means of support. The shoes are too big, but otherwise, everything's a perfect fit.

"No craving?" There's a fleck of ash in the A of the doctor's name tag. He picks at it with a fingernail. "You're not feeling the need of a drink right now?"

"Maybe I just *want* one," Landsman says. "Did you ever think of that?"

"Maybe," the doctor says. "Or maybe you are fond of large, salivating dogs."

"Okay, knock it off, Doc," Landsman says. "Let's not play games."

"All right." Dr. Rau turns his plump face to Landsman. The irises of his eyes are like cast iron. "Based on my examination, I would guess that you are going through alcoholic withdrawal, Detective Landsman. In addition to exposure, you're also suffering from dehydration, tremors, palpitations, and your pupils are enlarged. Your blood sugar is low, which tells me you probably haven't been eating. Loss of appetite is another symptom of withdrawal. Your blood pressure is elevated, and your recent behavior appears to have been, from what I gather, quite erratic. Even violent."

Landsman tugs on the wrinkled lapels of the collar of his chambray work shirt, trying to smooth them out. Like cheap window blinds, they keep rolling themselves up.

"Doctor," he says, "from one man with X-ray eyeballs to another, I respect your keenness, but tell me, please, if the country of India were being canceled, and in two months, along with everyone you loved, you were going to be tossed into the jaws of the wolf with nowhere to go and no one to give a fuck, and half the world had just spent the past thousand years trying to kill Hindus, don't you think you might take up drinking?"

"That or ranting to strange doctors."

"The dog with the brandy never gets wise with the frozen guy," Landsman says wistfully.

"Detective Landsman."

"Yes, Doc."

"I have been examining you for the last eleven minutes, and in that time you have produced three prolonged speeches. Rants, I would call them."

"Yes," Landsman says, and now his blood begins to flow for the first time: into his cheeks. "It happens sometimes."

"You like to make speeches?"

"They come and go."

"Verbal jags."

"I've heard them called that."

For the first time Landsman notices that Dr. Rau is secretly chewing something, working it with his back teeth. The faint smell of anise leaks from his frosting-pink lips.

The doctor makes a note on Landsman's chart. "Are you currently under the care of a psychiatrist or taking any medication for depression?"

"Depression? I seem depressed to you?"

"It's really just a word," the doctor says. "I'm looking at possible symptoms. From what Inspector Dick has told me, and from my examination of you, it seems at least possible that you might possibly have some kind of mood disorder."

"You aren't the first person to say that," Landsman says. "I'm sorry to have to break it to you."

"Are you taking medication?

"No, not really."

"Not really?"

"No. I don't want to."

"You don't want to."

"I'm, you know. Afraid I might lose my edge."

"That explains the drinking, then," the doctor says. His words seem tinged with a sardonic whiff of licorice. "I hear it does wonders for one's edge." He goes to the door, opens it, and an Indian noz comes in to take Landsman away. "In my experience, Detective Landsman, if I may," the doctor concludes his own jag, "the people who worry about losing their edge, often they fail to see they already lost the *blade* a long time ago."

"The swami speaks," says the Indian noz.

"Lock him up," the doctor says, tossing Landsman's file into the tray mounted to the wall.

The Indian noz has a head like a redwood burl and the worst haircut Landsman has ever seen, some kind of ungodly hybrid of a high-and-tight and a pompadour. He leads Landsman through a series of blank hallways, up a flight of steel stairs, to a room at the back of the St. Cyril jail. It has an ordinary steel door, no bars. It's reasonably clean and reasonably well lit. The bunk has a mattress, a pillow, and a blanket, folded trim. The toilet has a seat. There's a metal mirror bolted to the wall.

"The VIP suite," says the Indian noz.

"You should see where I live," Landsman says. "It's almost as nice as this."

"Nothing personal," the noz says. "The inspector wanted to make sure you knew that."

"Where is the inspector?"

"Dealing with this. We get a complaint from those people, he has nine flavors of shit to deal with." A humorless grin contorts his face. "You fucked up that gimpy little Jew pretty bad."

"Who are they?" Landsman says. "Sergeant, what the fuck are those Jews up to over there?"

"It's a retreat center," the sergeant says with the same burning lack of emotion that Dr. Rau put into his questions about Landsman's alcoholism. "For wayward Jew youth trapped by the scourge of crime and drugs. Anyways, that's what I heard. Have yourself a nice nap, Detective."

After the Indian noz leaves, Landsman crawls into the bunk and pulls the blanket over his head, and before he can prevent himself, before he has time even to feel something and know that he is feeling it, a sob gets wrenched loose from some deep niche and fills his windpipe. The tears that burn his eyes are like his alcoholic tremors: They have no use, and he can't seem to get on top of them. He clamps his pillow down over his face and feels for the first time how utterly alone Naomi left him.

To calm himself, he goes back to Mendel Shpilman on the bed in room 208. He imagines himself lying on the pulldown bed in that wallpapered cell, running through the moves of Alekhine's second game against Capablanca at Buenos Aires in 1927, while the smack turned his blood into a flood of sugar and his brain into a lapping tongue. So. Once he had been fitted for the suit of the Tzaddik Ha-Dor and then decided that it was a straitjacket. All right. Then a lot of wasted years. Hustling chess for drug money. Cheap hotels. Hiding himself from the incompatible destinies chosen for him by his genes and by his God. Then one day some men dig him up and dust him off and take him away to Peril Strait. A place with a doctor, a facility built through the generosity of the Barrys and the Marvins and the Susies of Jewish America, where they can clean him up, patch him together. Why? Because they need him. Because they intend to restore him to practical use. And he wants to go with them, these men. He agrees to do so. Naomi never would have flown Shpilman and his escorts if she sniffed any kind of coercion in the job. So there is something in it—money, the promise of healing or recaptured glory, reconciliation with the family, an eventual payoff in drugs—for Shpilman. But when he arrives at Peril Strait to start his new life, something changes Shpilman's mind. Something that he learns, or realizes, or sees. Or maybe he just gets cold feet. And turns for help to the woman who served any number of people, generally the most lost, as the only friend they had in the world. Naomi flies him out again, changing her flight plan en route, and finds him a ride to a cheap motel with the pie man's daughter. In payment for her hubris, these mystery

Jews crash Naomi's airplane for her. Then they go out hunting for Mendel Shpilman, gone to ground again. Hiding from his possible selves. Lying there in his room at the Zamenhof, facedown on the bed, too far gone to think about Alekhine and Capablanca and the Queen's Indian Defense. Too far gone to hear the knock on the door.

"You don't have to *knock*, Berko," Landsman says. "This is a jail."

There's a rattle of keys, and then the Indian noz throws open the door. Berko Shemets stands behind him. He has dressed himself as for a safari deep into the bush. Jeans, flannel shirt, lace-up leather hiking boots, a grayish-brown fisherman's vest equipped with seventy-two pockets, sub-pockets, and sub-sub-pockets. At first glance, he looks almost like a typical if rather large Alaskan bush runner. You can hardly make out the polo-player insignia that ornaments his shirt. Berko's usual discreet skullcap has been laid aside in favor of an outsize embroidered number, cylindrical, a dwarf fez. Berko always lays on the Jew a little thick when he is obliged to travel to the Indianer-Lands. Landsman can't tell from here, but his partner is probably wearing his Star of David cuff links, too.

"I'm sorry," Landsman tells him. "I know I'm always sorry, but this time, believe me, I could not be sorrier."

"We'll see about that," Berko says. "Come on, he wants to see us."

"Who does?"

"The emperor of the French."

Landsman gets up from the bed, goes to the sink, throws some water on his face.

"Am I free to go?" he asks the Indian noz as he walks out the door of the cell. "You're telling me I'm free to go?"

"You're a free man," says the noz.

"Don't you believe it," says Landsman.

 33

From his corner office on the ground floor of the St. Cyril station house, Inspector Dick has a fine view of the parking lot. Six Dumpsters plated and hooped like iron maidens against bears. Beyond the Dumpsters a subalpine meadow, and then the snow-capped ghetto wall that keeps the Jews at bay. Dick is slouched against the back of his two-thirds-scale desk chair, arms crossed, chin sunk to his chest, staring out the casement window. Not at the mountains or the meadow, grayish green in the late light, tufted with wisps of fog, or even at the armored Dumpsters. His gaze travels no farther than the parking lot—no farther than his 1961 Royal Enfield Crusader. Landsman recognizes the expression on Dick's face. It's the expression that goes with the feeling Landsman gets when he looks at his Chevelle Super Sport, or at the face of Bina Gelbfish. The face of a man who feels he was born into the wrong world. A mistake has been made; he is not where he belongs. Every so often he feels his heart catch, like a kite on a telephone wire, on something that seems to promise him a home in the world or a means of getting there. An American car manufactured in his far-off boyhood, say, or a motorcycle that once belonged to the future king of England, or the face of a woman worthier than himself of being loved.

"I hope you're dressed," Dick says without turning from the window. The wistful flicker in his eyes has been snuffed. There is no longer anything happening in his face at all. "Because the things I witnessed in those woods—Christ, I almost had to fucking burn my motherfucking bearskin." He affects to shudder. "The Tlingit Nation doesn't pay me anywhere near enough to make up for having to look at you standing around in your underpants."

"The Tlingit Nation," says Berko Shemets, pronouncing it like the name of a notorious scam or a claim about the location of Atlantis. He intrudes his bulk on the furnishings of Dick's office. "So, what, they still pay the salaries around here? Because Meyer was just telling me it might be otherwise."

Dick turns, slow and lazy, and hikes up a corner of his upper lip to bare a few incisors and cuspids. "Johnny the Jew," he says. "Well, well. Beanie and all. And clearly you haven't had any difficulties lately saying the holy blessing over the Filipino donut."

"Fuck you, Dick, you anti-Semitic midget."

"Fuck you, Johnny, and your chickenshit insinuations about my integrity as a police officer."

In his rich but rusty Tlingit, Berko expresses a wish to one day see Dick lying dead and shoeless in the snow.

"Go shit in the ocean," Dick says in flawless Yiddish.

They step toward each other, and the large man takes the small one into his embrace. They pound at each other's backs, searching for the tubercular spots in their slowly dying friendship, sounding the depths of their ancient enmity like a drum. In the year of misery that preceded his defection to the Jewish side of his nature, before his mother was crushed by a runaway truckload of rioting Jews, young John Bear discovered basketball and Wilfred Dick, then a four-foot-two point guard. It was hatred at first sight, the kind of grand romantic hatred that in thirteen-year-old boys is indistinguishable from or the nearest they can get to love.

"Johnny Bear," Dick says. "What the fuck, you great big Jew?"

Berko shrugs, rubbing at the back of his neck in a sheepish way that makes him look like a thirteen-year-old center who has just watched something small and nasty squirt past him on a drive to the basket. "Yeah, hey, Willie D.," he says.

"Sit down, you fat motherfucker," Dick says. "You, too, Landsman, and all those ugly freckles on your ass crack."

Berko grins, and they all sit down, Dick on his side of his desk, the Jewish policemen on theirs. The two chairs for visitors are standard scale, along with the bookshelves and everything else in the office apart from Dick's desk and chair. The effect is fun house, nauseating. Or maybe that's another symptom of alcoholic withdrawal. Dick takes out his black cigarettes and pushes an ashtray across the desk toward Landsman. He leans back in his chair and puts his boots up on the desk. He wears the sleeves of his Woolrich shirt rolled back. His forearms are ropy and brown. Curling gray hairs peep over his open collar, and his chic eyeglasses are folded in the pocket of his shirt.

"There are so many people I would rather be looking at right now," he says. "Literally millions."

"Then close your fucking eyes," Berko suggests.

Dick complies. His eyelids are dark and glossy, bruised-looking. "Landsman," he says, as if enjoying the blindness, "how was your room?"

"The sheets had a touch more lavender water than I care for," Landsman says. "Other than that, I really have no complaints."

Dick opens his eyes. "It has been my good fortune as an agent of law enforcement on this reservation to have relatively few dealings with Jews over the years," he begins. "Oh, and before either of you starts cinching up his sphincter on me over my supposed anti-Semitism, let me just stipulate right now that I don't give a flying fuck whether I offend your pork-shunning asses or not, and on balance, I would say that I hope I do. The fat man there knows perfectly well, or he should, that I hate everyone equally and without favor, regardless of creed or DNA."

"Understood," says Berko.

"We feel the same way about you," Landsman says.

"My point is that Jews mean bullshit. A thousand laminated layers of politics and lies buffed to a high sheen. Therefore, I believe precisely ass point two percent of anything that was told to me by this supposed Dr. Roboy, whose credentials, by the way, check out as legitimate but with a certain amount of mud at the bottom, about how you came to be scooting down that road in your skivvies, Landsman, with a Jew cowboy taking potshots at you out the window of his car."

Landsman starts to explain, but Dick holds up one of his girlish hands, the nails neat and glossy.

"Let me finish. Those gentlemen, no, Johnny, they do not pay my salary, fuck you very much. But through means not given to me to understand, and that I don't have the stomach to speculate about, those gentlemen have friends, Tlingit friends, who do pay my salary, or to be specific, who sit on the council that does. And if those wise tribal elders were to indicate to me that they would not take it amiss if I booked your partner here, and held him on charges of trespassing and burglary, not to mention conducting an illegal and unauthorized investigation, then that is what I would have to do. Those Jewish squirrels out there at Peril Strait, and I know you know it pains me to say this, for better or worse, they're *my* motherfucking Jewish squirrels. And their facility, for as long as they occupy it, comes under the full color and protection of Tribal law enforcement. Even if, after I go to all the trouble to save your freckle-assed life out there, Landsman, and drag you down here and house you at considerable expense, fuck if those Jews don't seem to lose all interest in you."

"Talk about verbal jags," Landsman says to Berko. To Dick he says, "They got a doctor here, I really think you ought to see him."

"But much as I'd like to send you back to get your ass hung on a hook by that ex-wife of yours, Landsman," Dick barrels on, "and try as I might, I can't seem to let you go without asking just

one question, even knowing in advance that you're both Jews, of
a sort, and that any answer you give me is only going to add to
the layers of bullshit that are already blinding me with their high
Jewish shine."

They wait for the question, and it comes, and Dick's manner
hardens. All traces of verbosity and teasing vanish.

"Are we talking about a homicide?" he says.

"Yes," Landsman says at the same time that Berko says,
"Officially, no."

"Two," Landsman insists. "Two, Berko. I make them for Naomi,
too."

"Naomi?" Berko says. "Meyer, what the fuck?"

Landsman goes over it from the beginning, leaving out nothing
relevant, from the knock on the door of his room at the Zamenhof
to his interview with Mrs. Shpilman, from the pie man's daughter
who sent him into the FAA records to the presence of Aryeh
Baronshteyn at Peril Strait.

"Hebrew?" Berko says. "Mexicans speaking Hebrew?"

"That's what it sounded like to me," Landsman says. "Not
synagogue Hebrew, either." Landsman knows Hebrew when he
hears it. But the Hebrew he knows is the traditional brand, the
one his ancestors carried with them through the millennia of their
European exile, oily and salty as a piece of fish smoked to preserve
it, its flesh flavored strongly by Yiddish. That kind of Hebrew is
never employed for human conversation. It's only for talking to
God. If it was Hebrew that Landsman heard at Peril Strait, it was
not the old salt-herring tongue but some spiky dialect, a language
of alkali and rocks. It sounded to him like the Hebrew brought over
by the Zionists after 1948. Those hard desert Jews tried fiercely
to hold on to it in their exile but, as with the German Jews before
them, got overwhelmed by the teeming tumult of Yiddish, and by
the painful association of their language with recent failure and
disaster. As far as Landsman knows, that kind of Hebrew is extinct
except among a few last holdouts meeting annually in lonely halls.

"I only caught a word or two. It was fast and I couldn't follow it. I guess that was the idea."

He tells them about waking in the room where Naomi wrote her epitaph on a wall, about the barracks and the training course and the groups of idle young men with guns.

As he tells it, Dick gets more and more interested in spite of himself, asking questions, poking his nose into the affair with an instinctive, stubborn love of stinks.

"I knew your sister," he says when Landsman winds up at the rescue in the woods of Peril Strait. "I was sorry when she died. And this holy fudge-packer sounds like exactly the kind of stray mutt she would have risked her ass for."

"But what did they want from Mendel Shpilman, these Jews with their visitor who doesn't like messes?" Berko says. "That's the part I don't get. What are they *doing* out there?"

The questions strike Landsman as inevitable, logical, and key, but they seem to cool Dick's ardor for the case.

"You have nothing," he says, his mouth a bloodless hyphen. "And let me tell you, Landsman, with these Peril Strait Jews, such is far from the case. They have so much weight behind them, gentlemen, let me tell you, they could make you a diamond out of a fossilized turd."

"What do you know about them, Willie?" Berko says.

"I don't know shit."

"The man in the Caudillo," Landsman says. "The one you went over and talked to. He was also an American?"

"I would say not, a shriveled-up raisin of a yid. He didn't care to tell me his name. And I'm not supposed to inquire. Being as how the Tribal Police official policy on that place, as I think I may have already mentioned, is 'I don't know shit.'"

"Come on, Wilfred," Berko says. "We're talking about Naomi."

"I appreciate that. But I know enough about Landsman here— fuck, I know enough about homicide detectives period—to know that sister or no sister, this is not about finding out the truth. It's not about getting the story right. Because you and I, we know, gentlemen, that the story is whatever we decide it is, and however nice and neat we make it, in the end a story is never going to make a damn bit of difference to the dead. What you want, Landsman, is to pay those fuckers back. But that is never going to happen. You are never going to get them. No fucking way."

"Willie boy," Berko says. "Come clean. So, don't do it for him. Don't do it because his sister, Naomi, was such a great fucking kid."

By means of the silence that follows, he supplies a third reason for Dick to clue them in.

"You're saying," Dick says, "that I should do it for you."

"I am saying that."

"Because of all we once meant to each other in the springtime of our lives."

"I might not go that far."

"That is so fucking touching," Dick says. He leans forward and pushes the button on his intercom. "Minty, get my bearskin out of the trash and bring it in here, so I can throw up on it." He lets up on the button before Minty can reply. "I'm not doing fuck-all for you, Detective Berko Shemets. But because I liked your sister, Landsman, I'll tie the same knot in your brain that those squirrels have tied in mine, and let you try to figure out what the hell it means."

The door opens, and a young, wide woman comes in, half again as tall as her boss, carrying the bearskin cloak like it contains the photoresidue of the risen body of Jesus Christ. Dick springs to his feet, grabs the cloak, and, with a grimace, as if fearing contamination, knots it around his neck by the thong.

"Find that one a coat and a hat," he says, jerking a thumb toward Landsman. "Something with a nice stink on it, salmon guts or muscatel. Take the coat off Marvin Klag, he's passed out in A7."

🔹 34 🔹

In the summer of 1897, members of the party of the Italian mountaineer Abruzzi, fresh from their conquest of Mount Saint Elias, inflamed barflies and telegraph operators in the town of Yakutat with a tale of having seen, from the slopes of the second-highest Alaskan peak, a city in the sky. Streets, houses, towers, trees, moving crowds of people, chimneys trailing smoke. A great civilization, in the midst of the clouds. A certain Thornton in the party passed around a photograph; the city captured on Thornton's blurred plate was afterward identified as Bristol, England, some twenty-five hundred transpolar miles away. Ten years later, the explorer Peary blew a fortune in a bid to strike Crocker Land, a land of lofty peaks that he and his men had glimpsed dangling in the sky on a prior journey north. Fata morgana, the phenomenon was called. A mirror made of weather and light and the imagination of men raised on stories of heaven.

Meyer Landsman sees cows, red-spotted white milk cows milling like angels in a wide green afterlife of grass.

The three policemen drove all the way back down to Peril Strait so that Dick could wow them with this doubtful vision. Crammed for two hours into the cab of Dick's pickup, they smoked and

abused one another, bumping along Tribal Route 2. Back through
deep miles of forest. Potholes the size of bathtubs. Rain tossed in
vandalistic handfuls at the windshield. Back through the village
of Jims, a row of steel roofs along an inlet, houses jumbled like the
last ten cans of beans on a grocery shelf before the hurricane hits.
Dogs and boys and basketball hoops, an old flatbed embodied by
weeds and spiky sprays of crowberry, a chimera of truck and leaf.
Just past the portable Assembly of God church the paved tribal
route gave way to sand and gravel. Five miles farther, it devolved to
a mere slash cut through the ooze. Dick swore and fought the stick
as his big GMC surfed the tides of mud and grit. The brake and gas
were rigged to suit a man of his stature, and he handled them like
Horowitz sailing through a storm of Liszt. Every time they hit a
bump, some critical piece of Landsman was crushed by a tumbling
slab of Shemets.

When they ran out of mud, they abandoned the truck and
hiked down through a dense growth of hemlock. The footing was
slippery, the trail a suggestion offered by scraps of yellow police
tape stuck to the trees. Now the trail has led, after ten minutes'
squelching and splashing in a dense mist that verged at moments
on outright rain, to an electrified fence. Concrete pylons driven
deep, wires taut and even. A well-made fence, a stark fence. A
brutal gesture for Jews to make on Indian land, and one that has no
precedent or license, as far as Landsman knows.

On the other side of the electric fence, the fata morgana
shimmers. Grass. Pastureland, rich and glossy. A hundred good-
looking freckled cattle with delicate heads.

"Cows," Landsman says, and the word sounds like a moo of
doubtfulness.

"They look like dairy cows," Berko says.

"They're Ayrshires," says Dick. "I snapped some pictures last
time I came out here. A professor of agriculture down in Davis,
California, ID'd them for me. 'A Scottish breed.'" Dick works his

voice up into his nose, mocking that Californian professor. "'Known for its hardiness and ability to thrive in northern latitudes.'"

"Cows," Landsman says again. He can't shake the eerie sense of dislocation, of mirage, of seeing something that is not there. Something that nonetheless he knows, recognizes, a half-remembered reality out of stories of heaven or his own past. From the days of the "Ickes colleges," when the Alaskan Development Corporation dispensed tractors and seed and sacks of fertilizer to the fugitive boatloads, Jews of the District have dreamed and despaired of the Jewish farm. "Cows in Alaska."

The Polar Bear generation suffered two great disappointments. The first and stupidest was due to the total absence, here in the fabled north, of icebergs, polar bears, walruses, penguins, tundra, snow in vast quantities, and, above all, Eskimos. Thousands of Sitka businesses still bear bitter and fanciful names such as Walrus Drug, or Eskimo Wig and Hairpiece, or Nanook's Tavern.

The second disappointment was celebrated in popular songs of the period, like "A Cage of Green." Two million Jews got off the boats and found no rolling prairies dotted with buffalo. No feathered Indians on horseback. Only a spine of flooded mountains and fifty thousand Tlingit village-dwellers already in possession of most of the flat and usable land. Nowhere to spread out, to grow, to do anything more than crowd together in the teeming style of Vilna and Lodz. The homesteading dreams of a million landless Jews, fanned by movies, light fiction, and informational brochures provided by the United States Department of the Interior—snuffed on arrival. Every few years some utopian society or other would acquire a tract of green that reminded some dreamer of a cow pasture. They would found a colony, import livestock, pen a manifesto. And then the climate, the markets, and the streak of doom that marbled Jewish life would work their charm. The dream farm would languish and fail.

Landsman feels that he's looking at that dream, lustrous and verdant. A mirage of the old optimism, the hope for the future on which he was raised. That future itself, it seems to him—that was the fata morgana.

"There's something funny about that one," Berko says, staring through the binoculars that Dick brought along, and Landsman can hear the tug in his voice, a fish playing at the end of his line.

"Give me," Landsman says, taking the binoculars and raising them to his face. He tries, but they're all just cows to him.

"That one. By the two over there, facing the other way." Berko guides the lenses with a brusque hand, settling them on a cow whose mottled hide is perhaps a richer red than its sisters', a more dazzling white, its head sturdier, less ladylike. Like avid fingers, its lips tear at the grass.

"There's something different," Landsman allows. "But so what?"

"I'm not sure," Berko says. It sounds slightly less than truthful. "Willie, do you know for sure these cows belong to our mystery Jews?"

"We saw the little buckaroo Jewboys with our own eyes," Dick says. "The ones from the camp or school or whatever it is. Rounding them up. Driving them that way, toward the campus. They used some kind of bossy Scottish dog to help them. Me and my boys followed them a ways."

"They didn't see you?"

"It was getting dark. Anyway, what the fuck do you think, of course they didn't see us, we're Indians, God damn it. About half a mile in, there's a state-of-the-art dairying barn. A couple of silos. It's a medium-small operation, and it's definitely all Jew."

"So what is going on here?" Landsman says. "Is it a rehab center or a dairy farm? Or is it some kind of weird commando training facility pretending to be both?"

"Your commando likes his milk fresh from the cow," Dick says.

They stand there looking at the cows. Landsman fights an urge to lean on the electric fence. There's a fool of a devil in him that wants to feel the thrum of current. There's a current in him that wants to feel the devil in the wire. Something bothers him, nags at him, about this vision, this Crocker Land of cows. However real it may be, it's also impossible. It should not be here; no yid should have been able to swing such a feat of real estate. Landsman has known or had dealings with many of the great and the wicked Jews of his generation, the rich men, the mad utopians, the so-called visionaries, the politicians who turn the law on their lathes. Landsman considers the warlords of the Russian neighborhoods with their stockpiles of weapons and diamonds and sturgeon roe. He runs through his mental docket of smuggler kings and gray-market moguls, gurus of minor cults. Men with influence, connections, unlimited funds. None of them could have pulled off something like this, not even Heskel Shpilman or Anatoly Moskowits the Wild Beast. No matter how powerful, every yid in the District is tethered by the leash of 1948. His kingdom is bound in its nutshell. His sky is a painted dome, his horizon an electrified fence. He has the flight and knows the freedom only of a balloon on a string.

Meanwhile, Berko is jerking on the knot of his necktie in a way that Landsman has come to associate with the imminent emergence of a theory.

"What is it, Berko?" he says.

"She's not a white cow with red spots," Berko says with finality. "She's a *red* cow with white spots."

He sets his hat on the back of his head and purses his lips. He takes several backward steps away from the fence, and hikes up his trouser legs. Slowly at first, he lopes toward the fence. And then, to Landsman's horror, shock, and mild elation, Berko leaps. His bulk leaves the ground. He sticks out one leg and hooks the other behind him. His trouser cuffs pull back to reveal green socks and pale shins. Then he comes down, with a gust of exhalation, on the other side of the fence. He staggers under his own impact, then plunges forward into the world of cows.

"What the fuck," Landsman says.

"Technically, I have to arrest him now," says Dick.

The cows react to the intrusion with complaint and protest but little in the way of emotion. Berko makes straight for the one that's bothering him, marches right up to it. It shies away, lowing. He holds up his arms, palms outward. He speaks to it in Yiddish, American, Tlingit, Old and Modern Bovine. He circles it slowly, looking it up and down. Landsman sees Berko's point: This cow is not like the others, in contour or coloration.

The cow submits to Berko's inspection. He puts a hand on its crop, and it waits, hoofs spread, knock-kneed, head canted at a listening angle. Berko ducks down and peers at its underside. He runs his fingers along its ribs, up its neck, to the poll of its head, then back along its flank to the tentlike rigging of its hips. There his hand stops, in the middle of a white patch of hide. Berko raises the fingers of his right hand to his mouth, moistens the tips, then rubs in a circular motion against the white patch of the cow's rump. He takes his fingers away, contemplates them, smiles, frowns. Then he lumbers back across the field and stops at the fence, opposite Landsman.

He holds up his right hand as if in solemn parody of the salute of a cigar-store Indian, and Landsman sees that his fingers are streaked with flakes of white.

"Fake spots," Berko says.

He backs up and comes at the fence again. Landsman and Dick get out of his way, and he's up and airborne, and then the ground rings with the impact of him.

"Show-off," Landsman says.

"Always was," says Dick.

"So," says Landsman, "what are you saying? The cow is wearing a disguise?"

"That's what I'm saying."

"Somebody painted white spots on a red cow."

"So it appears."

"This fact has significance to you."

"In a sense," Berko says. "In a certain context. I believe that cow may be a red heifer."

"Get out of here," Landsman says. "A red heifer."

"This is a Jew thing, I take it," Dick says.

"When the Temple in Jerusalem is restored," Berko says, "and it's time to make the traditional sin offering, the Bible says you need a particular kind of cow. A red heifer, without blemish. Pure. I guess they're pretty scarce, pure red heifers. In fact, I believe there have been only nine of them since the beginning of history. It would be pretty cool to find one. It would be like finding a five-leaf clover."

"When the *Temple* is restored," Landsman says, thinking of Buchbinder the dentist and his mad museum. "That's after Messiah comes?"

"Some people," Berko says slowly, beginning to understand what Landsman is beginning to understand, "say Messiah will tarry until the Temple is rebuilt. Until altar worship gets restored. Blood sacrifices, a priesthood, the whole song and dance."

"So if you got hold of a red heifer, say. And you had all the tools ready, right? And the funny hats and stuff. And you, um, you built the Temple . . . you could basically *force* Messiah to come?"

"Not that I'm a religious man, God knows," Dick puts in. "But I feel compelled to point out that the Messiah already *came*, and you bastards fucking killed the motherfucker."

They hear a human voice in the distance, amplified through a loudspeaker, speaking that strange desert Hebrew. At the sound, Landsman's heart turns over, and he takes a step toward the truck.

"Let's get out of here," he says. "I have spent some time with these men, and my strong impression is that they are not very nice."

When they get safely back to the truck, Dick starts the engine but keeps it in neutral with the brake on. They sit there, filling up the cab with cigarette smoke. Landsman bums one of Dick's black ones and is forced to concede that it's a fine example of the roller's craft.

"I'm just going to go ahead and say this now, Willie," Landsman says after he's smoked the Nat Sherman halfway down. "And I'd like you to try to deny it."

"I'll do my best."

"On the way out here, we were talking, and you alluded to a certain amount of, uh, odorousness coming out of this place."

"I did."

"A stink of money, you said."

"There is money behind these buckaroos, no doubt about that."

"But from the minute I first heard about this place, something's been bothering me. Now I figure I've seen most of the operation. From the sign on the floatplane dock to those cows. And it's bothering me even more."

"And what's that?"

"That is, I'm sorry, I don't care how much money they throw around. I buy that a member of your tribal council might take a bribe from a Jew every now and then. Business is business, a dollar's a dollar, and so forth. Who knows, I have heard people argue that the flow of illegal funds back and forth over the Line is the closest that Jews and Indians ever come to peace, love, and understanding."

"That's sweet."

"Obviously, these Jews, whatever it is they're doing, they don't want to share the news with other Jews. And the District is like a house with too many people and not enough bedrooms. Everybody knows everybody's business. Nobody has a secret in Sitka, it's just a big shtetl. You have a secret, it makes sense to try to hide it out here."

"But."

"But odor or not, business or not, secret or not, I'm sorry, there is no way in hell the Tlingit are ever going to let a bunch of Jews come in here, in the heart of the Indianer-Lands, and build all this. I don't care how much Jewish coin gets thrown around."

"You're saying not even us Indians are that gutless and debased. To give our worst enemy that kind of toehold."

"How about, let's say, us Jews are the world's most evil schemers, we run the world from our secret headquarters on the dark side of the moon. But even we have our limitations. Do you like that better?"

"I'm not going to argue the point."

"The Indians would never allow it unless they were expecting some kind of big payoff. Really big. As big as the District, let's say."

"Let's say," Dick says, his voice sounding tight.

"I figured the American angle in all this was whatever channel somebody used to get Naomi's crash file pulled. But no Jew could ever guarantee a payoff like that."

"Penguin Sweater," Berko says. "He fixes it so the Indians get the District under Native sovereignty once we're gone. For that, the Indians help the Verbovers and friends set up their secret dairy farm out here."

"But what does Penguin Sweater get out of it?" Landsman says. "What's in it for the U.S.?"

"You have now arrived at a place of great darkness, Brother Landsman," Dick says, putting the truck into gear. "Which I fear you will have to enter without Wilfred Dick."

"I hate to say this, cousin," Landsman says to Berko, putting a hand on his shoulder. "But I think we have to go down to the Massacre Spot."

"God fucking damn it," says Berko in American.

 35

Forty-two miles south of the Sitka city limits, a house crafted from salvage planks and gray shingles teeters on two dozen pilings over a slough. A nameless backwater, riddled with bears and prone to methane flatulence. A graveyard of rowboats, tackle, pickup trucks, and, somewhere deep down, a dozen Russian fur hunters and their Aleut dog-soldiers. At one end of the slough, back in the bushes, a magnificent Tlingit longhouse is being dismantled by salmonberry and devil's club. At the other end stretches a rocky beach, littered with a thousand black stones on which an ancient people etched the shapes of animals and stars. It was on this beach, in 1854, that those twelve *promyshlenniks* and Aleuts under Yevgeny Simonof met a bloody end at the hands of a Tlingit chief named Kohklux. Over a century later, the great-great-granddaughter of Chief Kohklux, Mrs. Pullman, became the second Indian wife taken by a five-foot-six Jewish chess player and spymaster named Hertz Shemets.

At chess, as in secret statecraft, Uncle Hertz was known for his sense of the clock, an excess of prudence, and a tiresome depth of preparation. He read up on his opponents, made a fatal study of them. He sought the pattern of weakness, the unresolved complex, the tic. For twenty-five years he conducted a secret campaign against the people on the far side of the Line, trying to weaken their hold on the Indianer-Lands, and in that time he became a recognized authority on their culture and history. He learned to savor the Tlingit language, with its sucking-candy vowels and its chewy consonants. He undertook profound research into the fragrance and heft of Tlingit women.

When he married Mrs. Pullman (no one ever called the lady, may she rest in peace, Mrs. Shemets), he developed an interest in her great-great-grandfather's victory over Simonof. He spent hours in the library at Bronfman, poring over Tsarist-era maps. He annotated interviews conducted by Methodist missionaries with ninety-nine-year-old Tlingit crones who were six-year-old girls when those war hammers went to work on all those thick Russian skulls. He discovered that in the USGS survey of 1949, the one that set the proper boundaries of the District of Sitka, the Massacre Spot somehow got drawn as Tlingit land. Even though it lies west of the Baranof range, the Massacre Spot is legally Native, a green badge of Indianness daubed on the Jewish side of Baranof Island. When Hertz discovered this error, he had Berko's stepmother buy up the land with money—as Dennis Brennan later documented— taken from his COINTELPRO slush fund. He built his spider-legged house on it. And when Mrs. Pullman died, Hertz Shemets inherited the Simonof Massacre Spot. He declared it the world's crummiest Indian reservation, and himself the world's crummiest Indian.

"Asshole," Berko says, with less rancor than Landsman might have expected, contemplating his father's rickety dwelling through the windshield of the Super Sport.

"When's the last time you saw him?"

Berko turns to his partner with his eyes rolled back as if to search an inner file on Landsman for the record of a question that needed less answering. "Let me ask you this, Meyer. If you were me, when would you have seen him last?"

Landsman parks the Super Sport behind the old man's Buick Roadmaster, a mud-streaked blue beast with fake wood panels

and a bumper sticker advertising, in Yiddish and American, the
WORLD-FAMOUS SIMONOF MASSACRE SPOT AND GENUINE TLINGIT
LONGHOUSE. Although the roadside attraction has been defunct
for a while, the bumper sticker is bright and crisp. There are still a
dozen cartons of them stacked in the longhouse.

"Give me a hint," Landsman says.

"Jokes about foreskins."

"Oh, right."

"Every single joke about a foreskin ever devised."

"I had no idea there were so many," Landsman says. "It was an
education."

"Come on," Berko says, climbing out of the car. "Let's get this
over with."

Landsman eyes the hulk of the Genuine Longhouse, off in the
dry thicket of berry vines and devil's club, a gaudy-painted wreck.
In fact, there is nothing genuine about the Longhouse. Hertz
Shemets built it with the help of two Indian brothers-in-law, his
nephew Meyer, and his son Berko one summer after the boy came to
live on Adler Street. He built it for fun, with no thought of turning
it into the roadside attraction that he tried and failed to make of
it after his ouster. Berko was fifteen that summer, and Landsman
twenty. The kid crafted every surface of his personality to conform
to the curvature of Landsman's. He devoted two solid months to
the task of training himself to operate a Skilsaw, as Landsman did,
with a papiros jiggling on his lip and the smoke stinging his eyes.
By then Landsman was already set on taking his police exams,
and that summer Berko declared his identical ambition, but if
Landsman had been talking about becoming a blowfly, Berko would
have found a way to learn to love dung.

Like most policemen, Landsman sails double-hulled against
tragedy, stabilized against heave and storm. It's the shallows he
has to worry about, the hairline fissures, the little freaks of torque.
The memory of that summer, for example, or the thought that he
has long since exhausted the patience of a kid who once would have

waited a thousand years to spend an hour with him shooting cans off a fence with an air rifle. The sight of the Longhouse breaks some small, as yet unbroken facet of Landsman's heart. All of the things they made, during their minute in this corner of the map, dissolved in brambles of salmonberry and oblivion.

"Berko," he says as they crunch across the half-frozen mud of the world's crummiest Indian reservation. He takes his cousin by the elbow. "I'm sorry I've been such a mess."

"You don't need to apologize," Berko says. "It's not your fault."

"I'm good now. I'm back," Landsman says, and the words ring true to his own ear in the moment. "I don't know what did it. The hypothermia, maybe. Or getting into this whole thing with Shpilman. Or, fine, laying off the booze. But I'm back to my old self."

"Uh-huh."

"Doesn't it seem that way to you?"

"Sure." Berko might be agreeing with a child or a nut. He might not be agreeing at all. "You seem all right."

"Ringing endorsement."

"I don't want to get into it now, tell me, do you mind? I just want to go in there, hit the old man with our questions, and get back home to Ester-Malke and the boys. That okay with you?"

"That's fine, Berko. Of course."

"Thank you."

They tramp through a congealed sludge of mud and patchy gravel, frozen puddles, each one stretched with a thin drumhead of ice. A cartoon stairway, splintered, wigwagging, leads to a weather-gray cedar front door. The door hangs crooked, crudely winterized with thick strips of rubber.

"When you say it's not my fault," Landsman begins.

"Man! I need to piss."

"The implication is, you think I'm crazy. Mentally ill. Not responsible for my actions."

"I'm knocking on this door now."

He knocks twice, hard enough to imperil the hinges.

"Not fit to wear a shield," Landsman says, truly wishing he could let the subject drop. "In other words."

"Your ex-wife made that call, not me."

"But you don't disagree."

"What do I know about mental illness?" Berko says. "I'm not the one who was arrested for running naked through the woods, three hours from home, after braining a man with an iron bed frame."

Hertz Shemets comes to the door, the shave on his jowls as fresh as two droplets of blood. He's wearing a gray flannel suit over a white shirt, with a poppy-red necktie. He smells like vitamin B, spray starch, smoked fish. He's tinier than ever, jerky as a wooden man on a stick.

"Old boy," he calls Landsman, breaking a few of the bones in his nephew's hand.

"Looking good, Uncle Hertz," Landsman says. Taking a closer look, he sees that the suit is shiny at the elbows and knees. The necktie bears testimony to some past meal of soup and has been knotted through the soft lapels not of a shirt but of a white pajama top jammed hastily into the trousers. But Landsman is hardly one to criticize. He's wearing his emergency suit, popped loose from its crevice at the back of his trunk and unballed, a black number in viscose and wool blend with gold buttons meant to look like Roman coins. He borrowed it once, for a last-minute funeral he forgot he was planning to attend, from an unlucky gambler named Gluksman. It manages to look both funereal and gaudy, has fierce wrinkles, and smells of Detroit trunk.

"Thanks for the warning," Uncle Hertz says, letting go of the wreckage of Landsman's hand.

"That one there was all for surprising you," Landsman says, nodding toward Berko. "But I knew you'd want to go out and kill something."

Uncle Hertz puts his palms together and bows. Like a true hermit, he takes his duties as a host very seriously. If the hunting is poor, then he will have dragged something well marbled out of the deep freeze and put it on the stove with some carrots and onions and a crushed handful of the herbs that he grows and hangs up in a shed behind his cabin. He will have seen to it that there is ice for the whiskey and cold beer for the stew. Above all, he will have wanted to shave and put on a tie.

The old man tells Landsman to go into the house, and Landsman obeys him, which leaves Hertz standing there to face his son. Landsman watches, an interested party like all Jewish men from the moment that Abraham got Isaac to lie down on that mountaintop and bare his pulsing rib cage to the sky. The old man reaches out and takes hold of the sleeve of Berko's lumberjack shirt. He rolls the fabric between his fingers. Berko submits to the examination with a look of genuine pain on his face. It has to be killing him, Landsman knows, to appear before his father wearing anything but his best Italian finery.

"So, where's the Big Blue Ox?" the old man says at last.

"I don't know," Berko says. "But I think he may have your pajama bottoms."

Berko smooths the pinched place that his father made in his sleeve. He walks past the old man and comes into the house. "Asshole," he says, under his breath, almost. He excuses himself to use the toilet.

"Slivovitz," the old man says, going for the bottles, a huddled skyline like a miniature replica of the Shvartser-Yam on a black enamel tray. "Isn't that it?"

"Seltzer," Landsman says. When his uncle arches an eyebrow, he shrugs. "I got a new doctor. Indian fellow. Wants me to give up booze."

"And since when do you listen to doctors or Indians?"

"Since never," Landsman admits.

"Self-medication is a Landsman tradition."

"So is being a Jew," Landsman says. "Look where that's got us."

"Strange times to be a Jew," the old man agrees. He turns from the bar and presents Landsman with a highball glass fitted with a lemon-slice yarmulke. Then he pours himself a generous shot of slivovitz and raises it to Landsman with an expression of humorous cruelty that Landsman knows well and in which he long since ceased to see any humor.

"To strange times," the old man says.

He eases it back, and when he looks at Landsman, he glows like a man who just said something witty that broke up a room. Landsman knows how much it must be killing Hertz to watch the skiff he poled for so many years, with all his craft and strength, drifting ever nearer to the falls of Reversion. He pours himself a second quick one and knocks it back with no show of pleasure. Now it's Landsman's turn to raise an eyebrow.

"You have your doctor," Uncle Hertz says. "I have mine."

Uncle Hertz's cabin is a single large room with a loft that goes all the way around three sides. All the trim and furnishing is horn, bone, sinew, hide, and pelt. You reach the loft by a steep companionway at the back, next to the kitchenette. In one corner is the old man's bed, neatly made. Beside the bed, on a small, round table, stands a chessboard. The pieces are rosewood and maple. One of White's maple knights is missing its left horse ear. One of Black's rosewood pawns has a blond flaw on its knob. The board has a neglected, chaotic air; a Vicks inhaler stands amid the pieces at one end, a possible threat to White's king at e1.

"I see you're playing the Mentholyptus Defense," Landsman says, turning the board to get a better look. "Correspondence game?"

Hertz is crowding Landsman, exhaling his breath of plum brandy, the undernote of herring so oily and sharp you can feel the little bones in it. Jostled, Landsman tips the whole thing to the ground with a clatter.

"You were always the master of that move," Hertz says. "The Landsman Gambit."

"Shit, Uncle Hertz, I'm sorry." Landsman crouches and gropes around under the old man's bed for the pieces.

"Don't worry about it!" the old man says. "It's all right. It wasn't a game, I was just fooling around. I don't play by mail anymore. I live and die by the sacrifice. I like to dazzle them with some crazy, beautiful combination. Tough to do that on a postcard. Do you recognize the set?"

Hertz helps Landsman return the pieces to their box, also maple, lined with green velveteen. The inhaler he slips into a pocket.

"No," Landsman says. Landsman is the one, executing the Landsman Gambit during a tantrum many years ago, who cost the White knight its ear.

"What do you think? You gave it to him."

There are five books stacked on the nightstand by the old man's bed. A Yiddish translation of Chandler. A French biography of Marcel Duchamp. A paperback attack on the wily agenda of the Third Russian Republic that was popular in the U.S. the year before. A Peterson field guide to marine mammals. And something called *Kampf*, in the original German, by Emanuel Lasker.

The toilet flushes, and there is the sound of Berko dashing water over his hands.

"Suddenly, everybody's reading Lasker," Landsman says. He picks up the book, heavy, black, the title embossed in gilded black letter, and is mildly surprised to discover that it has nothing to do with chess. No diagrams, no figurine queens and horses, just page after page of thorny German prose. "So the man was a philosopher, too?"

"He considered it his true calling. Even though he was a genius at chess and higher mathematics. I'm sorry to say, as a philosopher, maybe he wasn't such a genius. Why, who else is reading Emanuel Lasker? Nobody reads Emanuel Lasker anymore."

"That's even more true now than it was a week ago," Berko says, coming out of the bathroom, drying his hands on a towel. He gravitates naturally toward the dinner table. The big wood-block table is laid for three. The plates are enameled tin, the glasses plastic, and the knives have bone handles and fearsome blades, the kind you might use to cut the liver still throbbing from the abdomen of a bear. There is a pitcher of iced tea and an enameled pot of coffee. The meal that Hertz Shemets has prepared is plentiful, hot, and heavily weighted toward moose.

"Moose chili," the old man says. "I ground the meat last fall, I have it in vacuum bags in the deep freeze. Killed the moose, too, of course. A cow, a thousand-pounder. The chili I made today, the beans are kidney beans, and I threw in a can of turtle beans I had lying around. Only I wasn't sure it would be enough, so I heated up a few more things I had in the freezer. There's a quiche lorraine— that's egg, naturally, with tomato and bacon, the bacon is moose bacon. I smoked it myself."

"The eggs are moose eggs," Berko says, duplicating perfectly his father's mildly pompous tone.

The old man points to a white glass bowl piled high with uniform meatballs in a reddish-brown gravy. "Swedish meatballs," he says. "Moose meatballs. And then some cold roast moose, if anybody wants a sandwich. I baked the bread myself. And the mayonnaise is homemade. I can't abide mayonnaise from a jar."

They sit down to eat with the lonely old man. Years ago his dining room was a lively region, the only table in these divided islands at which Indians and Jews regularly sat down together to eat good food without rancor. There was California wine to drink and be expatiated upon by the old man. Silent types, hard cases, and the odd special agent or lobbyist from Washington mingled with totem carvers, chess bums, and Native fishermen. Hertz submitted to the raillery of Mrs. Pullman. He was the kind of domineering old cutthroat who chose to marry a woman who would knock him down a peg or two in front of his friends. Somehow it only made him look stronger.

"I put in a call or two," Uncle Hertz says after several minutes of chess-deep concentration on his food. "After you called to say you were coming down."

"Did you?" Berko says. "A call or two."

"That's right." Hertz has a way of smiling, or of producing a smile-like effect, where he lifts only the upper lip on the right side of his mouth, and only for half a second, flashing one yellow incisor. It looks like someone has caught him by the lip on an invisible fishhook and is giving the line a sharp tug. "From what I gather, you have been making a nuisance of yourself, Meyerle. Unprofessional conduct. Erratic behavior. Lost your badge and gun."

Whatever else he may have been, for forty years Uncle Hertz was a sworn officer of the law with a federal shield in his billfold. Though he undersells it, the note of reproach is unmistakable. He turns to his son. "And I don't know what you think you're doing," he says. "Eight weeks away from the void. Two children and, mazel tov and kaynahora, a third on the way."

Berko doesn't bother to ask how his father knows that Ester-Malke is pregnant. It would only feed the old man's vanity. He just nods and puts away a few more moose meatballs. They are good, the meatballs, moist with hints of rosemary and smoke.

"You are right," Berko says. "It's madness. And I don't say that I love or care for that buffalo there, look at him, with no badge and no gun, bothering people and running around with frostbite on his kneecaps, any more than I do for my wife or my children, because I don't. Or that it makes any sense for me to take risks with their future on his behalf, because it doesn't." As he contemplates the bowl of meatballs, his body emits a weary sound, a Yiddish sound, halfway between a belch and a lamentation. "But if we're talking about voids, what can I say, that's not the type of circumstances I want to be facing without Meyer around."

"You see how loyal," Uncle Hertz tells Landsman. "That's just how I felt about your father, may his name be for a blessing, but the coward left me high and dry."

His tone aspires to lightness, but the subsequent blot of silence seems to darken the remark. They chew their food, and life feels long and ponderous. Hertz gets up and pours himself another shot.

He stands by the window, watching the sky that is like a mosaic pieced together from the broken shards of a thousand mirrors, each one tinted a different shade of gray. The winter sky of southeastern Alaska is a Talmud of gray, an inexhaustible commentary on a Torah of rain clouds and dying light. Uncle Hertz has always been the most competent, self-assured man Landsman knows, neat as an origami airplane, a quick paper needle folded with precision, impervious to turbulence. Accurate, methodical, dispassionate. There were always hints of shadow, of irrationality and violence, but they were contained behind the wall of Hertz's mysterious Indian adventures, hidden on the far side of the Line, covered over by him with the careful backward kicks of an animal concealing its spoor. But now a memory surfaces in Landsman from the days following his father's death, of Uncle Hertz sitting crumpled like a wad of tissue in a corner of the kitchen on Adler Street, shirttails hanging, no order to his hair, shirt misbuttoned, the dwindling contents of a bottle of slivovitz on the kitchen table beside him marking like a barometer the plummeting atmosphere of his grief.

"We have ourselves a puzzle, Uncle Hertz," says Landsman. "Is why we're here."

"That and the mayonnaise," Berko says.

"A puzzle." The old man turns from the window, his eyes hard again and wary. "I hate puzzles."

"We're not asking you to solve any," Berko says.

"Don't take that tone with me, John Bear," the old man snaps. "I don't care for it."

"Tone?" Berko says, his voice stacked like a measure of musical score with a half-dozen tones, a chamber ensemble of insolence, resentment, sarcasm, provocation, innocence, and surprise. *"Tone?"*

Landsman gives Berko a look that is meant to remind him not of his age and station in life but of the manifest uncoolness of bickering with one's relatives. It's an old and well-worn facial expression dating from the time of Berko's first strife-filled years with the Landsmans. It never takes longer than a few minutes, whenever they get together, for everyone to revert to the state of nature, like a party marooned by a shipwreck. That's what a family is. Also the storm at sea, the ship, and the unknown shore. And the hats and the whiskey stills that you make out of bamboo and coconuts. And the fire that you light to keep away the beasts.

"There's something we're trying to explain," Landsman begins again. "A situation. And there are aspects of the situation that reminded us of you."

Uncle Hertz pours another shot of slivovitz, carries it to the table, and sits down. "Start from the start," he says.

"The start is a dead junkie in my hotel."

"Aha."

"You've been following it."

"I heard something on the radio," the old man says. "Maybe I read a little something in the paper, too." He always blames the newspapers for the things he knows. "He was the son of Heskel Shpilman. The one they had such high hopes for when he was a kid."

"He was murdered," Landsman says. "Contrary to what you might have read. And when he died, he was in hiding. He'd been in hiding, from one thing and another, for most of his life, but when he died, I think he was trying to duck some men he had run out on. I was able to trace his movements back to the Yakovy airport last April. He showed up there the day before Naomi died."

"This has something to do with Naomi?"

"These men who were looking for Shpilman. And who, we're assuming, killed him. Last April they hired Naomi to fly the guy out to a farm they run, supposed to be some kind of a therapy facility for troubled kids. Out in Peril Strait. But when he got there, he panicked. He wanted out. He came to Naomi to help him, and she sneaked him out of there and flew him back to civilization. To Yakovy. She died the next day."

"Peril Strait?" the old man says. "These are Natives, then? You're saying *Indians* killed Mendel Shpilman?"

"No," Berko says. "These men with the youth rehab. On a good thousand acres just north of the village there. It seems to have been built with money from American Jews. The people running it are yids. And as far as we can tell, the place is a front for their real operation."

"Which is what? Growing marijuana?"

"Well, for one thing, they have a herd of Ayrshire dairy cows," Berko says. "Maybe a hundred head of them."

"That's for one thing."

"For another, they seem to be running some kind of paramilitary training facility. Their leader might be an old man, a Jew. Wilfred Dick got a look at him, he was there. But the face meant nothing to Dick. Whoever he is, he seems to have ties to the Verbovers, or at least to Aryeh Baronshteyn. But we don't know why or what kind."

"There was an American there, too," Landsman says. "He flew in for a meeting with Baronshteyn and these other mysterious Jews. They all seemed a little worried about the American. They seemed to think he might not be happy with them or how they were running things."

The old man gets up from the table and goes to a hutch that separates his eating from his sleep. From a humidor he takes a cigar and rolls it between his palms. He rolls it a long time, back and forth, until it seems to disappear from his thoughts entirely.

"I hate puzzles," he says finally.

"We know that," Berko says.

"You know that."

Uncle Hertz runs the cigar back and forth under his nose, inhaling deeply, eyes closed, taking pleasure not only in the smell, it seems to Landsman, but in the coolness of the smooth leaf against the flesh of his nostrils.

"This is my first question," Uncle Hertz says, opening his eyes. "Maybe my only one."

They wait for the question while he trims the cigar, fits it to his narrow lips, works them up and down.

"What color were the cows?" he says.

36

There was a red one," Berko says, slow, a bit grudging, like he missed it when the coin got palmed, even though he was staring hard at the magician's hands.

"All red?" the old man says. "Red from horn to tail?"

"She was disguised," Berko says. "Sprayed with some kind of white pigment. I can't think of any reason you'd want to do that unless you had something about her that you wanted to hide. Such as that she was, you know." He winces. "Without blemish."

"Oh, for God's sake," the old man says.

"Who are these people, Uncle Hertz? You know, don't you?"

"Who are these people?" Hertz Shemets says. "They're yids. Yids with a scheme. I know that's a tautology."

He can't seem to make up his mind to light the cigar. He sets it down, picks it up, sets it down again. Landsman gets the feeling he's weighing a secret rolled tight in its dark-veined leaf. A course of action, a tricky exchange of pieces.

"All right," Hertz says at last, "so I lied: Here's another question for you. Meyer, maybe you remember a yid, when you were a little boy, he used to come around the Einstein Chess Club. He used to joke with you, you had quite a thing for him. Yid named Litvak."

"I saw Alter Litvak the other day," Landsman says. "At the Einstein."

"Did you?"

"He lost his voice."

"Yes, he was in an accident, his throat was crushed by the wheel. His wife was killed. It was out on Roosevelt Boulevard, where they planted all those chokecherry trees. The only one that didn't die, that was the tree they hit. The only chokecherry tree in the Sitka District."

"I remember when they planted those trees," Landsman says. "For the World's Fair."

"Don't get wistful on me," the old man says. "God knows I've had my fill of wistful Jews, starting with myself. You never see a wistful Indian."

"That's because they hide them when they hear you're coming around," Berko says. "The women and wistful Indians. Shut up and tell us about Litvak."

"He used to work for me," Hertz says. "For many, many years."

His tone goes flat, and Landsman is surprised to see that his uncle is angry. Like all Shemetses, Hertz was handed down a hot temper, but it served him ill in his work, so at some point he had it killed.

"Alter Litvak was a federal agent?" Landsman says.

"No. He was not. The man has not drawn an official government salary, as far as I know, since he was honorably discharged from the U.S. Army thirty-five years ago."

"Why are you so angry at him?" Berko says, watching his father through the lantern slits of his eyes.

Hertz is startled by the question, tries to hide it. "I never get angry," he says. "Except with you, son." He smiles. "So he still goes to the Einstein. I didn't know that. He was always more of a cardplayer than a patzer. He did better in games that favor the bluff. Deceit. Concealment."

Landsman remembers the pair of tough-looking young men whom Litvak introduced as his grandnephews. There was one of them in the woods at Peril Strait, he realizes, driving the Ford Caudillo with the shadow in the backseat. The shadow of a man who didn't want Landsman to get a look at his face.

"He was there," Landsman tells Berko. "At Peril Strait. He was the mystery man in the car."

"What did Litvak do for you?" Berko says. "For all those many, many years?"

Hertz hesitates, looking from Berko to Landsman and back. "Some of this, some of that. All strictly off the books. He had a number of useful skills. Alter Litvak may be the most talented man I ever met. He understands systems and control. He is patient and methodical. He used to be incredibly strong. A good pilot, a trained mechanic. Wonderful at orienteering. Very effective as a teacher. As a trainer. Shit."

He stares down in mild wonder at the snapped halves of his cigar, one in each hand. He drops them onto his plate of sauce streaks and spreads a napkin over the evidence of his emotion. "The yid betrayed me," he says. "To that reporter. He collected evidence on me for years and then handed it all over to Brennan."

"Why would he do that?" Berko says. "If he was your yid?"

"I really can't answer your question." Hertz shakes his head, hating puzzles, faced for the rest of his life with this one. "Money, maybe, though I never knew him to take an interest in the stuff. Certainly not his beliefs. Litvak has no beliefs. No convictions. No loyalty except to the men who serve under him. He saw how things were going when this bunch took over in Washington. He knew that I was through before I knew it myself. I suppose he decided the moment was ripe. Maybe he got tired of working for me, he wanted the job for himself. Even after the Americans got rid of me and shut down their official operations, they still needed a man in Sitka. They really couldn't find anyone better for their money than Alter Litvak. Maybe he just got tired of losing to me at chess.

Maybe he saw a chance to beat me, and he took it. But he was never my yid. Permanent Status never meant anything to him. Neither, I'm certain, does the cause he's working for now. "

"The red heifer," Berko says.

"And so the idea, forgive me," Landsman says, "but talk me through it. Fine, you have a red heifer without a single flaw. And somehow or other, you get it over to Jerusalem."

"Then you kill it," Berko says. "And you burn it to ashes, and you make a paste of the ashes, and you dab a little of that on your priests. Otherwise they can't go into the Sanctuary, in the Temple, because they are unclean." He checks with his father. "Do I have that right?"

"More or less."

"Okay, but here's the thing I don't get. Isn't there—what's it called?" Landsman says. "That mosque. On the hill there where the Temple used to be?"

"It isn't a mosque, Meyerle. It's a shrine," Hertz says. "Qubbat As-Sakhrah. The Dome of the Rock. The third holiest site in Islam. Built in the seventh century by Abd al-Malik, on the precise site of the two Temples of the Jews. The spot where Abraham went to sacrifice Isaac, where Jacob saw the ladder reaching up to heaven. The navel of the world. Yes. If you wanted to rebuild the Temple and reinstitute the old rituals, as a way of hastening the coming of Messiah, then you would need to do something about the Dome of the Rock. It's in the way."

"Bombs," Berko says with an exaggerated nonchalance. "Explosives. That part of the package with Alter Litvak?"

"Demolitions," the old man says. He reaches for his drink, but it's gone. "Yes, the yid is an expert."

Landsman pushes back from the table and stands up. He gets his hat from the door. "We need to get back," he says. "We need to talk to somebody. We need to tell Bina."

He opens his phone, but there's no signal this far out from Sitka. He goes to the telephone on the wall, but Bina's number kicks him right over to voice mail. "You need to find Alter Litvak," he tells her. "Find him and hold him and do not let him go."

When he turns back to the table, he sees father and son still sitting there; Berko is putting some intense question to Hertz Shemets without saying anything. Berko has his hands folded in his lap like a well-behaved child, but he is not a well-behaved child, and if he keeps his fingers intertwined, then it is only to prevent them from enacting some mischief or harm. After an interval that feels to Landsman like a very long time, Uncle Hertz looks down.

"The prayer house at St. Cyril," Berko says. "The riots."

"The St. Cyril riots," Hertz Shemets agrees.

"God damn it."

"Berko—"

"God damn it! Indians always *said* it was the Jews that blew it up."

"You have to understand the pressure we were under," Hertz says. "At the time."

"Oh, I do," Berko says. "Believe me. The balancing act. The fine line."

"Those Jews, those fanatics, the people moving into the disputed areas. They were endangering the status of the entire District. Confirming the Americans' worst fears about what we would do if they gave us Permanent Status."

"Uh-huh," Berko says. "Yeah. Okay. And what about Mom? Was she endangering the District, too?"

Uncle Hertz speaks then, or rather the wind emerges from his lungs through the gates of his teeth in a way that resembles human speech. He looks down at his lap and makes the sound again, and Landsman realizes that he's saying he's sorry. Speaking a language in which he has never been schooled.

"You know, I think I must have always known," Berko says, getting up from the table. He takes his hat and coat from the hook. "Because I never liked you. Not from the first minute, you bastard. Come on, Meyer."

Landsman follows his partner out. Going through the door, he has to get out of the way so that Berko can go back in. Berko tosses aside his hat and coat. He hits himself in the head twice, with both hands at once. Then he crushes an invisible sphere, roughly the size of his father's cranium, between his outspread fingers.

"I tried my whole life," he says finally. "I mean, fuck, look at me!" He snatches the skullcap from the back of his head and holds it up, contemplating it with a sudden horror as if it's the flesh of his scalp. He flicks it toward the old man. It hits Hertz on the nose and falls onto the pile with the napkin, the broken cigar, the moose gravy. "Look at this shit!" He grabs the front of his shirt and yanks it open in a skitter of buttons. He exposes the homely white panel of his fringed four-corners, like the world's flimsiest flak jacket, his holy white Kevlar, trimmed with a stripe of sea-creature blue. "I hate this fucking thing." The four-corners comes up over his head, and he shrugs and whips it off, which leaves him in a white cotton tee. "Every damn day of my life, I get up in the morning and put this shit on and pretend to be something I'm not. Something I'll never be. For *you*."

"I never asked you to observe the religion," the old man says, not looking up. "I don't think I ever put any kind of—"

"It has nothing to do with *religion*," Berko says. "It has everything to do, God damn it, with *fathers*."

It comes through the mother, of course, one's being or not being a Jew. But Berko knows that. He's known it since the day he moved to Sitka. He sees it every time he looks into a mirror.

"It's all nonsense," the old man goes on, a little mumbly, half to himself. "A slave religion. Tying yourself up. Bondage gear! I've never worn that nonsense in my life."

"No?" Berko says.

It catches Landsman off guard, how quick and how massive is the transfer of Berko Shemets from the doorway of the cabin to the dining table. Before Landsman can quite understand what is happening, Berko has jerked the ritual undergarment down over the old man's head. He cradles the head in one arm while, with the other, he winds the knotted fringes around and around, defining in fine strands of wool the contours of the old man's face. It's as if he's packing a statue for shipment. The old man kicks, rakes at the air with his fingernails.

"You never wore one, eh?" Berko says. "You never fucking wore one! Try mine! Try mine, you prick!"

"Stop." Landsman goes to the rescue of the man whose addiction to tactics of sacrifice led, maybe not predictably but directly, to the death of Laurie Jo Bear. "Berko, come on. Stop now." He takes hold of Berko's elbow and drags him aside, and when he's got himself between the two, he starts shoving the big man toward the door.

"Okay." Berko throws up his hands and lets Landsman push him a couple of feet in that direction. "Okay, I'm done. Get off me, Meyer."

Landsman eases up, letting go of his partner. Berko tucks his tee into his trousers and starts to button his shirt, but all the buttons have flown away. He leaves it, smooths down the black badger of his hair with a wide palm, stoops to retrieve his hat and coat from the floor, and walks out. Night comes curling with the fog into the house on its stilts above the water.

Landsman turns back to the old man, who is sitting there with his head shrouded in the four-corners, like a hostage who cannot be permitted to see the faces of his captors.

"You want some help, Uncle Hertz?" Landsman says.

"I'm fine," the old man says, his voice faint, muffled by the cloth. "Thank you."

"You just want to sit there like that?"

The old man doesn't reply. Landsman puts on his hat and walks out.

They are just getting into the car when they hear the gunshot, a boom that in the darkness maps the mountains, lights them up with reflected echoes, then fades away.

"Fuck," Berko says. He is back inside the house before Landsman has even reached the stairs. By the time Landsman runs in, Berko has crouched down beside his father, who has assumed a strange attitude on the floor beside his bed, a hurdler's stride, one leg drawn to his chest and the other flung out behind him. In his right hand, he keeps a loose grip on a black snub-nosed revolver; in his left hand, the ritual fringe. Berko straightens his father out, rolls him over onto his back, and feels for a pulse at the throat. There is a slick red patch on the right side of the old man's forehead, just above the corner of his eye. Scorched hair matted with blood. A poor shot, from the look of it.

"Oh, shit," Berko says. "Oh, shit, old man. You fucked it up."

"He fucked it up," Landsman agrees.

"Old man!" Berko shouts, and then he lowers his voice to a guttural rasp and croons something, a word or two, in the language that he left behind.

They stop the bleeding and pack the wound. Landsman looks around for the bullet and finds the wormhole that it chewed through the plywood wall.

"Where'd he get this?" Landsman says, picking up the gun. It's a homely thing, worn at the edges, an old machine. "The .38 Detective Special?"

"I don't know. He has a lot of guns. He likes guns. That's the one thing we had in common."

"I think it might be the gun that Melekh Gaystik used in the Café Einstein."

"That wouldn't surprise me at all," Berko says. He shoulders the burden of his father, and they carry him down to the car and lay him in the backseat on a pile of towels. Landsman switches on the undercover siren that he has used maybe twice in five years. Then they drive back up over the mountain.

There is an urgent-care center at Nayeshtat, but many have died there so they decide to take him all the way in to Sitka

General. Along the way, Berko calls his wife. He explains to her, not very coherently, that his father and a man named Alter Litvak were indirectly responsible for his mother's death during the worst Indian-Jew violence in the sixty-year history of the District, and that his father has shot himself in the head. He tells her that they are going to dump the old man at the Sitka General ER, because he is a policeman, God damn it, and he has a job to do, and because the old man can go and die for all he cares. Ester-Malke appears to accept this project as stated, and Berko hangs up the phone. They disappear into a zone without cellular telephone coverage for ten or fifteen minutes, and when they emerge from it, having said nothing, they are nearly to the city limits and the Shoyfer is ringing.

"No," Berko says, and then, more angrily, "No." He listens to his wife's reasoning for a little under a minute. Landsman has no idea what she's saying to him, whether she's preaching from the text of professional conduct, or of common decency, or of forgiveness, or of the duty of a son to a father that transcends or precedes them all. In the end Berko shakes his head. He looks over the backseat at the old Jew stretched out there. "All right." He closes the telephone.

"You can drop me off at the hospital," he says, sounding defeated. "Just call me when you find that fucking Litvak."

37

I need to speak to Katherine Sweeney," Bina says into the telephone. Sweeney, the assistant United States Attorney, is earnest and competent and may very well listen to what Bina has called her to say. Landsman reaches over, darts his hand across her desk, and cuts the connection with a fingertip. Bina stares at him with great slow wingbeats of her eyelids. He has taken her by surprise. A rare feat.

"They are behind this," Landsman says, his finger on the button.

"Kathy Sweeney is behind this," she says, keeping the receiver to her ear.

"Well, no. I doubt that."

"The Sitka U.S. Attorney's office is behind it?"

"Maybe. No, probably not."

"But you're saying the Justice Department."

"Yes. I don't know. Bina, I'm sorry. I just don't know how high up it goes."

The surprise has faded; her gaze is steady and unblinking. "Okay. Now, you listen to me. First of all, take your hairy damned finger off of my telephone."

Landsman withdraws the offending digit before the laser beams from her eyes can sever it cleanly at the knuckle.

"Don't you touch my telephone, Meyer."

"Never again."

"If the story you have been telling me is true," Bina says, a teacher addressing a roomful of imbecile five-year-olds, "then I need to tell Kathy Sweeney. I probably need to tell the State Department. I may even need to get hold of the Department of Defense."

"But—"

"Because I don't know if you are aware of this, but *the Holy Land is not part of this precinct*."

"Granted, of course. But listen. Someone with weight, serious weight, got into the FAA database and vanished that file. The same kind of weight promised the Tlingit Council they could have the District back if they let Litvak run his program out of Peril Strait for a little while."

"Dick told you that?"

"He suggested it strongly. And with all due respect to the Lederers from Boca Raton, I am sure that same weight has been writing checks for the clandestine side of the operation. The training facility. Weapons and support. The cattle breeding. They are behind this."

"The U.S. Government."

"This is what I'm saying."

"Because they think the idea of a bunch of crazy yids running around Arab Palestine, blowing up shrines and following Messiahs and starting World War Three is a really good idea."

"They're just as crazy, Bina. You know they are. Maybe they're *hoping* for World War Three. Maybe they want to crank up a new Crusade. Maybe they think if they do this thing, it will make Jesus come back. Or maybe it has nothing to do with any of that, and it's all really about oil, you know, securing their supply of the stuff once and for all. I don't know."

"Government conspiracies, Meyer."

"I know how it sounds."

"Talking chickens, Meyer."

"I'm sorry."

"You promised."

"I know."

She picks up the telephone and dials the AUSA.

"Bina. Please. Hang up the phone."

"I have been in a lot of dark corners with you, Meyer Landsman," she says. "I'm not going to go to this one."

Landsman guesses he can't blame her for that.

When she gets Sweeney on the line, Bina fills her in on the rudiments of Landsman's tale: The Verbovers and a group of messianic Jews have banded together and are planning to attack an important Muslim shrine in Palestine. She leaves out the supernatural and completely speculative elements. She leaves out the deaths of Naomi Landsman and Mendel Shpilman. She manages to make it sound just far-fetched enough to be credible.

"I'm going to see if we can maybe track this Litvak down," she tells Sweeney. "Okay, Kathy. Thanks. I know it does. I hope it is."

She hangs up the phone. She picks up the souvenir globe on the desk, with its miniature skyline of Sitka, gives it a shake, and watches the snow come down. She has moved everything else out of the office, the bric-a-brac, the photographs. Just the snow globe and her sheepskins in frames on the wall. A rubber tree and a ficus and a white-spotted pink orchid in a green glass pot. It's all still as pretty as the underside of a bus. Bina sits in the middle of it in another grim pantsuit, her hair piled up and held in place by metal clasps, rubber bands, and other useful items from her desk drawer.

"She didn't laugh," Landsman says. "Did she?"

"She's not the type," Bina says. "But no. She wants more information. For what it's worth, I got the feeling this wasn't the first she'd heard about Alter Litvak. She said she'd like to maybe bring him in if we can find him."

"Buchbinder," Landsman says. "Dr. Rudolf Buchbinder. You remember, he was going out of the Polar-Shtern the other night when you were coming in."

"That dentist from down on Ibn Ezra Street?"

"He told me he was relocating to Jerusalem," Landsman says. "I thought he was talking nonsense."

"The Something Institute," she remembers.

"With an M."

"Miryam."

"Moriah."

She gets on her computer and finds a listing for the Moriah Institute in the unlisted-number directory, at 822 Max Nordau Street, seventh floor.

"Eight-twenty-two," Landsman says. "Huh."

"Isn't that your block?" Bina dials the telephone number she found.

"Right across the street," Landsman says, feeling sheepish. "The Blackpool Hotel."

"Machine," she says. She kills the call with a fingertip and punches in a four-digit. "This is Gelbfish."

She arranges for patrolmen and plainclothes officers to stake out the doors and entryways of the Hotel Blackpool. She returns the phone to its cradle and then sits there, looking at it.

"Okay," Landsman says. "Let's go."

But Bina doesn't move.

"You know, it was nice not having to live with all your bullshit. Not having to put up with twenty-four-hour Landsmania."

"I envy you that," Landsman says.

"Hertz, Berko, your mother, your father. All of you." She adds in American, "Bunch of fucking nut jobs."

"I know."

"Naomi was the only sane person in the family."

"She used to say the same thing about you," Landsman says. "Only she used to say, 'in the world.'"

Two quick raps on the door. Landsman gets up, thinking it's going to be Berko.

"Hi, there," says the man at the door in American. "I don't think I've had the pleasure."

"Who are you?" Landsman says.

"Me is your burial societies," the man says in wretched but energetic Yiddish.

"Mr. Spade is here to oversee the transition," Bina says. "I think I mentioned that he might be coming, Detective Landsman."

"I think you did."

"Detective Landsman," Spade says, lapsing mercifully into American. "The notorious."

He's not the potbellied golf type Landsman imagined. He's too young, plain-faced, big around the chest and shoulders. He's wearing a gray worsted suit buttoned over a white shirt with a necktie the stippled blue of video static. His neck is a mass of razor bumps and missed whiskers. The protrusion of his Adam's apple suggests unfathomable depths of earnestness and sincerity. In his lapel he wears a pin in the shape of a stylized fish.

"How about you and I sit down with your commanding officer for a moment?"

"All right," Landsman says. "But I prefer to stand."

"Suit yourself. How about we get out of the doorway, though."

Landsman steps aside, waving him into the room. Spade shuts the door.

"Detective Landsman. I have reason to believe," Spade says, "that you have been conducting an unauthorized and, given the fact that you are currently under suspension—"

"With pay," Landsman says.

"—illegal investigation into a case that has been officially designated inactive. With help from Detective Berko Shemets, also unauthorized. And, taking a wild guess, well, I wouldn't be surprised if you turned out to have been helping him, too, Inspector Gelbfish."

"She has been nothing but a pain in the ass, actually," Landsman says. "To be honest. No help at all."

"I just called the AUSA's office," Bina says.

"Did you really?"

"They may be taking this one over."

"For real?"

"It's out of my jurisdiction. There's been—there may have been—a threat. Against a foreign target. By District residents."

"Huh-uh!" Spade looks at once scandalized and pleased. "A threat? Get out of town!"

A cold dense fluid fills Bina's gaze, somewhere between mercury and sludge. "I'm trying to find a man named Alter Litvak," she says, a great weariness dragging at the corners of her voice. "He may or may not be involved with this threat. In any case, I'd like to see what he knows about the murder of Mendel Shpilman."

"Uh-huh," Spade says amiably, a little distracted, maybe, like someone pretending to take an interest in the minutiae of your life while surfing some inner Internet of his mind. "Okay, but, see, the thing is, ma'am. Speaking as— What do you call it again? The man from the, uh, Burial Society who sits with the corpse when it's a Jew?"

"They call that a shoymer," Bina says.

"Right. Speaking as the local shoymer around here, I have to say: No. What you are going to do is to leave this mess, and Mr. Litvak, alone."

Bina waits a long time before saying anything. The weariness of her voice seems to flow into her shoulders, her jaw, the lines of her face. "Are you mixed up in this, Spade?" she says.

"Me personally? No, ma'am. The transition team? Huh-uh. The Alaska Reversion Commission? No way. The truth is, I don't know very much about this mess at all. And what I do know, I'm not at liberty to say. I'm in resource management, Inspector. That's what I do. And I'm here to tell you, with all due respect, that enough of your resources have already been wasted on this matter."

"They are my resources, Mr. Spade," Bina says. "For two more months, I can talk to whatever witnesses I want to talk to. I can arrest whoever I want to arrest."

"Not if the AUSA tells you to back off."

The telephone rings.

"That will be the AUSA," Landsman says.

Bina picks up the phone. "Hello, Kathy," she says. She listens for a minute, nodding, saying nothing. Then she says, "I understand," and hangs up the phone. Her voice is calm and devoid of feeling. There's a tight smile on her face, and she ducks her head in humility, as if she has been beaten fair and square. Landsman can feel that she is deliberately not looking at him, because if she looks at him, she might tear up. And he knows how outraged Bina Gelbfish has to get before there is any danger of tears.

"And I had everything fixed up so nice," she says.

"And this place, let me tell you," Landsman says. "Before you got here, it was a shambles."

"I was just going to hand it all over to you," she tells Spade. "All wrapped up. Free of crumbs. No loose strings."

She worked it with such care, accumulated the credits, kissed the asses that needed to be kissed. Swept out the stables. Tied up Sitka Central and attached herself to the top like a decorative bow.

"I even got rid of that wretched love seat," she says. "What the hell is going on here, Spade?"

"I honestly don't know, ma'am. And even if I did know, I would say that I didn't."

"Your orders are to keep things smooth on this end."

"Yes, ma'am."

"The other end being Palestine."

"I don't know much about Palestine," Spade says. "I'm from

Lubbock. My wife is from Nacogdoches, though, and that's only about forty miles from Palestine."

Bina looks blank for a moment, and then understanding seems to redden her cheeks like anger. "Don't you stand there and make jokes," she says. "Don't you dare."

"No, ma'am," Spade says, and it's his turn to go a little red.

"I take this job very seriously, *Mr.* Spade. And you had better, let me tell you, you had better fucking take me seriously."

"Yes, ma'am."

Bina gets up from behind the desk and takes her orange parka from its hook. "I am going to bring in Alter Litvak. Question him. Possibly arrest him. You want to stop me, try to stop me." Parka whuffing, she brushes past Spade, who's caught off guard by the move. "But if you try to stop me, things will not be *smooth* on your end. I promise you that."

And she's gone for a second. Then she sticks her head back into the doorway, pulling on her dazzling orange coat.

"Hey, yid," she tells Landsman. "I could use a little backup."

Landsman puts on his hat and goes after her, nodding to Spade on his way out.

"Praise the Lord," Landsman says.

 38

The Moriah Institute is the sole occupant of the seventh and uppermost story of the Hotel Blackpool. There is fresh paint on the walls of the corridor and a spotless mauve carpet on the floor. At the far end, beside the door to 707, small black characters on a discreet brass plate spell out the name of the Institute in American and Yiddish, and beneath that, in roman characters: SOL AND DOROTHY ZIEGLER CENTER. Bina pushes a buzzer. She looks up into the lens of the security camera that looks down at them.

"You remember the deal," Bina tells him. It's not a question.

"I am to shut up."

"That's such a small part of it."

"I am not even here. I don't even exist."

She buzzes again, and just as she raises her knuckles to knock, Buchbinder opens the door. He is wearing a different enormous sweater-jacket, this one in cornflower blue with flecks of pale green and salmon, over baggy chinos and a Bronfman U. sweatshirt. His face and hands are smudged with ink or grease.

"Inspector Gelbfish," Bina says, showing him her badge. "Sitka Central. I'm looking for Alter Litvak. I have reason to believe he may be here."

A dentist is not a man of guile, as a rule. Buchbinder's face reads plainly and without concealment: He was expecting them.

"It is very late," he tries. "Unless you——"

"Alter Litvak, Dr. Buchbinder. Is he here?"

Landsman can see Buchbinder wrestling with the mechanics and trajectories, the wind shear of telling a lie.

"No. No, he is not."

"Do you know where he is?"

"No. No, Inspector, I do not."

"Uh-huh. Okay. Any chance you might be lying to me, Dr. Buchbinder?"

There is a brief, dense pause. Then he closes the door in their faces. Bina raps, her fist the relentless head and bill of a woodpecker. A moment later, Buchbinder opens the door, tucking his Shoyfer away into a pocket of his sweater. He nods, his cheeks, jowls, and the twinkle in his eye arranged to genial effect. Someone has decanted a small hopper of molten iron into his spine.

"Please come in," he says. "Mr. Litvak will see you. He is upstairs."

"Isn't this the top floor?" Bina says.

"There is a penthouse."

"Fleabags don't have penthouses," Landsman says. Bina shoots him a look. He's supposed to be invisible, inaudible, a ghost.

Buchbinder lowers his voice. "It used to be for the maintenance man, I gather. But they have fixed it up. This way, please, there is a back stair."

The internal walls have been knocked out, and Buchbinder leads them through the gallery of the Ziegler Center. It's a cool, dim space, painted white, nothing like the grimy old ex-stationery shop on Ibn Ezra Street. The light emerges from a gridwork of glass or Lucite cubes set atop carpeted pedestals. Each cube displays its object, a silver shovel, a copper bowl, an inexplicable garment like something worn by the Zorvoldian ambassador in a space opera. There must be more than a hundred objects on display, many of them worked in gold and gemstones. Each of them advertises the names of the American Jews whose generosity made their construction possible.

"You've come up in the world," Landsman says.

"Yes, it's wonderful," Buchbinder says. "A miracle."

A dozen large packing crates have been lined up at the far end of the room, spilling exuberant coils of shaved pine. A delicate silver handle protrudes from the excelsior, chased with gold. At the center of the room, on a low, broad table, a scale model of a stone-furrowed bare hill soaks up the glow of a dozen halogen spots. The hilltop, where Isaac waited for his father to pry the muscle of life from his body, is as flat as a place mat on a table. On its flanks, stone houses, stone alleys, tiny olive and cypress trees with fuzzy foliage. Tiny Jews wrapped in tiny prayer shawls contemplate the void at the top of the hill, as if to illustrate or model the principle, thinks Landsman, that every Jew has a personal Messiah who never comes.

"I don't see the Temple," Bina says, seemingly in spite of herself.

Buchbinder emits an odd grunt, animal and contented. Then he presses a button in the floor with the toe of one loafer. There follows a soft click and the hum of a tiny fan. And then, built to scale, the Temple, erected by Solomon, destroyed by the Babylonians, rebuilt, restored by the same king of Judaea who condemned Christ to die, destroyed by the Romans, sealed and built over by the Abbasids, resumes its rightful place at the navel of the world. The technology generating the image imparts a miraculous radiance to the model. It shimmers like a fata morgana. In design, the proposed Third Temple is a restrained display of stonemason might, cubes and pillars and sweeping plazas. Here and there a carved Sumerian monster lends a touch of the barbaric. This is the paper that God left the Jews holding, Landsman thinks, the promise that we have been banging Him a kettle about ever since. The rook that attends the king at the endgame of the world.

"Now turn on the choo-choo," Landsman says.

At the back of the space there's a narrow stair, open on one side and flush against the wall on the other. It leads up to an enameled black steel door. Buchbinder gives a soft knock.

The young man who opens the door is one of the grandnephews from the Einstein, the driver of the Caudillo, the plump, broad-shouldered American kid with the pink nape.

"I believe Mr. Litvak is expecting me," Bina says brightly. "I'm Inspector Gelbfish."

"You can have five minutes," says the young man in serviceable Yiddish. He can't be older then twenty. He has a turned-in left eye and more acne than beard on his baby cheeks. "Mr. Litvak is a busy man."

"And who are you?"

"You can call me Micky."

She steps right up to him and jams her chin toward the meat of his throat. "Micky, I know this makes me a bad person in your eyes, but I don't really care how busy Mr. Litvak is. I need to talk to him for as long as it takes me to do that. Now take me to him, sweetness, or you're not going to be busy at all for a very long time."

Micky shoots a look at Landsman as if to say, *What a ballbreaker.* Landsman pretends not to understand.

"If you will excuse me, please," Buchbinder says with a bow to each of them. "I have very much work to do."

"Are you going somewhere, Doctor?" Landsman says.

"I already told you this," the dentist says. "Maybe you ought to try writing things down."

The penthouse of the Blackpool Hotel is nothing special. A two-room suite. The outer room holds a sleeper couch, a wet bar and mini-fridge, an armchair, and seven young men in dark suits and bad haircuts. The bed is all folded away, but you can smell that the room has been slept in by young men, maybe as many as seven.

The piped corner of a bedsheet pokes from the crack of the seat cushion like a shirttail caught in a fly.

The young men are watching a very large television tuned to a satellite news channel. On the screen, the prime minister of Manchuria is shaking hands with five Manchurian astronauts. The box that the television came in is sitting on the floor beside its former contents. Bottled sports drinks and bags of sunflower seeds on the coffee table, scattered among drifts of sunflower hulls. Landsman marks three guns, automatics, two jammed into waistbands, one into a sock. Maybe the butt of a fourth under somebody's thigh. Nobody is happy to see the detectives. In fact, the young men seem sullen, keyed up. Anxious to be anywhere else but here.

"Show us the warrant." It's Gold, the sharpened little prison shank of a mexican from Peril Strait. He peels himself from the couch and comes toward them. When he recognizes Landsman, his single eyebrow gets tangled at its apex. "Lady, that one has no right to be here. Get him out."

"Take it easy," Bina says. "What's your name?"

"He's Gold," says Landsman.

"Ah, yes. Gold, look at the situation. There are one, two, three, seven of you. There are two of us."

"I'm not even here," Landsman says. "You're just imagining me."

"I am here to talk to Alter Litvak, and I don't need a piece of paper to do that, sweetness. Even if I wanted to arrest him, I could always get the warrant later." She gives him her winning smile, slightly shopworn. "Honest."

Gold hesitates. He starts to check with his six comrades to see what they think he should do, but some aspect of that process, or of life in general, strikes him as pointless. He goes to the door of the bedroom and knocks. On the other side of the door, a set of punctured bagpipes gives out a dying wheeze.

The room is as spartan and neat as Hertz Shemets's cabin,

complete with chessboard. No television. No radio. Just a chair and a bookshelf and a folding cot in the corner. A steel blind that reaches to the floor rattles in the wind off the Gulf. Litvak sits on the cot, knees together, a book open on his lap, sipping some kind of canned nutritional shake through a flexible green drinking straw. When Bina and Landsman walk in, Litvak sets the can down on the bookshelf beside the marbled pad. He marks his place with a length of ribbon and closes his book. Landsman can see that it is an old hardback edition of Tarrasch, possibly *Three Hundred Chess Games*. Then Litvak looks up. His eyes are two dull pennies. His face is nothing but hollows and angles, an annotation in the yellow leather of his skull. He waits as if they have come to show him a card trick, a complicated grandfatherly expression on his face, prepared both to be disappointed and to pretend to be amused.

"I'm Bina Gelbfish. You know Meyer Landsman."

I know you, too, say the old man's eyes.

"Reb Litvak doesn't speak," Gold says. "He's crippled in the voice box."

"I understand," says Bina. She takes measure of the devastation wrought by time, injury, and physics on the man with whom, seventeen, eighteen years ago, she danced the rumba at the wedding of Landsman's cousin Shifra Sheynfeld. Her brash lady-shammes manner has been put away, though not abandoned. Never abandoned. Holstered, say, with the safety off, and one hand poised, fingers flexing, at her hip. "Mr. Litvak, I have been hearing some pretty wild stories about you from my detective here."

Litvak reaches for the pad, crossed with the sleek ebony cigar of his Waterman. He opens the pad with the fingers of one hand, spreads it on his knee, studying Bina the way he studied the chessboard at the Einstein Club, looking for his opening, seeing twenty possibilities, eliminating nineteen. He unscrews his pen. He's on the very last page. He marks it.

You don't care for wild stories

"No, sir, I don't. That's right. I have been a police detective for a lot of years, and I can count on one hand the number of times that somebody's wild story of what happened in a case turns out to be useful or true."

Tough break—to favor simple explanations in a world full of Jews

"Agreed."

A hard lot to be a Jewish policeman then

"I like it," Bina says simply, with feeling. "I'm going to miss it when it's done."

Litvak shrugs as if to suggest that he would like to sympathize, if only he could. His hard, bright red-rimmed eyes slide to the doorway and, with one arched eyebrow, form a question for Gold. Gold shakes his head. Then he goes back to the watching the TV.

"I realize it's not easy," Bina says. "But suppose you tell us what you know about Mendel Shpilman, Mr. Litvak."

"And Naomi Landsman," Landsman puts in.

You think I killed Mendel you're as clueless as he is

"I don't think anything at all," Bina says.

Lucky you

"It's a gift I have."

Litvak checks his watch and makes a broken sound that Landsman takes for a patient sigh. He snaps his fingers, and when Gold turns, Litvak waves the filled-in notepad. Gold goes into the outer room and comes back holding a fresh pad. He crosses the room and passes it to Litvak, along with a look that offers to dispense with or dispose of the annoying visitors by any one of a number of interesting methods. Litvak waves the kid away, sends him back to the doorway with one hand. Then he slides over and pats the vacated space beside him. Bina unzips her parka and sits down. Landsman drags over the bentwood chair. Litvak opens the notepad to its first fresh page.

Every Messiah fails, writes Litvak, *the moment he tries to redeem himself*

39

They had a pilot of their own, a good one, a Cuba veteran named Frum who flew the bus run from Sitka. Frum had served under Litvak at Matanzas and in the bloody debacle of Santiago. He was both faithful and without a shred of faith, a combination of traits prized by Litvak, who found himself obliged to contend on every side with the sometimes voluntary treachery of believers. The pilot Frum believed only what his instrument panel said. He was sober, meticulous, competent, quiet, tough. When he landed a load of recruits at Peril Strait, the boys left Frum's airplane with a sense of what kind of soldier they wanted to become.

Send Frum, Litvak wrote when they received the news from the case handler, Mr. Cashdollar, of a miraculous birth in Oregon. Frum left on a Tuesday. On Wednesday—how, the believers would say, could this be mere chance?—Mendel Shpilman stumbled into Buchbinder's cabinet of wonders on the seventh floor of the Blackpool Hotel, saying he was down to his last blessing and ready to spend it on himself. By now the pilot Frum was a thousand miles away, on a ranch outside of Corvallis, where Fligler and Cashdollar, who flew out from Washington, were having trouble coming to terms with the breeder of the magical red animal.

There were, of course, other pilots available to fly Shpilman out to Peril Strait, but they were outsiders, or young believers. An outsider could never be trusted, and Litvak worried that Shpilman might disappoint a young believer and start the evil tongues wagging. Shpilman was in a very fragile condition, according to Dr. Buchbinder. He was agitated and crotchety, or sleepy and listless, and he weighed only fifty-five kilos. Really, he was not much in the way of a Tzaddik Ha-Dor at all.

On such short notice, there was one other pilot whom Litvak considered, another one utterly without faith, but discreet and reliable, and with an ancient tie to Litvak on which he dared to pin his hopes. At first he tried to dismiss the name from his thoughts, but it kept returning. He was worried that if they hesitated, they would lose Shpilman again; twice already the yid had backed out of a promise to seek treatment with Roboy at Peril Strait. So Litvak ordered this faithless, reliable pilot tracked down and offered the job. She took it, for a thousand dollars more than Litvak had intended to pay.

"A *woman*," said the doctor, shifting his queenside rook, a move that gave him no advantage that Litvak could see. Dr. Roboy, in Litvak's measured view, had a vice common to believers: He was all strategy and no tactics. He was prone to move for the sake of moving, too focused on the goal to bother with the intervening sequence. "Here. In this place."

They were sitting in the office on the second floor of the main building, with a view of the strait, the ragtag Indian village with its nets and crazed boardwalk, the jutting arm of the brand-new floatplane dock. The office was Roboy's, with a desk in the corner for Moish Fligler when he was around and could be kept behind a desk. Alter Litvak preferred to do without the luxury of a desk, an office, a home. He slept in guest rooms, garages, on somebody's couch. His desk was a kitchen table, his office the training ground, the Einstein Chess Club, the back room of the Moriah Institute.

We have men in this place who are less manly, Litvak wrote in his notepad, *I should have hired her before*

He forced an exchange of bishops, opening a sudden breach in White's center. He saw that he had mate, in one of two ways, within four moves. The prospect of victory was tedious. He wondered if he had ever cared at all for the game of chess. He took up his pen and wrote out an insult, even though, in almost five years, it had proved impossible to get a rise out of Roboy.

If we had a hundred like her I would be cleaning your clock by now on a terrace overlooking the Mount of Olives

"Humph," said Dr. Roboy, fingering a pawn, watching Litvak's face as Litvak watched the sky.

Dr. Roboy sat with his back to the window, a dark parenthesis bracketing the chessboard, his long, jutting face slack with the effort of guessing at the bleakness of his immediate chess future. Behind him the western sky was all marmalade and smoke. The crumpled mountains, folds of green that looked black, and purple that looked black, and luminous blue fissures of white snow. To the southwest a full moon was setting early, sharp-edged and gray, looking like a high-resolution black-and-white photograph of itself pasted to the sky.

"Every time you look out the window," Roboy said, "I think it's because they're here. I wish you would stop. You're making me nervous." He tipped over his king, pushed back from the board, and unfurled his great mantis body one joint at a time. "I can't play, I'm sorry. You win. I'm too keyed up."

He started to stalk back and forth across the office.

I don't see what you are so worried about you have the easy job

"Is that so?"

He has to redeem Israel, you just have to redeem him

Roboy stopped pacing and turned to face Litvak, who put down his pen and set about returning the pieces to their maple box.

"Three hundred boys are ready to die at his back," Roboy said, peevish. "Thirty thousand Verbovers will be staking their lives and fortunes on this man. Uprooting their homes, putting their families at risk. If others follow, then we are talking about millions.

I'm glad you can make jokes about that. I'm glad it doesn't make you nervous to look out that window and watch the sky and know that he is finally on his way."

Litvak stopped putting away the pieces and looked out the window again. Cormorants, gulls, a dozen fanciful variations on the basic duck, having no names in Yiddish. At any moment any one of them, wings spread against the sunset, might be taken for an approaching Piper Super Cub, coming in low from the southwest. Looking at the sky was making Litvak nervous, too. But theirs was not by definition an endeavor that attracted men with the talent for waiting.

I hope that he is the Tz H-D I really do

"No, you don't," Roboy said. "That's a lie. You're just in it for the stakes. For the game."

Following the accident that took Litvak's wife and his voice, it was Dr. Rudolf Buchbinder, the mad dentist of Ibn Ezra Street, who had rebuilt his jaw, restored its masonry in acrylic and titanium. And when Litvak found himself addicted to painkillers, it was the dentist who had sent him for treatment to an old friend, Dr. Max Roboy. Years later, when Cashdollar asked his man in Sitka for help fulfilling the divinely inspired mission of the president of America, Litvak thought at once of Buchbinder and Roboy.

It had taken a lot longer, not to mention every last ounce of chutzpah Litvak had, to work Heskel Shpilman into the plan. Endless pilpul and haggling through Baronshteyn. Stiff resistance from career men at Justice who viewed Shpilman and Litvak—with justice—as a ganglord and a hatchetman. At last, after months of false alarms and cancellations, a meeting with the big man at the Ringelblum Avenue Baths.

A Tuesday morning, snow twisting down in sloppy helixes, four inches of new snow on the ground. Too new, too early for the snowplow. At the corner of Ringelblum and Glatshteyn, a chestnut vendor, snow on his red umbrella, hiss and shimmer of the roasting box, parallel grooves of his cart wheels framing the slurry of his footprints in the snow. So quiet you could hear the clockwork thunking in the traffic signal box and the vibration of the pager on the hip of the gunman by the door. A pair of gunmen, those great red bears they kept to guard the body of the Verbover rebbe.

As the Rudashevsky biks handed Litvak along from the door, up the cement stairs with the vinyl treads, down the mine shaft of a hallway to the front door of the baths, the fists of their faces all cupped a minor light. Mischief, pity, the glint of a prankster, a torturer, a priest preparing to uncover the cannibal god. As for the ancient Russian cashier in his steel cage, the burly attendant in his bunker of folded white towels, these yids had no eyes at all, as far as Litvak ever knew. They kept their heads down, blinded by fear and discretion. They were elsewhere, drinking coffee at the Polar-Shtern, still at home in their beds with their wives. The baths were not even open for business at this hour. There was nobody here, nobody at all, and the attendant who slid a pair of threadbare towels across the counter to Litvak was a ghost serving up a winding sheet to a dead man.

Litvak stripped and hung up his clothes on two steel hooks. He could smell the tidal flux of the baths, chlorine and armpit and a ripe salt vapor that might on second thought have been the pickle factory on the ground floor. There was nothing to weaken him, if that was part of the intent, in obliging him to take off his clothes. His scars were numerous, in certain instances horrible, and they had their effect. He heard a low whistle from one of the two Rudashevskys working the locker room. Litvak's body was a parchment scribed by pain and violence on which they could only hope to make the barest exegesis. He slipped his pad from the hip pocket of his jacket on its hook.

Like what you see?

The Rudashevskys could not agree on a fitting reply. One nodded; the other shook his head. They exchanged responses, to the satisfaction of neither. Then they gave him up and sent him through the misty glass door to the steam room, to confront the body they guarded.

That body, the horror and the splendor of it, naked as a giant bloodshot eyeball without a socket. Litvak had seen it only once before, years ago, topped with a fedora, rolled tight as a wad of Pinar del Río into a stiff black greatcoat that swept the toes of his dainty black boots. Now it emerged ponderous from the steam, a slab of wet limestone webbed with a black lichen of hair. Litvak felt like a fogbound airplane buffeted by updrafts into the surprise of a mountain. The belly pregnant with elephant triplets, the breasts full and pendulous, each tipped with a pink lentil of a nipple. The thighs great hand-rolled marbled loaves of halvah. Lost in the shadows between them, a thick umbilicus of grayish-brown meat.

Litvak lowered the uninsulated armature of his frame to the hot grid of tiles opposite the rabbi. The time he had passed Shpilman in the street, the man's eyes lay in the ambit of shadow cast by the sundial of his hat brim. Now they were trained on Litvak and his vandalized body. They were kindly eyes, Litvak thought, or eyes whose employer had schooled them in the uses of kindliness. They read Litvak's scars, the puckered purple mouth on his right shoulder, the slashes of red velour on his hip, the pit in his left thigh deep enough to hold an ounce of gin. They offered sympathy, regard, even gratitude. The war in Cuba was notorious for its futility, brutality, and waste. Its veterans had been shunned on their return. No one had offered them forgiveness, understanding, a chance at healing. Heskel Shpilman was offering Litvak and his war-torn hide all three.

"The nature of your handicap," the rebbe said, "has been explained to me, along with the substance of your offer." His girlish voice, baffled by steam and porcelain tile, seemed to emerge from someplace other than the kettledrum chest. "I see you've brought along your pad and a pen, in spite of my clear instructions that you were to carry nothing at all."

Litvak held up the offending items, beaded with steam. He could feel the warp, the buckle, in the pages of his pad.

"You won't need them." The birds of Shpilman's hands roosted on the rock of his belly, and he closed his eyes, depriving Litvak of their sympathy, real or feigned, and leaving Litvak to stew for a minute or two in the steam. Litvak had always hated a shvitz. But this fixture of the old Harkavy, secular and squalid, was the only place that the Verbover rebbe could contrive to do private business away from his court, his gabay, his world. "I don't plan to require any further response or inquiry from you."

Litvak nodded and prepared to stand. His mind told him that Shpilman would not have bothered to summon him to this nude and one-sided interview if he planned to turn Litvak down. But he felt in his gut that the errand was doomed, that Shpilman had called him down to Ringelblum Avenue to deliver the refusal in all the elephantine authority of his person.

"I want you to know, Mr. Litvak, that I have been giving a great deal of consideration to this proposal. I have attempted to follow its logic from every angle.

"Let's begin with our southern friends. If it were simply a case of their wanting something, some tangible feature or resource . . . oil, for example. Or if they were prompted by a more purely strategic concern with regard to Russia or Persia. In either case, they clearly don't need us. However difficult a conquest the Holy Land might be, our physical presence, our willingness to fight, our arms, can't make a great difference to their battle plan. I have studied their claims of support for the Jewish cause in Palestine, and their theology, and to the extent that I can, based on Rabbi Baronshteyn's reports, I have tried to form a judgment of the gentiles and their aims. And I can only conclude that when they say they wish to see Jerusalem restored to Jewish sovereignty, they mean it. Their reasoning, the so-called prophecies and apocrypha whose supposed authority underlies this wish, maybe it all strikes me as laughable. Abominable, even. I pity the gentiles for their childlike trust in the imminent return of one who never in the first place departed, let alone arrived. But I am quite sure that they, in turn, pity us our own tardy Messiah. As a foundation for a partnership, mutual pity is not to be despised.

"As for your angle in this matter, that is easy, yes? You are a soldier for hire. You enjoy the challenge and the responsibility of generalship. I understand that. I do. You like to fight, and you like killing, as long as those who die aren't your men. And, I dare say, after all these years with Shemets—and now, on your own behalf— you are long in the habit of appearing to please the Americans.

"For the Verbovers, there is great risk. Our entire community could be lost in this adventure. Wiped out in a matter of days, if your troops are ill prepared or simply, as seems not unlikely, outmanned. But if we stay here, well, then we are finished, too. Scattered to the winds. Our friends in the south have made that clear. That is the 'stick.' Reversion as the fire in the seat of the pants, yes? A restored Jerusalem as the bucket of ice water. Some of our younger men argue for making a stand here, daring them to dislodge us. But that is madness.

"On the other hand, if we agree, and you are successful, then we have regained a treasure of such incalculable value—I mean Zion, of course—that the mere thought of it opens a long-shuttered window in my soul. I have to shield my eyes from the brilliance."

He raised the back of his left hand to his eyes. His thin wedding band was engulfed in his fingers like an ax head lost in the flesh of a tree. Litvak felt the pulse in his throat, a thumb plucking over and over at the lowest string of a harp. Dizziness. A sensation of ballooning in his feet and arms. It must be the heat, he thought. He took shallow timid breaths of rich burning air.

"I am dazzled by that vision," the rebbe said. "Maybe as blinded by it, in my own way, as the evangelicals. So precious is the treasure. So incalculably sweet."

No. It was not, or not only, the heat and ripeness of the shvitz that were making Litvak's pulse thrum and his head spin. He felt certain of the wisdom of his gut: Shpilman was about to reject his proposal. But as that likelihood drew nearer, a new possibility began to dizzy him, to course through him. It was the thrill of a dazzling move.

"Still, it's not enough," the rebbe was saying. "I long for Messiah as I long for nothing else in this world." He stood up, and his belly poured over his hips and groin like scalded milk foaming down the sides of a pot. "But I am afraid. I'm afraid of failure. I'm afraid of the potential for great loss of life among my yids and the utter destruction of everything we've worked for these last sixty years. There were eleven Verbovers left at the end of the war, Litvak. *Eleven.* I promised my wife's father on his deathbed that I would never let such destruction befall us again.

"And, finally, truthfully, I fear this all may be a fool's errand. There are numerous and persuasive teachings against acting in any way to hasten the coming of Messiah. Jeremiah condemns it. So do the Oaths of Solomon. Yes, of course, I want to see my yids settled in a new home with financial assurances from the U.S., offers of assistance and of access to all the unimaginably vast new markets your success in this operation would create. And I want Messiah like I want to sink, after this heat, into the cold dark waters of the mikvah in the next room. But, God should forgive me these words, I am afraid. So afraid that even the taste on my lips of Messiah is not enough. And you can tell them that down in Washington. Tell them the Verbover rebbe was afraid." The idea of his fear seemed almost to entrance him with its novelty, like a teenager thinking of death or a whore of the chance of an immaculate love. "What?"

Litvak held up his right index finger. He had something, one more thing to offer the rebbe. One more clause for the contract. He had no idea how he would deliver it or if indeed it could be delivered. But as the rebbe prepared to turn his massive back on Jerusalem and on the complicated hugeness of the deal that Litvak had been putting together for months, he felt it well up in him like a chess brilliancy, notated with double exclamation marks.

He scrambled to open his pad. He scrawled two words on the first clean leaf, but in his haste and panic, he pressed too hard and his pen ripped through the wet paper.

"What is it?" Shpilman said, "You have something more to offer?"

Litvak nodded, once, twice.

"Something more than Zion? Messiah? A home, a fortune?"

Litvak got up and padded across the tile floor until he stood just beside the rebbe. Naked men bearing the tales of their ruined bodies. Each of them, in his way, bereft, alone. Litvak reached out and, with the force and inspiration of that loneliness, and with the tip of his finger, inscribed two words in the vapor condensed on a white square of tile.

The rebbe read them and looked up, and they beaded over once more and were gone.

"My son," the rebbe said.

It's more than a game, Litvak wrote now, in the office at Peril Strait, as he and Roboy awaited the arrival of that wayward and unredeemed son. *I would rather fight to take a prize however doubtful than wait to see what scraps I may be fed*

"I suppose there's a credo in there someplace," Roboy said. "Maybe there's hope for you yet."

In return for providing them with manpower, a Messiah, and financing beyond their wildest dreams, the only thing that Litvak had ever asked of his partners, clients, employers, and associates in this venture was that he never be expected to believe the nonsense that they believed. Where they saw the fruit of divine wishes in a newborn red heifer, he saw the product of $1 million in taxpayer dollars spent secretly on bull semen and in vitro fertilization. In the eventual burning of this little red cow, they saw the purification of all Israel and the fulfillment of a millennia-old promise; Litvak saw, at most, a necessary move in an ancient game—the survival of the Jews.

Oh I wouldn't go that far

There was a knock at the door, and Micky Vayner put in his head.

"I came to remind you, sir," he said in his good American Hebrew.

Litvak stared blankly at the pink face with its peeling eyelids and baby-fat chin.

"Five minutes before twilight. You said to remind you."

Litvak went to the window. The sky was striped in the pink, green, and luminous gray of a salmon's hide. Sure enough, he saw a star or planet overhead. He nodded his thanks to Micky Vayner. Then he closed the box of chessmen and hooked the clasp.

"What's at twilight?" Roboy said. He turned to Micky Vayner. "What's today?"

Micky Vayner shrugged; as far as he knew, it was, by the lunar calendar, an ordinary day in the month of Nisan. Though, like his young comrades, he had been trained to believe in the foreordained reestablishment of the biblical kingdom of Judaea and in the destiny of Jerusalem to be the eternal capital of the Jews, he was no more strict or nice in his observance than any of the others. The young American Jews at Peril Strait observed the principal holidays, and for the most part, they kept the dietary laws. They wore the skullcap and the four-corners but kept their beards in military trim. They avoided work and training on the Sabbath, though not without exception. After forty years as a secular warrior, Litvak could stomach that much. Even in the wake of the accident, with his Sora gone, with the wind whistling through the hole she had left in Litvak's life, with a thirst for meaning and a hunger for sense and an empty cup and a barren dish, Alter Litvak could not have taken a place among truly religious men. He never could have fallen happily, for example, among the black hats. In fact, he could not abide black hats, and since the meeting at the baths, he had kept to a minimum his contacts with the Verbovers, as they prepared in secret to be airlifted en masse to Palestine.

Today is nothing, he wrote before he pocketed the notepad and walked out of the room. *Call me when they arrive*

In his room Litvak took out his dental plates and dropped them with a chime of dice into a drinking glass. He unlaced his boots and sat down heavily on a folding cot. Whenever he came out to Peril Strait, he slept in this tiny room— on the blueprints, it had been shown as a utility closet— down the hall from Roboy's office. His clothes he hung on a hook behind the door, his kit he stashed under the cot.

He leaned back against the cold wall of painted cinder block and looked at the wall, over the steel shelf that held the glass with his teeth. There was no window, so Litvak imagined an early star. A wheeling duck. The photograph moon. The sky slowly turning to the color of a gun. And an airplane, coming in low from the southeast, bearing the man who was, in Litvak's plan, both prisoner and dynamite, tower and trapdoor, bull's-eye and dart.

Litvak stood up slowly, with a grunt of pain. There were screws in his hips, which ached; his knees thudded and gonged like the pedals of an old piano. There was a constant thrum of wire in the hinges of his jaw. He ran his tongue across the empty zones of his mouth with their feel of slick putty. He was accustomed to pain and breakage, but since the accident, his body no longer seemed to belong to him. It was something sawed and nailed together out of borrowed parts. A birdhouse built of scrap wood and propped on a pole, in which his soul flapped like a fugitive bat. He had been born, like every Jew, into the wrong world, the wrong country, at the wrong time, and now he was living in the wrong body, too. In the end maybe it was that sense of wrongness, that fist in the Jewish belly, binding Alter Litvak to the cause of the yids who had made him their general.

He went over to the steel shelf that was bolted to the wall under his notional window. Alongside the drinking glass that held the proof of Buchbinder's genius, there stood a second glass.

That one contained a few ounces of paraffin hardened around a piece of white string. Litvak had bought this candle in a grocery store not quite a year after his wife died, with the intention of burning it on the anniversary of her death. Now a number of such anniversaries had come and gone, and Litvak had evolved his own quaint tradition. Every year he brought the yahrzeit candle out, and looked at it, and thought about lighting it. He imagined the shy flutter of a flame. He envisioned himself lying in the darkness with the memorial candle's light dancing over his head, scattering an alefbeys of shadows across the ceiling of the tiny room. He pictured the glass empty at the close of twenty-four hours, the wick consumed, the paraffin combusted, the metal tab drowned at the bottom in waxy dregs. And after that—but here his imagination tended to fail him.

Litvak rummaged in the pockets of his suit pants for his lighter, just to give himself the option, the chance of finding out, if he could bring himself to do it, what it might mean to set fire to the memory of his wife. The lighter was a steel Zippo etched with the Rangers insignia in worn black lines on one side, and on the other dented deeply where it had deflected some oncoming bit of the car, or the road, or the chokecherry tree, from piercing Litvak's heart. For the sake of his throat, Litvak no longer smoked; the lighter was only a habit, a token of his survivorship, an ironical charm that never left his bedside or his pants. But now it was in neither place. He patted himself down with the sheepish method of old man. He stepped backward through his day, working his way to that morning, when, as every morning, he had slid the lighter into his hip pocket. Hadn't he? All at once he could not remember having pocketed his Zippo that morning, or laying it on the steel shelf last night when he went to sleep. Perhaps he had been forgetting it for days. It might be in Sitka, in the back room at the Blackpool Hotel. It might be anywhere. Litvak lowered himself to the ground, dragged his kit from under the cot, and ransacked it, his heart pounding. No lighter. No matches, either. Only a candle in a juice glass, and a man who did not know how to light it even when he had a source of fire. Litvak turned to the door just as he heard someone approach. A soft knock. He slipped the yahrzeit candle into the hip pocket of his jacket.

"Reb Litvak," said Micky Vayner. "They're here, sir."

Litvak put in his teeth and tucked in his shirt.

I want everyone in quarters I don't want anybody to see him now

"He isn't ready," Micky Vayner said, a little doubtfully, wanting to be reassured. He didn't know, had never seen Mendel Shpilman. He had only heard stories of long-ago boyish miracles and perhaps caught an acrid whiff of spoiled goods that sometimes curled in the air over the mention of Shpilman's name.

He is unwell but we will heal him

It was neither part of their doctrine nor necessary to the success of Litvak's plan for Micky Vayner or any of the Peril Strait Jews to believe that Mendel Shpilman was the Tzaddik Ha-Dor. A Messiah who actually arrives is no good to anybody. A hope fulfilled is already half a disappointment.

"We know he's just a man," said Micky Vayner dutifully. "We all know that, Reb Litvak. Only a man and nothing more, and this is bigger than any man, what we're doing."

It isn't the man I'm worried about, Litvak wrote. *Everyone in quarters*

As he stood on the floatplane dock and watched Naomi Landsman help Mendel Shpilman down from the cockpit of her Super Cub, Litvak considered that if he did not know better, he would have taken them for old lovers. There was a brusque familiarity in the way she gripped his upper arm, fished his shirt collar from the lapels of his rumpled pin-striped jacket, picked a string of cellophane from his hair. She watched his face, only his face, as Shpilman eyed Roboy and Litvak; she was tender as an engineer looking for cracks, fatigue in the material. It seemed inconceivable that they had known each other, as far as Litvak was aware, for slightly under three hours. Three hours. That was all it had taken for her to seal up her fate with his.

"Welcome," Dr. Roboy said, posed beside a wheelchair with his necktie flapping in the breeze. Gold and Turteltoyb, a Sitka boy, jumped down from the plane to the dock, Turteltoyb heavy enough to make it ring like a slammed telephone. The water smacked the pilings. The air smelled of rotten netting and brackish puddles in the bottoms of old boats. It was almost dark, and they all looked vaguely green in the light of the floods on the standards, except for Shpilman, who looked white as a feather and as hollow. "You are genuinely welcome."

"You didn't need to send an airplane," Shpilman said. He had a wry, actorish voice, his diction studied, excellent, with a low, soft underthrob of the sorrowful Ukraine. "I'm perfectly capable of flying on my own."

"Yes, well—"

"X-ray vision. Bulletproof. The whole bit. Who is the wheelchair for, *me*?"

He outspread his arms, laid his feet primly side by side, and gave himself a slow once-over, looking prepared to be shocked at what he found. Ill-fitting pin-striped suit, hatless, tie loosely knotted, one shirttail hanging out, something teenage in his unruly ginger curls. Impossible to see in that slender fragile frame, that sleepy face, any hint of the monstrous father. Or maybe a little, around the eyes. Shpilman turned to the pilot, affecting to be surprised, even hurt, by the implication that he was so far gone as to need a wheelchair. But Litvak saw that he was putting it on to cover his real surprise and hurt at the implication.

"You said I looked all right, Miss Landsman," Shpilman said, teasing her, appealing to her, pleading with her.

"You look terrific, kid," the Landsman told him. She was dressed in blue jeans tucked into high black boots, a man's white oxford shirt, an old Sitka Central firing-range jacket that said LANDSMAN over the pocket. "You look fabulous."

"Ah, you're lying, you liar."

"You look like thirty-five hundred dollars to me, Shpilman," the Landsman said, not unkindly. "How about we leave it at that?"

"I won't be needing the wheelchair, doctor," Shpilman said without reproach. "But thank you for thinking of me."

"Are you ready, Mendel?" Dr. Roboy asked him in his gentle and sententious way.

"Do I need to be ready?" Mendel said. "If I need to be ready, we may have to push this back a few weeks."

The words emerged from Litvak's throat like a kind of verbal dust devil, a tangle of grit and gusts, unbidden. An awful sound, like a glob of burning rubber plunged into a bucket of ice.

"You don't need to be ready," Litvak said. "You only need to be *here.*"

They all looked shocked, horrified, even Gold, who happily could have read a comic book by the light of a burning man. Shpilman turned slowly, a smile tucked into one corner of his mouth like a baby carried on the hip.

"Alter Litvak, I presume," he said, holding out his hand, scowling at Litvak, affecting to be tough and masculine in a way that mocked toughness and masculinity and his own relative lack of both qualities. "What a grip, oy, it's like a rock."

His own grip was soft, warm, not quite dry, eternally a schoolboy's. Something in Litvak resisted it, the warmth and softness of it. He was himself horrified by the pterosaur echo of his own voice, by the fact that he had spoken at all. He was horrified to see that there was something about Mendel Shpilman, about his puffy face and his bad suit, his kid-prodigy smile and his brave attempt to hide the fact that he was afraid, that had prompted Litvak, for the first time in years, to speak. Litvak knew that charisma was a real if indefinable quality, a chemical fire that certain half-fortunate men gave off. Like any fire or talent, it was amoral, unconnected to goodness or wickedness, power or usefulness or strength. He felt, shaking Shpilman's hot hand, how sound his tactics were. If Roboy could get Shpilman up and running again, then Shpilman could inspire and lead not merely a few hundred armed believers or thirty thousand black-hatted hustlers looking for new turf, but an entire lost and wandering nation. Litvak's plan was going to work because there was something about Mendel Shpilman that could make a man with a broken voice box want to speak. It was against the something in Shpilman that something in Litvak pushed back, revulsed. He felt an urge to crush that schoolboy hand in his own, to break the bones of it.

"What's up, yid?" the Landsman said to Litvak. "Long time."

Litvak nodded, and he shook the Landsman's hand. He was torn, as he had always been, between his natural impulse to admire a competent practitioner of a difficult trade and his suspicion that the woman was a lesbian, a human category that he failed almost on principle to understand.

"All right, then," she said. She was still holding on to Shpilman, and as the wind picked up, she moved closer to him and put her arm around his shoulder, drawing him to her, giving him a squeeze. She scanned the greenish faces of the men who waited for her to hand over the cargo. "You going to be all right, then?"

Litvak wrote in his pad and passed it to Roboy.

"It's late," Roboy said. "And dark. Let us put you up for the night."

She appeared to consider rejecting the offer for a long moment. Then she nodded. "Good idea," she said.

At the bottom of the long, winding stair, Shpilman stopped to take in the particulars of the climb and the platform of the inclined elevator, and he seemed to suffer a qualm—a foreshock, a sudden access of understanding of everything that would from now on be expected of him. With a certain drama, he collapsed into Roboy's wheelchair.

"I left my cape at home," he said.

When they reached the top, he stayed in the chair and allowed the Landsman to wheel him into the main building. The strain of travel or the step he had finally taken or the plummeting level of heroin in his bloodstream was beginning to tell. But when they reached the room on the ground floor that had been prepared for him—a bed, a desk, a chair, and a fine English chess set—he rallied. He reached into the pocket of his creased suit and took out a black and bright-yellow cardboard package.

"Nu, I understand a mazel tov is in order?" he said, passing out half a dozen fine-looking Cohiba cigars. The smell of them, even unlit and three feet from his nostrils, was enough to whisper promises to Litvak of well-earned respite, clean sheets, hot water, brown women, the quiet aftermath of brutal battles. "They tell me it's a girl."

For a moment nobody knew what he was talking about, and then they all laughed nervously, except for Litvak and Turteltoyb, whose cheeks turned the color of borscht. Turteltoyb knew, as each of them knew, that Shpilman was not to be provided with any details of the plan, including the newborn heifer, until Litvak gave the order.

Litvak knocked the cigar from Shpilman's soft hand. He scowled at Turteltoyb, hardly able to see him through the blood-red broth of his own anger. The certainty he had felt down on the dock that Shpilman would serve their needs was turned abruptly on its head. A man like Shpilman, a talent like Shpilman's, could never serve anyone; it could only be served, above all by the one who wielded it. No wonder the poor bastard had been hiding from it for so long.

Out

They read his message and filed one by one out of the room, last of all the Landsman, who made a point of asking where she would be sleeping and then of telling Mendel pointedly that she would see him in the morning. At the time Litvak had a vague idea she might be arranging a tryst, but his notion of her as a lesbian canceled it out before he had time to give it any consideration. It didn't occur to Litvak that the Jewess, in her readiness for any adventure, was already laying the groundwork for the daring escape that Mendel had not yet decided to attempt. The Landsman struck a match, puffed at her cigar to get it lit. Then she sauntered out.

"Don't hold it against the boy, Reb Litvak," Shpilman said when they were alone. "People have a way of telling me things. But I guess you noticed that. Please, have a cigar. Go on. It's a very good one."

Shpilman picked up the corona that Litvak had knocked from his grasp, and when Litvak neither accepted nor refused it, the yid lifted it to Litvak's mouth and fitted it gently between his lips. It hung there, exuding its smells of gravy and cork and mesquite, cuntish smells that stirred old longings. There was a click, and a scrape, and then Litvak leaned wonderingly forward and poked the end of the cigar into the flame of his own Zippo lighter. He felt the momentary shock of a miracle. Then he grinned and nodded his thanks, feeling a kind of giddy relief at the belated arrival of a logical explanation: He must have left the lighter back in Sitka, where Gold or Turteltoyb had found it and brought it along on the flight to Peril Strait. Shpilman had borrowed it and, with his junkie instincts, pocketed it after lighting a papiros. Yes, good.

The cigar caught with a crackle and flared. When Litvak looked back up from the glowing coal, Shpilman was staring at him with those strange mosaic eyes, flecks of gold and green. Good, Litvak told himself again. A very good cigar.

"Go ahead," Shpilman said. He pressed the Zippo into Litvak's hand. "Go, Reb Litvak. Light the candle. There's no prayer you say. There's nothing you have to do or feel. You just light it. Go on."

As logic drained away from the world, never entirely to return, Shpilman reached into Litvak's jacket pocket and took out the glass and the wax and the wick. For this trick, Litvak could make himself no explanation. He took the candle from Shpilman and set it on a table. He struck the flint with a scratch of his thumb. He felt the intense warmth of Shpilman's hand on his shoulder. The fist of his heart begin to slacken its grip, the way it might when the day came that he finally set foot in the home where he was meant to dwell. It was a terrifying sensation. He opened his mouth.

"No," he said in a voice that had in it, to his wonder, a note of the human.

He snapped the lighter shut and knocked Shpilman's hand aside with such violence that Shpilman lost his balance, stumbled, and hit his head on the metal shelf. The force of the blow jarred loose the candle and sent it crashing to the tile floor. The glass cracked into three large pieces. The cylinder of wax split in two.

"I don't want it," Litvak croaked. "I'm not ready."

But when he looked down at Shpilman, sprawled on the floor, dazed, bleeding from a cut on his right temple, he knew that it was already too late.

40

Just as Litvak lays down his pen, you can hear a tumult outside: half a curse, glass breaking, the wind huffing out of somebody's lungs. Then Berko Shemets comes promenading into the bedroom. He has Gold's head nestled under one arm like a nice roast and the rest of Gold draggling along behind. The ganef's heels plow deep furrows in the carpet. Berko slams the door behind them. He has his sholem out, and it hungers like a compass needle for the magnetic north of Alter Litvak. Hertz's blood is mapped across Berko's hunting shirt and jeans. Berko's hat is pushed back in a way that makes his face look all brow and eye whites. The head of Gold glares oracular from the crook of Berko's arm.

"You should shit blood and pus," Gold intones. "You should get scabies like Job."

Berko's gun swings around to get a look at the young yid's brain in its breakable container. Gold stops struggling, and the gun resumes its one-eyed inspection of Alter Litvak's chest.

"Berko," Landsman says. "What's this craziness?"

Berko heaves his gaze toward Landsman like a great burden. He opens his lips, closes them, draws a breath. He seems to have something important that he wants to express, a name, a spell, an equation that can bend time or unknit the strings of the world. Or maybe he's trying to keep from coming unknit himself.

"That yid," he says, and then softer, his voice a little husky, "My mother."

Landsman has maybe seen a photograph of Laurie Jo Bear. He manages to scare up a vague memory of teased black bangs, pinkish glasses, a wiseass smile. But the woman is not even a ghost to him. Berko used to tell stories about life in the Indianer-Lands. Basketball, seal hunts, drunks and uncles, Willie Dick stories, the story of the human ear on the table. Landsman doesn't remember any stories about the mother. He supposes that he always knew there had to be some kind of cost to Berko in turning himself inside out the way he did, some kind of heroic feat of forgetting. He just never bothered to think of it as a loss. A failure of imagination, a worse sin in a shammes than going into a hot place with no backup. Or maybe it was the same sin in a different form.

"No doubt," Landsman says, taking a step toward his partner. "Bad guy. Worth a bullet."

"You have two little boys, Berko," Bina says in her flattest tone. "You have Ester-Malke. You have a future not to throw away."

"He does not," Gold says, or tries to say. Berko puts a deeper squeeze on him, and Gold gags, trying to turn over, to gain purchase with his feet.

Litvak scrawls something in the back of the pad without taking his eyes off of Berko.

"What is it?" Berko says. "What did he say?"

No future here for any Jew

"Yeah, yeah," says Landsman. "We get it already."

He grabs the pen and the pad away from Litvak. He flips over the last page and writes, in American, DON'T BE AN IDIOT! YOUR ACTING LIKE ME! He tears out the sheet of paper, then tosses the pad and pen back to Litvak. He holds the sheet up in front of Berko's face so that his partner can read it. It's a fairly persuasive argument. Berko lets go of Gold right as the yid is turning a bruised color all over. Gold drops to the floor, gasping for breath. The gun in Berko's fist wavers.

"He killed your *sister*, Meyer."

"I don't know if he did or not," Landsman says. He turns to Litvak. "Did you?"

Litvak shakes his head and starts to write something out on the pad, but before he finishes, a cheer goes up in the outer room. The heartfelt but self-conscious whoop of young men watching something great on television. A goal has been scored. A girl playing beach volleyball has fallen out of her bikini top. A moment later, Landsman hears the cheer echoing, the sound of it carried through the open window of the penthouse as if on a wind from far away, the Harkavy, the Nachtasyl. Litvak smiles and puts down the pad and pen with a strange finality, as if he has nothing left to say. As if his whole confession was leading to—was made possible by—only this moment. Gold crawls to the door, drags it open, and then staggers to his feet and into the outer room. Bina goes over to Berko and holds out her hand, and after a moment Berko lays the gun across her palm.

In the outer room of the penthouse, the young believers hug one another and jump up and down in their suits. Their yarmulkes tumble from their heads. Their faces shine with tears.

On the big television screen, Landsman gets his first look at an image that will soon be splashed across the front page of every newspaper in the world. All over town, pious hands will clip it and tape it to their front doors and windows. They will frame it and hang it behind the counters of their shops. Some hustler, inevitably, will work the thing up as a full-size poster, two feet by three. The hilltop in Jerusalem, crowded with alleys and houses. The broad empty mesa of paving stone. The jagged jawbone of burnt teeth. The magnificent plume of black smoke. And at the bottom the legend, in blue letters, AT LAST! These posters will sell at the stationers' for between ten dollars and $12.95.

"Sweet God. What are they doing? What did they do?"

There is a lot that shocks Landsman about the image on the television screen, but the most shocking thing of all is simply that an object eight thousand miles away has been acted upon by Jews from Sitka. It seems to violate some fundamental law of the emotional physics that Landsman understands. Sitka space-time is a curved phenomenon; a yid could reach out in any direction as far as he was able and end up only tapping himself on the back.

"What about Mendel?" he says.

"I guess they were too far along to stop," Bina says. "I guess they just went ahead without him."

It's perverse, but for some reason, the thought makes Landsman feel sad on Mendel's behalf. Everything and everyone, from now on, will be going ahead without him.

For a couple of minutes Bina stands there watching the boys carry on, her arms folded, her face without expression except at the corners of her eyes.

The way she looks reminds Landsman of an engagement party they went to years ago, for a friend of Bina's. The bride-to-be was marrying a mexican, and as a kind of joke, the party had a Cinco de Mayo theme. They hung a papier-mâché penguin from a tree in the yard. Children were blindfolded and sent forth, armed with a stick, to deal the penguin blows until it broke open. The children beat the penguin with savagery, and then the candy came showering down. It was just a bunch of wrapped toffees, peppermint, butterscotch, the kind your great-aunt could be relied upon to supply from a dusty crevice of her handbag. But as it rained from the sky, the children swarmed with a bestial joy. And Bina stood there watching them with her arms folded and a pleat at the corners of her eyes.

She passes Berko back his sholem and unholsters her own.

"Shut up," Bina says, and then in American, "Shut the fuck up!"

Some of the young men have taken out their Shoyfers and are trying to call people, but everyone in Sitka must be trying to call people. They show one another the error messages they are getting on their telephones' screens. The network is busy. Bina goes over to the television and kicks its cord. The plug snaps out of the wall. The television sighs.

Some dark fuel seems to drain from the young men's tanks when the television goes off.

"You are under arrest," Bina says gently, now that she has their attention. "Go over and put your hands on the wall. Meyer."

Landsman pats them down one by one, crouching like a tailor measuring an inseam. From the six along the wall, he collects eight handguns and two expensive hunting knives. As he finishes with each one, he tells him to sit down. His third search recovers the Beretta that Berko lent to him before he left for Yakovy. Landsman holds it up for Berko to enjoy.

"Little cutie," Berko says, keeping his big sholem level.

When Landsman is through, the young believers take their seats, three on the couch, two in a pair of armchairs, one in a dining chair pulled from an alcove. All at once, sitting in their chairs, they look young and lost. They are the runts. The ones that have been left behind. They turn as one, faces flushed, to the door of Litvak's bedroom, looking for guidance. The door to the bedroom is closed. Bina opens the door, then pushes it wide with a toe. She stands, looking in, for a full five seconds.

"Meyer. Berko."

The blind rattles in the wind. The bathroom door stands open, the bathroom dark. Alter Litvak is gone.

They look in the closet. They look in the shower. Bina goes over to the rattling blind and jerks it high. A sliding glass door stands open, wide enough to admit an intruder or an escapee. They go out onto the roof and look around. They search behind the air-conditioner unit, and all around a water tank, and under a tarp that conceals a pile of folding chairs. They peer over the cornices. There is no shattered portrait of Litvak drawn in oils on the surface of the parking lot. They go back down to the penthouse of the Blackpool.

In the middle of his cot lie Litvak's pen and pad and an ill-used gunmetal Zippo. Landsman picks up the pad to read the last words that Litvak wrote before he laid it down.

I didnt kill her she was a good man

"They smuggled him out," Bina says. "Those bastards. Those bastard U.S. Army Ranger friends of his."

Bina calls to the men down around the hotel's doors. None of them saw anyone leave nor anything unusual, for example, a squad of coal-faced warriors on rappelling cables being lowered from a Black Hawk.

"Bastards," she says again, in American this time, and with greater heat. "Fucking Bible-thumping Yankee motherfuckers."

"Language, lady, jeez!"

"Yeah, whoa, take it easy, there, ma'am."

Some Americans in suits, a number of them, too many and too bunched up for Landsman to count accurately, call it six, have arranged their shoulders in the doorway to the outer room. Big men, well fed, loving their jobs. One wears a snappy olive-drab duster and an apologetic smile under his white-gold hair. Landsman almost doesn't recognize him without the penguin sweater.

"Okay, now," says the man who must be Cashdollar. "Let's everybody try to calm down."

"FBI," says Berko.

"Close enough," says Cashdollar.

41

Landsman pisses away the next twenty-four hours in the hum of a chalk-white room with a milk-white carpet on the seventh floor of the Harold Ickes Federal Building on Seward Street.

In teams of two, six men with the variegated surnames of doomed crewmen in a submarine movie rotate in and out of the room in four-hour shifts. One is a black man and one a Latino, and the others are fluid pink giants with haircuts that occupy the neat interval between astronaut and pedophile scoutmaster. Gum chewers, overgrown boys with good manners and Bible-school smiles. In each of them at moments Landsman sniffs out the diesel heart of a policeman, but he is baffled by the fairings of their southern and gentile glamour. Despite the smoke screen of back talk that Landsman puts up, they make him feel rattletrap, a two-stroke old beater.

No one threatens him or tries to intimidate him. Everyone addresses him by rank, taking care to pronounce Landsman's name the way he prefers. When Landsman turns surly, flippant, or evasive, the Americans display forbearance and schoolteacher poise. But when Landsman dares to give out with a question of his own, an extinguishing silence rains down like a thousand gallons of water dropped from a plane. The Americans will say nothing about the whereabouts or situation of Detective Shemets or Inspector Gelbfish. They have nothing to say, either, about Alter Litvak's vanishing act, and they appear never to have heard of Mendel Shpilman or Naomi Landsman. They want to know what Landsman knows, or thinks he knows, about U.S. involvement in the attack on the Qubbat As-Sakhrah, and about the perpetrators, principals, ancillaries, and victims of that attack. And they do not want him to know what they know, if anything, about any of that. They have been so well trained in their art that they are deep into the second shift before Landsman realizes that the Americans are asking him the same roughly two dozen questions over and over, inverting and rephrasing and coming at them from odd angles. Their questions are like the fundamental moves of the six different chess pieces, endlessly recombined until they number with the neurons in the brain.

At regular intervals Landsman is provided with terrible coffee and a series of increasingly rigid apricot and cherry Danish. At one point he is shown into a break room and invited to inhabit a sofa. The coffee and Danish rotate in and out of the chalk-white room of Landsman's brain while he jams his eyes shut and pretends to nap. Then it is time to go back to the steady white noise of the walls, the laminate tabletop, the squeak of vinyl under his ass.

"Detective Landsman."

He opens his eyes and sees woozy black moire on brown. Landsman's cheekbone is numb from the pressure of the tabletop against it. He hoists his head, leaving behind a puddle of spit. A sticky filament connects his lip to the table, then snaps.

"Ick," says Cashdollar. He takes a little package of Kleenex out of the right pocket of his sweater and slides it across the table to Landsman, past an open box of Danish. Cashdollar has on a new sweater, a dark gold cardigan with front panels of coffee-brown suede, leather buttons, suede patches on the elbows. He's sitting upright on a metal chair, necktie knotted, cheeks smooth, blue eyes softened by attractive jet-pilot wrinkles. His hair is the precise gold of the foil in a package of Broadways. He smiles without enthusiasm or cruelty. Landsman wipes his face and the mess he made on the table during his nap.

"Are you hungry? Would you like a drink?"

Landsman says he would like a glass of water. Cashdollar reaches into the left pocket of his sweater and takes out a small bottle of mineral water. He tips it on its side and rolls it across the table to Landsman. He is not a young man, but there is something boyishly serious about the way he aims the bottle and launches it and steers it with body English to its destination. Landsman uncaps the bottle and takes a swallow. He doesn't really care for mineral water.

"I used to work for a man," Cashdollar says. "The man who had this job before me. He had a lot of cute catchphrases he liked to drop into a conversation. It's kind of a common trait among people who do what I do. We come out of the military, you know, we come out of the business world. We tend to like our catchphrases. Shibboleths. That's a Hebrew word, you know. Judges, Chapter 12. Are you sure you aren't hungry? I can get you a bag of potato chips. Cup of noodles. There's a microwave."

"No, thanks," Landsman says. "So. Shibboleths."

"This man, my predecessor. He used to say, 'We are telling a story, Cashdollar. That's what we do.'" The voice he adopts to quote his former superior is bigger and not as folksy as his own prim tenor twang. More pompous. "'Tell them a story, Cashdollar. That's all the poor suckers want.' Only he didn't say 'suckers.'"

"People who do what you do," Landsman says. "Meaning what? Sponsor terrorist attacks on Muslim holy places? Start in with the Crusades all over again? Kill innocent women who never did anything but fly their small airplanes and try to help somebody out of a jam once in a while? Shoot defenseless junkies in the head? Excuse me, I forget what it is you do, you people with your shibboleths."

"First of all, Detective, we had nothing to do with Menashe Shpilman's death." He pronounces Shpilman's Hebrew name

"Men-ashy." "I was as shocked and puzzled by that as anybody. I never met the fellow, but I know he was a remarkable individual with remarkable abilities, and we are very much worse off without him. How about a cigarette?" He holds out an unopened package of Winstons. "Come on. I know you like to smoke. There you go." He produces a package of matches and passes them with the Winstons across the table.

"Now, as for your sister, hey, listen. I am so very sorry about your sister. No, I really am. For what it's worth, and I suppose that's not a lot, you have my sincere apology on that. That was a bad call made by the man who preceded me in this job, the fellow I was just talking about. And he paid for it. Not with his life, of course." Cashdollar bares his big square teeth. "Maybe you wish he had. But he paid. He was wrong. The man was wrong about a lot of things. For one, huh-uh, sorry." He gives his head a gentle shake. "But we aren't telling a story."

"No?"

"Huh-uh. The story, Detective Landsman, is telling us. Just like it has done from the beginning. We're part of the story. You. Me."

The book of matches comes from a place in Washington, D.C., called Hogate's Seafood, at Ninth and Maine Avenue, SW. The very restaurant, if he remembers his history, in front of which Delegate Anthony Dimond, prime opponent of the Alaskan Settlement Act, was run down by a taxicab while chasing an errant rum bun into the street.

Landsman strikes a match.

"Jesus?" he says, looking up cross-eyed over the flame.

"Jesus, too."

"Jesus is okay with me."

"I'm glad. He's okay with me, too. And Jesus wasn't keen on killing, on hurting people, on destruction. I know that. The Qubbat As-Sakhrah was a fine old piece of architecture, and Islam is a venerable religion, and other than the fact that it's completely mistaken on a fundamental level, I have no quarrel with it per se. I wish there was some way to do this job that didn't require taking such actions. But sometimes there isn't. And Jesus knew that. 'Whoso shall offend one of these little ones which believe in me, it were better for him that a millstone were hanged about his neck, and that he were drowned in the depth of the sea.' Right? I mean, those are Jesus' words. The man could be fairly harsh when he needed to be."

"He was kick-ass," Landsman suggests.

"Yes, he was. Now, you might not credit the fact, but the end times are coming. And I for one very much look forward to seeing them come. But for that to happen, Jerusalem and the Holy Land have to belong to the Jews again. That's what it says in the Book. Sadly, there is no way to do that without some bloodshed, unfortunately. Without a certain amount of destruction. That's just what is written, you know? But I am trying very hard, unlike my immediate predecessor, to hold all that down to the absolute minimum. For Jesus' sake and for the sake of my own soul and all our sakes. To keep things running clean. Hold this operation together until we have it sorted out over there. Lay us down some facts on the ground."

"You don't want anybody to know you're behind it. You people who do what you do."

"Well, but, that's kind of our MO, if you know what I mean."

"And you want me to keep my mouth shut."

"I know it's asking a lot."

"Just until you lay these facts down on Jerusalem. Move some Arabs out and some Verbovers in. Rename a few streets."

"Just until we get some of that good old critical mass going. Straighten out some of the noses this has put out of joint. And then get busy, you know. Fulfilling what is written."

Landsman takes a swallow of mineral water. It's warm and tastes of the inside of the pocket of a cardigan. "I want my gun and my badge," he says. "And that's what I want."

"I love policemen," Cashdollar says without much enthusiasm.

"I really do." He covers his mouth with one hand and takes a contemplative breath through his nostrils. His hand sports a manicure, but one thumbnail has been gnawed. "It's going to get awfully Indian around here, mister. Just between you and me. You get your gun and badge back, you don't stand to hold on to them for very long. Tribal P won't be hiring too many Jewboys to serve and protect."

"Maybe not. But they'll take Berko."

"They aren't taking anyone who doesn't have the paper."

"Oh, yeah," Landsman says. "That's the other thing I want."

"You're talking about a lot of paper, Detective Landsman."

"You need a lot of quiet."

"Indeed I do," Cashdollar says.

Cashdollar studies Landsman for a long second or two, and Landsman understands from a certain alertness in the man's eyes, a look of anticipation, that there is a gun concealed somewhere on Cashdollar's person and an itch in his finger to go with it. There are more direct ways of keeping Landsman's mouth shut than buying him off with a gun and some documentation. Cashdollar gets up from the chair and returns it carefully to its place under the table. He starts to work his thumb into his teeth but thinks better of it.

"If I could just get my Kleenex back?"

Landsman tosses the package, but it goes awry, and Cashdollar fumbles the catch. The package of Kleenex splats down into the box of stale Danish, landing in a shiny patch of red jelly. Anger opens a seam in Cashdollar's placid gaze, through which you can see the banished shades of monsters and aversions. *The last thing he wants*, Landsman remembers, *is any hint of a mess*. Cashdollar tweezes a Kleenex from the package and uses it to wipe the package off, then tucks the rest back into the safety of his right pocket. He fidgets the bottom button of his sweater back through its buttonhole, and in the brief tug of woolen waistband over hip, Landsman spots the bulge of the sholem.

"Your partner," he tells Landsman, "has a great deal to lose.

A very great deal. So does your ex-wife. A fact that they both recognize all too well. Maybe it's time you came to the same conclusion about yourself."

Landsman considers the things that remain his to lose: a porkpie hat. A travel chess set and a Polaroid picture of a dead messiah. A boundary map of Sitka, profane, ad hoc, encyclopedic, crime scenes and low dives and chokeberry brambles, printed on the tangles of his brain. Winter fog that blankets the heart, summer afternoons that stretch endless as arguments among Jews. Ghosts of Imperial Russia traced in the onion dome of St. Michael's Cathedral, and of Warsaw in the rocking and sawing of a café violinist. Canals, fishing boats, islands, stray dogs, canneries, dairy restaurants. The neon marquee of the Baranof Theatre reflected on wet asphalt, colors running like watercolor as you come out of a showing of Welles's *Heart of Darkness*, which you have just seen for the third time, with the girl of your dreams on your arm.

"Fuck what is written," Landsman says. "You know what?" All at once he feels weary of ganefs and prophets, guns and sacrifices and the infinite gangster weight of God. He's tired of hearing about the promised land and the inevitable bloodshed required for its redemption. "I don't care what is written. I don't care what supposedly got promised to some sandal-wearing idiot whose claim to fame is that he was ready to cut his own son's throat for the sake of a hare-brained idea. I don't care about red heifers and patriarchs and locusts. A bunch of old bones in the sand. My homeland is in my hat. It's in my ex-wife's tote bag."

He sits down. He lights another cigarette.

"Fuck you," Landsman concludes. "And fuck Jesus, too, he was a pussy."

"Tick a lock, Landsman," Cashdollar says softly, miming the twist of a key in the hole of his mouth.

42

When Landsman steps outside the Ickes Building and fits his hat to his voided head, he finds that the world has sailed into a fog bank. The night is a cold sticky stuff that beads up on the sleeves of his overcoat. Korczak Platz is a bowlful of bright mist, smeared here and there with the pawprints of sodium lamps. Half-blind and cold in his bones, he trudges along Monastir Street to Berlevi Street, then over to Max Nordau Street, with a kink in his back and an ache in his head and a sharp throbbing pain in his dignity. The space recently occupied by his mind hisses like the fog in his ears, hums like a bank of fluorescent tubes. He feels that he suffers from tinnitus of the soul.

When he drags himself into the lobby of the Zamenhof, Tenenboym hands him two letters. One is from the board, informing him that the hearing into his conduct in the deaths of Zilberblat and Flederman has been scheduled for nine A.M. tomorrow morning. The other letter is a communication from the hotel's new ownership. A Ms. Robin Navin of the Joyce/Generali Hotel Group has written to inform Landsman that exciting changes are afoot in the coming months for the Zamenhof, to be known as of January 1 as the Luxington Parc Sitka. Part of the general excitement stems from the fact that Landsman's monthly lease has been terminated, effective on December 1. All the pigeonholes behind the front desk contain long white envelopes, each one slotted with the same fatal bend sinister in twenty-pound laid. Except for the pigeonhole labeled 208. Nothing in that one.

"You heard about what happened?" Tenenboym says after Landsman has returned from his epistolary journey into the bright, gentile future of the Hotel Zamenhof.

"I saw it on the television," Landsman says, though the memory feels secondhand, fogged-over, a construct that his interrogators implanted through persistent questioning.

"At first they said it was a mistake," Tenenboym says, gold toothpick jiggling in a corner of his mouth. "Some Arabs making bombs in a tunnel under the Temple Mount. Then they said it was deliberate. The ones fighting the other ones."

"Sunnis and Shiites?"

"Maybe. Somebody got careless with a rocket launcher."

"Syrians and Egyptians?"

"Whoever. The president was on, saying they might have to go in. Saying it's a holy city to everybody."

"That didn't take long," Landsman says.

His only other piece of mail is a postcard advertising a deep discount on lifetime membership at a gym where Landsman worked out for a few months after his divorce. The suggestion was made at the time that exercise might help his moods. It was a good suggestion. Landsman can't remember if it proved correct or not. The card depicts a fat Jew to the left and a thin Jew to the right. The Jew to the left is haggard, sleepless, sclerotic, straggly, with cheeks like two spoonfuls of sour cream, and two bright, mean little eyes. The Jew to the right is lean, tanned, and trim-bearded, relaxed, self-confident. He looks a lot like one of Litvak's young men. The Jew of the future, Landsman thinks. The unlikely claim is made by the postcard that the left-hand Jew and the Jew on the right are one and the same person.

"Did you see them out in the neighborhoods?" Tenenboym says, the golden pick clicking against a bicuspid. "On the television?"

Landsman shakes his head. "I imagine there was dancing?"

"Such dancing. Fainting. Crying. A mass orgasm."

"Not on an empty stomach, I beg you, Tenenboym."

"Blessing the Arabs for fighting with each other. Blessing the memory of Mohammed."

"That seems cruel."

"One of these black hats was on there saying how he's going to move over to the Land of Israel, get himself a good seat for when Messiah shows up." He removes the toothpick and surveys its tip for a hint of treasure, then returns it, disappointed. "Ask me, I say put all those nut jobs on a great big airplane, send them all the hell over there, a black year on them. "

"That what you say, Tenenboym?"

"I'll fly that airplane myself."

Landsman stuffs the letter from the Joyce/Generali Hotel Group back into its envelope and slides it across the counter to Tenenboym. "Toss that for me, would you?"

"You have thirty days, Detective," Tenenboym says. "You will find something."

"You bet I will," Landsman says. "We'll all find something."

"Unless something finds us first, am I right?"

"What about you? They going to let you keep your job?"

"My status remains under review."

"That sounds hopeful."

"Or hopeless."

"One or the other."

Landsman takes the elevatoro to the fifth floor. He walks down the corridor, his overcoat slung on a crooked fingertip from one shoulder, loosening his necktie with the other hand. The door to his room hums its simple lyric: five-oh-five. It means nothing. Lights in the fog. Three Arabic numerals. Invented in India, actually, like the game of chess, but disseminated by Arabs. Sunnis, Shiites. Syrians, Egyptians. Landsman wonders how long it will take the various contending factions in Palestine to figure out that none of them was responsible for the attack. A day or two, maybe a week. Just long enough for terminal confusion to set in, Litvak to get his boys in place, Cashdollar to send in the air support. Next thing you know, Tenenboym's working as the night manager of the Jerusalem Luxington Parc.

Landsman gets into bed and takes out the pocket chess set. His attention flits along the lines of force, hops from square to square in pursuit of the killer of Mendel Shpilman and Naomi Landsman. Landsman finds, to his surprise and relief, that he already knows who the killer is—it is the Swiss-born physicist, winner of the Nobel Prize, and mediocre chess player Albert Einstein. Einstein with his fog of hair and his enormous sweater-jacket and his eyes like tunnels reaching deep into the darkness of time itself. Landsman pursues Albert Einstein across the milk-white, chalk-white ice, hopping from square to shadowed square across relativistic chessboards of culpability and atonement, across the imaginary land of penguins and Eskimos that the Jews never quite managed to inherit.

His dream makes a knight move, and with characteristic fervor, his little sister, Naomi, begins to explain to Landsman Einstein's famous proof of the Eternal Return of the Jew and how it can be measured only in terms of the Eternal Exile of the Jew, a proof that the great man deduced from observing the wobble in the wing of an airplane and the drift of a dark bloom of smoke rising from the slope of an ice mountain. Landsman's dream calves other slow iceberg dreams, and the ice hums with fluorescence. At some point the humming that has plagued Landsman and his people since the dawn of time, which some in their foolishness have mistaken for the voice of God, gets trapped in the windows of room 505 like sunlight in the heart of an iceberg.

Landsman opens his eyes. In the seams of the venetian blinds, daylight buzzes like a trapped fly. Naomi is dead again, and that fool of an Einstein is innocent of all wrongdoing in the Shpilman case. Landsman knows nothing at all. He feels an ache in his abdomen that he takes at first for sorrow before determining, a moment later, that what he's feeling is hunger. The desire, in fact, for stuffed cabbage. He checks his Shoyfer for the time, but the battery has died. The day clerk reports, when Landsman calls down to the desk, that it is 9:09 A.M., Thursday. Stuffed cabbage! Every Wednesday night is Rumania night at the Vorsht, and Mrs. Kalushiner always has something left over the next morning. The old bat serves the finest sarmali in Sitka. At once light and dense, favoring hot pepper over sweet-and-sour, drizzled with fresh sour cream, topped with sprigs of fresh dill. Landsman shaves and dresses in the same blown suit and a tie from off the doorknob. He is ready to consume his own weight in sarmali. But when he gets downstairs, he glances at the clock over the mail slots and realizes that he is nine minutes late for his hearing before the review committee.

By the time Landsman comes scrabbling like a dog on slick tile down the corridor of the Administration modular, into room 102, he is twenty-two minutes late. He finds nothing but a long veneer table with five chairs, one for each member of the review board, and his commanding officer, sitting on the edge of the table, legs dangling, crossed at the ankle, her pointy-toed pumps aiming straight for Landsman's heart. The five big high-backed leather chairs are empty.

Bina looks like hell, only hotter. Her seagull-brown suit is rumpled and misbuttoned. Her hair appears to be tied back with a plastic drinking straw. Her panty hose are long gone, her legs bare and dappled with pale freckles. Landsman recalls with a strange pleasure the way she would trash a laddered pair of stockings, shredding them into a pompon of rage before tossing them into the can.

"Stop looking at my legs," she says. "Cut it out, Meyer. Look at my face."

Landsman complies, staring right down the bores of her double-barreled gaze. "I overslept," he says. "I'm sorry. They kept me for twenty-four hours, and by the time—"

"They kept me for thirty-one hours," she says. "I just got out."

"So fuck me and my whining, for starters."

"For starters."

"How was it by you?"

"They were so nice," Bina says bitterly. "I totally folded. Told them everything."

"Same here."

"So," she says, gesturing to the room around them with upturned hands, like she just made something disappear. Her jocular tone is not a good sign. "Guess what?"

"I'm dead," Landsman tries. "The board sprinkled me with quicklime and plowed me under."

"As a matter of fact," she says, "I got a call on my mobile this morning, in this room, at eight-fifty-nine. After I made a total ass of myself and screamed my head off until they let me out of the Federal Building, so I could get down here and make sure I was in that chair behind you, on time and ready to stand up and support my detective."

"Um."

"Your hearing was canceled."

Bina reaches into her bag, rummages around, and comes out with a gun. She adds it to the battery comprising her rifled gaze and the toes of her pointed shoes. A chopped M-39. A manila tag dangles on a string from its barrel. She arcs it toward Landsman's head. He manages to catch the gun but fumbles the badge holder that comes flying after it. Then comes a little bag with Landsman's clip. Another brief search of her bag produces a murderous-looking form and its triplicate henchmen. "After you go ahead and break your head on this DPD-2255, Detective Landsman, you will have been reinstated, with full pay and benefits, as an active member of the District Police, Sitka Central Division."

"I'm back on the job."

"For, what is it, five more weeks? Enjoy."

Landsman weighs the sholem like a Shakespearean hero contemplating a skull. "I should have asked for a million dollars," he says. "I'll bet he would have coughed it up."

"God damn him," Bina says. "God damn them all. I always knew they were there. Down there in Washington. Up there over our heads. Holding the strings. Setting the agenda. Of course I knew that. We all knew that. We all grew up knowing that, right? We are here on sufferance. Houseguests. But they ignored us for so long. Left us to our own devices. It was easy to kid yourself. Make you think you had a little autonomy, in a small way, nothing fancy. I thought I was working for *everyone*. You know. Serving the public. Upholding the law. But really I was just working for Cashdollar."

"You think I should have been discharged, don't you?"

"No, Meyer."

"I know I go a little too far. Play the hunches. The loose-cannon routine."

"You think I'm angry because they gave you back your badge and your gun?"

"Well, not so much that, no. But the hearing being canceled. I know how much you like things done by the book."

"I do like things done by the book," she says, her voice tight. "I believe in the book."

"I know you do."

"If you and I had played it by the book a little more," she says, and something dangerous seems to well up between them. "You and your hunches, a black year on them."

He wants to tell it to her then: the story that has been telling him for the past three years. How, after Django was husked from her body, Landsman stopped the doctor in the hall outside the operating room. Bina had instructed Landsman to ask this good doctor whether there was some use, some aim or study, to which the half-grown bones and organs might be put.

"My wife was wondering," Landsman began, then faltered.

"Whether there was any visible defect?" the doctor said. "No. Nothing at all. The baby appeared to be normal." He remarked, too late, the look of horror blooming on Landsman's face. "Of course, that doesn't mean there was nothing wrong."

"Of course," Landsman said.

He never saw this doctor again. The ultimate fate of the little body, of the boy Landsman sacrificed to the god of his own dark hunches, was something he had neither the heart nor the stomach to investigate.

"I made the same fucking deal, Meyer," Bina says before he can confess to her. "For my silence."

"That you get to keep being a cop?"

"No. That you do."

"Thanks," Landsman says. "Bina, thanks a lot. I'm grateful."

She presses her face into her hands and massages her temples. "I'm grateful to you, too," she says. "I'm grateful for the reminder of just how messed up all of this is."

"My pleasure," he says. "Glad I could help."

"Fucking Mr. Cashdollar. The man's hair doesn't move. It's like it's welded to his head."

"He said he had nothing to do with Naomi," Landsman says. He pauses and nibbles on his lip. "He said it was the man who had the job before him."

He tries to keep his head up while he says it, but after a moment he finds himself looking at the stitches of his shoes. Bina reaches, hesitates, then gives his shoulder a squeeze. She leaves her hand on him for all of two seconds, just long enough to rip a seam or two in Landsman.

"Also he denied any involvement in Shpilman. I forgot to ask him about Litvak, though." Landsman looks up, and she takes her hand away. "Did Cashdollar tell you where they took him? Is he on his way to Jerusalem?"

"He tried to look mysterious about it, but I think he was just without a clue. I overheard him on his cell phone, telling somebody they were bringing in a forensic team from Seattle to go over the room at the Blackpool. Maybe that was something he wanted me to hear. But I have to say they all seemed nonplussed about our friend Alter Litvak. They seem to have no idea where he is. Maybe he took the money and ran. He could be halfway to Madagascar by now."

"Maybe," Landsman says, then, more slowly, "maybe."

"God help me, I sense another hunch coming on."

"You said you're grateful to me."

"In a backhanded, ironical way. Yeah."

"Look, I could use a little backup. I want to have another look at Litvak's room."

"We can't get into the Blackpool. The whole joint is under some kind of secret federal lockdown."

"Only I don't want to get into the Blackpool. I want to get under it."

"Under it?"

"I heard there might be some, well, some tunnels down there."

"Tunnels."

"Warsaw tunnels, I heard they're called."

"You need me to hold your hand," she says. "In a deep dark nasty old tunnel."

"Only in the metaphorical sense," he says.

⊒ 43 ⊑

At the top of the stairs, Bina takes a key-ring flashlight from her cowhide bag and passes it to Landsman. It promotes or possibly allegorizes the services of a Yakovy funeral home. Then she moves aside some dossiers, a sheaf of court documents, a wooden hairbrush, a mummified boomerang that may once have been a banana in a Ziploc, a copy of *People*, and comes up with a slack black harness suggestive of sadomasochistic sex play, equipped with a kind of round canister. She plunges her head into the midst of it and involves her hair with the black webbing. When she sits up and turns her head, a silver lens flares and wanes, raking Landsman's face. Landsman can feel the imminent darkness, can feel the very word "tunnel" burrowing through his rib cage.

They go down the steps, through the lost-articles room. The taxidermy marten leers at them as they pass. The loop of rope on the door of the crawl space dangles. Landsman tries to recall if he returned it to its hook before his inglorious retreat last Thursday night. He stands there, racking his memory, and then he gives up.

"I'll go first," Bina says.

She gets down on her bare knees and works herself into the crawl space. Landsman hangs back. His throbbing pulse, his dry tongue, his autonomic systems are caught up in the tiresome history of his phobia, but the crystal set that is handed out to every Jew, tuned to receive transmissions from Messiah, resonates at the sight of Bina's ass, the long indented arc of it like some kind of magic alphabet letter, a rune with the power to roll away the stone slab behind which he has entombed his desire for her. He is pierced by the knowledge that no matter how potent a spell it still casts over him, he will never again find himself permitted, wonder of wonders, to bite it. Then it vanishes into the darkness, along with the rest of her, and Landsman is left stranded. He mutters to himself, reasons with himself, dares himself to go in after her, and then Bina says, "Get in here," and Landsman obeys.

She spans an arc of the plywood disk with her fingertips, lifts it, and passes it to Landsman, her face flickering with the glow of his flashlight and with a prankish solemnity he has not seen in years. When they were kids, he would climb to her bedroom in the night, sneaking in and out the window to sleep with her, and this was the face she wore as she eased up the sash.

"It's a *ladder*!" she says. "Meyer, you didn't go down this? When you came here that night?"

"Well, no, I was kind of, I wasn't really—"

"Yeah, okay," she says gently. "I know."

She lowers herself down one steel cleat at a time, and again Landsman goes after her. He can hear her grunt as she lets herself drop, the metallic scrape of her shoes. Then he falls down into the darkness. She catches hold of him and half succeeds in keeping him on his feet. The lamp on Bina's forehead splashes light here, here, here, making a hasty sketch of the tunnel.

It's another aluminum pipe, running perpendicular to the one they just came down. Landsman's hat brushes against the arc of it when he stands erect. It ends behind them in a curtain of dank black earth and runs straight away from them, under Max Nordau Street, toward the Blackpool. The air is cold and planetary, with an iron taint. A floor of plywood has been laid, and as they clunk along it, their lights pick out the imprints of the boots of passing men.

When they reckon themselves to be about halfway across Max
Nordau, they meet another pipeline running away to the east and
west, linking this tunnel to the network laid against the likelihood
of future annihilation. Tunnels leading to tunnels, storehouses,
bunkers.

Landsman considers the cohort of yids who arrived with his
father, those who were not broken by suffering and horror but
rather somehow resolved. The former partisans, the resisters,
Communist gunmen, left Zionist saboteurs—the rabble, as they
were styled in the newspapers of the south—who showed up in
Sitka after the war with their vulcanized souls and fought with Polar
Bears like Hertz Shemets their brief, doomed battle for control of
the District. They knew, those bold and devastated men, knew as
they knew the flavor of their tongues in their mouths, that their
saviors would one day betray them. They walked into this wild
country that had never seen a Jew and set about preparing for the
day when they would be rounded up, sent packing, forced to make
a stand. Then, one by one, these wised-up, angry men and women
had been coopted, picked off, fattened up, set against one another,
or defanged by Uncle Hertz and his endless operations.

"Not all of them," Bina says, her voice, like Landsman's,
caroming off the aluminum walls of the tunnel. "Some of them
just got comfortable here. They started to forget a little bit. They
felt at home."

"I guess that's how it always goes," Landsman says. "Egypt.
Spain. Germany."

"They weakened. It's human to weaken. They had their lives.
Come on."

They follow the planks until they come to another pipe that
opens overhead, also fitted with cleats.

"You go first this time," Bina says. "Let me check out your ass
for a change."

Landsman hoists himself up to the lowest cleat and then mounts
to the top. A swatch of weak light shows through a break or hole

in the lid that caps this end of the pipe. Landsman pushes against the hatch and it shoves back, a thick sheet of plywood that doesn't budge or buckle. He puts his shoulder into it.

"What's the matter?" Bina says from beneath his feet, her lamp wobbling into his eyes.

"It won't move," Landsman says. "There must be something on it. Or—"

He feels for the hole, and his hand brushes against something cold and rigid. He recoils, then his fingers return to work out the sense of an iron rod, a cable, pulled taut. He shines his light. A rubberized cable, knotted and fed through the finger hole from the top side, then drawn tight and lashed to the topmost cleat of the ladder underneath.

"What is it, Meyer? What did they do?"

"They tied it shut behind them so that nobody could follow them back down," Landsman says. "Tied it with a nice big piece of string."

44

A ganef wind has blown down from the mainland to plunder the Sitka treasury of fog and rain, leaving behind only cobwebs and one bright penny in a vault of polished blue. At 12:03 the sun has already punched its ticket. Sinking, it stains the cobbles and stucco of the platz in a violin-colored throb of light that you would have to be a stone not to find poignant. Landsman, a curse on his head, may be a shammes, but he is no stone.

Driving onto Verbov Island, coming west on Avenue 225, he and Bina catch strong whiffs at every corner of the bubbling tzimmes that is cooking up all over town. The smell blows more intense and richer with both joy and panic on this island than anywhere else. Signs and banners announce the imminent proclamation of the kingdom of David and exhort the pious to prepare for the return to Eretz Yisroel. Many of the signs look spontaneous, sprayed in dripping characters on bed linens and sheets of butcher paper. In the side streets, crowds of women and handlers yell at one another, trying to hold down or hyperinflate the price of luggage, concentrated laundry soap, sunscreen, batteries, protein bars, bolts of tropical-weight wool. Deeper into the alleys, Landsman imagines, in the basements and doorways, a quieter market burns like a banked fire: prescription drugs, gold, automatic weapons.

They drive past huddled groups of street-corner geniuses spinning commentary on which families are to be given which contracts when they reach the Holy Land, which of the wiseguys will run the policy rackets, the cigarette smuggling, the gun franchises. For the first time since Gaystik took the championship, since the World's Fair, maybe for the first time in sixty years, or so it feels to Landsman, something is actually happening in the Sitka District. What that something will turn out to be, not even the most learned of the sidewalk rebbes has the faintest idea.

But when they reach the heart of the island, the faithful replica of the lost heart of old Verbov, there is no hint of the end of exile, rampant price gouging, messianic revolution. Down at the wide end of the platz, the house of the Verbover rebbe stands looking solid and eternal as a house in a dream. Smoke hastens like a remittance from its lavish chimney, only to be waylaid by the wind. The morning's Rudashevskys loiter darkly at their posts, and on the ridge of the house, the black rooster perches, coattails flapping, with his semiautomatic mandolin. Around the platz, women describe the ordinary circuits of their day, pushing strollers, trailing girls and boys too young for school. Here and there they stop to knit and unravel the skeins of breath that tangle them together. Scraps of newsprint, leaves, and dust get up impromptu games of dreydl in the archways of the houses. A pair of men in long coats leans into the wind, making for the rebbe's house, sidelocks swinging. For the first time the traditional complaint, tantamount to a creed or at least a philosophy, of the Sitka Jew—*Nobody gives a damn about us, stuck up here between Hoonah and Hotzeplotz*—strikes Landsman as having been a blessing these past sixty years, and not the affliction they had all, in their backwater of geography and history, supposed.

"Who else is going to want to live in this chicken coop?" Bina says, echoing his thought in her own fashion, zipping her orange parka up past her chin. She slams the door of Landsman's car and trades ritual glares with a gathering of women across the lane from the boundary maven's shop. "This place is like a glass eye, it's a wooden leg, you can't pawn it."

In front of the somber barn, the bachelor torments a rag with a broom handle. The rag is sloshed in solvent with a psychotropic odor, and the boy has been exiled to three hopeless islands of automobile grease on the cement. He jabs and caresses the rag with the end of his pole. When he takes note of Bina, he does so with a satisfying mixture of horror and awe. If Bina were Messiah come to redeem him in an orange parka, the expression on the pisher's face would be more or less the same. His gaze gets stuck to her, and then he has to detach it with brutal care, like someone removing his tongue from a frozen pump.

"Reb Zimbalist?" Landsman says.

"He's there," says the bachelor, nodding toward the door of the shop. "But he's really busy."

"As busy as you?"

The bachelor gives the rag another desultory poke. "I was in the way." He makes the citation with a flourish of self-pity, then aims a cheekbone at Bina without implicating any of his other features of his face in the gesture. "She can't go in there," he says firmly. "It isn't appropriate."

"See this, sweetness?" Bina has fished out her badge. "I'm like a cash gift. I'm always appropriate."

The bachelor takes a step backward, and the mop handle disappears behind his back as if somehow it might incriminate him. "Are you going to arrest Reb Itzik?" he says.

"Now," Landsman says, taking a step toward the bachelor, "why would we want to do that?"

One thing about a Yeshiva bachelor, he knows his way around a question.

"How should I know?" he says. "If I was a fancy-pants lawyer, tell me, please, would I be standing out here slopping around with a rag on the end of a stick?"

Inside the shop, they have gathered around the big map table, Itzik Zimbalist and his crew, a dozen strapping Jews in yellow coveralls, their chins upholstered with the netted rolls of their beards. The presence of a woman in the shop flits among them like a bothersome moth. Zimbalist is the last to look up from the problem spread out on the table before him. When he sees who has come with the latest thorny question for the boundary maven, he nods and grunts with a suggestion of huffiness, as if Landsman and Bina are late for their appointment.

"Good morning, gentlemen," Bina says, her voice weirdly fluting and unpersuasive in this big male barn. "I'm Inspector Gelbfish."

"Good morning," says the boundary maven.

His sharp and fleshless face is illegible as a blade or a skull. He rolls up the plan or chart with practiced hands, ties it in a length of cord, and turns to sheath it in the rack, where it disappears among a thousand of its fellows. His movements are those of an old man to whom haste is a forgotten vice. His step is herky-jerk, but his hands mannered and accurate.

"Lunch is over," he tells the crew, though there is not a trace of food to be seen.

The men hesitate, forming an irregular eruv around the boundary maven, ready to shield him from the secular trouble that stands hung with a couple of badges in their midst.

"Maybe they'd better stick around," Landsman says. "We might need to talk to them, too."

"Go wait in the vans," Zimbalist tells them. "You're in the way."

They start across the supply area to the garage. One of the crew turns back, pressing doubtfully at the roll of his beard.

"Seeing as how lunch is over, Reb Itzik," he says, "is it all right with you if we have our supper now?"

"Eat your breakfast, too," Zimbalist says. "You're going to be up all night."

"Lot of work to do?" Bina says.

"Are you kidding? It's going to take them years to pack up this mess. I'm going to need a cargo container."

He goes to the electric tea kettle and begins to set up three glasses. "Nu, Landsman, I heard maybe you lost the use of that badge of yours for a little while," he says.

"You hear a lot, don't you?" Landsman says.

"I hear what I hear."

"Have you ever heard that people dug tunnels all under the Untershtot, just in case the Americans turned on us and decided to stage an *aktion*?"

"I'd say it rings a bell," Zimbalist says. "Now that you mention it."

"So you wouldn't happen to possess, by any chance, a plan of those tunnels? Showing how they run, where they connect, et cetera?"

The old man still has his back to them, tearing open the paper envelopes that hold the tea bags. "If I didn't," he says, "what kind of a boundary maven would I be?"

"So if, for whatever reason, you wanted to get somebody, say, into or out of the basement of the Hotel Blackpool on Max Nordau Street without being seen. Could you do that?"

"Why would I want to do that?" Zimbalist says. "I wouldn't board my mother-in-law's Chihuahua in that fleabag."

He unplugs the kettle before the water has boiled and soaks the tea bags one-two-three. He puts the glasses on a tray with a pot of jam and three small spoons, and they sit down at his desk in the corner. The tea bags surrender their color unwillingly to the tepid water. Landsman hands around papiroses and lights them. From the vans come the sounds of men shouting, or laughing, Landsman isn't quite sure.

Bina walks around the workshop, admiring the mass and variety of string, stepping carefully to avoid a tumbleweed of knotted wire, gray rubber with a blood-red copper stump.

"Ever make a mistake?" Bina asks the boundary maven. "Tell someone he can carry where he's not allowed to carry? Draw a line where no line needs to be drawn?"

"I don't dare to make mistakes," Zimbalist says. "Carrying on the Sabbath, it's a serious violation. People start thinking they can't rely on my maps, I'm through."

"We still don't have a ballistic fingerprint on the gun that killed Mendel Shpilman," Bina says with care. "But you saw the wound, Meyer."

"I did."

"Did it look like it was made by, say, a Glock, or a TEC-9, or any kind of an automatic?"

"In my humble opinion," Landsman says, "no."

"You spent a lot of quality time with Litvak's crew and their firearms."

"And loved every minute."

"Did you see anything in their toybox that was not an automatic?"

"No," Landsman says. "No, Inspector, I did not."

"What does that prove?" Zimbalist says, easing his tender bottom down onto the inflatable-donut cushion of his desk chair. "More importantly, why should I care?"

"Aside from your general, personal interest in seeing justice done in this matter, of course," says Bina.

"Aside from that," Zimbalist says.

"Detective Landsman, do you think Alter Litvak killed Shpilman or ordered him killed?"

Landsman looks right into the boundary maven's face and says, "He didn't. He wouldn't. He didn't just need Mendel. The yid had started to *believe* in Mendel. "

Zimbalist blinks and fingers the blade of his nose, thinking this over, as if it is the rumor of a newborn creek that will force him to redraw one of his maps.

"I do not buy it," he concludes. "Anybody else. Everybody else. Not that yid."

Landsman doesn't bother to argue. Zimbalist reaches for his tea. A vein of rust twists in the water like the ribbon in a glass marble.

"What would you do if something you had been telling everybody was one of the lines on your map," Bina says, "turned out to be, say, a crease? A hair. A stray pen mark. Something like that. Would you tell anyone? Would you go to the rebbe? Would you admit that you made a mistake?"

"It would never happen."

"But if it did. Would you be able to live with yourself?"

"If you knew you had sent an innocent man to prison for many years, Inspector Gelbfish, for the rest of his life, would you be able to live with yourself?"

"It happens all the time," Bina says. "But here I am."

"Well, then," the maven says. "I guess you know how I feel. By the way, I use the term 'innocent' very loosely."

"As do I," says Bina. "No doubt about it."

"My whole life, I knew only one man I would use that word to describe."

"You're ahead of me, then," Bina says.

"Me, too," says Landsman, missing Mendel Shpilman as if they had been, for many years, the best of friends. "I am very sorry to say."

"You know what people are saying?" Zimbalist says. "These geniuses I dwell among? They're saying Mendel's coming back. That it's all happening just the way it was written. That when they get to Jerusalem, Mendel is going to be there, waiting for them. Ready to rule over Israel."

Tears start to run down the boundary maven's sallow cheeks. After a moment Bina removes a handkerchief from her bag, clean and pressed. Zimbalist takes it and looks at it for a moment. Then he blows a great tekiah on his shofar of a nose.

"I would like to see him again," he says. "I will admit it."

Bina hoists her bag to her shoulder, and it resumes its steady mission to drag her down. "Get your things together, Mr. Zimbalist."

The old man appears startled. He puffs his lips as if trying to light an invisible cigar. He picks up a loop of rawhide thong lying on his desk, ties a knot in it, and puts it down again. Then he picks it up and unties it. "My things," he says finally. "Are you saying I'm under arrest?"

"No," Bina says. "But I would like you to come down so that we can talk some more. You might want to call your lawyer."

"My lawyer," he says.

"I think you took Alter Litvak out of his hotel room. I think you've done something with him, put him on ice, possibly killed him. I'd like to find out."

"You have no evidence," Zimbalist says. "You're just guessing."

"She has a little evidence," Landsman says.

"About three feet," says Bina. "Can you hang a man with three feet of rope, Mr. Zimbalist?"

The maven shakes his head, half irritated, half amused, his poise and his bearings regained. "You're just wasting my time and yours," he says. "I have a huge amount of work to do. And you, by your own admission, by your own theory, have not found whoever it was that killed Mendele. So with all due respect, why don't you just worry about that, all right, and leave me alone? Come back when you've caught the supposed actual killer, and I'll tell you what I know about Litvak, which at the moment, by the way, is officially and everlastingly nothing."

"It doesn't work that way," Landsman says.

"All right," says Bina.

"All right!" Zimbalist says.

Landsman looks at Bina. "All right?"

"We catch whoever killed Mendel Shpilman," Bina says, "you give us information. *Helpful* information about Litvak's disappearance. If he's still alive, you give me Litvak."

"You have a deal," the boundary maven says. He thrusts out his right claw, all spots and knuckles, and Bina shakes it.

Landsman, feeling stunned, gets up and shakes hands with the boundary maven. Then he follows Bina out of the shop into the waning day, and his shock intensifies when he finds that Bina is crying. Unlike Zimbalist's, hers are tears of fury.

"I can't believe I *did that*," she says, availing herself of a tissue from her endless stash. "That is the kind of thing *you* would do."

"People I know keep having that problem," Landsman says. "Suddenly acting like me."

"We're law officers. We uphold the law."

"People of the book," Landsman says. "As it were."

"Fuck you."

"Do you want to go back in there and arrest him?" he says. "We can. We have the cable from the tunnel. We can hold him. Start from there."

She shakes her head. The bachelor on his map of stains is staring at them, hitching up the seat of his black serge trousers and taking it all in. Landsman decides he'd better get her out of there. He puts his arm around her for the first time in three years and ushers her over to the Super Sport, then goes around to his side and climbs in behind the wheel.

"The law," she says. "I don't even know what law I'm talking about anymore. Now I'm just making this shit up."

They sit silently as Landsman wrestles with the perennial detective problem of being obliged to state the obvious.

"I kind of like this new crazy, confused Bina and all," he says. "But I feel I have to point out that we have no real leads on the Shpilman case. No witnesses. No suspect."

"Well, then, you and your partner had better fucking *get* me a suspect," she says. "Hadn't you?"

"Yes, ma'am."

"Let's go."

He starts the ignition, puts the Super Sport in gear.

"Hold on," she says. "What's that?"

Across the platz, a big black four-by-four pulls up around the east side of the rebbe's house. Two Rudashevskys get out of it. One goes around to open the rear gate of the vehicle. The other waits at the bottom of the side steps, hands knotted loosely behind him. A moment later, two more Rudashevskys come out of the house, humping several hundred cubic meters of what appears to be hand-painted French luggage. Quickly and with little regard for the laws of solid geometry, the four Rudashevskys manage to fit all of the trunks and bags into the back of the four-by-four.

Once they have accomplished that feat, a big chunk of the house itself breaks off and falls into their arms, wearing a gorgeous fawn-colored alpaca coat. The Verbover rebbe does not look up, or back, or around at the world he rebuilt and is now abandoning. He lets the Rudashevskys do their quantum origami on him, folding him and his canes into the backseat of the four-by-four. The yid just joins his luggage and rolls on.

Fifty-five seconds later, a second four-by-four pulls up, and two women in long dresses, heads covered, are helped into the back along with their city of baggage and a number of children. The process is repeated with females and children and black four-by-fours for the next eleven minutes.

"I hope they have a very big airplane," Landsman says.

"I didn't see her," Bina says. "Did you see her?"

"I don't think so. I didn't see Big Shprintzl, either."

Half a second later, Bina's Shoyfer rings.

"Gelbfish. Yes. We did wonder. Yes. I understand." She snaps the phone shut. "Drive around the back of the house," she says. "She saw your car."

Landsman guides the Super Sport through a narrow alley and into a courtyard behind the rebbe's house. Apart from the car, there is nothing that would have been out of place a hundred years ago.

Stone flags, stucco walls, leaded glass, a long half-timbered gallery. The flags are slick, and water drips from a row of potted ferns that hang from the underside of the gallery.

"She's coming out?"

Bina doesn't answer, and after a moment, a blue wooden door opens in a low wing of the great high house. The wing is set at a crooked angle to the rest of the building, and it sags with picturesque accuracy. Batsheva Shpilman is still dressed more or less for a funeral, her head and face wrapped in a long, sheer veil. She doesn't cross the gap of perhaps eight feet separating her from the car; she just stands on the doorstep with the faithful bulk of Shprintzl Rudashevsky looming in the shadows behind her.

Bina rolls down the window on her side. "You aren't leaving?" she says.

"Did you catch him?"

Bina doesn't play games or act stupid. She just shakes her head.

"Then I'm not leaving."

"It might take a while. It might take longer than we really have."

"I certainly hope not," says Mendel Shpilman's mother. "That man Zimbalist is sending his idiots in their yellow pajamas over here to number every stone in this house so that it can be disassembled and then reassembled in Jerusalem. If I'm still here in two weeks, I'm going to be sleeping in Shprintzl's garage."

"It would be my very great honor," says what is either a very grave talking donkey or Shprintzl Rudashevsky from behind the rebbe's wife.

"We will catch him," Bina says. "Detective Landsman just swore me an oath to that effect."

"I know what his promises are worth," Mrs. Shpilman says. "So do you."

"Hey!" Landsman says, but she has already turned and gone back into the crooked little building from which she emerged.

"All right," Bina says, clapping her hands together. "Let's get started. What do we do now?"

Landsman taps the wheel, considering his promises and their worth. He was never unfaithful to Bina. But there is no doubt that what broke the marriage was Landsman's lack of faith. A faith not in God, nor in Bina and her character, but in the fundamental precept that everything befalling them from the moment they met, good and bad, was meant to be. The foolish coyote faith that could keep you flying as long as you kept kidding yourself that you could fly.

"All day I've been craving stuffed cabbage," he says.

45

From the summer of 1986 to the spring of 1988, when they defied the wishes of Bina's parents and moved in together, Landsman sneaked in and out of the Gelbfish home to make love with her. Every night unless they were quarreling, and sometimes in the thick of a quarrel, Landsman climbed the drainpipe and tumbled in through Bina's bedroom window to share her narrow bed. Just before dawn she would send him back down again.

Tonight it took him longer and cost him more effort than his vanity would care to admit. As he passed the halfway mark, just above Mr. Oysher's dining room window, Landsman's left loafer slipped, and he dangled free and thrilling over the black void of the Gelbfish backyard. The stars overhead, the Bear, the Snake, exchanged places with the rhododendron and the wreckage of the neighbors' sukkoh. In regaining a purchase, Landsman tore the leg of his trousers on the aluminum bracket, his old enemy in the struggle for control of the drainpipe. Foreplay between the lovers commenced with Bina balling up a tissue to blot the cut on Landsman's shin. His shin with its blotches and freckles, with its strange midlife bloom of black hair.

They lie there on their sides, a couple of aging yids stuck together like pages of an album. Her shoulderblades dig into his chest. The knobs of his patellas are notched against the soft moist backs of her knees. His lips can blow softly across the teacup of her ear. And a part of Landsman that has been the symbol and the site of his loneliness for a very long time has found shelter inside of his commanding officer, to whom he was once married for twelve years. Although, it's true, his tenure inside her has grown precarious. One good sneeze could pop him loose.

"The whole time," Bina says. "Two years."

"The whole time."

"Not once."

"Not even."

"Weren't you lonely?"

"Pretty lonely."

"And blue?"

"Black. But never black or lonely enough to kid myself that having sex with a random Jewess was going to make me feel any less."

"Actually, random sex only makes it worse," she says.

"You speak from experience."

"I fucked a couple of men in Yakovy. If that's what you want to know."

"It's strange," Landsman says upon reflection. "But I think I do not."

"A couple or three."

"I don't need a report."

"So, nu," she says, "so you just beat off?"

"With a discipline you might find surprising in a yid so unruly."

"And what about now?" she says.

"Now? Now is madness," he says. "Not to mention uncomfortable. Plus I think my leg is still bleeding."

"I meant," she says, "what about now, do you feel *lonely*."

"You're kidding, right? Squashed into this bread box?"

He buries his nose in the thick soft rasp of Bina's hair and takes a deep breath. Raisins, vinegar, a salt whiff of the sweat of her nape.

"What does it smell like?"

"It smells red," he says.

"It does not."

"It smells like Rumania."

"You smell like a Rumanian," she says. "With shockingly hairy legs."

"I've become such a geezer."

"Me, too."

"I can't even climb stairs. My hair's falling out."

"My ass is like a topographical map."

He confirms this information with his fingers. Ridges and depressions, here and there a pimple in high relief. He threads his hands under and over her waist and reaches around to weigh a breast in each hand. At first he retrieves no memory of their former size or estate to compare them with, and he panics a little. Then he decides that they are the same as they have always been, spanned exactly by his palm and his outstretched fingers, formed from some mysterious compound of gravity and give.

"I'm not going back down that drainpipe," he says. "I can tell you that much."

"I said you could just take the stairs. The drainpipe was your idea."

"It was all my idea," he says. "It was always my idea."

"Don't I know it," she says.

They lie there for a long time without saying anything more. Landsman can feel the skin beside him slowly filling with dark wine. A few minutes later, Bina begins to snore. There is no doubt that her snoring has not changed in two years. It has a double-reeded hum, the bumblebee continuo of Mongolian throat-singing. It has the slow grandeur of a whale's respiration. Landsman begins to drift across the surface of her bed and of the susurration of Bina's breath. In her arms, in the scent of her on the bed linens—a strong but pleasant smell like new leather gloves—Landsman feels safe for the first time in ages. Drowsy and content. Here you go, Landsman, he thinks. Here is the smell and the hand on your belly that you traded for a lifetime of silence.

He sits up, wide awake and hateful to himself, craven, more unworthy than ever of the fine kidskin woman in his arms. Yes, all right, Landsman understands, so go shit in the ocean, that he made not the right but the only choice. He understands that the necessity of covering up for the dark deeds of the boys in the top drawer is one that nozzes have been making into a virtue since the dawn of police work. He understands that if he were to try to tell someone, say Dennis Brennan, what he knows, then the boys in the top drawer would find another way to silence him, this time on their own terms. So why is his heart running like a jailbird's steel cup along the bars of his rib cage? Why does Bina's fragrant bed suddenly feel like a wet sock, a pair of underpants riding up on him, a wool suit on a hot afternoon? You make a deal, take what you can get, move on. Get over it. So distant men in a sunny country have been lured into killing one another so that while their backs are turned, their sunny country can be boosted and fenced. So the fate of the Sitka District has been sealed. So the killer of Mendel Shpilman, whoever it was, is walking around free. So, so what?

Landsman gets out of the bed. Discontentment gathers like ball lightning around the chessboard in the pocket of his coat. He unfolds it and contemplates it and thinks, I missed something in the room. No, he didn't miss anything; but if he missed something, it's gone by now. Only he didn't miss anything in the room. But he must have missed something.

His thoughts are a tattoo needle inking the spade on an ace. They are a tornado going back and forth over the same damn pancaked trailer. They narrow and darken until they describe a tiny black circle, the hole at the back of Mendel Shpilman's head.

He re-creates the scene in his imagination, as he saw it that night when Tenenboym knocked on his door. The freckled expanse of pale back. The white underpants. The broken mask of the eyes, the right hand tumbled from the bed to brush the floor with its fingers. The chessboard on the nightstand.

Landsman lays the board on Bina's night stand, in the pale of dim light from the lamp, a yellow porcelain affair with a big yellow daisy on the green shade. White facing the wall. Black—Shpilman, Landsman—facing the middle of the room.

Maybe it's the context at once familiar and strange, the painted bedstead, the daisy lamp, the daisies on the wallpaper, the dresser in whose top drawer she used to keep her diaphragm. Or maybe it's the lingering traces of endorphin in his bloodstream. But as Landsman stares at the chessboard, staring at a chessboard, for the first time in his life, feels good. It feels pleasurable, in fact. Standing there, moving the pieces in his mind, seems to slow or at least to dislodge the needle inking over the black spot in his brain. He focuses on the promotion at b8. What if you changed that pawn to a bishop, a rook, a queen, a knight?

Landsman reaches for a chair to take White's place at the board, to sit down in his imagination for a friendly game against Shpilman. There's a chair at the desk, painted to match the daisy-green bed, in the corner of Bina's room. It's right about where the fold-down desk would be in relation to the bed in Shpilman's room at the Zamenhof. Landsman lowers himself into the green chair, eyes on the board.

A knight, he decides. And then Black has to move the pawn at d7—but to where? He settles in to play it out, not because of some forlorn hope that it might lead him to the killer, but because he really needs, all of a sudden, to play the game out. And then, as if the seat is wired to administer a charge, Landsman leaps to his feet. He yanks the green chair one-handed into the air. Four round indentations in the low-pile white carpet, faint but distinct.

He always assumed that Shpilman, as the reception clerks all reported, never had visitors, that the game he left behind was a form of chess solitaire played from memory, from the pages of *Three Hundred Chess Games*, maybe just against himself. But if Shpilman did have a visitor, maybe that visitor pulled up a chair to sit down at the board across from his opponent. Across the cardboard chessboard from his victim. And that phantom patzer's chair would have left indentations in the carpet. No doubt by now they have faded or been vacuumed over. But they might be visible in one of Shpringer's photographs, boxed up in some storage room at the forensic lab.

Landsman steps into his trousers, buttons his shirt, knots his tie. He takes his coat from the door and, carrying his shoes, goes to pull the covers more snugly over Bina. As he bends to switch off the bedside light, a rectangle of paper falls out of his coat pocket. It's the postcard he received from the gym that he used to frequent, with its offer of a lifetime membership good for the next two months. He studies the glossy side of the card, with its enchanted Jew. Before; after. Fat; thin. Start here; finish there. Wise; happy. Chaos; order. Exile; homeland. Before, a neat diagram in a book, its grid carefully crosshatched at the black squares and annotated like a page of Talmud; after, a battered old chessboard with a Vicks inhaler at b8.

Landsman feels it then. A hand laid on his, two degrees warmer than normal. A quickening, an unfurling like a banner in his thoughts. Before and after. The touch of Mendel Shpilman, moist, electric, conveying some kind of strange blessing on Landsman. And then nothing but the cold air of Bina Gelbfish's childhood bedroom. The flowering O'Keeffe vagina on the wall. The stuffed Shnapish sagging on a bookshelf beside Bina's wristwatch and her cigarettes. And Bina, sitting up in bed, propped on an elbow, watching him, sort of the way she watched those kids go after that hapless penguin piñata.

"You still do that humming thing," she says. "When you're thinking. Like Oscar Peterson, only with no piano."

"Fuck," Landsman says.

"What, Meyer?"

"Bina!" It's Guryeh Gelbfish, that old whistling marmot, from across the hall. An ancient terror momentarily seizes Landsman. "Who is there with you?"

"Nobody, Pa, go to sleep!" Again she says, in a low whisper, "Meyer, what?"

Landsman sits down on the edge of the bed. Before; after. The exaltation of understanding; then understanding's bottomless regret.

"I know what kind of a gun killed Mendel Shpilman," he says.

"All right," Bina says.

"It wasn't a chess game," Landsman says after a moment. "On the board in Shpilman's room. It was a *problem*. It seems obvious now, I should have seen it, the setup was so freaky. Somebody came to see Shpilman that night, and Shpilman posed him a problem. A tricky one." He moves the pieces of the pocket chess set, his grasp of them sure, his hand steady. "White is all set up to promote his pawn, see. And he wants to promote it to a knight. That's called underpromotion, because usually, you want to get yourself a queen. With a knight here, he has three different ways to mate, he thinks. But that's a mistake, because it leaves Black—that was Mendel—with a way to drag the game out. If you're White, you have to ignore the obvious thing. Just make a dull move with the bishop, here at c2. You don't even notice it at first. But after you make it, every move Black has leads directly to a mate. He can't move without finishing himself. He has no good moves."

"No good moves," Bina says.

"They call that *Zugzwang*," Landsman says. "'Forced to move.' It means Black would be better off if he could just pass."

"But you aren't allowed to pass, are you? You have to do something, don't you?"

"Yes, you do," Landsman says. "Even when you know it's only going to lead to you getting checkmated."

Landsman can see it starting to mean something to her, not as evidence or proof or a chess problem, but as part of the story of a crime. A crime committed against a man who found himself left with no good moves at all.

"How'd you do that?" she says, unable to suppress completely a mild astonishment at this evidence of mental fitness on his part. "How'd you get the solution?"

"I *saw* it, actually," Landsman says. "But at the time I didn't know I was seeing it. It was an 'after' picture—the *wrong* picture, actually—to the 'before' picture in Shpilman's room. A board where White had three knights. Only chess sets don't come with three White knights. So sometimes you have to use something else to stand in for the piece you don't have."

"Like a penny? Or a bullet?"

"Any kind of thing a man might have in his pocket," Landsman says. "Say a Vicks inhaler."

46

"The reason you never developed at chess, Meyerle, is because you don't hate to lose badly enough."

Hertz Shemets, sprung from the hospital with a nasty flesh wound and that Sitka General smell on him of onion broth and wintergreen soap, is lying on the couch in his son's living room, his thin shanks sticking out of his pajamas like two uncooked noodles. Ester-Malke has a ticket for Berko's big leather armchair, with Bina and Landsman in the cheap seats, a folding stool and the armchair's leather ottoman. Ester-Malke looks sleepy and confused, hunkered down in her bathrobe, her left hand fiddling with something in the pocket that Landsman figures for last week's pregnancy test. Bina's shirt is untucked, and her hair is a mess; the effect partakes of shrubbery, some kind of ornamental hedge. Landsman's face in the pier glass on the wall is an impasto of shadows and scurf. Only Berko Shemets could look sharp at this little hour of the morning, perched on the coffee table by the couch, clad in a pair of rhinoceros-gray pajamas, neatly creased and cuffed, his initials worked over the pocket in mouse-gray crewel. Hair combed, cheeks eternally innocent of whisker or blade.

"I actually prefer losing," Landsman says. "To be honest. I start winning, I get suspicious."

"I hate it. Most of all I hated losing to your father." Uncle Hertz's voice is a bitter croak, the voice of his own great-aunt calling out from beyond the grave or the Vistula. He's thirsty, tired, rueful, and in pain, having refused any medication stronger than aspirin. The inside of his head has got to be ringing like the slammed hood of a car. "But losing to Alter Litvak. That was almost as bad."

Uncle Hertz's eyelids flutter, then settle over his eyes. Bina claps her hands, one-two, and the eyes snap open.

"Talk, Hertz," Bina says. "Before you get tired or go into a coma or something. You knew Shpilman."

"Yes," Hertz says. His bruised eyelids have the veined luster of purple quartz or the wing of a butterfly. "I knew him."

"You met him how? At the Einstein?"

He starts to nod, then tilts his head to one side, changing his mind. "I met him when he was a boy. But I didn't recognize him. When I saw him again. He had changed too much. He was a fat little boy. Not a fat man. Thin. A junkie. He started coming around the Einstein, hustling chess for drug money. I would see him there. Frank. He wasn't the usual patzer. From time to time, I don't know, I would lose five, ten dollars to him."

"Did you hate that?" Ester-Malke says, and though she knows nothing about Shpilman at all, she seems to have anticipated or guessed at his answer.

"No," her father-in-law says. "Strangely, I didn't mind."

"You liked him."

"I don't like anybody, Ester-Malke."

Hertz licks his lips, looking pained, sticking out his tongue. Berko gets out of the chair and takes a plastic tumbler from the coffee table. He holds it to his father's lips, and the ice jingles in the tumbler. He helps Hertz to drain half of it without spilling. Hertz doesn't thank him. He lies there for a long time. You can hear the water sluicing through him.

"Last Thursday," Bina says. She snaps her fingers. "Come on. You went to his room. At the Zamenhof."

"I went to his room. He invited me. He asked me to bring Melekh Gaystik's gun. He wanted to see it. I don't know how he knew I had it, I never told him. He seemed to know a lot about me that I never told him. And he told me the story. How Litvak was pressing him to play the Tzaddik again, to rope in the black hats. How he'd been hiding from Litvak, but he tired of hiding. He had been hiding his whole life. So he let Litvak find him again, but he regretted it right away. He didn't know what to do. He didn't want to keep using. He didn't want to stop. He didn't want to be what he wasn't, he didn't know how to be what he was. So he asked me if I would help him."

"Help him how?" Bina says.

Hertz purses his lips, gives a shrug, and his gaze sidles toward a dark corner of the room. He is nearly eighty years old, and before this he has never confessed to anything.

"He showed me that damned problem of his, the mate in two," Hertz says. "He said he got it off some Russian. He said if I solved it, then I would understand how he felt."

"Zugzwang," Bina says.

"What's that?" Ester-Malke says.

"It's when you have no good moves," Bina says. "But you still have to move."

"Oh," says Ester-Malke, rolling her eyes. "*Chess*."

"It's been driving me crazy for days," Hertz says. "I still can't get a mate in fewer than three moves."

"Bishop to c2," Landsman says. "Exclamation point."

It takes Hertz what feels to Landsman like a long time, with his eyes closed, to work it out, but at last the old man nods.

"Zugzwang," he says.

"Why, old man? Why would he think you would do that for him?" Berko says. "You barely knew each other."

"He knew me. He knew me very well, I don't really know how. He knew how badly I hate losing. That I couldn't let Litvak bring about this foolishness. I couldn't. Everything I worked for all my life." There must be a bitter taste in his mouth; he makes a face. "And now look what happened. They did it."

"You got in through the tunnel?" Meyer says. "Into the hotel?"

"What tunnel? I walked in the front door. I don't know if you've noticed, Meyerle, but it's not exactly a high-security building you live in."

Two or three long minutes unwind from their spool. Out on their closed-in balcony, Goldy and Pinky mutter and curse and hammer at their beds like gnomes at their forges deep beneath the earth.

"I helped him fix himself up," Hertz says finally. "I waited till he was under. Way, deep down under. Then I took out Gaystik's gun. I wrapped it in the pillow. Gaystik's .38 Detective Special. Rolled the boy over onto his belly. Back of the head. It was quick. There was no pain."

He licks his lips again, and Berko is there with another cool swallow.

"Too bad you couldn't do as good a job on yourself," Berko says.

"I thought I was doing the right thing, that it would put a stop to Litvak." The old man sounds plaintive, childish. "But then the bastards went ahead and decided to try it without him."

Ester-Malke takes the lid from a glass jar of mixed nuts on the table beside the couch and stuffs a handful into her mouth. "Don't think I'm not totally disturbed and horrified by all of this, friends," she says, hoisting herself to her feet. "But I'm a tired lady in her first trimester, and I'm going to bed."

"I want to sit with him, sweetness," Berko says. He adds, "In case he's faking and he tries to steal the television once we're asleep."

"Don't worry," Bina says. "He's already under arrest."

Landsman stands by the couch, watching the old man's chest rise and fall. Hertz's face has the hollows and facets of a flaked arrowhead.

"He's a bad man," Landsman says. "And he always was."

"Yes, but he made up for it by being a terrible father." Berko stares at Hertz for a long time with tenderness and contempt. The old man looks like some kind of demented swami in that bandage. "What are you going to do?"

"Nothing, what do you mean what am I going to do?"

"I don't know, you have that twitchy thing happening. You look like you're going to do something."

"What?"

"That's what I'm asking you."

"I'm not going to do anything," Landsman says. "What can I do?"

Ester-Malke walks Bina and Landsman down the hall to the front door of the apartment. Landsman puts on his porkpie hat.

"So," Ester-Malke says.

"So," say Bina and Landsman.

"I note that the two of you are leaving together."

"You want us to leave separately?" Landsman says. "I can take the stairs and Bina can ride down in the elevator."

"Landsman, let me tell you something," Ester-Malke says. "All these people rioting on the television in Syria, Baghdad, Egypt? In London? Burning cars. Setting fire to embassies. Up in Yakovy, did you see what happened, they were dancing, those fucking maniacs, they were so happy about all this craziness, the whole floor collapsed right onto the apartment underneath. A couple of little girls sleeping in their beds, they got crushed to death. That's the kind of shit we have to look forward to now. Burning cars and homicidal dancing. I have no idea where this baby is going to be born. My murdering, suicidal father-in-law is sleeping in my living room. Meanwhile, I'm getting this very strange vibration from the two of you. So let me just say that if you and Bina are planning to get back together, excuse me, but that's all I need."

Landsman considers this. Any kind of wonder seems likely. That the Jews will pick up and set sail for the promised land to feast on giant grapes and toss their beards in the desert wind. That the

Temple will be rebuilt, speedily and in our day. War will cease, ease and plenty and righteousness will be universal, and humankind will be treated to the regular spectacle of lions and lambs cohabiting. Every man will be a rabbi, every woman a holy book, and every suit will come with two pairs of pants. Meyer's seed, even now, may be wandering through darkness toward redemption, striking at the membrane that separates the legacy of the yids who made him from that of the yids whose errors, griefs, hopes, and calamities went into the production of Bina Gelbfish.

"Maybe it would be better if I took the stairs," Landsman says.

"You go right ahead and do that, Meyer," says Bina.

But then when he finally makes it all the way down, he finds her at the bottom, waiting for him.

"What took you so long?" she says.

"I had to stop a time or two on the way."

"You need to quit smoking. Quit again."

"I do. I will." He fishes out his package of Broadways, fifteen left to burn, and arcs it into the lobby trash can like a dime carrying a wish into a fountain. He's feeling a little giddy, a little tragic. He is ripe for the grand gesture, the operatic mistake. Manic is probably the word. "But that's not what held me up."

"You're really hurt. Tell me you're not really hurt, walking around so tough and macho when you need to be in the goddamn hospital." She reaches for his windpipe with the fingers of both hands, ready, as ever, to choke the life from Landsman to show how much she cares. "Are you hurt badly, you idiot?"

"Only in my soul, sweetness," Meyer says. Though he supposes it's possible that Rafi Zilberblat's bullet creased more than his skull. "I just had to stop a couple of times. To think. Or not to think, I don't know. Every time I let myself try to, you know, *breathe*, just for ten seconds, with the air full of this thing we're letting them get away with, I don't know, I feel like I'm suffocating a little bit."

Landsman sinks onto a sofa whose bruise-colored cushions

give off a strong Sitka odor of mildew, cigarettes, a complicated saltiness that is part stormy sea, part sweat on the lining of a wool fedora. The lobby of the Dnyeper is all blood-purple velvet and gilded crust, blown-up hand-tinted postcards of the great Black Sea resorts in Tsarist times. Ladies with their lapdogs on sun struck promenades. Grand hotels that never housed a Jew.

"It's like a stone in my belly, this deal we made," Landsman says. "Just lying there."

Bina rolls her eyes, hands on her hips, glances at the door. Then she comes over and drops her bag and plops down beside him. How many times, he wonders, can she have enough of him, already, and still have not quite enough?

"I can't really believe you agreed to it," she says.

"I know."

"I'm supposed to be the brownnose around here."

"Tell me about it."

"The ass licker."

"It's killing me."

"If I can't rely on you to tell the big shots to fuck off, Meyer, why do I keep you around?"

He tries to explain to her, then, the considerations that led him to make his own personal version of the deal. He names some of the small things—the canneries, the violinists, the marquee of the Baranof Theatre—that it pleased him to cherish about Sitka when he was coming to terms with Cashdollar.

"You and your goddamned *Heart of Darkness*," Bina says. "I'm not sitting through that movie ever again." She shrinks her mouth down to a hard mark. "You forgot something, asshole. On your sweet little list. You were one item short, I'd say."

"Bina."

"You have no place for me on that list of yours? Because I hope you know you're at the fucking top of mine."

"How is that possible?" Landsman says. "I just don't see how that could be."

"Why not?"

"Because, you know. I failed you. I let you down. I feel like I just let you down so badly."

"In what way?"

"Because of what I made you do. To Django. I don't know how you can even stand to look at me."

"*Made* me? You think you *made* me kill our baby?"

"No, Bina, I—"

"Let me tell you something, Meyer." She grabs his hand, digging her nails into his skin. "The day you *ever* have that much control over my behavior, it will be because somebody's asking you, should she get the pine box or a plain white shroud?" She discards his hand, then retrieves it and strokes at the fiery little moons she carved into his flesh. "Oh my God, your hand, I'm sorry. Meyer, I'm sorry."

Landsman, of course, is sorry, too. He has already apologized to her several times, alone and in the presence of others, orally and in writing, formally in measured phrases and in untrammeled spasms: *Sorry I'm sorry I'm so, so sorry.* He has apologized for his craziness, his erratic behavior, his glooms and jags, for the years of round-robin exaltation and despair. He has apologized for leaving her, and for begging her to take him back again, and for breaking down the door to their old apartment when she declined to do so. He has abased himself, and rent his garments, and groveled at her shoes. Most of the time Bina has, good and caring woman that she is, offered Landsman the words he wanted to hear. He has prayed to her for rain, and she has sent cool showers. But what he really requires is a flood to wash his wickedness from the face of the earth. That or the blessing of a yid who will never bless anyone again.

"It's all right," Landsman says.

She gets up and goes over to the lobby trash can and fishes out Landsman's package of Broadways. From her coat pocket she pulls a dented Zippo, bearing the insignia of the 75th Ranger regiment, and lights a papiros for each of them.

"We did what seemed right at the time, Meyer. We had a few facts. We knew our limitations. And we called that a choice. But we didn't have any choice. All we had was, I don't know, three lousy facts and a boundary map of our own limitations. The things we knew we couldn't handle." She takes her Shoyfer out of her bag and hands it to Landsman. "And right now, if you're asking me, and I kind of got the idea you were, you also don't really have any choice."

When he just sits there, holding the phone, she flips it open and dials a number and puts it into his hand. He raises it to his ear.

"Dennis Brennan," says the chief and sole occupant of the Sitka bureau of that major American daily.

"Brennan. It's Meyer Landsman."

Landsman hesitates again. He covers the mouth hole of the phone with a thumb.

"Tell him to get his big head down here and watch us arrest your uncle for murder," Bina says. "Tell him he has twenty minutes."

Landsman tries to weigh the fates of Berko, of his uncle Hertz, of Bina, of the Jews, of the Arabs, of the whole unblessed and homeless planet, against the promise he made to Mrs. Shpilman, and to himself, even though he had lost his belief in fate and promises.

"I didn't have to wait for you to drag your lamentable hide down those lousy stairs," Bina says. "You know that. I could just have walked out the goddamned door."

"Yeah, so why didn't you?"

"Because I know you, Meyer. I could see what was going through your mind, sitting up there, listening to Hertz. I could see you had something you needed to say." She pushes the phone back to his lips and brushes them with hers. "So just go ahead and *say* it already. I'm tired of waiting."

For days Landsman has been thinking that he missed his chance with Mendel Shpilman, that in their exile at the Hotel Zamenhof, without even realizing, he blew his one shot at something like redemption. But there is no Messiah of Sitka. Landsman has no home, no future, no fate but Bina. The land that he and she were promised was bounded only by the fringes of their wedding canopy, by the dog-eared corners of their cards of membership in an international fraternity whose members carry their patrimony in a tote bag, their world on the tip of the tongue.

"Brennan," Landsman says. "I have a story for you."

AUTHOR'S NOTE

I am grateful for the help of the following people, works, websites, institutions, and establishments:

The MacDowell Colony, Peterborough, New Hampshire; Davia Nelson; Susie Tompkins Buell; Margaret Grade and the staff of Manka's Inverness Lodge, Inverness, California; Philip Pavel and the staff of the Chateau Marmont, Los Angeles, California; Bonnie Pietila and her fellow denizens of Springfield; Paul Hamburg, librarian for the Judaica Collections, University of California; Ari Y. Kelman; Todd Hasak-Lowy; Roman Skaskiw; the Alaska State Library, Juneau, Alaska; Dee Longenbaugh, Observatory Books, Juneau, Alaska; Jake Bassett of the Oakland Police Department; Mary Evans; Sally Willcox, Matthew Snyder, and David Colden; Devin McIntyre; Kristina Larsen, Lisa Eglinton, and Carmen Dario; Elizabeth Gaffney, Kenneth Turan, Jonathan Lethem; Christopher Potter; Jonathan Burnham; Michael McKenzie; Scott Rudin; Leonard Waldman, Robert Chabon, and Sharon Chabon; Sophie, Zeke, Ida-Rose, and Abraham Chabon, and their mother; *The Messiah Texts*, Raphael Patai; *Modern English-Yiddish Yiddish-English Dictionary*, Uriel Weinreich; *Our Gang*, Jenna Joselit; *The Meaning of Yiddish*, Benjamin Harshav; *Blessings, Curses, Hopes and Fears: Psycho-Ostensive Expressions in Yiddish*, James Matisoff; *English-

Yiddish Dictionary, Alexander Harkavy; *American Klezmer*, Mark Slobin; *Against Culture: Development, Politics, and Religion in Indian Alaska*, Kirk Dombrowski; *Will the Time Ever Come? A Tlingit Source Book*, Andrew Hope III and Thomas F. Thornton, eds.; *The Chess Artist*, J. C. Hallman; *The Pleasures of Chess*, Assiac (Heinrich Fraenkel); *Treasury of Chess Lore*, Fred Reinfeld, ed.; Mendele (http://shakti.trincoll.edu/~mendele/index.utf-8.htm); Chessville (www.chessville.com); *Eruvin in Modern Metropolitan Areas*, Yosef Gavriel Bechhofer (http://www.aishdas.org/baistefila/eruvp1.htm); Yiddish Dictionary Online (www.yiddishdictionaryonline.com); and Courtney Hodell, editor and redeemer of this novel.

The Hands of Esau brotherhood was founded by and appears here with the kind permission of its grand chairman and president for life, Jerome Charyn; the Zugzwang of Mendel Shpilman was devised by Reb Vladimir Nabokov and is presented in his *Speak, Memory*.

This novel was written on Macintosh computers using Devonthink Pro and Nisus Writer Express.

GLOSSARY

[PREPARED BY PROF. LEON CHAIM BACH, WITH THE ASSISTANCE OF SHERRYL MLEYNEK]

alefbeys alphabet (esp. the Hebrew alphabet, which Yiddish employs)

bik (*Rus., Sitka slang, lit. "bull"*) bodyguard, heavy

bulgar type of traditional dance tune played by **klezmorim**

dybbuk parasitical spirit, a restless ghost that takes possession of a living soul

emes truth

feh (*int.*) yuck, ick

forspiel small reception held before a wedding at the home of the bride-to-be

freylekh type of traditional dance tune played by **klezmorim**

gabay assistant to the rabbi; in Chasidic life, private secretary or personal assistant to a rebbe

ganef thief, criminal

goy non-Jew, gentile, pl. goyim

haskomo an official letter of rabbinic approval

kaddish loosely, the Mourner's Kaddish, a prayer sanctifying and praising God, recited in remembrance of the dead

kaynahora formula (*shorthand for kayn ayn hora, "no evil eye"*), prophylactically used after some good fortune or a happy outcome has been mentioned

kibitzer one who pesters by making unwanted comments

klezmorim musicians who play the lively instrumental dance music of Eastern European Jews

koyenim the priestly class of pre-exilic Israel

kreplach filled dumplings, typically boiled in soup

kugel a baked casserole, sweet or savory, usually made from potatoes or noodles

latke (*Sitka slang*) Uniformed patrolman, beat cop; lit., "pancake," in joking reference to the patrolman's flat-crowned hat

luftmensh (*lit. "air-man", pl. luftmenshen*) dreamer, a space-case

macher big shot, important or self-important person

maven expert, guru

mazel (*lit. "astrological sign"*) luck

mikvah bath used by observant Jews for ritual immersion and purification

momzer bastard

noz (*Sitka slang; lit., "nose"*) cop

nu so, well, as I feared, please go on, what's up?

oy (*int.*) oh, as in oy, vey

oy, vey (*int., lit "oh, woe"*) oh, no; shorter form of oy, vey iz mir "oh, woe is me."

patzer (*Ger., chess slang, lit. "blunderer"*) lousy chess player

papiros cigarette

pisher (*lit., "pisser"*) squirt, young pup

purimspiel comic play presented at Purim, early-spring holiday that is a Jewish variant of the "feast of fools," in which the parts of Queens Vashti and Esther are typically played by men in drag, one of them often a rabbi or other dignitary

rebbe master, mentor; leader of a Chasidic movement

shammes (*Sitka slang, lit., "sexton of a synagogue"*) police detective

Shavuous Jewish holiday celebrating the revelation of the

Torah at Mount Sinai

shaydl wig worn by married Jewish women who follow the Laws of Tznius (modesty)

sheygets non-Jewish male

shiva ritual period of intense mourning observed by Jews for seven days after burial

shkotz (*form of sheygets, lit., "gentile boy"*) rascal

shlemiel sad sack, loser, hump

shlosser (*Sitka slang, lit., "mechanic"*) hit man

sholem (*Sitka slang, lit., "peace"*) gun; ironic bilingual pun on American slang "piece"

Shoyfer (*lit., "ram's horn," ritual musical instrument*) brand of tselularer telefone (Sitka slang: tselke) manufactured in the District of Sitka

shoymer (*Sitka slang, lit. "watchman" and fig. "one who fulfills the requirement that a body be watched over between death and burial"*) member of the government task force overseeing the reversion of the District of Sitka to Alaskan state sovereignty

shpilkes nervous energy, "on pins and needles"

shtarker (*Sitka slang sense of "gangster"*) strongman

shtekeleh (*Sitkaism, lit., "a little stick"*) local variant on the Filipino donut or "bicho bicho"

shtetl village, small town

shtinker (*Sitka slang*) informer, stool pigeon

shul synagogue

Shvartser-Yam the Black Sea

shvitz (*short for shvitzbad, lit. "sweat bath"*) a steam bath, a Turkish bath

slivovitz plum brandy

smikha rabbinic ordination

tallis prayer shawl

patsh tanz type of traditional dance tune played by **klezmorim**

tekiah (*Heb.*, "*blast*") one of three prescribed sounds to be played on the shofar at High Holy Days

tefillin pair of small boxes, each containing a miniature scroll of sacred text, which an observant Jewish man binds each morning to his forehead and to one arm by means of leather straps

tzaddik righteous one

Tzaddik Ha-Dor "the righteous one of his generation"; a potential Messiah

Untershtot (*Sitkaism, lit.* "*downtown*") The oldest, central neighborhood of Jewish Sitka

vorsht (*Yid. musician's slang, lit.* "*sausage*") clarinet

yekke a German Jew

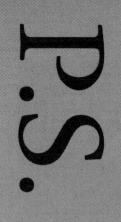

Insights,
Interviews
& More . . .

Meet **Michael Chabon**

© 2007 Stephanie Rausser

MICHAEL CHABON was twenty-four years old when he wrote his first novel, *The Mysteries of Pittsburgh*, in a crawl space illuminated by a single naked bulb; he did so seated on a folded chair perched ruinously atop a steamer trunk. "I found that if I held very still, typed very chastely, and never, ever, rocked back and forth, I would be fine." Written to fulfill his master's requirement at University of California, Irvine, the novel became a national bestseller. "There's a delicacy as well as sheer abundance here," declared the *Pittsburgh Post-Gazette*, "a high-style elegance reminiscent of Cheever or even Fitzgerald."

He next worked five years on *Fountain City*, a novel about the construction of the perfect baseball stadium. His manuscript did not, however, correspond to his idea of the perfect novel. He ditched it. He completed a draft of his second novel, *Wonder Boys*, in less than seven months. *The Washington Post Book World* dubbed him "the young star of American letters, 'star' not in the current sense of cheap celebrity but in the old one of brightly shining hope." The book's adaptation to the screen starred Michael Douglas, Tobey Maguire, and Frances McDormand.

Chabon's success traces back to three requirements:

talent, luck, and discipline. "Discipline," he says, "is the one element of those three things that you can control, and so that is the one that you have to focus on controlling, and you just have to hope and trust in the other two."

His third novel made quite a ripple. *The Amazing Adventures of Kavalier & Clay* unfolds the tale of two boys who create a comic superhero, the Escapist, against the backdrop of New York City's cultural and commercial life in the thirties and forties. The sweeping narrative closes in on a number of themes, among them the Holocaust, McCarthyism, homophobia, friendship, and the relationship between art and political resistance. The *New York Post* food columnist Pia Nordlinger called the book "an excellent novel that deserves every award and palm frond it has garnered." Most conspicuous amid these fronds and awards was the Pulitzer Prize, which *The Amazing Adventures of Kavalier & Clay* won in 2001. A signed first edition recently cropped up on eBay; it was priced at three hundred dollars and bore an almost illegible inscription, the spasmodic irregularity of which suggested great perturbation or duress.

Chabon wrote his fourth novel, *Summerland*, for young adults. The novel casts back to an adolescent boy's Technicolor world of baseball and fantasy. Chabon "spins some typically lovely turns of phrase and ideas," said *Time Out*, "while never talking down to his younger audience: there's neat, uncondescending wit, death, even intimations of sex—not something you get in *Harry Potter*."

In *The Final Solution* (2005), Chabon condensed his boundless vision to create a short, suspenseful tale of compassion and wit that re-imagines the classic 19th-century detective story. "The writing," observed the *Baltimore Sun*, "is everything that Chabon's fans expect—gorgeous, muscular, mildly melancholic . . . wonderfully executed."

His next novel, *Gentlemen of the Road*, appeared serially in the *New York Times Magazine* before publication (Del Ray, October 2007). *Publishers Weekly* called the book "a terrifically entertaining modern pulp adventure replete with marauding armies, drunken Vikings, beautiful prostitutes, rampaging elephants and mildly telegraphed plot points that aren't as they seem."

He is also the author of two collections of short stories, *A Model World and Other Stories* and *Werewolves in Their Youth*. His story "Son of the Wolfman" was chosen for the 1999 O.Henry Prize collection and for a National Magazine Award.

> *". . . marauding armies, drunken Vikings, beautiful prostitutes, rampaging elephants . . ."*

He lives in Berkeley, California, with his wife, novelist Ayelet Waldman, and four children. He is "handsome, brilliant, and successful," wrote Waldman in a *New York Times* article. "But he can also be scatterbrained, antisocial, and arrogant. He is a bad dancer, and he knows far too much about Klingon politics and the lyrics to Yes songs."

The Frozen Chosen

by Patricia Cohen

"The Frozen Chosen" appeared in the New York Times, *Sunday April 29, 2007. Reprinted by permission of the* New York Times.

Aside from geography, Sitka, a boomerang-shaped island in the southeastern panhandle of Alaska, has very little in common with the imaginary city named Sitka conjured up by Michael Chabon in his latest book, *The Yiddish Policemen's Union.*

In this fourth novel, . . . Mr. Chabon takes a historical footnote, a pie-in-the-sky proposal to open up the Alaska Territory in 1940 to European Jews marked for extermination, and asks: What if? What if this proposal, which in real life was supported by the secretary of the interior, Harold Ickes, but killed in Congress, had actually passed? What if Jews had poured into a frigid island instead of the Middle Eastern desert, and the state of Israel had never been created? What if the small settlement of Sitka had grown into a teeming Jewish homeland, a land not of milk and honey but of salmon and lumber?

Mr. Chabon (pronounced SHAY-bon), tucking into a breakfast of eggs, wheat toast and reindeer sausage at Sitka's Westmont Hotel, said he took the first, unwitting step down this road-not-taken a decade ago. That's when Mr. Chabon, who won the Pulitzer Prize in 2001 for *The Amazing Adventures of Kavalier & Clay*, wrote a controversial essay about *Say It in Yiddish,* a 1958 phrase book for travelers that he found both poignant and funny. "Where would be the most fabulous kingdom you could have taken this phrase book to, if the Holocaust hadn't happened?" he wondered. To him, the phrase book was predicated on the ultimate "Yiddishland," a place "where you might need to say 'Help, I need a tourniquet'" (which the phrase book thoughtfully provides).

"Oh yeah? That offended you? Well, I'm going to write a goddamn novel . . . Just wait."

After Mr. Chabon's essay appeared, he was attacked for mocking the language and prematurely announcing its demise. He had not realized that its revered authors, Uriel and Beatrice Weinreich, wrote the book at the request of the publisher because Yiddish was spoken widely in Israel in the 1950s and in other Yiddish communities around the world. "I had a double reaction," Mr. Chabon said. "I don't like having my ignorance pointed out to me. I was embarrassed and shamed. I had the nice Jewish boy impulse that I disrespected my elders and caused pain and embarrassment. But I also felt a total sense of irritation and spite."

In Yiddish the word is "tsalooches," he explained. "Oh yeah? That offended you? Well, I'm going to write a goddamn novel, and you think that was offensive? Just wait."

It wasn't until 2003 that Mr. Chabon began to transform this momentary flight of fancy into *The Yiddish Policemen's Union*, a detective story in the hard-boiled style of Raymond Chandler, where the dead body and the detective both make their appearance on the first page.

The following year he visited Alaska and chose Sitka (it "sounds kind of Yiddish") as home for the three million

European Jews—and their children and grandchildren—
his imagination saved from the Holocaust.

This is his first trip back to the Russian-accented city
since then, and while the herring boats in Sitka's harbor
announce the arrival of spring, large feathery flakes of snow
have been falling. Mr. Chabon is wearing Ugg boots, which
keep out the wet slush but are not that comfortable to walk
around in. He stops at the corner of Monastery Street, a
narrow road with boxy, pastel-colored houses, and an-
nounces, "This is where the Zamenhof Hotel is," a rundown
flophouse that can be found only in his novel.

Mr. Chabon, 43, grew up in Columbia, Md., a newly
formed community with a utopian flavor and very few
people and houses. "It only existed on paper," he explained,
"but we had this map, a project map of how it was going to
be. And then it came into being as we lived there. So I got
really into this early on, that you could imagine a place and
it would come into being."

With Sitka, he said, "I was just repeating what I had seen
done in the town I grew up in." The Sitka he created is far
from utopian, though. On the eve of "Reversion"—when the
territory is to be returned to Alaskans, and the Jews, suspended between hopelessness and oblivion, are to be kicked
out—the book's Sitka is a grim, choked place, desperate
and despairing, more like Jake Gittes's Chinatown than the
"fabulous kingdom" of Yiddishland.

In reality, the 4,710-square-mile island, much of it
mountains and national forest, has a population of 8,947,
of which no more than 35 adults are Jewish, according to
Aryeh Levenson, whose home phone rings when you dial
the listing for Sitka's Jewish Community Center. But once
Dr. Levenson, who works for the Indian Health Service
and wears a colorful tapestry yarmulke, has alerted the tiny

network, it almost seems as if we have stepped into Yiddish-land. David Voluck, a Philadelphia boy who worked for the tribal bureau as a lawyer before becoming a Hasidic Jew, heard we were in town, so he called a Jewish friend, Davey Lubin, to take us out on his boat, a 28-foot aluminum cruiser built by another friend, also Jewish.

The boat is named *Esther G.*, after the grandmother of Mr. Lubin's wife, Lisa Busch. The couple met here and had the city's first Jewish wedding. They flew in bagels from H&H in Manhattan. Ms. Busch is studying for her master's in Northern studies, and as we head across the inner Sitka sound, warm inside the heated cabin, she says she just wrote a paper on Mr. Ickes's resettlement plan.

"No one here had ever heard about it," she tells Mr. Chabon.

Esther G. bounces along the sound. It is snowing again, tiny hard pellets that resemble a beanbag's innards. The giant spruce that cover the island's mountains are thoroughly dusted, as if someone shook out too much powdered sugar. They match Mr. Chabon's hat, whose furry black earflaps are flecked with snow, and his few days of stubble, which shows some gray whiskers among the black. Mr. Lubin spots a few dozen brown-pointed snouts bobbing in and out of the water, sea lions, near a few glistening black seals on a rock. He is standing in the cabin doorway with a wide grin: "This is my homeland."

Later in the afternoon, we head toward the airport. At the back of the terminal, past the mounted heads of moose, ram and bear, hangs a wooden sign with a long arrow that looks as if it came from a Motor Vehicle Bureau in the 1960s, except that it points the way to "PIE" instead of license renewals. Follow it and you can buy the Nugget

Restaurant's banana cream pie, famous throughout Alaska. In *Policemen's Union,* the detective Meyer Landsman is sitting with a slice when he discovers a crucial clue. Disappointingly, the only kind left when we arrive is peanut, but Mr. Chabon orders it anyway, à la mode.

> *"I felt like I had to invent a whole new language, a dialect."*

The Russian writer Isaac Babel is partly responsible for his writing a detective story, Mr. Chabon explains, after declaring the peanut pie pretty good. "There was some strange kinship between Babel writing in translation and hard-boiled detective fiction, a kinship to Chandler," he says.

For *Policemen's Union,* he adds, "I felt like I had to invent a whole new language, a dialect. The thing that took the longest for me was finding the right voice. The sentences are much shorter than usual for me."

Mr. Chabon wrote a 600-page draft in the first person that he ended up trashing after a year. It had the same characters—Landsman; his ex-wife, Bina Gelbfish, also a policeman; and his cousin and partner, a half-Indian, half-Jew named Berko Shemets—but a completely different story. He feels as if *Policemen's Union* is its sequel, he says.

For the book, Mr. Chabon dug into New York's underworld slang, filling in at spots with his own linguistic creations. A latke is a beat cop and a sholem is a gun—a bit of wordplay, as "sholem" in Yiddish means peace, and "piece" is slang for gun in English.

The powerful local mafia is made up of Hasidic Jews with payess, long curling sidelocks. Along with the rest of Alaska's Jews, they are part of what Jews living in the rest of America call "the Frozen Chosen."

Since Mr. Chabon envisioned a "story that would

encompass many levels of society," he needed a character who would have access to them all. "That's why writers have been using detectives," he says, mentioning Inspector Bucket in Dickens's *Bleak House.* Such examples haven't saved detective stories or narratives in general from contemporary disdain, he complains. "Telling stories well is a neglected and undervalued element of what is thought to be a 'real' writer's job. There is a bias against any kind of narrative in which plot is foregrounded."

To Mr. Chabon, the detective and the writer share a bond: "A detective suffers about a case. Writers tend to be recriminators; they go back over the same turf."

Does he?

"Oh, definitely," Mr. Chabon says. As he goes back and refines his characters, there is always "that sense of 'Oh, I missed something here.'"

His detective, Meyer Landsman, is like many of Mr. Chabon's protagonists, empty, disaffected men who have never quite come to terms with their (physically or spiritually) absent fathers. Landsman's damaged father, salvaged from the death camps, is brilliant at chess. He played "like a man with a toothache, a hemorrhoid, and gas," writes Mr. Chabon, and helped teach "his son to hate the game he himself loved." Mr. Chabon learned chess from his own father, who separated from his wife and left their home when Michael was 11. "I was good at it, like Meyer," he said. "I grew up hating it. I transferred a lot of my own feelings" about the game to the character.

Mr. Chabon, who lives in Berkeley, Calif., with his wife, the writer Ayelet Waldman, is more available to his two boys and two girls, 4 to 12, getting them ready for school, breaking from work when they return in the afternoons.

As a teenager, he said, he thought a lot about what kind of father he would like to be—unusual musings for an adolescent.

Mr. Chabon's novels are dominated by men, and this one is no different—although Bina is one of his most developed female characters. Writing fully rounded, complex women, he said, "is something I've been working on."

With *Policemen's Union*, Mr. Chabon was aiming not only for a classic detective story with a twisting, page-turning plot, but also for rich characters and detail, psychological depth and cosmic truth—or at least cosmic questions. The book's mysteries are manifold. There is the mystery of a murder and a chess problem, the larger conspiracy it may be linked to, the fate of the Jews without a homeland, and then the ultimate mystery of existence itself.

"Is there a plan for us, is there destiny or fate?" Mr. Chabon says. "Are we chosen? Chosen for what? Is that a good thing or a bad thing?" Are things "bashert" (meant to be)?

Thinking about what the world would look like without the state of Israel was "one of the motivating impulses of writing the book," he says. "How mad it seems that this tiny little scrap of land" should be at the center of global conflicts. "I have a very strong feeling of complete ambivalence about a world without Israel," Mr. Chabon says. "I didn't come in with a point to prove or an agenda."

Whether because of that or despite it, Jews, Muslims and Christians will no doubt be able to find something in the book to hate or love.

That evening, Mr. Voluck and his wife, Esther, have invited most of Jewish Sitka to their small blue bungalow to meet Mr. Chabon and have a dinner of fish tacos. Kosher, of course. (Nearly everything is flown in from Seattle.)

Mr. Voluck's impish laugh contrasts with his severe

black suit and starched white shirt, buttoned to the collar. The fringes of his prayer shawl hang out the back, and a black velvet yarmulke is on his head. On the wall, he points out pictures of Joseph Isaack Schneersohn and his son-in-law Menachem Mendel Schneerson, whom many within the Chabad-Lubavitch sect believe was the messiah.

"I took his name," Mr. Chabon says, referring to Mendel, a character in the book.

"I knew you did," Mr. Voluck responds with a smile. "I'm on to you."

Mr. Chabon explains that he also used the name of the Russian town that he thinks his grandmother came from, Verbov, for the Hasidic sect that runs Sitka.

Why not, says Mr. Voluck, they're your family, "your mishpokhe."

He points to a picture on the opposite wall of his own mishpokhe, his wife's great-grandparents. Only two of 14 siblings made it out of Poland after the Holocaust. "We're here on a thread," he says, "so close to being lost."

A galley of the book has been making the rounds, and Mr. Voluck is needling Mr. Chabon about some of the plot points. But the next morning, when we meet him at the Back Door, a coffee shop behind the bookstore, he makes a point of telling Mr. Chabon how authentic and moving he found a funeral scene in the novel. "It hit me right between the eyes," he says, putting a forefinger above the bridge of his nose.

John Straley, a mystery author and the writer laureate of Alaska, is there, and they start talking about Babel and the language of the detective novel. "There is a lot of Eastern European street talk that's made it into the language," Mr. Straley says.

Those immigrants later "created this underworld cash culture," Mr. Voluck responds. "A moral netherworld," Mr. Straley says. Mr. Chabon nods: "I just took that one more step."

The bagels—which taste and look like muffins—are finished. "I've got to go to jail," says Mr. Straley, who works as an investigator for the public defender's office. Mr. Chabon has to catch his plane. He is already at work on other projects. Finishing a novel is always bittersweet, he says, as he realizes "I'm not coming back to these people anymore, that this is it."

Still, he adds, "the world of the book still feels pretty close to me. When I was landing and the stewardess announced that we were arriving in Sitka, I had this 'What? Oh yeah, it's the real Sitka.' For so long, the only Sitka is the Sitka I made up. I forgot for a minute there was this real Sitka."

Guidebook to a **Land of Ghosts**
by Michael Chabon

The following essay, reprinted by courtesy of the author, appeared in the June/July 1997 issue of Civilization *and the October 1997 issue of* Harper's Magazine.

Probably the saddest book that I own is a paperback copy of *Say It in Yiddish,* edited by Uriel and Beatrice Weinreich. I bought it new, in 1993, but the book was originally published in 1958. According to the back cover, it's part of the *Say It* book series, with which I'm otherwise unfamiliar. I've never seen *Say It in Swahili, Say It in Hindi,* or *Say It in Serbo-Croatian,* nor have I ever been to the countries where any of them might come in handy. As for the country in which I'd do well to carry a copy of *Say It in Yiddish,* naturally I've never been there either. I don't think anyone ever has.

When I first came across *Say It in Yiddish,* on a shelf in a big chain bookstore in Orange County, California, I couldn't quite believe that it was real. There was only one copy, buried in the back of the language section. It was like a book in a story by Borges: unique, inexplicable, possibly a hoax. The first thing that really struck me about it was, paradoxically, its unremarkableness, the conventional terms of its self-promotion. "No other phrase book for travellers," it claimed, "contains all these essential features." It boasted of "over 1,600 up-to-date practical entries" (up-to-date!), "easy pronunciation transcription," and a "sturdy binding—pages will not fall out."

What were they thinking, the Weinreichs? Was the original 1958 edition simply the reprint of some earlier, less heartbreakingly implausible book? At what time in the history of the world was there a place of the kind that the Weinreichs imply, a place where not only the doctors and waiters and trolley conductors spoke Yiddish but also the airline clerks, travel agents, and casino employees? A place where you could rent a summer home from Yiddishspeakers, go to a Yiddish movie, have your bridge repaired by a Yiddish-speaking dentist? If, as seems likelier, the book first saw light in 1958, a full ten years after the founding of Israel—which turned its back once and for all on the Yiddish language, condemning its native speakers to a headlong race for extinction with the twentieth century itself—then the tragic dimension of the joke looms larger and makes the Weinreich's intentions even harder to divine. *Say It in Yiddish* seems an entirely futile effort on the part of its authors, a gesture of embittered hope, of valedictory daydreaming, of a utopian impulse turned cruel and ironic.

The Weinreichs have laid out, in painstakingly categorized numerical entries, the outlines of a world, of a fantastic land, in which it would behoove you to know how to say, in Yiddish:

> 250. What is the flight number?
> 1372. I need something for a tourniquet.
> 1379. Here is my identification.
> 254. Can I go by boat/ferry to __ ?

The blank in the last of those phrases, impossible to fill in, tantalizes me. Whither could I sail on that boat/ferry, in the solicitous company of Uriel and Beatrice Weinreich, and from what shore?

I dream of two possible destinations. The first might be a modern independent state very closely analogous to the state of Israel. Call it the state of Yisroel: a postwar Jew-ish homeland created during a time of moral emergency, located presumably, but not necessarily, in Palestine. Here, perhaps, that minority faction of the Zionist movement that favored the establishment of Yiddish as the national language of the Jews was able to prevail over its more nu-merous Hebraist opponents. There is Yiddish on the official currency, of which the basic unit is the herzl, or the dollar, or even the zloty.

There are Yiddish-speaking color commentators for soc-cer games, Yiddish-speaking cash machines, Yiddish tags on the collars of dogs.

I can't help thinking that such a nation, speaking its es-sentially European tongue, would, in the Middle East, stick out among its neighbors to an even greater degree than Isra-el does now. But would the Jews of a Mediterranean Yisroel be impugned and admired for having the kind of character that Israelis, rightly or wrongly, are taken to have, the clas-sic sabra personality: rude, hardheaded, cagey, pushy? Is it living in a near-permanent state of war, or is it the Hebrew language that has made Israeli humor so barbed, so cynical, so untranslatable?

I can imagine a different Yisroel, the youngest nation on the North American continent, founded in the former Alaska territory during World War II as a resettlement zone for the Jews of Europe. (I once read that Franklin Roosevelt was briefly sold on such a plan.) Perhaps after the war, in this Yisroel, the millions of immigrant Polish, Romanian, Hungarian, Lithuanian, Austrian, Czech, and German Jews held a referendum, and chose independence over prof-fered statehood in the United States. The resulting country is a cold, northern land of furs, paprika, samovars, and one long, glorious day of summer. It would be absurd to speak Hebrew, that tongue of spikenard and almonds, in such a place.

These countries of the Weinreichs are in the nature of a wistful toy theater, with miniature sets and furnishings to arrange and rearrange, all their grief concealed behind the scrim, hidden in the machinery of the loft, sealed up beneath trapdoors in the floorboards. But grief haunts every mile of the places to which the Weinreichs beckon. Grief hand-colors all the postcards, stamps the passports, sours the cooking, fills the luggage. It keens all night in the pipes of old hotels. By taking us to Yisroel, the Weinreichs are, in effect, taking us home, to the "old country." To a Europe that might have been.

In this Europe the millions of Jews who were never killed produced grandchildren, and great-grandchildren, and great-great-grandchildren. The countryside retains large Yiddish speaking pockets, and in the cities there are many more for whom Yiddish is the language of kitchen and family, of theater and poetry and scholarship. A surprisingly large number of these people are my relations. I can go visit them, the way Irish-Americans I know are always visiting second and third cousins in Galway or Cork, sleeping in their strange beds, eating their strange food, and looking just like them. Imagine. Perhaps one of my cousins might take me to visit the house where my father's mother was born, or to the school in Vilna that my grandfather's grandfather attended. For my relatives, although they will doubtless know at least some English, I will want to trot out a few appropriate Yiddish phrases, more than anything as a way of reestablishing the tenuous connection between us. In this world Yiddish is not, as it is in ours, a tin can with no tin can on the other end of the string.

What is this Europe like, with its twenty-five, thirty, or thirty-five million Jews? Are they tolerated, despised, ignored by, or merely indistinguishable from their fellow modern Europeans? What is the world like, never having felt the need to create an Israel, that hard bit of grit in the socket that hinges Africa to Asia? What phrases would I need to know in order to speak to these millions of unborn phantoms to whom I belong? Just what am I supposed to do with this book?

Have You Read?
More by Michael Chabon

THE MYSTERIES OF PITTSBURGH

A funny, tender, beautiful coming-of-age novel that introduces Art Bechstein, every bit the voice of confusion and heartache for the Cusper Generation (post-Boomer/pre-GenX-er) that Holden Caulfield was for his. Chabon's first novel marked the unmistakable arrival of a rare literary talent, a writer who could be—and who has proved to be—one of the most important and enduring voices of his generation.

"Absolutely terrific. . . . Anybody can write a realistic account of his first postgraduation summer of growing up and making love, but to make such a story the stuff of legend, as Chabon has done here—and Fitzgerald did before him—takes something close to genius."
—*Los Angeles Times*

"Chabon's writing is deft and delicate—almost every page includes a delightful phrase or two. He mingles dialogue, the Pittsburgh cityscape, descriptions of the characters . . . to achieve that magical illusion good novels give—that the reader is living the character's life with all its savors, jokes and pangs."
—*Boston Herald*

A MODEL WORLD AND OTHER STORIES

A magnificent collection of eleven tales— ironic, understated stories about growing up and growing wise—stories in which people attempt to create and inhabit their own model worlds, only to watch them collapse in the face of the real world.

"Chabon manages to locate those fleeting moments that define a young man's initiation into the complexities of the grown-up world, and to memorialize those moments with such precision that they glow with the hard, radiant energy of one's own remembered past."
—Michiko Kakutani, *New York Times*

"Chabon moves across powerful emotional ground with certainty and delicacy. There are heartbreaking moments in these stories, but they are rendered so precisely, through incidents that capture the subtlest of feelings, that the reader can only smile at Chabon's skill."
—*Chicago Tribune*

THE FINAL SOLUTION: A STORY OF DETECTION

Retired to the English countryside, an eighty-nine-year-old man, rumored to be a once-famous detective, is more concerned with his beekeeping than with his fellow man. Into his life wanders Linus Steinman, nine years old and mute, who has escaped from Nazi Germany with his sole companion: an African gray parrot.

What is the meaning of the mysterious strings of German numbers the bird spews out—a top-secret SS code? The keys to a series of Swiss bank accounts? Or do they hold a significance both more prosaic and far more sinister?

Though the solution may be beyond even the reach of the once-famous sleuth, the true story of the boy and his parrot is subtly revealed in a wrenching resolution.

"Chabon's writing here is elegant and limber. . . . [*The Final Solution*] is a little mystery story with big ideas."
—*San Francisco Chronicle*
(Best Books of 2004)

"A profound pleasure."   —*New York* magazine